ANNE MACLEOD studied medicine in Aberdeen and now works as a dermatologist. Her poetry and fiction have been widely published and her first novel *The Dark Ship* was nominated for the Saltire and IMPAC awards. Anne now lives on the Black Isle with her husband, four children, and two dogs.

The Blue Moon Book

ANNE MACLEOD

Luath Press Limited

EDINBURGH

www.luath.co.uk

First published 2004

Anne MacLeod has asserted her rights
under the Copyright, Designs and Patents Act 1988
to be identified as the author of this work.

The paper used in this book is recyclable.
It is made from low-chlorine pulps produced in a low-energy,
low-emission manner from renewable forests.

The publisher acknowledges subsidy from the Scottish Arts Council

Scottish
Arts Council

towards the publication of this volume.

Printed and bound by
Creative Print and Design, Ebbw Vale

Typeset in 10.5 point Sabon

For Jim

Acknowledgements

The Blue Moon Book is fiction grounded in the current expanding field of medical narrative. It is not based on lived experience, nor is it *roman à clef*. The characters are real – in the pages, in my heart – but any similarity to persons living or dead, whether in name or narrative event, is coincidental. If Jess's story resembles yours, I salute your bravery. You have travelled a difficult road.

I apologise, in advance, to the good folk of Edinburgh, Glasgow, Kraków and Ross-shire for having made free with the physical beauty of street or landscape while imposing a fictional population. As they will know, there is no Central Hospital in Edinburgh, no daily *Standard* in Glasgow, no Portnahurach in Ross-shire. Please forgive me for abducting Tarbatness and renaming it Tarvat.

There are many people who must be thanked for the advice they gave me in the making of this story. I am grateful to Speech and Language Therapists Sharmilla Bramley and Hilary Cowie; to Carole Pound and Susie Parr for the wonderful conference at Connect. Without Groam House and their excellent selection of Pictish literature, I would have found it much more difficult to research the historical background. I am grateful to Elizabeth Sutherland for *The Picts*; to Dr Ronnie Moore of Dublin for bringing Ian Adamson's published work on the Cruthin to my attention; to Toby Ritty in Waterstone's Inverness for directing my football reading, and to James Macleod, my resident expert in the field. I am indebted to Mark Janssens whose advice on surgical matters enabled me to paint the picture of a modern A&E department. To those who read the story in its early form – May Marshall, Joanne Macleod, James Macleod, Elaine Macneil – thank you for your kindly offered advice. Any errors are, of course, my own.

Further thanks are due to my agent Jenny Brown, editor Jennie Renton and the team at Luath. Last – but not least – I would like to thank my long-suffering family who make things happen.

Edinburgh is not an easy city to drive in if you don't know your route that well. The one-way system is jammed with tourists, all in the wrong lane, wrestling the taxis and impatient buses. There's nowhere to park, nowhere easy; and traffic in the centre becomes quite impossible long before Festival when congested roads coagulate into no-go areas and tourists swarm on foot across even the widest streets, ignoring traffic and red light alike. Indifferent, they jaywalk, as if expecting this capital city to be no different from any village anywhere, Lowland or Highland, European, Asian; assuming cars will stop with a good comfort zone in each and almost every emergency.

Then there are the cobbles. Hard-wearing, picturesque, they probably have preservation orders slapped on them. Noisy. Slippery in wet weather, ice. Natural traffic calming.

In August the Edinburgh traffic grinds so slowly that for the most part there are less problems than you might expect; or that's how it feels when you're marooned in the wrong, unmoving lane, unable to segue into the forward traffic. You've been here a good ten minutes. Every time the lights change, cars behind and to your left cut quickly into the dissolving breach ahead, leaving you immobile, stranded. Between sullen, unsuccessful stabs at movement you're at liberty to watch St Andrews Square, the shoppers, the tourists and tour buses, sweeping round and down towards Princes Street. There are a great many of these buses. Most of them look modern, with doors in the middle or near the driver's end. Most of them are open-topped. All of them are garish; red or green-and-yellow, scrawled with loud advertisements in untidy lettering. (It's the fashion.) The one you notice most catches your eye first because its entrance is different – one of them, at least. It yawns at the back corner, unravelling a spiral stair. This bus is open-topped too, crowded. Its driver has cut into the current expertly, beginning to accelerate. You see the whole thing clearly.

The wooden platform. (Most of them are steel.)

You've known buses just like this; wooden, slatted platforms clogged with litter, matches, cigarette ends. (One of your pet hates as a child.) You used to run for buses.

And now, as you keep watching, someone's running for this bus. You notice her because she looks so happy.

Also because she's running, waving, and the long skirt is a pretty colour (just like the lilac bush that finally came into bloom this spring in your garden. After four years too.) Her dark hair shines, glints auburn in the afternoon sun. She's wearing sandals you wouldn't care to run in. Strappy, high. Stilettos. They match the leather jacket.

She's crazy. It can't be easy, running in a long dress like that. Running in those heels. And she's not that great a runner, obviously quite uncertain of the traffic. She seems to slow down, stop; but the bus hesitates momentarily. She tries again, speeds up, makes a jump for it.

You hold your breath.

Who in their right mind would run for a tour bus? Why? There are half a dozen idle at the kerb. Who would try that leap in a long, too-straight dress, and Jimmy Choo absurdities?

She would.

She does.

You hold your breath. The girl is jumping. The tour bus lurches forward. She lands, yes, gains the wooden deck; stretching for the safety of the perpendicular and shining rail. You're almost breathing easier.

But her hand slips as the bus jolts forward once again.

And she's falling, thrown backwards, back on to the road. She's falling back, back. You close your eyes.

How long does it take?

Perhaps a second. Perhaps no time.

It seems very long, that fall, that glimpse of darkness.

When you open your eyes, you see the bus still kangarooing and the lilac skirt flailing, the girl dragged along, helpless, head raking the tarmac, left shoe snagged in the wooden deck.

She's hanging limp and twisted. There's blood streaking the road, spurting fountain-like. If the bus doesn't stop, her face will smash into the pavement edge. The concrete kerb will taste that blood-stained face.

Your horn blares. The black cab next to you jolts to a halt. The tourist behind him smacks into his rear. You hear metal scraping, buckling, see the girl jerked hard against the kerb.

The bus stops. Finally.

beginning

JESS OPENS THE window, letting in the afternoon warmth, the city sounds. The drifting bus tour commentary. Naked, framed in shivering beech shadow, she leans against the sill. A passing tour bus fades.. Rebus.. red-light district.. the Scottish Parliament. She stretches, laughs. Laughs too when a brisk pedestrian (male, elderly), catching sight of her, averts his eyes, cheeks scarlet.

The sky is bluer now, less cloud. No, it won't rain. Easy enough to read that sky. Harder to decide what she should wear.

She leaves the window. Odd how confident, how free, she feels. And not alone. The bed, unmade, still holds the outline of him. Even the air is different. She breathes lighter, more easily, wonders at the smiling face, the figure with her eyes, her hair, trapped in the mahogany-dark mirror.

She should have been working. She should, at this very moment, be sitting in the depths of the conference hall, making serious and full notes on Celtic Heritage, the Celtic Year, Picts and Scots. Adomnan. Instead she has been drifting in a daze of remembered light. Picts, though.. she has learned something about Picts.

His area is Picts, he is passionate about them; dazzled, dazzling. Jess finds this touching.

'Not that we can be all that sure about the culture though, of course, we have their wonderful symbols.'

His face was very close; his eyes bluer, smaller, without the steel-rimmed glasses.

'How many symbols?'

'That depends who's counting.' Fingers running up and down her spine, cradling each individual vertebra. 'Anything from twenty-eight to sixty.'

She stroked his neck, his shoulder. Neat shoulders. She'd liked the shape of him right from that very first minute she saw him across the hall, towering over Julia. Julia in organising mode.

'Twenty-eight to sixty? Within confidence limits?'

He laughed, 'It's all a game of definitions. But if we take the symbols individually,' the man grew serious now, earnest, couldn't stop himself, 'take, for instance, the snake. Fourteen times it's found on Class I stones. They're the simplest, earliest.'

'I know.'

'And half of them crossed with a z-rod, the only animal and

geometric symbols shown together.. think about it.'

She stroked his chest, her fingers gliding, serpent-like.

'So what d'you think it means?'

'The snake has always stood for wisdom. Everywhere but Ireland, where there are no snakes and they make do with salmon.'

'Snakes? *Wisdom?*'

'It's a standard thing.' Michael raised himself on one elbow, reaching for the glass of red wine on the bedside cabinet. He sipped the wine, said thoughtfully, 'Snakes are wise *and* dangerous. Life and death. Healing. Rebirth.'

'And what about the.. what did you call them.. z-rods?'

He set the glass down gently, drew her closer to him. 'Ah, no-one knows. There's so much no-one knows. If it hadn't been an oral culture, if they'd written more down.. all we have are the stones, the ever more intricate carving, the religious ideology obviously changing. Very few words.'

'No written words at all?'

'Only King lists. Place-names. River names, occasionally. The odd rune here and there. The Book of Kells.'

'That's Irish!'

'Not necessarily: some say it was made, or could have been, at Tarvat, sent to Ireland for safety. They've uncovered a vellum workshop there. And the monks certainly knew all the patterns.'

'You're sure about this?'

'No. But when the Book of Kells was being made, Kells was insignificant. Tarvat was flourishing. A centre of the arts. Rich too. They even owned a mill.' He stroked the soft skin on her stomach. 'What do you know about vellum?'

'Was it made from reeds?'

His touch defined her body; the fingers moved on, dancing, dancing.

'Calf-skin. You only got two sheets of vellum from a calf. Two sheets. Think about that, Jess. Think how many calves died for the Book of Kells.'

'Not to mention substandard pages.'

'No.'

'Not vegetarian, then.'

'Jess.'

'Michael, what are you doing? That hurts!'

'Making you an honorary Pict.' He traced a serpent on her shoulder, digging his nail in slightly, so the weal shone, fading slowly. 'Bless you, Jess.' He kissed her forehead. 'May the serpent protect you from all evil. Bring you wisdom. Rebirth.'

She tried to answer lightly.

'I bet you say that to all the girls.'

Afternoon sun has now moved round the crescent. Glimmering beech-shadows quiver across the carpet, sneak into the bathroom. Three o'clock. Jess is to meet Michael at six, in a carefully distressed café-bar by the museum. They arranged this last night. He told her when to come and where, even where to sit, exactly where he'd look for her. He went over and over this. He was, she came to realise, nervous about the lecture.

'Relax. You've done this kind of thing before.'

'I know. I'm not usually worried about talking, but..'

'And I'll be there.'

That was, she saw suddenly, what was bothering him.

'That's no reason to be nervous! Look at you!'

He shrugged.

'Michael,' she stretched her hand towards him, nearly said it, held back just in time, changed the word, 'I.. have.. every confidence in you. You'll be wonderful.'

Too early to say it. Much too early.

In the beginning was the word. *Love*. A four-letter word, not to be used carelessly.

Not to be scattered to the four winds. Not to be squandered. Not to be uttered without certainty of its return.

Flesh. Another possibility. Five letters. *Flesh*.

She shivers. She has no idea who she has become. All she knows is flesh; how flesh, dissolving words, healed the old wounds, all of them.

She'd skip the shower if she could. Preserve the knowledge of him, the shock of skin on skin. But the luxury of water on her neck, her back, pooling round her breasts, grazing the landfall of her hips, is soothing, centres her.

Twenty-four hours ago she had not known of his existence.

This hotel is one of the few Jess has ever known to offer really good thick towels, large and soft. The kindness of these voluminous bath sheets would make her want to stay here again though the wallpaper is over-ornate, and the curtains, no, the window treatment, the heaviest, least beguiling flight of Victoriana north of Watford. But those soft white towels! She wraps herself in one, combs spritzer through her hair, wrinkling her nose at the smell of it, an unstable mix of coconut and chemical.

Her mouth is dry. She could do with a cup of coffee. Where's the kettle? There is one, she's seen it. Arriving the day before, she'd gone through all the cupboards. No minibar, the hotel too small. An ugly television taking up three quarters of the heavy mahogany dressing table, hiding the mirror. The wardrobe saved the day with its full-length mirror, too narrow, and in rather a shadowy corner. She'd hung up her jackets and dress, flung underwear on the internal shelves, shoes in the bottom.

Hairdryer? In the bathroom.

Kettle and cups are, she remembers now, secreted in the bedside cabinet. She fishes out the tray, takes the white plastic kettle over to the sink for water. UHT milk. For such a small kettle it makes a lot of noise, roaring so fiercely she scarcely hears the mobile. It makes her heart jump. Michael. Is he ill? Is there a change of plan? Her voice is hoarse with emotion and the morning's silence.

'Hello?'

'Sorry to trouble you at the conference.'

For a moment she does not understand. Makes no sense of this intrusion.

'Jess? Can you hear me?'

She sits down, makes an effort to control her disappointment, her surprise.

'Dan. Something's wrong?'

'Not wrong, no. I need to know exactly when your holidays end. I've been on to the travel agent and they want the dates today if we're to get the discount.'

'Let me find my diary.' Jess sounds calm enough. Where is her bag? Not on the dressing table, no. Not in the wardrobe. Not hanging on the back of her door. Where is it?

'Are you okay, Jess?'

'Why shouldn't I be okay?'

'You sound different.'

'Can't find my diary. No, here we go.' With some relief, she spots the bag under a pile of tumbled bedclothes. 'Here it is.. let me see now.. yes.. I pencilled in the first three calendar weeks in September.'

'Right, that'll do it, I should think. Are you having a good time?'

'Excellent.'

'And will it be useful?'

Jess didn't answer right away.

'Am I breaking up at your end?'

'Just a little, Dan. Useful? I don't know. We'll have to see. It has been interesting, certainly.'

'That's okay then. See you at the station.'

'Yeah. See you then.'

'Take care.'

'Bye.'

The instant coffee is particularly bitter. Jess drinks it slowly, every drop. Thinking about Michael, the touch of him, the smell of him. Thinking she has no words, no adequate language for what has happened. Thinking he has transformed her world. That things cannot go on the way they used to.

She can still feel him; it's as if he's holding her still.

But Dan. What can she say, do, about Dan?

No words. No words for either. The only one that comes to mind – guilty – she discards.

She takes great care with her make-up. Shimmering eye shadow. War-paint. It makes her laugh, for the first time since Dan phoned. It takes her back to Michael, on the matter of formal dress.

'What should I wear tonight?'

'Come as you are.'

'What?' They were wrapped only in the sheet.

'Come as you are. We're sure to find blue paint in the museum. Perhaps in the Early Living section. You can stand beside the Cadboll Stone. They'll all think you're a model.'

'Yeah, right.'

'See,' Michael laughed, 'I'll tell them. This is not Jess Kavanagh, fiercely intellectual freelance journalist (half-Irish, but she can't do the accent.) No, I'll say, it's just a model who looks a little like her. Examine her closely,' he stroked the nearest nipple, 'touch and see. You can tell by the lack of wrinkles. This one's much, much younger.'

That was when Jess kicked him out of bed, pushing slowly, inexorably, till he fell, laughing, on the floor. She had the wall behind her, an advantage then, but not when he crawled back in, pinning her against it, tickling.

'No, stop, please! Sorry. I said sorry!'

'What will you wear tonight?'

'Clothes.'

'Wrong answer.'

'No! No more tickling. I give in. Keys! Keys..'

'What will you wear?' Eyes creased with mischief.

'Blue paint. Like you said.'

'That's better.'

'Michael.' Her head was on his shoulder now. Still breathless, still laughing.

'Comfortable?'

'Hmm.' Her ribs were aching. She shivered, couldn't help it.

'Cold?'

'Not cold.'

The dress, lilac silk, goes really well with this eye shadow. She puts on the new sandals too, still a bit uneasy at their height, at the thinness of the heels. She's practised walking in them. They're elegant, but not secure.

Dan thought them unsafe. 'You'll break your neck! Women! I don't know.'

She dismisses the memory. They'll get a taxi back, and if her feet ache in the museum she can take the shoes off, go barefoot. She takes her leather jacket too, slings it across her arm.

Four o'clock. She still has time for that city tour.

Janet

'HOW ARE WE daein?'

Janet Pringle checked the drip rate, monitored blood pressure and pulse. Shrugged.

Even driving, Kev must see, must know. He'd told her once that he could tell how things were going just by the set of her shoulders.

She was thrown too near the window as the ambulance jerked through the evening rush-hour.

'Is she stable?' he asked again.

Janet shook her head.

'Don't like this pulse. Thready. Kev, the sooner we get this one in the better. I've a bad feeling about this trip. Where on earth was Medic One?'

'You ken fine! They're awa tae that pile-up on the ring-road.'

'Well, keep the right foot down.'

'I'm daein fit I can. Who is she?'

'Driver's licence says Jess Kavanagh, White Street, Glasgow.'

Janet bent down, shouted in Jess's ear.

'Jess! Can you hear me, Jess? We're taking you to the Central Infirmary. You've had a wee accident, Jess. But we'll soon have you sorted out.'

'I dinna ken why you bother.'

'Aye, you do. Fuck it, Kev!' The ambulance spun squealing round a corner, throwing her off balance.

'It wis you telt me to step on it!'

'Aye, well, you don't want to be driving two bloody head injuries, do you?'

Janet gazed down on her patient, shook her head again. The face so badly bruised, so swollen, the lass wouldn't recognise herself if she were conscious. The scalp lacerations bound, for the moment, with pad and bandage; shoulders soaked in blood, swollen lips skewed further by the endotracheal tube and securing tape.

'Jess! Can you hear me, Jess? Don't worry, Jess, we're nearly there. Just another minute or two. Then you'll be okay. Keep with it, Jess. Hang in there. Nearly there, Jess. Nearly there..'

'Okay!' Kev swept the ambulance smoothly to a halt, jumped

out, flung the doors open. 'Let's hand her over.. I dinna ken, Janet, really I dinna,' he complained as they slid the stretcher out of the ambulance, 'I never should have ta'en you to see that film wi thon American medic, that Nick Cage.. the language has been just a mite *colourful* ever since.'

'I wonder who friggin learnt me it? Don't you listen to him, Jess, he's feeble. Typical man, eh? You're here now. Safe. We've got you to the hospital. You'll make it. You can do this. For me. For you. Just hang on in there, babe.'

'See what I mean? American. All the time, you're talkin bloody American. We're friggin Scots! Highland, Doric. You should be talking Gaelic!'

'If your mother heard you cry the Doric friggin Scots, you'd have your head in your hands,' laughed Janet. 'Just as well for you she's in Aberdeen!'

'An if *your* mother heard half o your swearin you'd be blawin bubbles every time you opened yer mou!'

'Aye, well,' Janet bent down, speaking into Jess's ear. 'You'll be okay, Jess. You'll be okay now. Just hang on in there.'

They slid the trolley straight through to the crash room, where a staff-nurse waited, already gloved.

'Fit like, Helen?'

'Janet, Kev. What have we here?'

'Jess Kavanagh. Head injury from Princes Street. Jumped on a bus. Fell out the back of it.'

'Drugs?'

'Dinna think it. Broken ankle. Maybe airm. Nae sure aboot the neck.'

'Nice dress,' said Helen. 'Shame. Okay. I'll take the drip. D'you want to slide her over?'

Kev nodded to Janet, raised the trolley till it matched the crash-room table height for height.

'One, two, three..'

A smooth lift. Janet bent down.

'Bye, Jess. We're off. Maybe see you later. This is Helen, the worst-tempered staff-nurse in the place. But she knows her stuff! You'll be safe enough with her. She'll introduce you to all the other guys.'

She backed off, giving way to a wave of nurses. Helen nodded dismissal, smiled, began checking vital readings. But Janet found it difficult to leave. She lingered by the door, waiting, holding it open for the registrar and senior house officer.

'Poor lass,' she said again, under her breath.

'Come on,' Kev ordered. 'Coffee. We could dae wi a break. We didnae get the full lunch hour, remember?'

'And whose fault was that?'

'Janet,' he soothed. 'I ken ye're nae in just the best form..'

'Come on, coffee!' she interrupted. 'Would you like some from the wee stand over the way?'

'Ye really think ye're Nick Cage, don't ye? Like we'd be roving the streets o Edinburgh, checkin oot the dossers..'

'Mightn't be a bad idea!' Janet shrugged. 'No, it's just the coffee's better. You know fine it is. Tell you what, I'll run and get some for us both. What d'you fancy? Latte?'

'Macchiatto.'

'Okay. Doughnut?'

'Fine. Why no? Three sugars, eh? See you in the staffroom.'

'Aye. See you.'

She was relieved to get out of the building. Pleased to get some fresh (well, maybe not that fresh, but at the very least not hospital) air into her lungs. Breathe. She had to breathe.

That poor lass, that Jess, hadn't a hope of surviving.

Not a hope in hell.

Ken

THE COFFEE MACHINE spluttered in the corner, hissed and fizzed. No-one paid a blind bit of attention; after checking that there were enough tokens to supply the meeting, they ignored the grumbling pyrotechnics. The commissioning team for the new Central Infirmary sipped scalding liquid from thin plastic tumblers, shrugging off Ken Groundwater's rhetoric. If they'd hoped their decisions would go through on the nod, they were disappointed.

'No. This is the machine we need. Do you want a flagship unit or not?'

'Ken,' the commissioning officer repeated, 'it's twice the price.'

'And five times as good,' Ken insisted. 'It's like the difference between Seventies' ventilators and the Evitas we're using today.

The one works, up to a point, but the other is state of the art.. damn. Excuse me, please.'

The sharp note of his pager needled Ken, startled everybody in the room. He stood up, glancing round.

'Phone just outside the door,' the secretary nodded.

'Thanks.' He slipped out, shutting the door behind him before he dialled the unit.

' Ken,' his younger colleague began. 'You said to call if anything major came up. RTA. Another *en route*. Possible pile-up on the ring-road.'

'Be right there.'

He popped his head back round the door, smiling ruefully.

'Emergency. Sorry. Don't take that decision without me.'

'Ken..'

'Sorry. Got to go.'

Ken ran. He swept into the duty room, out of breath.

'Right, John, what've we got?'

The younger doctor slid an unruly sheaf of x-rays from their envelope, capturing them, sticking them on the viewing box. John hadn't worked in A&E that long. He was still in awe of his consultant colleague. Whenever he spoke, his tone was over-confident in compensation.

'Female head-injury. Fell off a bus. Tib and fib rotational fracture here.. see.. chest okay.. abdomen, pelvis, unremarkable.. no obvious skull fractures..' he summarised. 'Skin damage, of course, road rash.. she was dragged a fair few yards.. the Plastic boys will sort that later. Still unconscious.'

'CAT scan?'

'Just fixed up. Couldn't get the on-call radiologist earlier.'

'Better get the neurosurgeons in as well. We'll need their overview. Have we reached the relatives?'

John sighed. 'Not yet. Jean's getting on to the police to look up all Jess Kavanaghs in Glasgow in case the address we found in her papers isn't current.'

'What did you say?' Ken looked round sharply. '*Who?*'

John hesitated, glanced down at the papers in his hand. 'Jess. Jess.. Kavanagh.'

'*The* Jess Kavanagh?'

'Don't know, Ken. Who do you mean by *the* Jess Kavanagh?'

Ken shook his head, exasperated. 'Don't you read anything but medical journals? Jess Kavanagh the journalist. Used to do features for the Scottish Sundays. Interviews. That type of thing. Famous, actually. It's not a common name.' He sipped the coffee the charge-nurse had handed him as he came in. Too strong. Too hot. He put the cup down quickly.

'Any more milk?'

'Sorry.' Mike shook the empty carton. 'We'll get more.'

'This Jess Kavanagh comes from Glasgow,' offered John. 'White Street.'

'Better see her, eh?'

Ken swept out of the staff-room, veering towards the crash-room, a room he sailed into day after day, his knowledge and skill the slender fulcrum equilibrating life and death for those stretched on the table. It came to him now that he'd never really looked at the room, not properly – its harsh fluorescent light, slightly shabby walls – the mounting plethora of machinery – the nurses solemn and intent around their central patient, guardian angels, purposeful. Their uniforms today were all different colours, pastel blues and pinks, surgical green; they bent across the patient, stooped like Dégas bathers, cleaning Jess's temple, shoulders, areas easily reached; and tar, disinfectant, blood oozing from gauze swabs, exposing ravaged areas where it looked as if the hair might not grow back.

'Could be worse,' Helen sighed. 'The leather jacket must have ridden up. Her shoulders took more of a scraping than the scalp. She won't have too much hair loss.'

'What about the shoulders?'

'Not pretty,' said Helen. 'But you can cover shoulders.'

Ken stared at the bruised and swollen face of the unconscious woman stretched out on the trolley before him and felt suddenly profoundly tired. He hesitated for a long moment, took a deep breath, nodded.

'Thanks, Helen. Come on, John,' he swung round to the waiting registrar. 'Let's get the rest of this show on the road. What was that address again?'

'14 White Street.'

'No telephone? No diary?'

'No, well..'

John could never quite work out when Ken was teasing him. He didn't seem to be teasing now, but last week when he'd put up those weird pictures in front of the whole team and asked for an opinion.. Ken hadn't felt it necessary to say it was a scan from a cat; the joke was CAT scan, obvious. Everyone else got it right away. John kicked himself afterwards. Ken hadn't meant to make him look a fool, got quite upset. Ken was okay. A bit off-beat. Tangential. You never knew quite what he might come up with. Like seeming to know all about Jess Kavanagh.

'There was a phone number in a notebook, and we tried it, but no success. No answer. Jean's phoning the police as we speak.'

'As I remember,' Ken pulled the X-rays down from the viewing box, shoving them back in the green protective envelope, 'Jess Kavanagh's partner is Dan McKie.'

' Dan *McKie*?' John's jaw dropped. Ken laughed.

'Different when it comes to sport, eh?

So if it's the same Jess Kavanagh, we ought to get in touch with Dan McKie. Look, I met him once. I'll find a number for the paper. You phone Neurosurgery. Straight away. Go.'

Ken flopped into the scruffy office chair, stretching for the phone, forcing his younger colleague to move to the nurses' room.

'Go on, John. Hurry up!'

He dialled 100, settling back into the chair's cushioned plastic. The telephonist took several seconds to answer. Ken doodled on the desk pad, waited, counting ring-tones.. eight, nine, ten.. busy tonight.. sometimes it took ages.. ages. Was it going to be one of those nights? No. Here goes.

'Mary, my love,' his voice was as tender as if he were addressing a dear friend, which indeed Mary had come to be; you got to know the folk you worked with, even the ones you only met by phone. Ken had never, to his knowledge actually *seen* Mary. 'Yes I know,' he laughed, 'I know I say that to all of you. I've been here too long, you've got me sussed. Know all my tricks.' He paused, listening to Mary, laughing again. 'And yes, I know Pete doesn't much like being called *Mary*.. can't imagine why.. it's a great compliment, don't you think? Anyway, Petal, would you have a number for the

Glasgow Standard? Great. Yes, there's a nine on this phone. Thanks, Mary. You're a pal.'

He put the receiver down, sat back for a moment, letting the nonsense wash out of his voice, gathering his thoughts before he took a deep breath, dialled nine, tried the outside number.

He had no trouble getting through. A short cascade of voices, departments and he'd reached the man he asked for. Much more quickly, thought Ken, than he might have got through to another department at the hospital. Sitting up, he modulated his tone. He found he had forgotten McKie's voice, its Northern Irish cast, almost Caithness-sounding. He had not forgotten the man, remembered him all too well. Dan was stocky and reddish-haired. Oddly charismatic. Not easily likeable, but then, in the circumstances..

'Mr McKie? Good of you to speak to me. No, you won't know me, though we did meet once when you were covering Inter-University football.. oh, ten years ago at least.. Ken Groundwater.. that's right, Aberdeen. That's right.. good memory.' Ken's surprise rang in his voice. 'It's not football I'm phoning about, actually. And I may be bothering you unnecessarily.. I apologise if that's the case.'

Now for the difficult bit. Ken was not surprised to find his throat dry. Offering bad news at such a distance. Not the ideal thing to do. Hard to gauge the effect of your words, even in easier circumstances.

'Would.. ah.. would I be right in thinking you live at 14 White Street, Glasgow? Yes, I know it's an odd question. I think you should sit down, Dan. You are sitting down. Good.' Ken forced himself to relax.

'These days, Dan, I'm in Accident and Emergency at Edinburgh Central.. consultant, yes.. and I wouldn't normally want to pass on this kind of news by phone.. but we've had a casualty just brought in who seems from her papers to be one Jess Kavanagh.. of 14 White Street, and I wondered.. yes. No. She's very ill, but not..' his voice grew soft now, soft and quiet. 'Head injury. Neurosurgeons are on their way.. yes. Yes. It would be good if you could get over here, I think. Get someone else to drive you.. no, I don't want to make any pronouncements at this stage. You'll need to talk to the neurosurgeons when they've seen the scan. That's just been organised. At the moment she seems relatively stable. She's been unconscious since it happened. Fell backwards off a bus. I think her heel broke.. Yes.. strappy sandals. Now, listen, Dan. This must be difficult news. I want you to get someone to drive you over. Have a cup of tea too, and make sure you've eaten.. Dan?'

Ken cradled the receiver for a moment, gently laid it down.

John came back to find him staring at his coffee cup, looking shrunken, shaken. He, on the other hand, grew increasingly confident, brisk.

'Neurosurgeons *en route*. Scan set up. Porter coming.'

'It is Jess Kavanagh.'

'We knew that.'

'No. *The* Jess Kavanagh. I spoke to Dan McKie.'

'I'd better tell Jean, then. She can let the police know.'

'Yes.'

'Oh, and there's a stabbing on its way.. and an M.I. No rest for the wicked.' John looked almost cheerful.

'Drink your coffee,' ordered Ken. 'Sounds like you're going to need it.'

Michael

FIVE PAST SIX. Maigret's was already busy. Michael flew in, breathless, to find the window table taken, and not by Jess. He'd expected her to be there early, watching for him, waiting, smiling as he came in.

All afternoon he had pictured her doing just that. Silly. And foolish to put such store on that window table too, but to sit there, watching the street, the swirling traffic, the seemingly endless trail of people passing, passing, was one of his favourite things, always had been. A good talking point, the rhythm of the city, the rhythm of its people, or at least of the people currently filling its streets, which is, as he would be the very first to admit, not the same thing, not the same thing at all.

Maigret's was full. Full and noisy; that incessant chatter of adults dining, drinking, rising voices reflecting off mirrors and plate glass.

There was no sign of Jess. He advanced further into the room, scanning the corners.

'Can I help?'

A blonde waitress stood at his elbow, smiling. Chirpy. Australian. Hip-skimming apron a little askew.

'I'm looking for my friend,' he nodded, uncertain. 'Smallish, dark-haired. Tell me,' his eyes still sweeping the café-crowd, searching, 'are you open downstairs?'

'Not today.'

'Ah. She can't be here yet. I'll wait.' Michael looked about the room, twisting, turning, could not see a space. 'Have you a table free?'

'One, I think. Over at the back, there, look.. right in the corner.'

'Hobson's choice.'

'When she comes in,' the girl smiled, ' I'll tell her where you're hiding.'

'Great,' he grinned slowly. 'How will you recognise her?'

'I won't. I'll just send every unattached female over. You can sort them out yourself.'

He laughed out loud at that.

'In that case, a glass of red wine wouldn't go amiss.'

'Keeping your strength up, eh?'

'Too right. Think of the droves I'm going to have to turn away.'

'Better make that a large red wine.'

Michael laughed again, his smile fading as the girl made her way back towards the bar, weaving a tortuous path through the closely-set tables. He watched her progress absently, checking his watch.

Ten past.

He didn't mind Jess being late. Frantic punctuality was never a good sign. He was not that punctual himself, always late for everything, except when it was something important, when he always made sure to be there really early.

Perhaps, the thought struck him, perhaps he was being unfair to punctual people. Perhaps punctuality was an art like any other, one he'd never quite mastered. He would have been here earlier tonight, for example, but for the Edinburgh traffic. Chaos induced by tourists.

'Your wine.'

'Thanks. D'you want me to pay for it now?'

'I'll put it on the bill. You can settle up on your way out, after your friend arrives.'

'Thank you.'

'No problem. I'm interested to see her.'

'Oh?' Michael looked up. 'Why?'

The blonde girl raised an eyebrow.

'Well, anyone who keeps a guy like you waiting..'

You've done this before, thought Michael, oddly grateful. This was a come-on, gentle, perfectly good-natured. He nodded, smiled.

'Let me know what you think.'

'Don't worry, mate. I will.'

He sat, sipping the wine, set the glass down carefully. He might as well benefit from this unexpected time. He'd always found that someone ten minutes late was as likely to be twenty, and it wouldn't harm to run over his lecture notes again, recheck the slides. He'd meant to do this earlier, but Julia insisted on dragging him and one or two others away from the conference floor and into town. She refused to take no for an answer.

'It's your half-day,' she said. 'If we'd wanted you to work, you'd be running seminars.'

The notes were, as he knew, in perfect order. And the slides. Still, one more glance wouldn't harm. After that, he could only trust to fate, and the adrenalin that coursed through the veins when performing, that elasticity of time that somehow allowed freedom to think of other things while you were speaking lines already framed, following arguments you had considered and found relevant.

Amazing what the mind would cope with; like a singer using circular breathing techniques, you could juggle two, three different areas, different concepts, as long as you didn't see something too upsetting, too stimulating while reaching out towards the audience.

Once, lecturing to a non-academic group, he'd been intrigued to see his host, the society's president, clasp hands with the honorary secretary. Briefly. The president's wife sat only two seats away, closely watched, as Michael saw, by her spouse. A hard, unforgiving word, spouse. Michael didn't even blink. Passed his eyes smoothly to a different row.

Two of them sleeping. He didn't blink at that either.

Perhaps, after all, it was better not to try too hard to read the disparate faces ranged before you. Though it could be quite fun seeing the odd person struggle desperately to stay awake, eyelids drifting, falling and the neck jerking stiffly. You could keep a book on how many would sink into sleep. Should. It didn't seem to depend on delivery or content. Michael took real pride in his lecturing skill. No. Whatever you did, no matter how fascinating the subject, you'd have folk whose attention wandered, some who were too tired to be there in the first place, who ate or drank too much.

He shut his briefcase, lifted his wineglass.

Six twenty-five. Jess should have been here by now. He drained the glass, looked at the door forlornly.

'Can I get you another?' The Australian girl again.

'Pardon?'

'Would you like another glass? Only I'm off at seven. After that you'll have to watch out for her by yourself.'

'Thanks,' he nodded.

'I'm sorry?'

'Thanks, I'd like another glass of wine.'

Six thirty. She couldn't be much later, surely? She had a partner. Some guy who worked with her on the paper. Julia had taken care to tell him that this afternoon. He'd kept his face carefully free of emotion.

That Julia, staring down her long thin nose telling him all about Jess's long time partner, some *talented* man.. Dan something-or-other. Michael had smiled politely. Julia didn't offer details.

Six thirty-five. Where could she be?

Michael sighed, glanced at the couple at the next table but one. They'd not long met, you could tell. He found his eyes drawn back and back to them. The woman, girl, was young, too thin, dark shadows circling her eyes. There was something about her, though. The man was older. He'd had his hair cut too short. One of those number one efforts. It made him look disturbingly like an ageing child.

They talked in fits and starts. Michael tried to listen, didn't pick up much of the conversation. It was like a foreign film without the subtitles. He was fascinated by them, by their embarrassment, the way their eyes locked, pulled away; they never quite held hands, but wanted to, kept touching each other shyly, reassuring, kept advancing, retreating. Perhaps one of them was married? Or both? That was not how things had been between him and Jess. No.

Six forty. What on earth had happened to her? Jess –

He reached for his mobile. Checked the battery.

Dead.

She'd probably been trying to reach him all afternoon. All afternoon while he'd been forced to squire Julia all over bloody Edinburgh, in and out of boring shops, then on that stupid bus some idiot tourist managed to fall off. They'd been at the front, on top. Saw nothing. Heard the screaming, that was all.

They hadn't realised, not immediately, that it was their bus the screaming came from. Shunted off by the police, and having nothing to contribute, they gave their names, and were duly sent on their way. By then the street was white with ambulances, green with paramedics. They'd seen nothing but the bloodstains on the road.

'Poor sod,' said Michael.

Julia shook her head. 'Probably on drugs.'

But they were both more shaken than they cared to show. Stopped for a medicinal quick one. As Julia put it. Hers was tea, camomile.

Michael stood, moved over to the bar. The Australian girl looked up, surprised, from the coffee she was preparing. Steam hissed.

'Hi. Not a sign.'

'No,' he said. 'I wondered.. do you, by any chance, have a phone in here?'

'Round the corner. See?'

'Thank you.' he smiled. 'And would there be a phone book?'

'No. Best try Directory Enquiries.'

'Good thinking.'

'Hope you find her, mate.'

Michael shrugged. 'So do I.'

'Fingers crossed. And toes..'

The girl continued shaking chocolate over frothing cappuccino, precariously balancing spoons and chocolate logs. She sighed as Michael disappeared round the corner.

'She must be crazy. Off her head.'

She offered this opinion to no-one in particular.

Dan

IT WAS SUNNY in Edinburgh though darker, thicker cloud was gathering to the west. In Glasgow, it was already raining, vengeful drops strafing the rush-hour traffic. Dan McKie sat a long time with the phone in his hand, did not close his window, barely noticed the storm. He couldn't move, couldn't, somehow, let go the receiver.

Jess injured? Jess unconscious? Hadn't he spoken to her, what.. an hour, maybe two.. before? She'd seemed a little distant, a little less than focused. But critically ill? In a coma?

Such an odd coincidence that Groundwater should be the one to phone.

He'd met them together, Jess and Ken. One November Saturday endless years ago. How many? What did Groundwater say? Ten years? More than ten, surely?

A desperate morning. Dreich and wet, not typical, he was assured, of Aberdeen in winter; but Aberdeen had seemed the greyest place on earth, and Johnston Hall a flight of grey impenetrability. The taxi dropped him beside a vaulting gate, leaving him to decipher the tangle of student residences.

'This is Johnston?'

'D'ye nae ken faur ye're goin, loon?'

'I..' Dan turned back to the middle-aged and balding driver, struggling to unscramble the dour reply. 'I wanted Johnston Hall. This the right place?'

'Ayewis wis.'

He gave up, making his way across the lawn to the building that seemed more residence-like, the dining hall resplendent with cutlery and glass. Empty. Though it should not, doubt insisted, have been empty at nine o'clock on a Saturday morning. It took a full ten minutes to find a porter and be redirected towards the uncompromising certainty he'd passed on his way in.

Modern, granite-faced, Johnston proved as difficult to negotiate as the Doric he'd encountered on every hand. No, this was not Lowland Scots; nor was it Lowland weather. It was raining, certainly, but not Irish rain, and not your mild Glasgow variety – this was fish-biting-through-flesh Aberdeen precipitation, salting skin, incising muscle and bone. It took some time to track down his friend, one J. Cavanagh. He found the name eventually, knocked briskly on a first-floor door.

'Come in!'

He knew at once he was in the wrong place. John did not sound like that. But he opened the door, hovering uncertain on the threshold, to find the owner of the voice standing by her window, red kimono loosely tied, brown hair combing narrow shoulders.

The room spilled out and over him. Barely-broken sleep, toothpaste, coffee not long made. And the faintest undertone of fragrance, fresh as broom in flower. Dan hesitated.

He had, from his earliest years, found himself possessor of an exquisite sense of smell. Not always a blessing, though sometimes it was; walking the shore at dusk, the streets at dawn. This room cried young girl, morning, as clear and undeniable as if the words had been painted above the door; as beguiling, as energising as the mix of wintergreen and sweat, shampoo and aftershave tasted in a winning dressing-room.

Thinking of that room now, he could smell it, feel it there in front of him.

'Can I help?' the girl looked slightly confused. 'I thought you were.. you sounded like.. like my friend Ken.'

Dan wondered who this Ken might be.

'I'm looking for John Cavanagh, Subwarden. Sorry.'

'John, did you say?'

The girl beckoned him over, pointing across the quadrangle.

'That's where you should go. That flat on the ground floor. Over there.'

She may have redirected him, but Dan was lost, he was in no doubt of that. He caught himself glancing back and back again at her window, smiling foolishly as he ploughed the rain-soaked grass.

'Oi! You there! Off the grass! D'you think it grows on trees?'

Dan swung round, chuckling. 'If it did, my friend, we couldn't play football on it!'

'Dan!' the subwarden's face registered amusement, then surprise. 'What the bloody hell do you think you're doing?'

'Trying to find you, John.'

'No chance of finding me in the female wing! Though I'm not surprised to see *you* coming from that direction. Old habits die hard.'

John was shouting, his voice echoing around the quadrangle, even in the rain. Dan glanced back at the girl in the kimono. She couldn't possibly have heard.

'What about this match? Cancelled, maybe?'

'Cancelled? This is Aberdeen! No – don't come any further. You're bloody soaking! I'll come out to you!'

Dan looked back to Jess's window. She was still there. From this distance he could not tell if she was watching. He dragged his gaze away as John Cavanagh emerged into the downpour, buttoning his jacket.

'Come on, man! Wake up! You're in a proper dwam. Let's move! We'll miss the kick-off.'

They pelted across College Bounds and on behind the cloistered grey and golden crown of King's College towards the playing fields. Rain was easing off, the wind dropping a little. And the match was sound, if desperately polite. *Ref, don't be so pedantic!* The supporters were students. No Doric. *Come on Aberdeen.. Where's your passion?*

For the moment, Dan forgot Jess, his passions inexorably fixing on the beautiful game, on midfield play. Yes, midfield held the key; what happened there gave shape to everything that followed, every good move.

And that left-winger..

'Groundwater,' said John, watching Dan, smiling. 'He's the one I wanted you to see. What d'you think?'

'Fucking brilliant.'

The boy was great. Intelligent. Instinctive.

His football career should have gone further. Ken could have done his bit for Scotland. Should have. Dan never heard why not. Over the years, he lost sight of Ken, supposed him to have given up football for his studies. So many did. It happened all the time, and medicine was nothing if not time-consuming.

After the match they had gone with Cavanagh to a nearby pub, where Dan in a flight of generosity amplified by the Machar's excellent beer implied – did not actually say – he would pass the lad's name to the National Coach.

'Would you?' Cavanagh looked up in awe. 'Would you?'

'Of course,' Dan nodded.

'D'you hear that, Ken?'

'Great.' Ken drained his beerglass, said no more. But body language talks. Even Cavanagh could read it.

Dan fled back to the bar. The National Coach – whisper it – was not his greatest fan. But how could Ken have known? Wasn't he, Dan, the coming man? On his way?

Everybody knew.

That afternoon Dan took himself back to Johnston Hall, looked for Jess's door again. Conversation, laughter, spattered round it, spiked the corridor. The noise might still, he hoped, be from the next room, or the floor below.

Jess was not alone. Another girl lounged in the corner chair and two male students, long legs tenting the tintawn floor, lolled against the bed. Dan didn't envy them; the rough sisal matting could not be comfortable. He recognised Groundwater.

'Ken,' he shrugged, 'we'll have to stop meeting like this.'

But Ken was only one reason for his lack of confidence. The other stood before him, wearing green now, something green and fitted.

'I just..' he blushed, smiling at Jess, 'wanted to.. to.. thank you for your help this morning.'

'In you come,' she said. 'Coffee?'

'Thanks, but no. Got to get back to Glasgow. Half an hour to catch the train.'

'You'll have to run,' volunteered Ken, 'Hope you're in training. College Bounds is longer than you think. And fairly steep.'

'Well,' said Dan. 'I've a..'

Jess didn't let him finish. 'I'll give you a lift,' she said. 'Come on. Clear up for me guys. I'll be back in half an hour.'

Dan blushed. Ken glowered. Jess stretched behind the door for her jacket.

'Come on,' she said. 'Don't just stand there! You haven't much time.'

Dan blushed again. He hadn't blushed in years and this bright girl, this nineteen-year-old (she must be nineteen, surely.. didn't seem like a first-year) so unsettled him that he might as well have been an undergraduate again himself.

Jess shrugged her jacket on, shook her hair free from the collar. Silky, shiny.

Second year, surely?

'You coming?'

Dan, conscious of the interest and ill-will directed at him by the other students, turned, pulling the door firmly shut. J. *Kavanagh*. Banging on her door this morning, he'd ignored the psychedelic daisies curling round the name. Now they seemed sinuous, insurgent.

'Come on!'

The rubber floor squeaked underfoot, pungent as if the linoleum had been laid the day before. The grey brick walls gave little away about the age of the building. Jess's room, though, had not looked all that new.

'When were these halls built?'

'Late Sixties.'

'That long ago?'

'You could have guessed that from the style, no?'

She led him through a maze of narrow corridors. Heavy, intersecting doors blocked their way at every turn, making progress slow. Deciding who would open each door proved a tricky business, one they found no easy answer to.

'My car's out the back,' she apologised as they reached the glass door by the porter's lodge. 'We could have walked across the quadrangle, but it's so wet.. as you found this morning.'

She stretched for the last handle. So did Dan. Their fingers touched. Both withdrew.

'I..'

'Yes?'

'I should tell you, Jess.. I did order a taxi.'

'That'll be it at the gate.' she nodded. 'Look. Over there.'

'I..'

'Yes?' She sounded friendly, natural. Dan cursed himself for feeling clumsy.

'Can I.. would you like.. my card?'

'Your card?'

'My business card. With my number on it. You could ring me sometime. Talk.'

If any of his colleagues or friends had heard him stuttering like this they would have laughed out loud. Dan? Dan McKie to sound so stilted? As if he was thirteen, and on his first date. Jess didn't answer, not immediately.

Maybe she thought him impossibly old? Was she first year after all? When at last she did reply, she seemed distracted.

'Business card. Yes, why not? Give me your card, Dan.'

He fumbled in his wallet.

'Here..'

'Your taxi's gone,' she said, watching it drive away. 'They never wait long. I should have warned you.' She looked down, embarrassed.

'I can get the next train.'

'We could still make the station.'

He shook his head. 'I'll catch the next one.'

'No big date tonight ?'

'No.' Dan did not meet her gaze.

'That's all right then,' she smiled, tucking the card in her pocket.

'What is it, Dan? What's wrong?'

He looked up. He had not heard Rachel enter the room. She was the only woman he knew, the only woman he had ever known, who managed to walk silently in high-heeled shoes.

'What is it?' Rachel was beautiful when, as now, she adopted an expression of concern.

Dan couldn't speak. Shook his head. 'Jess.'

'What now? Bumped the car again?'

'Fallen off a bus.'

Her laughter rang across the room, bell-like. When Dan did not join in, she slowly stopped. The smile faded. 'What? Is she hurt?' She smoothed her skirt flat against her hips, flicking at an imaginary piece of fluff. 'Did she twist an ankle? Do you want me to go and fetch her?'

He shook his head, sighing. 'She's in Edinburgh.'

'I know.'

'In hospital. Unconscious.'

'Oh.' She leaned against the desk, sat on the edge of it, folding her arms. 'It's serious, then? What exactly did they say?'

Dan sighed. 'The neurosurgeons haven't made a full assessment yet. They're waiting for a scan. Should be happening as we speak. I'll have to go through, Rache. Everything's under control at this end. You'll be able to finish up without me. '

'Do you want me to drive you?'

'No. Better go myself. I'll not be back tonight. Perhaps not for a day or two.'

'Yeah. See how things go.'

'I cancelled St Andrews.. phoned the hotel.'

Rachel looked up sharply. 'It's that bad? Our weekend's off?'

Dan shrugged. 'The consultant sounded worried. It wouldn't look great, you know, for us to be seen swanning round St Andrews and my partner of twelve years in Neurosurgery.'

'I could still go with George,' Rachel pouted.

Dan nodded his agreement. 'You could. Phone them up and re-book if you like. I said someone might.'

'I'll think about it.'

Dan stood up then, glancing restlessly about the office. There was nothing here he needed. He should be on his way. 'I'll need to go. Run home, fetch a shirt or two.'

'Don't forget your toothbrush.'

He smiled. 'No.' Silence gaped. There was nothing more to say. He shrugged. The door slammed shut after him.

Rachel stared down at her feet, then at the space where Dan had stood. She sat down, lifted the phone.

Michael

SEVEN TWENTY. THE central hall in the new museum had been almost completely filled with chairs. It was surprising how many it held. It was surprising how much noise subdued murmuring could make in an echoing building. Most of the chairs were now occupied. Michael studied the rows of faces, wondering if the sound system would cope with the echo in this soaring space. He could not see Jess anywhere. As Julia passed with a sheaf of leaflets, he threw caution to the wind, tapped her on the shoulder.

'Yes, Michael? Everything okay?' Julia seemed a little off-balance. The afternoon had upset both of them. Michael knew she'd disapproved of the double whisky he'd demanded while she sipped camomile tea. She's worried, he realised, that I may be drunk. He almost laughed out loud but controlled the impulse.

'Julia, have you seen Jess?'

'Jess?'

'Jess Kavanagh?'

Julia shook her head. 'No. No, I haven't. She must be somewhere round the place, though? There are still one or two folk lingering in the shop. If I see her, I'll tell her you were looking for her, shall I?'

'Please.'

Jess wasn't in the shop. Michael knew that for a fact.

He slipped out to the payphone. Tried the hotel one more time.

Julia gave her audience a few minutes to settle. At seven thirty-five she stood up, cleared her throat, and inaugurated the E.S. Wilson lecture, a lecture made possible, as she explained in detail, by a handsome and unexpected legacy.

'This is to be an annual event,' she nodded. 'The committee are, however, thrilled to have secured this year – for your erudition and delight – a young man who blends a deep love of early languages with anthropological and archaeological expertise. Michael Hurt's work may range far beyond the confines normally explored on such occasions as this; you may find it completely contrary to what you have accepted, what you have hitherto taken as firm knowledge. Of one thing I am sure.. you will not find it boring. Michael has asked me to say he welcomes debate and will leave ample time for questions at the end of the talk. He lectures, as you know from your conference notes, in..'

Michael's attention drifted. He hated fulsome introductions. Julia was covering her back, making sure her position would remain secure no matter how the lecture went. Well, why not? He had other, more important, things on his mind. He stood to one side of the hall, scanning the crowd. There were all the conference faces, some old friends, and one or two newcomers. No Jess.

With a shock he recognised the young Australian waitress from Maigret's. She hadn't seen him yet, didn't realise he was about to speak. Michael wondered briefly whether she had followed him. No. She'd left the café first, hadn't she?

Perhaps she was a student? Perhaps she was interested in archaeology, knew about the Tarvat dig? Perhaps her ancestors came from Pictish areas? That was often the way. Folk were drawn in by the past, attracted by its winsome lack of certainty. As he took centre stage, made contact with the audience, he registered her look of pleased surprise. He'd been right then, she didn't know. But where was Jess? Where was she?

'Some hold the Picts,' he began, 'to have been, like other Celts, Indo-European. Some posit that their roots were somewhat more ancient, their speech non-Indo European, though the Caledonian Picts in early Christian times did use P-Celtic.'

He paused, watching the faces, gauging their reaction to this statement. The microphone was good. Seemed somehow to counter the excessive resonance. His words were clear. He could speak normally, forget about projecting. Concentrate on ideas, not delivery.

'Adamson, in his work on the Cruthin, describes successive waves of invasion in Ireland, the Irish Picts, Pretani or Cruthin, overcome, driven to Argyll by an influx of Gaels. This view remains, of course, highly controversial, even being drawn into the sectarian debate, though Adamson would refute such interpretation, preferring to see the Irish as essentially pre-Indo-European, their language and culture altered and imposed by the influx of successive waves of conquerors and settlers; Gaelic imposed by Gaels on more ancient peoples.

'In many ways,' he smiled, 'this may reflect the situation here in Scotland, in the Highlands, where Pictish tribes held power. Picts are clearly documented. Tacitus described them but their language whether pre-Indo European or P-Celtic, remains a matter of speculation. Not that they were illiterate. Their druids, their monks, possessed the ability to write; indeed thirteen of the Pictish stones bear Ogham inscriptions.

'So far, so simple. Cummins has of course questioned all of the above, describing the language spoken in Pictish times, between 300 and 850, as, if you like, a palimpsest; Q-Celtic over-written by P, then reinfused by Q.

'What is clear is that the Picts had considerable sophistication; communicating with Gaelic-speaking Scots and Viking races. Even the classical languages were known to certain of them. That their own tongue has been lost has been a source of fascination, particularly in modern times. Was it quickly subsumed in the Q-Celtic of Dal Riata? It was different enough for Columba to need an interpreter when he made contact with the High King Brude.'

Immersed now in the lecture, in word and line of thought, Michael at last forgot to worry about Jess.

'There are never primitive peoples, only primitive circumstances. Like the Egyptian God, Ammon, the Celtic races relied on the spoken word, mistrusting the disruptive technology of their time. Egyptians held *writing* to have been invented by Thoth or Theuth as a Pharmakon, a cure for ignorance, a way of storing knowledge. Ammon, as you will know, concluded Thoth's invention was indeed a Pharmakon, more poison than cure; preventing true learning, giving the appearance of knowledge where there was none. Of course, it took a little longer for ideas and technologies to spread in those days,' he added, to general laughter.

'And just as the electronic revolution threatens our own systems and power bases – medicine, law, you name it – just as it threatens current knowledge hoards, threatens our religion of professionalism – the very fact of writing threatened the power base of the Druidic classes, their carefully guarded knowledge systems.

'We are ourselves at the beginning of an industrial revolution, the outcome of which is impossible to predict. Will, for instance, *books* survive? And in what form? Language is changing already, communication is being radically altered by the electronic medium, and I don't just mean the typos you're not supposed to correct! No, what we read and how we read it, how knowledge is stored and accessed, is in the greatest state of flux since writing was invented.

'The Picts *could* write, some of them. They've left us tantalisingly little to go on, so it's almost impossible to know how much of their culture survives in the Celtic melting pot. Frustrating when you compare this to the wealth of carved stone imagery, frustrating that the meanings were not not written about, preserved, *not* or *not apparently*, woven into the culture we inherit.' He was well away now, oblivious to audience.

'Unspoken language withers where spoken language grows, changes constantly. To strengthen and protect diversity takes energy

– almost as much energy as it must have taken to preserve, in unchanging words, an oral history, an oral tradition. The loss is unimaginable. Yet it must have taken time, generations, perhaps, to perpetrate.

'I have a friend who lived in Tanzania in the 1960s and used to travel with his father and uncles buying goods for their trading post. They had to know many local languages, but used to pretend they knew them less well than they did, so as to gain advantage in negotiation when tribesmen, assuming the traders could not understand, discussed their tactics openly. It must have been like that, I think.. such complex language skills are lost – or not cultivated – in monoglot times.

'Political imperatives, of course, may have ensured an older tongue was discouraged, driven, like religion, out of sight. And yet, and yet. Old ways die slowly in religious matters. There must be traces of the language still. How will we ever find them? We must start with the few texts we have, the King lists, place-names..'

Questions at the end went on and on. Michael felt suddenly exhausted, drained. There was still no sign of Jess when Julia turned towards him, smiling.

'One last question before dinner,' she said. 'And not a scientific one, I'm afraid. But Michael has shown us that he's not afraid to tackle philosophical and personal, even emotional, aspects of the problem. How do you think you would feel, Michael, *as a Pict*, to have lost the possibility of language, of your own tongue?'

He stared at Julia, shrugged.

'I can't speak for the Picts. But for myself.. to be unable to express oneself, not to have instinctive words for sea and sky.. for love and loss.. for happiness.. you'd be in the world, but without the defining sense of who you are, who you had been. Quite simply,' he concluded, 'you'd be lost. Totally, and completely, lost.'

Then the long queue formed. Book signing. Michael nodding, smiling patiently. Resigned. Why there were so many anxious to speak to him, he could not understand. The new book was (when were they not?) delayed; all that was on offer was earlier, well-known work.

'She's still not here?'

He looked up. The girl from Maigret's. He took the book she handed him.

She tried again. 'Great talk.'

'Thank you. Who shall I sign this for?'

'Oh, sign for me. Kerry.'

'Good to see you, Kerry. Thanks for your help earlier.'

'Wish it had been more successful. What about that drink?'

He smiled. 'Another time.'

Kerry did not move on. 'Maybe tomorrow?'

He shook his head. Sighed.

'The girl's got stamina, I'll say that for her.'

'Pardon?'

The elderly woman now standing before him was fortunately deaf.

'Pardon?' she shouted again.

what happened next

DAN PROWLED ROUND and round the narrow waiting area, a caged and fretting animal in a cramped old-fashioned zoo, detesting the green walls, fashionable though they no doubt were when the place was decorated. He'd never liked hospitals, never. He found them claustrophobic, hated the antiseptic nature of the corridors, even these days when lavatorial shiny brick was no longer in vogue, the walls more likely to be stippled with magnolia emulsion and large abstract pictures on loan from the Arts Council.

When at last he sat down, it was to find himself obsessively numbering the interlaced blue and gold lozenges festooning the navy ceiling border. Dan was used to waiting. He'd had to do a fair bit in his time, a lot of hanging around ready for action, ready for others' action, at least; which seemed much the same. This was the most difficult wait he'd ever known. Not that any thought or deed of his could alter the result, the news he waited for, breathless. Every passing minute streaked towards infinity. It was a great relief when Ken at last came in, looking scarcely a day older than when they'd last met. He'd filled out a bit, thought Dan, but only a little. He would have recognised Ken Groundwater.

They shook hands, sat down. Dan found it surprisingly difficult to speak. Words stumbled, died. Ken looked at him for a long moment as if assessing opposition, deciding tactics.

'I'm so sorry, Dan, that we should meet again like this, in such circumstances.'

Dan tried but could not follow what was being said, his mind not so much drifting as actively swerving, for all he clutched at scattered fragments.

Is this happening? Is this real?

He wished he had someone with him. No, not Rachel. Jack maybe, his friend Jack. He'd thought about phoning Jack, then remembered he had flown to London for a meeting. Bad timing.

Again and again he tried to focus, concentrate, but the words sailed round and over him, dissolving in mottled walls. All the technical stuff, details of the accident, the extent of Jess's injuries, the clearly-explained management plan – none of it made sense. No sense at all.

Dan floundered, did not know where to look. He bent forward, gripping and ungripping his hands, staring at the floor, at the ageing carpet tiles, curled over at the edges. Six, no, seven..

He suddenly became aware that Ken had fallen silent.

'Well, Dan? Have you any questions?'

Dan had taken nothing in. Nothing.

'Tomorrow,' Ken assured him, 'you'll see the neurosurgeons. They had to dash back to the Western. Another emergency, I'm sorry. And as I've explained, we've moved Jess up to High Dependency. Shall I take you there?'

Dan swallowed, nodded. Ken had lost little of that disconcerting clarity, that look that made you feel he was seeing through you, straight through each and every defensive layer. What was it made him able to do this? His expression; something, perhaps, about the set of his eyes. And the corridor didn't help, echoing mournfully as they swept along.

'Have you ever seen anyone on a ventilator?'

Dan found his voice at last, was surprised how calm, how cold it sounded.

'Can't say I have. Jess went to see her mother after she had the heart attack. I was off abroad.'

'Then I should warn you,' Ken said softly, 'not to be too alarmed by all the tubes, all the machines. Also..'

Dan was already feeling queasy. He'd never become used the sight of blood, not even in the boxing ring.

'Jess,' Ken hesitated, 'was badly bruised about the face. Lacerations to the scalp and shoulders. You may find it difficult to recognise her.'

'No problem.' Dan was brusque. 'Don't patronise me, Groundwater. I may not be a doctor but I'm at least ten years older than you. I remember you in short pants.'

'Football shorts, perhaps,' Ken smiled. 'Here we are. Let me introduce you to the staff looking after Jess. Ella this is Mr McKie, Jess's husband.'

'Partner.'

'Partner.' Ken remained determinedly affable. 'Dan, this is Nurse Stanfield, Ella to her friends. She'll be on overnight. She'll look after you; keep you informed.'

'Where is Jess?' Dan's eyes swept, angry, round the cluttered space. 'Where is she?'

Ella raised her eyebrows at Ken, who simply nodded.

'Don't hesitate to call if you need me. This is my home number.' He scrawled it on a piece of paper, handed it to Dan. 'Call any time.'

'Why are you doing all this?' Dan sounded far from grateful.

Ken shrugged. 'Let's say it's for an old friend. Do you want to see Jess now?'

'Why else would I be here?'

But Dan was shocked, truly shocked, at the poor bruised wreck they offered him. His knees felt weak. His palms were sweaty.

'Sit down,' said Ken, gently. 'We'll bring you a cup of tea. Sit on the other side,' he added, 'there's much less bruising.'

On the other side, the plethora of machines was as frightening to Dan as the swollen face before him. He couldn't take it in.

This was a mistake, surely? This wasn't Jess.. not Jess, this waxen dummy, pierced by tubes and drips, drooling mucus. This was not a real human being?

And as for calling that a bed, the hi-tech bench the broken form was stretched on.. his face worked. He felt tears stabbing his eyes. Any minute now he would choke. He struggled to suppress the bile rising in his throat.

Ken hovered. Ella beckoned him over to the desk.

'Has he anywhere to stay? A contact number?'

'Don't know,' said Ken. 'I'll ask.'

He stood behind Dan for a long moment before offering the mug of tea. 'We wondered,' he said at last, 'where you might be staying?'

'Ah,' said Dan, glad of something tangible to focus on. 'I thought about that in the train. It'll be difficult at Festival time to find a room. I thought I'd just use Jess's.'

'You came in the train?'

'Lost my licence last year,' Dan frowned. 'Don't you read your papers?'

Ken shook his head. 'Obviously not those pages. Look, Dan, Jess is not my patient any more. You could stay with me in Bruntsfield. It wouldn't be a problem.'

'Thanks, but no.'

Dan turned back to Jess, dismissing Ken who, much relieved, did nothing to persuade him.

Jess

THE BEDS IN Johnston Hall are surprisingly comfortable, wide enough for two. Jess's window is overlooked by the hall library, the games room, the television room. She can see them all from her bed, their dark plate-glass reflecting light from F Block. She's visible on every side. She hates to sleep with her curtains shut, but privacy dictates that she must.

'You locked the door?'

'Yes.'

'Are you sure?' Dan sits up. 'Are you sure?'

'Probably,' Jess laughs.

'Jess Kavanagh! It's not only not locked, you haven't even shut it. Look!' He slides off the bed. 'Where's your key?'

'Don't know.'

'What are you like? Anyone could waltz right in. Anyone!' Dan opens the door wide and they hear footsteps rushing down the stair, laughter. 'And look! You've left the key outside the bloody door!'

'So?'

'So what if your disapproving friend came round? He could have barged right in on us.'

'Leave Ken alone. He doesn't call you names.'

'A man of conviction, ground-breaking, eh? So he doesn't call me names? What does he say about me?'

'Nothing, Dan. We don't discuss you. Leave it alone.'

'Ground-breaking could at least be misconstrued as a compliment. Ground-*watering* on the other hand..'

'I said, leave Ken alone. What's he ever done to you?'

'He hates me.'

'Don't be silly.'

'Jess..'

Dan locks the door and takes the key over to the desk.

'What are you doing now?'

'Tidying your desk.'

He rearranges her books in neat piles, places lecture notes carefully to one side. She's so untidy. There's no system here, none. He couldn't work with a desk like this. He knows people who do.

They usually have a system.

'Dan.'

He snaps the light off. Shakes his head as the darkness settles round him, shawling, obliterating chaos and accentuating what he loves about his room, the freshness, the hint of flowers.

'Dan. Leave that.'

He shakes his head, lingers at the desk, breathes in and out, breathes quietly.

Sian

THE SUMMER EVENING stretched as grey, as inhospitable, as any November afternoon. Uneasy in the hi-tech shades of High Dependency, Dan found his tiny view of sky uncomforting; rain slashing against glass as dark, as strange as the body on the bed before him.

He did not, could not, recognise that form as Jess. Even the skin felt alien. He tried to touch the hand and withdrew his own, shuddering. Something about the temperature, lack of movement, lack of life, unmanned him. The hospital ambience held nothing that could soothe his panic. He felt sick, bereft, though the girl, the nurse, tried several times to reassure him.

He snapped her into silence. He was not the patient! But this was a new world, unknowable. He wished Groundwater had stayed; knew Ken would have, given the merest encouragement. Dan had offered none.

'Fuck!'

If he stayed here any longer he'd be sick, physically sick. He staggered to his feet and swept out of the ward without another word. He had to get out, had to find somewhere he could breathe.

In the corridor he hesitated. Which way had they come? How could he escape this echoing maze? The corridors now seemed oddly empty, empty and blurred. Eyes ripe with tears, Dan could make out nothing, could see none of the signs plastered on the walls, hanging from the ceiling. He leaned against a window, retching.

'Can I help?'

He ignored the voice behind him.

'Is there anything I can do?'

Dan sniffed, looked round. A small, dark-haired girl smiled up at him, her arms full of folders; case-notes, he guessed, clinging to the unimportance of the notion. It was somehow comforting. Her white coat was far too large, the shoulders sagging, the cuffs turned back several times. The things that save us, Dan thought.

'Are you lost?' she tried again. Her voice was not Edinburgh, but soft, probably Glasgow, the speech rhythms not quite right, hard to place.

He sighed. 'Can't remember how the fuck to get myself out.'

'I'll show you. This way.'

She did not quibble at his language. Dan was grateful for this.

'Don't go out of your way.. Ms Kinnon..' the badge on her lapel gave her name away.

'It's not a problem. Here you are. These are the main stairs,' she nodded. 'Once you reach the ground floor.. and you'll find that marked clearly on the wall.. follow the *Way Out* signs. You're sure you'll be okay?'

'Thanks, yes.' He set off down the stairs. 'Thank you,' he called again.

'No bother.'

She waited till he'd rounded the corner, then set off herself in the opposite direction. It was not unusual to find distraught and disorientated relatives caught at that window. Sian paused, looked through it. Not much of a view. Blank hospital walls, uncompromising. She shook her head again, bustled away. If she did not get on she'd never be finished, never get home.

Dan

DAN STRODE OUT of the hospital, was half away down the street before he realised he had only the vaguest idea of where the Meredith might be. He should have asked. Was it over towards Morningside? Bruntsfield way? Merchiston? Or was it in the New Town? Off the street?

He had Jess's diary in his pocket. Typically, she'd left it at home, on the kitchen table. The Meredith was all she'd written.

No address. No phone number. It would be on her mobile. They relied so much on mobiles now.

In the end he asked a taxi driver, found his way eventually, stumbling through drizzle that kept threatening to turn to rain. It did. Somehow the thunder helped, was even soothing. His hair and face felt fresher too, as if the downpour had washed the antiseptic away.

Hospitals. He hated them.

Not that the Meredith, a brownish sandstone townhouse set back from the road, was that appealing. It looked slightly down-at-heel.

'Can I help you?'

The receptionist did not, for her part, seem much impressed with him.

'Room 12A, please.'

The girl stared at him, questioning. She remembered Ms Kavanagh's friend perfectly well, a different man, taller, better looking than this one. More polite. Something about Dan told her not to mention this. Not to ask. This one might be, she thought, a troublemaker. She adopted her coolest, most official, voice.

'I'm sorry, sir. That room is taken. Do you have a booking? We're actually full. In Festival time..'

'It's my partner's room,' growled Dan.

The girl looked him up and down.

'I'm sorry, sir, it's not a double room. In any case, we'd need confirmation from Ms Kavanagh of any change of booking status.'

'That will be difficult,' Dan took pleasure in informing her, spitting out the words, slowly, clearly, 'as Jess is in the Central Infirmary. In Intensive Care. Unconscious.'

'I beg your pardon?'

Dan grew weary of this charade.

'For heaven's sake,' he spat, 'just give me a bloody key. Get your manager to check with the Central. It'll take you two minutes max. What harm can I possibly do in two minutes?'

Shaken, the receptionist handed him a keycard. '12A,' she said. 'First floor. Turn left.'

He was half way up the stairs before she'd finished speaking.

Opening the door, he was appalled to find the bed unmade,

damp towels in an untidy heap at the bathroom door. Not only unmade, the bed was virtually stripped, blankets kicked off at the foot, sheets hanging wrinkled to the floor. The receptionist had lied. It was a double bed. Typical of Jess, he thought, to sleep so late, so restlessly.

He lifted the phone by the bedside, dialled zero.

'This room has not been made up,' he stated without preamble. 'I want that remedied. Right away.'

'But sir..'

Dan was well aware that the housekeeping staff would be long gone.

'Now,' he repeated, slamming the phone down.

God, he thought, looking around him, this is a hideous room. What a place to have to spend the night, any night, never mind your last.. he stopped. Hadn't meant to think along those lines. It did no good. And nobody had said, not actually put that possibility in words.. that Jess might die.. but she was on the edge, even he could see that. What was left of her.

He flung open the wardrobe. Trousers and underwear stared mutely back. Jess's, he supposed. He wouldn't know. Never took notice of such things. He slammed the door, lifted the phone again.

'Is there a bar in this establishment?'

'Yes, sir, second floor.'

'Second floor? Christ!'

A dram, he thought. Or two. Or six.

What was he doing here? He sagged, flopped on the unmade bed. Jess had slept here last night. Jess, who didn't know what lay in store, how less than twenty-four hours later she'd be lying in intensive care, her face a livid wail of red and blue. Unconscious. Unknowing. He found himself hoping her last sleep had been at least refreshing.

The phone rang at that moment. Dan stirred, did not lift the receiver immediately. Who could be calling? Ken? The hospital? He didn't want to speak to anyone. Maybe, if he let it ring, the caller would go away. No. They knew he was here. They'd only try again. He sighed, lifted the receiver. 'Hello?'

There was no response at the other end.

'Room 12A,' Dan snapped. 'Dan McKie. Who the hell is speaking?'

'Sorry,' said a quiet male voice. Diffident. 'Sorry. Wrong number.'

Michael

EVEN HAD JESS turned up, Michael realised they would have had to stay for the conference dinner, now hovering between the fish and main courses. The organisers had gone to a deal of trouble arranging for the meal to be served in the museum itself, in the lower gallery, tables set on both levels, so that some of the delegates sat among the iron men, the rusted metal statues offering in glass cases some of Scotland's most ancient treasures; thick twisted silver chains, torques, brooches and rings of reddish gold.

He liked these statues, glorified exhibition-cases though they were. Liked the sense of humour that had caused the designer to site the glass exhibition-case in the head and hands of some and the gut and balls of others. He had little opportunity to study any of this. Sandwiched between Julia and her elderly, deaf, husband, he had rather a lean time of it.

'Did you find Jess?' Julia asked, knowing perfectly well that Jess had not appeared.

Michael shook his head.

'I think,' Julia nodded, setting down the glass of wine she'd hardly sipped, 'she must be ill. Don't think I've seen her all day.'

'Who haven't you seen?' her husband asked, too loud, his voice reverberating across the gallery.

'Jess, dear. Jess Kavanagh. The girl from the *Standard*. Michael was looking for her.'

'Looking for who?'

'Jess Kavanagh!'

Julia was shouting now, her words echoing across the marbled floor, skimming the soaring walls. Everyone in the conference must have heard.

'Excuse me,' Michael stood up. 'I'll just..'

He didn't finish, left the table. In the phone booth on the upper floor he dialled the Meredith again.

'Room 12A, please.'

'Certainly, sir. I'll put you through.'

Earlier, the girl had been less positive. 'I'll try that for you sir,' or 'I'm not sure she's in.' And now 'I'll put you through.'

Michael stared at the white-painted wall before him. Jess. Where have you been? Why aren't you here. Why..

'Hello?'

A male voice. Baffling. This must be the wrong room? A mistake?

'Room 12A,' Dan snapped. 'Dan McKie. Who the hell is speaking?'

'Sorry,' Michael choked. 'Sorry. Wrong number.'

He hung up, stood for several minutes staring at the phone. Went back to the dinner where the main course was now being served at the high table. He absently allowed the waiter to fill his glass and plate, then left both food and wine untouched.

Perhaps he should have rung again, asked for Jess? Perhaps Dan had come through unexpectedly and Jess had been unable to get away? Perhaps there was a family problem. Perhaps.. perhaps he should ring and simply ask for her, just to hear her voice, just to say hello. Just the simple word of greeting. He excused himself again, left the hall, making for the entrance, for the public telephone. He lifted the receiver. Hesitated. Dialled half the number. Put the phone down. What if this made trouble for her? He had no idea how things stood between them, between Jess and Dan. How could he wade right in there? But Dan wasn't to know.. how could he? All Michael had to do was tell the truth, say he was from the conference, wondering why Jess had not made an appearance at the dinner. Nothing wrong with that.

He dialled again.

'Meredith Hotel.'

'Room 12A please.'

The phone rang out. And out. And out. This time there was no answer. Where was Jess? Where were they? What were they doing? Michael leaned against the wall, forehead on cooling brick. The phone rang twenty, thirty times before he crashed the receiver down and blundered out into Edinburgh's rainy darkness.

Jess

TEN FIFTEEN. ELLA turns her patient, moving arms and legs, soothing sheets, examining pressure points. The lassie's back is a right mess. Her left leg, splinted, will need attention too. But the face looks worst of all.. so much swelling, so much bruising, particularly on the left. Her right side is not as bad, not nearly as bad. The surgeons seem to think there has been no serious bony damage, that it's all soft tissue swelling, broken teeth apart. If, when, she comes round she at least won't need her face set on a steel frame till the fractures heal. That always looks like mediaeval torture.

As she works, Ella murmurs. Chatting away. There's little logic in it. Jess is out of it, unconscious, sedated. They'll keep her sedated today, tomorrow, then..

'Sorry, Jess,' Ella apologises. 'Got to keep you ship-shape. You'll be hearing me soon enough.'

She looks out the window into the gathering dark.

'It's raining out there, stotting, Jess. If you were awake, you'd be wondering what the noise is. Always the same at Festival time, isn't it? Rain and wind. Anything to keep the crowds away.

Funny how they still come. Year after year. Enjoy themselves. Weather doesn't seem to matter.

There. That's better now. Okay Jess. I'll be back.'

Jess makes no response.

The crowding machines click on/off, registering her heart's confusion.

Dan

THE BAR AT the Meredith was even worse than the bedroom, dingy, its flock wallpaper redolent with nicotine; scratched, if polished, tables; and plush velvet chairs considerably worn. But there was a good selection of malts. That was something. Dan ordered a double Lagavulin, knocked it back. Jess, he thought, never could find a good hotel. It didn't seem to bother her, but he travelled so much he'd become fastidious. He liked his comforts. Needed them. To be fair, she'd registered at the last minute for this conference and this had been one of the recommended hotels. One of the cheaper ones. The better hotels, Jess had said, were full. He wasn't sure she'd been telling him the truth. It would be like Jess to come here just to avoid the other delegates. Well, he was stuck with it now. And he'd been so rude to the receptionists he doubted they'd find a bed for him tomorrow night. Dan slammed his glass back down on the counter.

'Same again.'

The barmaid swept the empty glass away, fetching a new one.

'Double? Lagavulin?'

'Yes,' said Dan. 'Please.'

The barmaid wasn't that bad-looking, but he was tired.

'I'll have another, for a nightcap. Can I take it up with me?'

'Certainly, sir. Room number?'

'12A.'

'I'll charge these to the room, then.'

'Thanks.'

He slouched from the bar, feeling less hollow. A little. It was an odd sensation this, an oddly indescribable predicament. To be wandering round a dingy Edinburgh hotel, not knowing if Jess..

He recognised the beginnings of anger growing in him. This was all so stupid, so unnecessary. What on earth had Jess thought she was doing? The lift, thick with dust, made his skin itch. That Seventies notion of using carpet instead of wallpaper. Tacky. Nor did he feel at all secure, formed the distinct impression that this lift was not that safe. It made an odd clacking noise. He should have taken the stairs. What kind of hotel had their bar on the second floor? Madness.

The phone in the bedroom rang as he fumbled with the keycard. He hated keycards. Had to put his whisky down, use both hands. Though the green light flashed obediently enough, his door refused to open. He tried the card again. The telephone was blaring, louder and louder, a dry and electronic sound, harsh as burning. Dan felt suddenly, illogically, enraged. Shoved the plastic card back in the door. This time it deigned to open, but pushing in and past the heavy door he knocked his whisky over, sending Lagavulin skiting right across the carpet.

'Fuck!' The glass was empty. All the whisky gone. The room smelled like a pub the morning after. 'Fucking hell!'

The phone stopped. They'll ring back, he thought. If they need to. Maybe it was Rachel. Good thing I was out. He couldn't bear to talk to Rachel about Jess. Not tonight. Rachel was becoming too possessive. Territorial. That was not in the equation, never would be, not even if..

The room at least looked tidier. He flicked the light on, reaching for the phone.

'Room service? Lagavulin. Double. 12A.'

He shrugged his jacket off. Loosened his tie. Unbuttoned his cuffs. Opened his shirt. That was better. They'd changed the bed, thank goodness. But he wouldn't call this perfect by any means.. He scanned the room. He should refuse to pay the bill.

Look at the unemptied bin nestling in the bathroom, underneath the sink. And the floor in here.. a piece of purple foil beneath the bed caught his eye. Dan, fastidious, bent to pick it up, would have tossed it in the bin, but his whisky arrived just at that moment. The knock on the door distracted him.

Laying the scrap of foil carefully on the porter's tray, Dan signed for the drink.

The porter flushed, looked quickly away, almost flinching.

Dan didn't understand the embarrassed look, the scared-cat behaviour, but followed the young lad's eye, his gaze fixed on the purple sliver winking on the tray.

Dan shivered.

What had *seemed* like foil was not. He snatched at the torn condom wrapper, cringing. The lad must have thought.. obviously did..

'This room,' Dan blustered. 'Rubbish everywhere.. do you *have* housekeepers? Look what they left lying on the floor.'

That the lad did not believe him was all too obvious.

Dan flopped into the uncomfortable armchair as the boy effected a hasty exit, red-necked.

'Fuck. Fuck. *Fuck.* Jess, what a one you are. Every hotel you ever chose.. every single one.'

It wasn't till much later, brushing his teeth, opening the new toothpaste and discarding the box, that Dan finally recognised the latex shine of used condoms gleaming through the tissues in the bathroom's overflowing bin.

'What the..? Who..?' he couldn't breathe. 'Jess?'
This time he didn't swear. He was in a cold sweat.
Cuckolded.
An old word.
Dan would sit up all night in the too-hard chair, unable to lay his head where she had lain with.. who? For now he bent across the bed, peeling the bedcovers back, smelling the sheets, every single inch of them. Nothing but starch. He systematically searched all the cupboards, all the drawers. Found nothing incriminating. Nothing. Nothing but Jess's unworn nightdress. He sat holding this, cradling it, as if it might somehow bring her back.

first light

IN THE EARLY morning light, rainwashed Edinburgh shone, uncannily beautiful. Although, it must be said, the green and sloping land of Orkney, the mist-soaked slopes and interweaving sea, would have looked better still, a marriage of distinct uncertainties.
Five a.m.

Ken, unable to sleep, had been wandering slowly through the rain down to Morningside and back. He passed his house. No. Liz's house. It was her house now.

He stood for fifteen, twenty minutes, watching in the rain. No lights. No car in the drive. Liz must be out. She always left a light on. The house looked dark, deserted; closed doors, empty windows.

He didn't cross the road, didn't feel inclined. Even the street seemed alien, too tidy, too precise. He felt more at home walking in the rain.

There were others, wandering, just like him, shoulders hunched, faces set, tendrils of rain rivuletting faces, necks. Let's face it, thought Ken, where can anyone go, grounded in their own unhappiness, the lack of possibility of cure? And walking in a city, even in the rain, while it might feel unpleasant, never seemed truly *outside*, never felt like freedom. Dangerous, perhaps, but never free. And never outside weather either, but movie-rain-effect, water thrown in buckets.

As cities went, though, Edinburgh was special; best at dawn, its streets serene and quiet before the thronging mass of city folk and tourists cluttered the uneven pavements. There was something about dawn-light.. hadn't it been dawn-light? Yes.. dawn-light, first light.. photos.. that award-winning exhibition where the camera persuaded ordinary Edinburgh people, women, to strip and pose naked in dawn-lit streets, tastefully arranged limbs echoing the city's dance of leaf and stone.

Female silhouettes sang against bark and brick. Pavements spoke of skin.

The story even made the Glasgow papers!

Now Ken can never look at these pavements, these stones, without thinking of warm flesh pressed against them. How did those women feel?

Lost? Liberated?

He checked his watch. Too late to go home.

Dan

ACROSS THE CITY, Dan McKie was wakeful, but not refreshed. The strengthening light, pouring through the high bay window, mocked his bleary, bloodshot eyes. He stretched, shifting uneasily in the brown and sagging chair, rubbed his neck. It was stiff, his back tender, aching. It had been a bad night. He felt at least a hundred. But the hospital hadn't phoned, hadn't called him in. Jess had made it. So far.

He squinted at the number Ella had written down for him, the neat script clear, easy to read. He reached for the bedside telephone, dialled, expecting the anonymity of the hospital switchboard. The answer left him shaking.

'Good morning. High Dependency. Nurse Stanfield speaking. How may I help you?'

'Christ, you sound like a cracked record,' Dan snarled. 'Do you really think that crap is necessary?'

'Mr McKie,' sighed Ella. 'What can I do for you?'

'What do you think you can do for me? Tell me how Jess is!'

'There's been no change, Mr McKie. No obvious improvement, but no deterioration either. The doctors will be round at eight. You should phone back then.'

'Why aren't the fucking doctors there right now?'

'Mr McKie, it's half past five.'

'Look, I want to speak to a bloody doctor! What else do we pay them for? I'm a taxpayer. They're well-paid.. far too well-paid if you ask me, and you tell me they're never on the bloody job!'

'Mr McKie..'

'Don't you Mr McKie me..' Dan hissed.

Ella laid the phone down, shaking with anger. Ken, measuring the Richter scale of Dan's temper from where he was standing, stretched across the desk and picked up the receiver.

'Good morning, Dan. What seems to be the problem?' The voice as cold as ice.

'Groundwater! Do you *never* go home?'

Ken waved Ella away.

'I've just popped by in passing. Jess is doing all we can expect. Yes, the neurosurgeons will visit later. Shall I ask the day staff to arrange an appointment for you? Would you find that helpful?'

The modulated male tones cut the feet from Dan, already undermined by his own aggression. Such outbursts used to calm him. They didn't help anyone around him, he'd been told that often.

'Would you find that helpful?' Ken repeated. 'Shall I ask the staff to make you that appointment?'

'Yes, please,' Dan said at length. 'Get them to phone me with the time. I'll be at the Meredith.'

'By the way,' added Ken, 'did you know they're running a story about Jess in the early editions of the *Standard*?'

'What?'

'I didn't think you had anything to do with it,' Ken's voice grew kinder now. 'I was just saying to Ella that you wouldn't have sanctioned it. We're not releasing any news, obviously. Perhaps you'd get on to the paper, tell the journalists to stop harassing our nurses.'

Dan hung up. Dialled the newspaper. Didn't find it at all difficult to trace who gave permission to run the story. Rachel. It was already too late to dampen the enthusiasm for it; tabloids on the scent. As he stood beside the window, phoning, clutching Jess's nightgown, Dan knew he was already being photographed.

One newish reporter, scouring the hotel staff, stumbled on the young night-porter's tale and rushed back to Glasgow, where his gleefully offered narrative was binned.

'Dan McKie?' the tabloid editor laughed in his face. '*Dan McKie* soliciting young *males*? Who fed you this crap? Young females maybe.. under-age waitresses perhaps.. Do you want us sued for everything we've got? You'd be laughed out of court! No, we'll stick with the broken-hearted husband. That's quite enough of a lie to be going on with.'

Sending the novice scuttling, Des Millen retrieved the pad he'd confiscated, tossed into the wicker bin. Re-read the shorthand carefully. How, he pondered, could that greenhorn have turned up something so unexpected?

Incredible.

He scanned the notes again, removed offending pages one by one, then flicked a switch, fed them to the shredder.

'Dan, you old wanker,' he shrugged, 'you fucking owe me.'

Michael

PACKED ONTO THE train, Michael was very glad Julia had insisted on booking him first class. Standard accommodation had standing room only, luggage overflowing into all the aisles. His first class carriage seemed an oasis of unfair calm.

'It's the least we can do,' she'd said, discussing travel arrangements a full year back. 'Festival time.. bound to be crowded. There'll be more leg-room in first class. If I remember rightly, you're quite tall.'

He was. She was right about the leg-room too and he was grateful for it. It was a longish stretch to Oxford.

His interest in the Pictish language predated these southern years. Even before university in Glasgow, Michael had been hooked on the symbol stones, spent one long summer (luckily dry, sunny) at the end of first year hitching all over the Highlands trying to find and see and draw as many stones as possible.

That summer changed his life. He thought of it now as The Summer of the Stones. The stones and Morna, it must be said. His first attempt at intimacy.

Their tiny tent did not prove an advantage in this last respect; nor the cold hard ground. Hemingway was wrong. You couldn't do it in a sleeping bag, not easily.

Early efforts were the most disastrous. The whole camp-site must have heard and understood the combination of giggling and bumping and moaning. And they knocked the tent pole over, and the tiny nylon space sagged, collapsing over them. On film (especially American) the camp-site folk would all have been standing round, clapping, cheering, as he and Morna crawled out of the wreckage. That's not how it was. Michael recalled pained, embarrassed looks, caravanned matrons *tisking* as they slunk past, blushing, trailing clouds of midges. The tent pole got bent too.

She still sent him a Christmas card every year. More often than not it had a tent drawn in the snow behind the crib; or three fat kings bore armfuls of gifts labelled baked beans, lager, condoms, gleefully decorated with holly and ivy. They hadn't met, not in a dozen years. Michael was a little afraid to suggest this now, in case marriage and childbirth had translated the reckless girl he knew into a wordy matron. Morna had two children. No, three. He must remember *three*, try to. Should have written it in the address book next to her husband's name.

He did not have Jess's address, or email, or phone number. She had been going to write these down for him. Nor, he remembered, had he got round to giving her his own. But Julia could help there. Julia loved to be useful. Julia would know where everybody was. He must phone her the minute he touched base. In fact, he sneezed, he could phone her now. Kerry – indefatigable Aussie that she was – had thought of everything, even his mobile phone.

Finding him that morning on the step outside Maigret's, Kerry had taken charge.

'What's happened? Are you okay?'

He was shivering, too wet, too cold to speak. He'd spent the night wandering between the Meredith and Maigret's, back and fore, back and fore.

'Have you been drinking?'

But he didn't smell of alcohol, just rain and misery. Kerry sighed. 'Wait there. No,' she changed her mind. 'Come in and wait.'

She dragged him into the restaurant, sat him in a chair next to a radiator.

'Coffee first.'

She slapped a mug of latte down.

'Drink.'

Michael obeyed.

'Right, Mike. I've phoned my friend. She'll come in early, stand in for me. Which hotel are you in?'

She'd gone with him in the taxi, seen him up to his room, run a bath and ordered him firmly into it.

'I don't understand,' she kept saying, 'what it is with you Scottish guys? I wouldn't stand you up like that. She did, and look at you! What a state! And you, you've got no pride! More stuck on her than ever. No self-respecting Aussie would behave this way.'

Michael retaliated, called out from the steamy bathroom.

'No self-respecting Aussie would take help from a girl!'

'Now, I wouldn't say that.'

'Kerry!' he yelled, wishing he had locked the door, 'stay out there! Or I'll call..'

'You'll call who?'

'Julia,' Michael said, in desperation.

'Julia who?'

'The woman organising the conference. Doctor Julia Goggins. Very fierce lady.'

'Don't I know it? My giddy aunt!' said Kerry. 'I mean, she's my mother's sister. Don't you see the resemblance? Why do you think I came to your lecture last night? Talk about three-line whip!'

'What?'

'And Michael, Aunt Julia was worried, and not a little offended, when you left the dinner. It was noticed. I think you should phone her.'

'My mobile's dead.'

'Soon fix that. What time did you say the train was, Michael?'

Now he fished out his mobile, flicked it on. Nearby passengers frowned at him; one was frankly glowering. He took no notice. It was, after all, almost an emergency. But Julia wasn't in. He left a message on her voicemail.

'Julia, hi. Michael here.' This was difficult. How could he approach things tactfully? First, apologise. 'Sorry, I felt ill last night, had to leave so urgently. Gastric thing. I hope the museum staff passed the message on. I'm a bit better now. I wondered, actually, if you'd be able to give me Jess Kavanagh's phone number and email address? I seem to have mislaid them. And thank you for everything. Lovely conference. Seamless.'

He hoped that didn't sound too interested, too personal, or too off-hand. Julia mustn't think it unimportant.

Or too important either.

As the trolley-assistant filled his cup with coffee for the third time (real coffee, real cup, free.. that's what you paid for in first class, was it, that and leg-room?) he tried to understand and measure how he was feeling. Here he was, trailing south, away from Edinburgh, miserable, certainly; but not without hope. That was what he really couldn't understand, the hopefulness that somehow refused to fade. Jess. The feel of her. Her body against his. His arm, the arm she touched that first day, still bore the gentle pressure of her. How? Why? It had never been like this. He had never been like this.

He'd been standing outside the museum that first morning, unable to bear the echoing din, wondering if he shouldn't nip across the road for coffee. He had registered and wasn't needed for an hour at least.

'Excuse me.'

A small hand touched his arm. The sort of hand that might inspire Japanese love poems. A light touch.

Michael stared.

'Excuse me, sorry. I can see you're with the conference. Where are we supposed to go?'

He'd looked up then. The hand was attached to a dark-haired woman standing beside him. She didn't look familiar but she carried the conference folder, wore a delegate's badge on her right lapel.

'Actually,' he said, 'I was just about to duck out for an illicit cappuccino.'

'Sounds.. ooh..' her voice grew solemn, 'reprehensible. And dangerous. If Julia were to catch you, she'd not allow you back in.'

'I think,' Michael said, 'she'd let me give my own lecture. Perhaps.'

The dark-haired woman nodded. 'We might risk the coffee then.'

'But I would hate,' he warned, playing the game, keeping face and voice as serious as hers, 'to be held responsible for putting anyone at risk of Julia's displeasure. Without due thought. You're sure you're up to it?'

'I was thinking,' said Jess, 'more of your protection. Julia's very tall. Strong.'

'And you'd protect me?' Michael loomed over her five feet four.

'I've a black belt.'

He was duly impressed. 'What in?'

'My suitcase. Back at the hotel.'

She smiled, suddenly.

'What?'

Her eyes danced. 'Pardon?'

'What are you grinning at?'

59

'Nothing.'

'It's that joke, isn't it?'

'What joke?'

'The joke in my last book.'

'No,' Jess shook her head. 'I haven't read it. But jokes for archaeologists can't be bad idea. Not that I know any.'

'No?' Michael frowned. 'Why do people hate archaeologists on site?'

'Don't know,' she grinned.

His eyes narrowed. 'Because they're.. entrenched.'

'Ah.'

'Their career is in ruins.'

'Oh.'

'And they're always pre-hysterical. Never on the level.'

She shook her head.

'Come on,' he said. 'Try. Why do people hate archaeologists on sight?'

Now she laughed at him again. 'Saves time.'

'More coffee, sir?'

'Thanks.' Michael laid his cup down. He was drinking too much coffee, and it was not, after all, that good. He sneezed. This was a proper cold.

Not so long now. He was struck by the conviction that Jess would have phoned Julia already. There would be a letter or email from her, asking for a reprint. Perhaps an interview request?

She'd come down. He would meet her at the airport, insist on it.

That small hand on his arm.

They wouldn't talk. There would be no need for words.

That small hand on his arm..

He sighed, stared through the window at the rolling land, subversive in its endless spread of possibility. Seductive. Disruptive. There was no limiting that lack of sharp horizon diffused in sky.

He felt the same on islands, though with less imposed connectedness. On Orkney, on Lewis, there was no escaping sky, as there was no escaping, anywhere (he knew this all too well) love that strikes out of the blue.

And mountains were like love, mountains proved life, *im*proved it. That quality of otherness, of land still on the move, emotion jarred in polaroid suspense. Of course, they differed widely – all wonderful, spectacular. He never could decide which mountains he loved best. (Always the last ones visited, the last ones climbed.)

There's nowhere like Assynt, he's heard himself declaring, often and sincerely. Those unexpected mountains, uncompromising, like swirling waves, twisters, floating on a sea of moor.

Or yet again, Moidart. Nowhere like it – sweeping tree-lined flanks, heartland to the Jacobites.

Or Kintail. Or Glencoe. Or the Cuillin.

Mountain sky everywhere demanding homage from the air, binding soft grey cloud to disparate peak.

No, there was nowhere like Scotland, yet here he was. South. College-bound, river-fed. And yet this lack of hills also tendered pleasure.. different pleasure. Sunlight. Thunder.

A vernacular of land and weather. Oxford, with its busy streets, its college spires was part of that.

And Jess.. Jess would have phoned, certainly.

Michael rented a flat the college found for him when he began his PhD. Folk kept telling him it was time he put down roots, bought his own place, and now and then he did consider it. But this flat suited him; its stretching upper room and open kitchen, facing south, so light and bright always. The owner, overseas, showed no sign of returning, and the flat was near the town centre, near the college. Home, he slammed the door, retrieved the stack of mail that spilled across the doormat, running upstairs with it. He flicked eagerly through the thick pile.

All the mail was formal, official. It was, of course, too early.

Voicemail proved just as bad. Plenty of messages; none from Jess. None from anyone he really wanted to hear about. Not even Julia. One from Kerry, however, made him smile.

'So you're back. No moping, eh? I'm off to Ireland, Mikey. Keep that chin up, right?'

Email was even worse. What could his friends be thinking of, plaguing him with trivialities? He deleted everything, everyone, pulled a beer out of the fridge.

One substantial pleasure of his flat was its antique and outsized bath. Michael could never imagine how they'd forced it up the stairs. The brass taps and gargantuan plumbing resonated at full flow, making an unearthly sound like a band of untuned, out-of-control pipers. (He'd lost more than one flannel down the enormous plughole.) To fill the bath took a swimming pool of water, a whole hot tank, but to bathe in it, even alone, always relaxed him. Today he filled it to the top, ignoring the cacophony, jumped in, splashing, spilling water. The bathroom's black and white tiling was used to this, fit for it. The students down below never complained.

So he was back. This was not Edinburgh, even though the street would not have looked amiss in Stockbridge. Voices floating through the window belied that appearance. In a different register, they displayed their indisputably *English* music. Or lack of music. And foreign voices too danced on the street's symphonic plane. Not Edinburgh. Oxford. He was back, the conference over. No word from Jess, but that would come. Given time.

Michael dozed off in the lukewarm water.

Not the safest thing perhaps, although his feet (he stretched over six feet) almost reached the end. Floating, dozing, dreaming, he sank only once, sat up coughing, drank more beer.

He was suddenly aware that the telephone was ringing. It sounded oddly distant.

He didn't wait for towels, catapulted from the bath, racing through the flat. He caught the phone on the seventh ring, just beating the answer-service, breathless.

'Michael here. Hi.'

He hoped his voice was not too gruff.

'Michael, hello.'

He sagged. Julia, not Jess.

'Got your message,' Julia boomed, 'A pleasure to have you here again, and such a controversial lecture. Thought-provoking. Not that we didn't expect it. Know your quality.'

'Thank you.' Michael could hardly get the words in edgeways.

'I'll look up those addresses,' Julia said. 'Send them to you next week. Will that be okay? Only I'm off up to Perthshire. Don't you always think there's nowhere like Perthshire?'

'Beautiful,' he agreed.

'Yes, well. I hear you met my niece Kerry. Nice girl. Wild.'

'I thought her very kind,' Michael understood the warning. 'A bit of a livewire.'

'She should be at home, at university,' snapped Julia, 'not trailing round the world.'

'The university of life?' Even as he said this, Michael knew his mistake.

'Some of us,' said Julia, 'think rather too much of life. Anyway, I'll get those numbers for you. Shall I give Jess yours? She's quite a good reporter, a good contact.'

'Please,' he sighed.

She hadn't been in touch then. Julia rabbited on for ten, fifteen minutes more, seeking his feedback on the conference, on parts of it he didn't see. Hadn't they been on the tour bus together? Didn't she remember? Perhaps, Michael thought, Jess reached the café before him, left because he wasn't there. He had arrived late. Or perhaps she came and somehow missed him. Did he have the time right? He checked his watch against the video. The figures were the same. No, that wasn't the problem. His thoughts were drifting, he was losing it, losing concentration, standing in a pool of water, skin completely dry, more or less.

The flat across the road, he saw, had new tenants at last. Must have. The blinds were different. There were fresh flowers on the windowsill. Two girls of student age were standing at the window opposite, staring back at him, at his full frontal manhood. Michael blushed, turned his back, exposing nothing but his sagging shoulders.

Work was the thing. Always. He hid himself in work. Slipped into his cluttered study, squandering time, wandering through books, deciphering stray thoughts and ideas other people first shared hundreds, thousands, of years before.

Sometimes he'd get side-tracked. Sometimes he would sit wondering how best to make ideas last, how best he might preserve them. Clay, vellum, paper, acetate, the brief dancing electron all bent to words, ideas on the move, immobile while unread. The meaning only programmed as far the decipherer, the reader, would allow; as far as mind and capability, experience and knowledge dictated.

Michael lost himself in books. It had always been his way.

'Michael!' his mother calling. 'Come for tea!'

Michael never heard.

'Michael!' Morna warning him. ' I'm leaving. I'm going *now*.'

Michael never heard.

'Michael! Will you get your head out of that dictionary long enough for me to at least throw something at you?'

Michael did not hear, did not look up.

And now again, this minute, when the phone rang, Michael, in his study, surrounded by books, by dictionaries, by computerised reconstructions of the Symbol Stones, simply did not hear.

'Did you get him, Aunt Julia?' Kerry looked up, anxious.

'No,' Julia shook her head. 'he didn't answer.'

Kerry glanced down at the paper, the smiling photograph of Jess. The inch-high headline. JOURNALIST IN FREAK ACCIDENT.

'Critically ill,' she read. 'And she looks nice enough.'

'She is nice,' Julia nodded. 'A lovely girl. A bit lonely, I always thought.'

'What did you say?'

'I said.. a bit lonely.'

'No,' Kerry cut her aunt off in midstream, 'what did you say to Michael?'

'Nothing. I told you. He didn't answer.'

'But you left a message, surely?'

'No.' Julia frowned. 'How could I possibly leave news like that as a message on an answering service? I'll send him her address, that's what I'll do. Then the boy can write. If she survives..'

'There's a question about that?

'Certainly there is. *If* she survives, and *if* she's not brain-damaged..'

'God,' Kerry sat down, dazed. 'I never thought of brain damage.'

'Has to be faced. Then there's the partner. Abrasive horror of a man. Goodness knows how he'll react.'

'It's all so difficult.'

'I'll just send the address, say I've no more information. That's the best thing. Come on, Kerry, lass, cheer up! You're off to Kerry, land of your father, for the next month. That'll do the trick!'

'I suppose.' Kerry seemed unconvinced. 'You don't think we should try to phone again?'

'I expect he gets the *Standard*, even in Oxford. Lots of exiled Scots do. Or they get it on the net. Now come on, Kerry, get cracking. Get packing! We're off in half-an-hour.'

'Okay. Sorry, Aunt Julia.'

When Julia swept out of the room, Kerry tried Michael's number again. Still no answer. And when it came to the bit, she found she couldn't leave a message either.

Jess

'SPORTS DESK. DAN McKie.'

'Hello.. I mean.. hi. Hi, Dan. It's me.'

Dan knows her instantly. It's Tuesday, and it's raining. All morning he's been thinking about her, the girl he met in Aberdeen. Too nice. Too young.

'Jess? Good to hear you.'

She sounds carefree, light. Surprised.

'I didn't think you'd..'

'Jess, it's great to talk. What's your weather doing in Aberdeen? Still freezing?'

'Think so.'

Dan laughs. 'What d'you mean, think so? Don't you know? It's nearly midday.'

'Yes.' She's playing with the telephone cord, twisting it round all her fingers, twisting and untwisting it. 'I know. I'm thinking about lunch. That's why I rang.'

'I'm thinking about lunch too. Chinese.'

'Oh.' A pause. 'You're going out?'

'When I finish up here.'

'Ah.'

Jess seems oddly tongue-tied. Dan helps out. 'How about you?'

'I.. well.. I was hoping to meet a friend. Not sure he's free.'

'He?'

She laughs. 'It's the correct pronoun, I believe. For a male friend.'

'But, Jess, think about it.. *lunch*. With someone of the *opposite* sex? That's serious. *Think*. Would your mother approve? And this guy.. are you sure his intentions are honourable?'

'Yes. No. No. Don't know.'

'What?' He swings his chair round, faces the window. It's not taking time to rain. It's stotting.

She translates. 'Yes, lunch. No, not serious. No, my mother wouldn't like him. And as for his intentions. Haven't asked. Yet.'

Yet, Dan almost hisses. 'So where's he taking you?'

'Well..'

'Always insist on knowing where you're going, Jess. That's good advice. Take it from me. I'm older. I know.'

Silence again.

'Jess,' Dan knows he shouldn't be saying this. 'Jess, next time I come up to Aberdeen *we*'ll go for lunch. Somewhere really posh.'

'I prefer simple.'

'Okay, simple.' She didn't say no. She didn't say no.

'Where are you going today, Dan?'

'Haven't decided.'

'Who are you going with?'

'Oh, some of the guys.'

'Which ones?'

'You wouldn't know them, Jess.'

'No, but tell me what they look like, what their names are.'

'Why?' Dan smiles, turns his chair round. The office lies before him. At every desk, almost every desk, a friend bends over the computer or the phone. Stray plants litter the scene, occasionally impede the view. Someone must water them. The cleaner, probably.

'Tell me about the office. Describe your friends. Tell me what they look like.'

'Have you enough money for this? Shall I ring you back?'

'I'm okay.'

'Right, here goes.'

'Where are you, Dan? Begin with you.'

'Right. Don't interrupt again.'

'Touchy, eh?'

'Just putting on my journalistic voice.'

'Very persuasive.'

'Indeed. Well, I'm sitting at my desk, with my computer in front of me. From here, I can see the whole room.'

'All of it?'

'The whole room. I'm as far away as it's possible to be from reception. It's oh..' Dan stands up, estimating the distance, 'at least twenty metres long.'

'Like a swimming pool?'

'That's right. And nearly as wet today. Every time someone squelches into reception they seem to bring a swimming pool of water with them.'

'That's Glasgow for you.'

'Yes.'

'How far are you from reception?'

'I told you. Twenty metres.'

'Can you see it, Dan?'

'When I'm standing up. If I've my glasses on.'

'And who's going to lunch with you?'

'I haven't arranged it yet. Probably Jack and Tom.'

'What are they wearing?'

'Jack always wears a suit. His desk is next to mine.'

'What's his hair like?'

'Hair?'

'Has he got hair? At all?'

'Well, now you come to mention it, no. None.'

'And Tom?'

'He's wearing a green pullover.'

'Yellow tie?'

'How did you guess that?'

'Go on..'

Dan notices a buzzing in the background, an electronic sound. Computers switching on?

'Jess, where are you? Where are you phoning from?'

It's unmistakable. That voice in the background.

I'll put you on hold.

'Where are you phoning from?'

He crams his glasses on, sees at last the tiny figure in reception, cradling the phone, her head barely visible above the high counter, her hair flattened by the downpour to the line of her skull. She's looking at him, waving.

'Jess, what are you doing here?'

She sighs. 'I'm really hungry, Dan.'

three weeks on

THREE WEEKS TO the day after Jess's accident, Dan McKie went back to work. Tried to. It was not a success. His desk was piled with memos, his subeditor off sick; his computer had developed a glitch, would do nothing right. Rachel was avoiding him. Well, that was over. He'd made that pretty clear when last they spoke, the morning after Jess's accident. He missed the attention, of course, the sinuous feel of her.. missed her in bed.

'How do you..'

'How do I what?'

'How do you *do* it like that? Make me feel..'

He laughed a little. 'It's all down to a strict upbringing.'

'Oh?'

'That and the plaque above the bed.'

'Dan McKie slept here?'

'No,' he stroked her tiny breast, springing the disproportionately large nipple – a tayberry, a loganberry – sharply to attention. Some women felt nipple changes quite acutely. Others didn't notice. Dan had always been fascinated by nipples, their feel in the cupped palm, their sudden hardness, the way they worked independently. Women's bodies. Women. Prickly, all of them, sharp as blackthorn, and as beautiful. As a student, he'd driven through the fields of Blair at blackthorn time. Weddings always put him in mind of Blair at blackthorn time. Lace and hidden barbs.

'Tell me, then.'

'Tell you what?'

'What was on the plaque, idiot.' Rachel sounding confident, knowing she'd made it, unafraid now to rib him a little.

'Oh, the plaque. It said,' Dan lied, '*Home sweet home.*'

Well, it might have, if there'd been a plaque. His piano teacher did have one hanging by the cold and uncomfortable carved oriental chair you sat on in her hall as you waited for the lesson, hearing her berate the child before you, who like yourself never practised.

Good, better, best
Never let it rest
Till your good is better
And your better best.

Dan might not have practised the piano, no, but he had taken that advice, applying it to football. All things physical. Nor was he sure he'd reached the best stage yet, but he knew he was good. You did know. Didn't have to be told. Not that he and Jess..

He was glad to be rid of Rachel, slender or not.

It made work tricky though, today, the need to dance around avoiding her, having to get other folk to act as intermediary without actually spelling out the situation. They all knew fine. This was the downfield downside of an office dalliance, the awkwardness during and after. The only time an office gig was ever truly good news was early on, before it started. Then, it was wonderful, the wishful thinking, the certainty of seeing, meeting, the possibility (always the possibility) of touching. Dan enjoyed these early rituals.

In fact, if he was honest, it was the ritual he was addicted to. Except with Jess; but even Jess had not proved able to hold his attention for more than the first few years, maybe three, maybe four.

Why did she do it? Who did she do it with?

He didn't like to think about that room in the Meredith. Or Jess in hospital. Neither seemed to fit with what he knew. And this was not the building they'd worked together in, but still her face kept floating in and through the office, sliding between him and his erratic screen. Phone calls were interrupted by her screaming or the silence that had latterly descended on them in White Street. Their home had become the quietest, least conversational house he'd ever known. They had nothing to talk about. No words. None kind.

Dan struggled with the day, spilled coffee on his failing keyboard, sat for hours distracted while the outer office hummed, apparently oblivious to all his problems. Not a good day. One disaster following another. The final straw came when the editor summoned him.

'Come in, Dan,' he said, 'sit down. How are you? Rachel says..'

'After *Rachel* running that fucking story about Jess, I'm surprised you fucking listen to her.'

Jack looked down, away. 'I was off that night..'

'I know.'

Jack leaned forward, gestured Dan into the leather chair opposite.

'I told you to sit down. How's she doing?'

Dan sat down at last, shaking. His fingers strummed the chair-arm. No words came. Truth was he was finding it harder and harder to talk about Jess, think about her. His own mood didn't help, veering between anger and jealousy and hopelessness. Not a state he'd ever thought to find himself in.

'She's not that great,' he said at last. 'Not great.'

'But she's regained consciousness?'

'Yes.' Dan did not elaborate.

'What happened?' Jack asked, innocently enough. 'Has she been able to tell you what she was doing when she fell?'

'It's obvious,' Dan laughed harshly. 'Running for the bus. In stupid shoes.'

'But why? Why that bus?'

'God only knows. I don't.'

Silence followed. Dan crossed his arms and legs, glanced uneasily about the room, avoiding his colleague's eyes, staring at each and every object, every corner, concentrating, as if memorising every detail. Jack broke first.

'There's often,' he offered, 'a bit of amnesia after a blow to the head.'

'Yes I know. It's not that.'

Dan's face crumpled now, and trickling down his cheeks were wet tracks Jack would have interpreted as tears on anybody other than Dan McKie.

'Not amnesia, Jack. She's lost.. seems to have lost.. the power..'

He didn't finish. Couldn't bring himself to use the words.

Jack waited, did not understand.

'I don't follow, Dan. What do you mean, she's lost the power?'

'The power of speech,' Dan said at last. Whispered. 'She.. Jess.. can't *speak*.'

'What?'

'Not a word. Not a single word. It's even hard to know if she takes in what you say to her. No. No, it's not!'

Dan's voice was rising. He was shouting now.

'I'm lying.. bloody lying, Jack. She doesn't take a thing in, not a single thing, lies cowering, a lump of bruises, broken bones. No understanding. Nothing. And Jack,' his voice faltered, broke, 'she screams all the time I'm there, like some fucking animal. I can't bear it, can't fucking bear it.

'The quacks call it traumatic *amnesia* and *aphasia*. Say it's because of where the bleed was in her brain. And I don't remember, Jack!' he started to shout again, furious with Jess, the world, the doctors. 'I can't seem to take anything in myself. They told me, they showed me, drew it for me, and still I can't remember. Can't remember anything at all for more than a few minutes at a time. Nothing.

'Nothing but this. Look what I found, Jack, in her fucking hotel room. Look what I found.. and a fucking bin full of used condoms..'

Embarrassed, Jack picked up the strip of purple foil Dan threw across the desk. Stared at it for a good ten seconds. Looked at Dan directly. Opened his mouth. Shut it. Sighed. Started over, his kind face working with pity and understanding. He stood up, walking to the window. Turned back, his face serious and pale.

'Be fair about this, Dan. You've been playing away from home for years. I've never quite known how Jess coped.'

Dan bristled.

'That's right! Hit me when I'm down!'

Jack's response was measured, quiet.

'How long have I known you? Do I ever lie?'

Dan smiled unwillingly.

'No. No you don't.'

'Then I won't start now. How many affairs have you had in the last two years, never mind the last ten?'

'Leave it, Jack. I warn you. Don't go there.'

'Then don't judge Jess, Dan. You know what they say.. people in glass houses. What's sauce for the goose..'

'Gander,' Dan snapped. 'Get the gender right, at least!'

Jack shrugged, looked away. Stared out of the window.

Rain. Why did it always rain?

Poor Jess. Poor, poor Jess.

He looked back at Dan, his friend of fifteen, twenty years. This had been hard on him. He'd lost weight. Aged. Shrunk.

'You're not fit to be here.'

'No.'

'A spell off work would help.'

'Hasn't helped so far. I don't need to be pensioned off. What

I need is something to get my teeth into.'

'You'll take a month off,' Jack said sternly. 'Look at you. Then, if you're fit, if Jess is coming on, we'll talk about that sabbatical you asked for last year.'

'No, Jack!'

'And that's my last word on the subject. Except..'

'Except what?'

'Margot's expecting you home with me tonight for dinner.'

'I've made plans.'

'Change them. Spend the rest of the day sorting out the odds and ends. Meet me here at six.'

'Six?'

'We'll go for a drink first. And don't tell me you're on the wagon. I can see you're not. You should be, but you're not.'

Dan sighed.

'That's next week's problem.'

Jess

FOR JESS, THE first few days after she opens her eyes bring drifting floods of pain and noise. Her throat, now empty of the laryngeal tube, is hot and dry, aching. Her face hurts even more; her scalp and shoulders, lacerated, scabbing, pillow her in grief. Her left leg has become a constant source of agony, all the more defeating because she has no words and cannot understand that there is life beyond the tearful sum of injuries. Her world is a burning desert of unpitying light and noise and she lies stranded in the wasteland, helpless.

She does not realise, does not remember, the possibility of words. Somehow she has forgotten language. When the nurses speak at her she feels only the rush and pointless impact of air fumbling her middle ear. When Ken and Ella whisper she has not an inkling that their voices mean any more than the noisy vacuum-cleaner the ward staff wheel past her every day. Not that she realises it passes her every day, twice a day. The noise itself overwhelms her every time it growls by, and she, totally unable, unequipped to cope with it, with no understanding, no reaction to that resonance except instinctive panic.

Her bed stands near a window. Once, the window open, she hears a blackbird sing. The trickling notes, cohesive, true, move her to tears. She cannot remember what the sound means, why she loves it; but she recognises beauty, weeps at the pleasure of it.

Other things. The starched hospital sheets chafe at her arms, her buttocks, leave her deeply uncomfortable, but the itch, so much less than her pain, is lost in the feeding maelstrom.

And when Dan comes in, makes noises at her – every time he comes, Jess frowns, stiffens, screams. Every time. It's not the words, not how he makes those indecipherable noises. No. His presence brings a vice-like increase in her pain, as if he's laid it on her, dementing agony. Not that she understands that, or could explain it if she did.

She has lost language. Time stands still.

Jess is so much, at this time, like a new-born child, all traumatised sensation. There is, however, somewhere at the back of her head, a store of memories, flickering pictures, technicolour. Silent movies. Any captions left are indecipherable, unrecognisable, no more than decoration.

Ken seems quite familiar to her, warm. Her stored reflections of Ken are happy, bright. Ella is completely new but somehow close, her voice familiar; as the other nurses are, as is the woman who comes to see her three, four times a day and blows sound at her, staring hopefully into her eyes. Jess watches her.

'See? She's in there,' Sian says. 'Ella, I guarantee she's in there. Give it a few days, and we'll get purpose, understanding. If only we could help her recognise her partner. It must be so difficult for the poor man.'

'She doesn't want to know him,' Ella frowns. 'It's like she needs to shut him out.'

'She's reacting to his grief. His fear.'

'That's possible.'

'It's what's happening, I tell you. The guy's a bit abrasive, but there's something about him.'

'Sian! He's appalling!'

'I don't think so. The guy is only stressed out of his skull.'

'I've seen folk stressed. That man is overbearing. Angry.'

'He's angry, certainly. Not an uncommon reaction.' Sian picks up all her books and papers. 'When will you be transferring her?'

'Transferring her?'

'To Glasgow. Don't they come from Glasgow?'

Ella nods. 'Dan the man has insisted that she stay here. Tell the truth, Sian, I'm glad. I don't think it would help her to be shunted across country – not like this. And I'm glad I shifted from High Dependency at the same time. Continuity may not be everything, but..'

Shivering, Sian looks across the ward, into Jess's staring eyes.

'Ella.. I suppose you bear in mind that Jess has no way to express her pain?'

'We try,' Ella nods again. 'But you're right, Sian. It's all too easy to forget.'

'Being aware is half-way to combating that.'

'Not the whole way, though,' Ella sighs. 'Don't you hate to think of her stuck in there, suffering?'

'You won't let that happen. Still, it's odd about the partner,' Sian sighs, bringing the conversation back to Dan. 'They've been together.. how long.. ten, twelve years? It can't all have been bad.'

'How are we to know? There's no way she can tell us. It's even difficult to tell what food she likes.'

'She's feeding herself now?'

'We feed her. She drinks well enough. The eating's harder work.'

'Think how sore her face must get, swallowing, chewing.'

'Well,' says Ella, 'what can you do? She's for theatre, tomorrow. More skin grafting – early afternoon.'

'I'll come in in the morning, then.'

'Make it early morning,' Ella suggests, 'before the pre-med kicks in.'

Sian

SIAN HAD NOT been in Edinburgh long enough to have lost her sense of wonder at the sheer diversity of buildings, all so closely packed together. The contrast of Princes Street Gardens, that green swathe cut between the Old Town and the New; the fairy-tale of painted buildings scrabbling up and over the Mound; the Old Town, so palpably an area where folk had lived and gossiped for centuries.

She counted herself lucky to be renting a flat behind the High Street, the close hidden from view, opening on a square rich with cherry trees. The blossom, when she first moved in last spring, had been thick, prolific, drifts of soft pink petals swathing the paving. Being off the High Street, well down the hill, almost at the Canongate, she didn't suffer from the traffic noise. The flat was double-glazed. That helped too.

Even laden with shopping, as she was at this moment, Sian enjoyed the walk. You could walk everywhere in Edinburgh. Sometimes she tried to imagine the High Street as it might have been three, four hundred years before; the animals, the folk, the muck, the sedan chairs. Imagine being bumped along in one of those, dependent on others' arms, others' legs. Pretty uncomfortable, you would have thought. A statement of power missing today – hospital stretchers, perhaps, the nearest equivalent – offering quite a different message. Only the eminent used sedans. There was one, in fact, in the Museum of Scotland, a narrow, confining box, coffin-like, which had belonged not to a nobleman, but the city's most prominent doctor.

She loved the new museum, the unexpected light and shade, the whiteness and richness of it. Even the way the steps were decorated with dark circles. So much attention to detail in its reaching for the past, in its offering the remnants to a present littered with all the detritus of the television age. She visited the museum often, always found something to catch her interest. She might go along that way tonight. It was late opening, should be.

Born and raised in Glasgow, Sian, coming to this job, found she knew surprisingly little of the capital. She'd been pleased to discover it so much less wet than its sister city; remembering all those years of forgetting umbrellas, of streaming hair and jackets steaming with rain. Edinburgh had its underside, its drug addicts, its share of vandalism. The shops were perhaps a little less vibrant than Glasgow's, the city's dress-style verging more towards the legal (or perhaps the parliamentary) dark suit than you'd have seen in her native city.

Glaswegians liked to sparkle. Edinburgh folk, she thought, tended towards the neat. That was okay. Not a problem.

And walking home was a delight these mild autumn evenings, the leaves not turning yet, not quite, although there had been one or two mornings with that gentle freshness you knew would turn to frost in a week, maybe two. She'd been shopping, food for the weekend, enough to see her well into next week. Sian loved to cook, took pleasure in exploring new exotic tastes. The language of food, the related mythology, always beguiled.

Not that she was thinking about food. She was turning over and over in her head a phrase she'd happened on in a magazine at work *the word has nothing absolute about it.* Balzac. Well, of course it didn't. Difficult, impossible to fix meaning, any meaning, even in simple words. As for his next assertion *we act more on the word than it acts on us*? She was not so sure about that.

Words were powerful tools. Spoken, written or simply thought, they built themselves into the body, translating into movement of nerve and muscle, sinew; even bone.

Words, she conjectured, warming to the notion, swam around the arteries and veins. They released or bound, not necessarily because of the symbols they represented.

Sound itself was emotive.

Words were music too.

'Penny for them.'

Sian looked up, startled.

'Mr McKie! What on earth are you doing here? Aren't you going back to Glasgow?'

Dan's expression was guarded, hard to read.

'No. Well, I did, but I wasn't all that useful. Couldn't concentrate. I've been told to take the next month off.'

'What will you do?'

He shoved his hands in the pockets of his crumpled raincoat, looked at the pavement.

'Haven't the faintest idea. I want to try to help Jess, somehow. I want to stop feeling like some bloody monster every time she screams at me.'

He trailed into silence, gazing down the hill towards Holyrood and all the street chaos associated with the building of the new Parliament. Sian let the silence stretch. Dan did not break it.

'I can see,' she offered at last, 'it must be difficult.'

'Impossible.'

He sighed, changed the subject, his tone noticeably brisker.

'So what about yourself?'

'I beg your pardon?'

'What are you doing here?'

'Me? I live quite near.'

She did not volunteer her address.

'Good,' he smiled. 'Then you'll be able to tell me where to find this fancy new restaurant everyone's talking about.'

'You've passed it. Further back, see?' Sian pointed up the street. 'I'm a little afraid it might be shut already. Winter closing hours.'

'Pity. Well, I'll run by it anyway. Thanks. Good to see you. Catch you later.'

He turned, strode off up the hill, shoulders set as if to counter great odds, heavy grief.

The word, thought Sian, was desperate. That man was desperate. She picked her bags up, ducked into her close. She did not see Dan, now moving across the street, look back, consciously noting her direction.

Dan

AS SIAN PREPARED her prawn and avocado salad, Dan trailed up the street regretting the impulse that brought him through to Edinburgh, regretting having taken the Tron flat for a whole month. He should have stayed in White Street.

No.

All those phone messages.

All of them for Jess.

Folk looking for her, unaware of all that happened, despite the nation-wide publicity after the accident. How could they have missed it? Didn't anyone read papers once they'd bought them?

Those who asked to speak to her upset him most. He shouted at them. Couldn't help it. Shouted, slammed the phone down. The phone calls left him shaking. And as for all those well-meaning callers, the incessant trundle of Jess's friends to his door. He never answered; watched them in retreat, wafting along White Street in all their variety. She made a lot of friends, Jess, always did. He studied them, trying to decide if any of these men might be the one.

He didn't think so. None of them seemed lost enough.

Whenever he thought about that bedroom in the Meredith his hands shook and his heart thumped too fast; rolling, rattling, caged but not safe. Not safe. No. Was any of these men the one? He couldn't tell. How could he? Seeing them only in reverse. What if.. he hadn't thought of this before.. what if there wasn't only one?

What if Jess, like himself, had taken a series of lovers? She could have done, and easily. He was always away, always busy. Always (the words slid unbidden through his head, couched in Jack's sensible and disapproving Highland tone) always *on the randan.*

He was outside *La Vie en Rose* now. That speech therapist.. he couldn't think what she was called.. did they ever tell him? Well, whatever her name was, she was right. The restaurant had closed over an hour ago. It looked pleasant enough, what he could see of it, peering into the inner darkness. He'd come back another time. For now he headed on up the hill.

Every bar he looked into was crowded, noisy; most of them with televisions blaring in high corners. Widescreen. He'd forgotten the match tonight. Rangers. Bayern Munich. Odd, but since the accident he'd found it less and less easy to maintain energy and enthusiasm for what had always been his life's main interest. Why should he suddenly question the meaning, the aesthetic, of it all ? Football was the only game. The beautiful game. The skilful game. The philosophical game. Music too: the football crowd's excited soughing always seemed to Dan like waves crashing the shore. Who could want background music in a pub when they could have football?

For twelve, fifteen, years he'd rushed around the world, watching twenty-two players locked in elegant combat. He'd seen so many dressing-rooms, board-rooms; so much corporate entertainment it had become diffused, a blur, something he had to deconstruct to sift any meaning from it all.

In the old days, his columns wrote themselves in bursts of intuition and delight. Now his over-intimacy with the game meant he had to work much longer, much more seriously, for the same effect. Word was, his new style had set a fashion. He didn't know. All he knew was, here and now, trailing up the Royal Mile, football was the last thing on his mind.

He needed help. Needed soothing.

He felt.. how did he feel?
Numb. Alone.
It had never been so difficult getting through the day.

Even food was difficult. He was seriously into food. Jess never
was, not really. Not that she didn't eat, she did, quite liked cooking.
Simple plain things. She never let herself be carried away by the
romance of it.
'What on earth have you got there?'
'Oysters. Champagne.'
It was her birthday. She laughed when the champagne exploded,
fizzing all over his new silk tie, the green one with stars that had
been a present from Rachel. She laughed at his handless (he has to
admit it was handless) attempt at opening the champagne bottle,
turned her nose up at the oysters.
'Mmm.'
Dan, relishing oyster after oyster, looked up, disappointed.
'What's wrong? Don't you like them?'
'They're a bit..' Jess thought about it, finally pronouncing, 'well,
genital, actually – definitely. Vaginal.'
'Jess!'
'You asked.'
Savouring the sea-tang, he thought about it. She was right.
'How do they compare,' he asked, 'with semen?'
She didn't blink.
'Not the same. Semen's fishier. Mildly anaesthetic.'
They lapsed into silence after this pronouncement.
Jess shook her head.
'Dan, about this conference next week. I've spoken to Julia and
she says there is a place, that she'll hold it for me. I'll be off on
Wednesday, back Saturday.'
'A long conference.'
'Only three days,' she pointed out, reasonably enough. 'You're
still going to that dinner in St Andrews at the weekend?'
'Think so,' Dan was carefully noncommittal. He was taking Rachel.
'When are you off?'
'Saturday.'
'I'll not see you till Sunday night then. Maybe Monday.'

Dan, feeling dismissed, insisted, 'I'll fetch you from the station.'

'Dan, you've lost your licence.'

'We'll take a taxi,' he said airily. 'You'll be back mid-morning, and the guys aren't coming for me till four o'clock.'

'See how you feel next week.' Jess gave him no encouragement. 'Your arrangements may well change. It's not as if I can't see myself home from Queen Street.'

'On the other hand,' Dan smiled, 'I might.. just might.. like to see you for half an hour when you've been away all week.'

'Fine,' she gave in, pouring the last of the champagne. He reached for the oysters, stirring, rattling empty shells.

'And not a pearl,' said Jess, 'among them.'

Dan could taste them still. Was not altogether sure he didn't prefer Guinness with oysters. Vaginal? Yes, they were.

'Jess,' he'd complained, 'Jess, how can you possibly know what a vagina tastes like?'

She laughed.

'Smell and taste, Dan, are one and the same.'

Why did he argue?

'Give or take a few thousand taste-buds.'

This set Jess off. 'They're similar enough. You of all people must know! Smell is under-rated.'

'Pheromones,' Dan shook his head. 'Old hat.'

She frowned.

'I don't think so. It's not just pheromones. Aroma, scent, call it what you will. I mean, think about it! Smell's the only thing that evokes atmosphere, memory – individual. Particular. And it does it all so subtly, so completely.. sweeps you back through years, across thousands of miles, right back to the precise place you remember it from. Like it's marked your body. Like it stimulates cell-memories.'

'How New Age!'

'It's science, Dan. Words and images are filtered through the conscious bit of our brains, but smell goes straight to the emotions.. hard-wired.. to what they call the limbic system. They know about these things. More than sexual behaviour is suggested to us by subtle odours we have known and loved. Or hated.'

'Rubbish. We may be animals, but at least we're rational.'

Fluid from the last of the oysters trickled down his chin. She handed him a napkin.

'You think so?'

Dan knew there was a sushi bar in the old *Scotsman* building, but that wasn't the kind of food he needed, not tonight. Pub food would have been best, but he couldn't face the football. Against his better judgement he crossed the road, drifted into a small Italian café, ordered lasagne. Red wine. Garlic bread.

The wine was almost drinkable. Mildly anaesthetic.

Sian

SIAN SWITCHED THE television on. News. *Neighbours*. She flicked it off, restless. Nothing worth watching and tonight the flat seemed tiny, cramped. She pulled her coat back on. No point in staying in when she felt like this. She'd go to the museum. Yes.

The High Street was still full of visitors. It was odd how they came and came. Festival time had been colourful, but quite impossible, pushing up and down the hill through massed crowds gathered round the armies of Fringe entertainers. After the first week she stopped being amused, began to find it an enormous nuisance, the buses slowed to stop and all the streets impassable on foot. The weather none too kind. She had tried a couple of shows, found them expensive.

She was still a little lonely here. Oh, the hospital was fine, gregarious enough, a social life of sorts; but after Matt, and with her twin Jamie still in England, still studying, she hadn't properly explored the local scene. Phone calls were a help. Email too. They made good use of it. Email lingered, could never be deleted. She liked that about it. Words that would not be dismissed, nor rubbed out. Stood to reason, you had to choose those words with care. She quickened her step, passing the designer jumper shop, eyes averted. She couldn't afford to go back in there, not till the payday after next.

On up the Royal Mile, past all the pubs, the model shop, the cafés, almost up to Gladstone's Land, then down past the library, towards Greyfriars Bobby chivvying the tourists across in Chambers

Street. This was a very long way round, but she liked the walk, found the folk encountered along it flamboyant, arresting.

Like that man in the crumpled raincoat walking ahead of her, briskly at times. Other times he stopped, stood completely still, shaking his head, perplexed. Then he'd seem to pull himself together, stride off into the distance again as if he didn't altogether know where he was going. He didn't seem quite of this world.

Perhaps, she thought, perhaps he was a newly-wingless angel, like in that Wim Wenders film – an angel who had lost his wings and armour. Now he was swallowed in a bus tour crowd, only to reappear outside the new museum, where she caught his face in profile, recognised the slightly too-pink skin, the vulnerable tone that only redheads have. Dan McKie. She should have known. There had been a familiar set to those marching shoulders, so reminiscent of the first time she'd glimpsed him, lost and hopeless, in the hospital corridor.

Ella was wrong about that man. Whatever drove him, it wasn't all anger. But Dan McKie belonged to the world of work. Sian didn't want to meet him now. She hung back, saw him move slowly along Chambers Street, ignoring the museum steps. Good. He'd be unlikely to disturb her.

She slipped into the entrance tower of the Museum of Scotland, ears singing in the resonance inherent to the space. It was almost palpable. Martello towers felt the same. She knew, having visited one as a child. And once, in Cape Breton, in the UCCB library, a Mi'kmaq room, a perfect oval round the Mi'kmaq star, reduced her to the same state of awe.

Wordless. Listening.

The attendant nodded. Sian smiled, moving on, past the white screen, the unexpected slitted shards of light.

She took herself from Hawthornden Court, the soaring white room at the heart of the new building and down a narrow, grey-stained stair. This led to the Early Living section, a much lower room, still white. Shallow steps ambled through a fist of iron men, over marbled floors to stones set upright in islands. Stones like broken hearts, like phalluses. Pictish stones. Intricately carved.

Sian would have liked to feel them, touch them. Surely stones like these were meant for touching? She knew better than to try, instead wove her way round and through the space.

Life from neolithic times was represented here, up till the dark ages: worked silver, gold that somehow escaped the grasp of time (often in hoards, buried for safety); a warrior's grave, where hands that once held weapons lay disintegrated, undignified – bones scattering beneath a hilt, or over the disappeared testicles. No doubt these bones had been placed exactly as found. They'd have been drawn, mapped. The warrior's lower jaw had shifted too, appeared now to be biting the remains of his skull. He had his comb with him. Sian wondered at that. Sailing in his stone boat to Valhalla, this warrior could comb his beard. She wandered back and back to the carved upright stones, moved by the sheer craft, the beauty of the carving, the life-drawn simplicity of the animal symbols, the impressive order of the battle scenes. These stones were older than the Viking grave, much older, their story more intricate, less clear.

The phrase she had been puzzling over earlier came back to her, the Balzac.. *The word has nothing absolute about it.. its force is due to the images we have acquired and associate with it..* images we have acquired and associate with it. These people, thought Sian, must have been masterful with language. Their symbols were unbearably strong.

On the way out she picked up a flyer with a Pictish stone emblazoned on the front of it. *The Riddle of the Picts.* Sian folded the paper, stuffed it in her pocket. She was almost hungry now. Turning into Chambers Street, she walked right into Dan McKie. Literally.

'It's our night for meeting.'

'What?' Dan seemed disorientated.

'Are you alright, Mr McKie? Are you not going home tonight?'

'No. I'm going for a drink,' he said thickly. 'Fancy coming?'

Sian smiled, 'Sorry. Work to do.' She hesitated. 'Do you know where you're going?'

'Do I look lost?'

She didn't take offence at his sharp tone, said firmly, 'Frankly, yes. But if you don't need help, I'll say goodnight. See you at the hospital.'

'Yes. At the hospital.'

She turned away, and was moving down the street when she heard muffled sobbing. Dan was crying openly. She couldn't leave him like that. 'Mr McKie,' she said, 'look. Come and have a cup of coffee. Maybe talking will help.'

She steered him across the road into a café bar, ordered for them both. Dan sat, eyes closed, collapsed against the high back of the soft settee. He tried in vain to stem the tears.

'There you go,' she said. 'Latte. Hope that's okay.'

They sat in silence, staring at their cups, at the table, at the floor.

If there was one thing Sian had learned to recognise beyond the need for words, it was the need for silence.

weeks later

THE KNOCK AT the duty room door interrupts the nursing report. Ella looks up, frowning. She has only reached the third set of notes and has, so far, endured four interruptions; six, if you count the phone.

'What now?' The tone is sharp.

'Fit like, Ella?'

The ambulance driver's expression is not in the least apologetic. His mouth may be unsmiling, but his eyes are quick with mischief.

'Sorry tae barge in. The wee bank nurse isnae sure fit ye'll be daein wi' Mrs McKendrick. The new wifie,' he adds. 'Fae Leith.'

Ella raises her eyebrows. All the nurses in the duty room sit up, hold their breath.

'We'll be looking after her, Kev. Bizarrely enough, that's what we're here for.'

He seems undismayed. 'Fit tae be tied, eh? They said you were.'

'You want your head in your hands?'

Tension is rising. Kev ignores or simply misses it.

'The lassie oot there disnae ken fit room ye want the patient in.'

Ella's face is like thunder. She glances up at the notice board.

'She's for Room Six. Oh, and Kev, the other patient in that room is not up to your banter. Seriously.' She looks him straight in the eye.

'Anither auld cratur?'

'Young. Head injury. Aphasic. And easily upset.'

'I'll mak Janet lay off, then.'

'You do that,' Ella nods, turning back to her nurses, to the report. 'Where was I? Minnie Corrance..'

Kev steps back into the corridor, mimicking the Highland sharpness.

'We'll be looking after her. That's what we're here for! As if!'

Janet pays no attention. Crouched at the entrance, she is blethering away to the bank nurse and the frail old woman on the stretcher. In the ambulance the auld biddie had been singing away – *The Twelve Days of Christmas* – a bit out of season and even more out of tune. Now in full flight, she's gabbing ten to the dozen, fairly enjoying it. A lonely old soul. It's a shame, thinks Kev, to put the cratur in a room with someone who can't talk back to her, someone as difficult as this other patient sounds.

'Okay boss?' Janet smiles as he saunters over. 'Got our marching orders?'

'Room Six.'

'Six geese a-laying, eh?'

Mariah McKendrick grins.

'I'd rather have the five gold rings.'

'Oh you would? Well, see and send them to the hospital safe.'

Janet keeps up the banter as Kev releases the brakes and they wheel the ambulance trolley down the corridor.

'So, here we are, Room Six. This is your stop, Mariah. Jenny's the boss from here. She'll soon have you settled.'

They slide the trolley alongside the bed, gently lifting the patient over.

'There you are. Right opposite the nursing station, see? There's usually someone sitting there. Don't worry. It won't feel strange for long. And Jenny will give you a buzzer. Press it if you need anything. The nurses and the young doctor will soon sort you out. In a day or two you won't know yourself. Well? What is it, Kev?'

His expression has changed. He looks puzzled. Wary.

'Have I forgotten something? Scratched something?'

She swings round, checking.

'What's wrong? What's the matter?'

'See that quine?' Kev's gaze lingers on the pale, still figure on the opposite bed. 'Thon's the quine fae the accident on Princes Street. The bus..'

Janet turns, whispering. 'God, so it is. And to think I didn't even notice. Jess, wasn't it? Jess.. I'm so sorry.. didn't mean to ignore you.'

She moves swiftly across the four-bedded room, checking the name scrawled in blue marker pen above the patient's wardrobe. *Jess Kavanagh.*

'How are you doing, Jess?'

There is little response, though Jess's eyes flicker briefly over them all. Janet tries once more.

'Are you feeling better?'

Again, no response. The pale face scarcely moves. Jess shuts her eyes.

Kev's bleeper erupts, sudden, loud. Jess flinches. Kev damps the volume, turns away.

'Sorry. I'll hae to get this.'

'Use the nursing station.'

'Aye.'

Janet walks round the bed, propping herself on the arm of the low chair beside it, assessing the thin pale cheeks, the patchy hair. Jess looks, she thinks, like a plant dying of lack of care, a plant that has been frosted.

'You won't remember. Kev and I brought you in after.. after the bus.'

Brown eyes settle on Janet, with no expression in them. Janet looks into them, wondering.

Kev waves impatiently from the corridor.

'We're awa! Janet! Hurry up!'

She shrugs.

'Och, Jess, I'll have to rush. Tell you what though, I'll come back and see you. After my shift. Do you fancy that?'

She leans forward, patting Jess's hand. Beside her, Jenny stiffens, bracing herself for the screaming that generally follows contact with a stranger. Jess can take hours to settle.

The screaming doesn't happen. The mouth opens, shuts.

'No.'

The word is barely audible. The lips hardly move.

'What did you say, Jess?' Janet bends forward.

'No.'

'You don't want visitors?'

'No.'

Jenny grips Janet's arm, pulls her away.

'You don't realise,' she says, 'Janet, that's the.. the.. first..'

'First what?'

'The first time she's spoken. Her first word.'

Janet doesn't follow.

'Since the coma,' Jenny insists.

'What?' Janet shakes her head. 'That can't be right, surely. Sure you've got the right patient? Is this true?'

'Janet!' Kev insists. 'Come oot o there! We hae tae hurry!'

Janet hesitates.

'Look,' she says at last. 'I'll come back. Are you on this evening?'

Jenny shakes her head.

'Ella is.'

'Right. Tell her I'll be back. See you later, Jess,' Janet smiles then turns back to the patient they've just left. 'See you too, Mariah.'

Mrs McKendrick nods.

'Thanks. Thank you, lass.'

'Janet!'

'Sorry, guys.. got to run.'

She backs the trolley out of the limited space, edging it through the door.

'See you later on.'

'No,' Jess insists. 'No.'

Janet

'SO WHAT DID Ella say to you? Tell me again.'

The ambulance edged its way past Haymarket Station.

'That the patient in Room Six wouldnae cope wi us. That she wis a head injury. Aphasic. Easily frightened.'

'Fucking hell.'

'An you telt me she spoke!'

'She did. Said no. Quite clearly.'

'Fit was the question?'

'I asked her would she like us to visit.'

Kev laughed. 'Nae sae daft then..'

'The wee bank nurse says it's the first word anyone has heard from her.'

'Christ,' whistled Kev. 'How long is that ?'

'Weeks ago, wasn't it?'

' Festival.'

'You're right. What a memory for faces you have,' Janet sighed, looked out the window. 'When you think what the poor lass was like. How d'you do it?'

'Dinna ken. It's like barcoding, I think. Or like drivin.. ken, like when ye dinna get more nor the briefest keek at the quine in the car racin directly at ye.. ken fit I mean, eh?'

'Oh, I'm not in your league, Kev. Chauvinists' brigade, is it? And where,' she asked suddenly, 'exactly are we going? What was all the rush? What are we doing here?'

'We're first on call.'

'So.. why are we suddenly at the zoo?'

'Tae see the lion-keeper.'

'What?'

'The lion's cut its paw. Someone has tae fix it.'

'Kev! Be serious!'

'Okay. Just a wee fib. The giraffe. Forgot itsel. Sat doon. Legless. We hae tae winch it up again.'

'Kev!'

'Ye're richt. I shouldnae tak the job hame wi me.'

'Kev. I want the proper briefing. Give me the information.'

'I telt ye. Ane o the lion-keepers..'

'Kev!'

'Cross my hert! And hope, somehow, nae tae dee!'

'Kev!'

'Look, quine. God's own truth. The lion-keeper slipped when he wis practisin Salsa dancin in the lions' enclosure..'

'I'm warning you..'

Kev chuckled. He could keep this up for ever.

Michael

MICHAEL WAS DRINKING too much. Every night he told himself this was the last time he'd open a bottle alone, that he shouldn't drink without company. Then, every night, he'd open a bottle, promising himself he would drink three glasses, no more. After all, red wine was good for you. Everybody said. Every night found him draining the dregs of the first bottle. Opening another.

Jess hadn't written back.

No letter.

No email.

No telephone message.

Julia sent only her home address, saying she'd mislaid the other details. This was not at all like her and Michael did wonder what it might imply. He took his courage in both hands, wrote anyway, sent a card, a friendly card, not spelling out anything; but giving his phone number, saying how good the conference had been. He had to be subtle. Patient.

Students were gathering; the new term would start soon. They were finalising timetables, updating the website. The day Lesley came to take his photograph for the departmental web page found Michael very low.

He'd written to Jess ten days before. So far, there had been no answer.

Lesley thought he needed cheering up. She tried hard, did her best, to make him smile.

'Come on, say cheese. Gorgonzola! Loch Ness Monster for Prime Minister! Anything! Just stop glowering!'

'I'm trying,' he fixed his eyes on her camera bag, on the badges. 'What's this? You were at the Fringe? Edinburgh? You were in Edinburgh?'

'Yes. Ah, of course..' she refocused the camera, 'so were you.'

'Not at the Festival, no. I was up at a conference. Picts!'

'I heard. Quite a buzz about it.'

'Oh?'

Lesley took this chance to flatter. He looked as if he needed it.

'Your lecture went down well. The *Scotsman* reviewed it.'

'Oh? '

'Michael,' she lowered the camera, spoke to him quite firmly. 'Look this way. Straight at me. And please, not so scary. First years check out the site most. You don't want to send them away in a panic.'

'Sorry.'

'That's better.'

She angled her shot carefully. The room was not that tidy.

'Now.. what was I on about?'

'Festival. The *Scotsman*.'

'Your lecture.. yeah. Don't think the *Standard* covered it. They went big on the story about that girl.. the one who fell off the tour bus.'

'I nearly saw that,' Michael nodded.

'Sit still, please.'

'Sorry,' he said again. 'I mean, I was on the bus. Upstairs. Right at the front. Couldn't see a thing. Never heard any more about it. So it was a girl? A young child?'

Lesley shook her head. 'No, a journalist. Terribly injured. I think she died. I think I heard that.'

Michael shivered.

'God. What a shame.'

He'd hardly thought about it and he'd been on that bus, his mind full of Jess. God – that woman *died*. She *died*. While he'd lost nothing. Pride, maybe.

Jess enjoyed the night, moved on. Hadn't he, in other circumstances, done the very same?

Why couldn't he do it here? Now? He shouldn't waste his time studying conference emails, studying endless lists of names attached to literature requests. Why would Jess's name be there?

(It might, hope still insisted. It just might.)

No. He ought to get on with his life, his work, touch base with friends neglected since coming back. He would do all of that. Tomorrow. Maybe.

He winced at his folly, and it was this lack of smile that Lesley captured.

'Fine. That'll do. I'll let you get on,' she packed her camera away, 'unless..'

'Unless?'

'You wouldn't fancy a coffee?' The tone was friendly. Unchallenging.

Michael shook his head. 'Deadlines. Sorry. Thanks.'

He saw her out. As he shut the door behind her, he sighed again. He should have taken her up on that invitation. Lesley was kind. Back to work? Back to waiting. These days work was salted into odd fragmented moments between longing and distraction. Jess. Where are you? Where have you gone?

And now – once again – his head jangled with squealing brakes, Edinburgh sirens. That poor, poor woman.

Lesley, catching none of this, swung away, off down the street, shaking her head. She'd edit out the empty bottles on the counter. Wouldn't do to have them showing. Students' parents wouldn't like it.

Michael had been back now for several weeks, Edinburgh a bruise at the back of his mind. Bruise upon bruise, layering. He drove himself, working too hard, swimming, running, cycling too; anything, everything, to leave his body so tired it couldn't but collapse when his head hit the pillow. A postcard informed him Kerry was now in Dublin, but flying back to Australia earlier than expected.

I won't see you after all, Mikey. Maybe next year if my dear sweet old-lady aunt allows me back in the country. Don't think she's so sure that's such a good idea.

He would have liked to see Kerry again. Ah well. On with the rest of the day.

Not such a good day. The computer was in bad tune, the library hadn't come up with the papers he asked for. He found himself restless. Easily distracted. When the phone rang, he heard it.

'Michael?'

'Hello..' he did not recognise this voice, wasn't sure what to say next, how to respond. 'Hello?'

'Michael, it's Morna.'

'Morna?'

'Yes, Michael! *Morna*. Look, it's not that long ago. Camping? Symbol Stones?'

'Morna.. God, *Morna*. Morna! Well.. I wasn't expecting.. no, I mean.. God... Morna..'

'Yes. That's my name. Now we've established that..'

'What can I do for you? Needing the tent?'

'Not today, thank you.'

'Good.'

'What do you mean, good?'

Michael sighed. 'I haven't got it any more.'

'I know.'

'How can you know?'

'Michael, I bought the tent. It was mine so I took it with me when I left.'

So that's where it had gone.

'Yes, that's what happened to it,' said Morna, as if he'd spoken the thought aloud, her voice grown reedy, petulant. More like the Morna who'd left.

'You know me,' sighed Michael.

'Yes. Yes I do. Nevertheless..'

'Nevertheless?'

'Nevertheless I've been asked to invite you to head up our conference.'

'Conference?'

'Next year. Here at Tarvat.'

'Since when have you been at Tarvat?'

'I live in Ross-shire, Michael. If you read your Christmas cards, you would know.'

Michael was blushing. Surely Morna felt it, six hundred miles away?

'I do read them. Know you have three kids. Married to Liam.. Rory.'

'Charlie.'

'I do read the cards, Morna. And the jokes. I look forward to them.'

Her silence upset him.

'Morna? Are you okay?'

'Fine.' She sounded suddenly as if she might be choking. 'Michael,' she sniffed, 'Do you check your email?'

'Yes.'

'Do you answer it?'

'Morna, of course I do.'

'I'll email you then. Got to rush.'

'Won't you need the address?'

'Got it from Google. At the Department. Bye, Michael.'

Morna was gone. Had she been crying? That silence. Michael knew he had not been kind to Morna, not at the end. But what could you do? When something was over, it was over.

Like Jess. Could he complain? He had no right. No-one had mentioned the word love, although he nearly had, nearly.

What could he do? Her silence spoke for her.

He slipped on his running shoes, fastened them carefully, raced downstairs. It was cold, raining heavily.

He ran five miles, six.

For her part, Morna laid the receiver down with exaggerated gentleness. She'd like to have thrown it, she'd like to have shouted.

'Christ, Michael, it's me! Don't you know? Don't you care?'

But his answer, retreat into silence, baffling, polite, would only have made her feel worse. Charlie wasn't like Michael. With Charlie you knew exactly how he felt, what he wanted. Wasn't that odd? With Michael the linguist, and Charlie the relatively silent engineer? It was Charlie who'd suggested she phone.

'An old student friend of yours, this Michael Hurt.'

'Yes, Charlie, but..'

'So if you speak to him, he'll come.'

'Why can't you do it?'

'He won't know me from Adam,' Charlie smiled, stroking his wife on the cheek. 'But who could forget you?'

Hope could be a funny thing. Oddly persistent. Even as Michael pounded the streets and paths along the riverside, racing the punts, most of them badly managed by out-of-season tourists, he was hoping this would be the day Jess would write.

Morna phoned. Jess would write.

She must be at least fond of him. They were good together. Couldn't have been better. Couldn't have been.

Maybe she was waiting, hoping, just like him.

Maybe the card didn't get there.

He stopped running, breathless now, caught by the possibility. Maybe his card had not arrived. You heard of mail endlessly, hopelessly delayed. Or Jess might be away, as she had been, when he phoned the *Standard*. Ms *Kavanagh*, the voicemail said, *is out of town*. Yes, she might be still away, and the card there all right, lying impotent on the door-mat, suffocating in a pile of bills. Or perhaps Dan was the jealous type and opened all the mail? That wouldn't matter, Michael reassured himself. There had been nothing in that card to spark off a jealous partner. No.

On the other hand, he wondered, on the other hand, perhaps he had made the card too cool, too impersonal? What if Jess needed more encouragement? Perhaps he should write again, more openly. No. He couldn't do that. No. By the sound of it she was as good as married. But if that were the case, why did any of it happen?

if winter comes

WEEKS ARE PASSING, days flying. Mornings have grown darker, evenings too. Jess doesn't notice. Her leg is still in plaster. She's walking now, managing the crutches. It's taken a while for her to get the hang of them.

At first, when she came round, life had been difficult, lacking shape, lacking organisation. Things are gradually assuming relevance, importance. Not that she thinks of it in that way. Not that she thinks of it at all.

Watching her from the door of the four-bedded ward, Sian notes considerable physical improvement. Jess is sitting up, beginning to take notice, and if she still has the slightly dazed expression of the newly awake, at least she is watching, listening. There's an element of euphoria too, none of the frustration you'd normally predict in someone denied speech who had used words creatively, lived by them. It is almost as if Jess has no need to communicate, feels happy enough surfing the relative calm of the ward. This isn't good enough. Sian wants to see greater recovery than this. She hopes they can achieve it. Only on the one occasion has she witnessed Jess striving to reach beyond immediate comfort.

Yesterday the tree outside the ward window, a rowan, had been filled with finches, snub-nosed, orange-breasted, stripping branch after branch of their shockingly red berries. Jess watched, fascinated, hobbled across the ward to the window. Tried to open it. It was too stiff, and perhaps, thought Sian, perhaps the catch was a little complicated for Jess's damaged fingers. She could not shift it, turned in panic, searching, caught Sian's eyes.

'No,' she said. 'No. No.'

She still had only the one word, though the range of expression she imbued it with was growing.

Sian had smiled. 'We can't open that window, Jess. It's stuck.'

'No.'

'I think they keep them locked for insurance purposes.'

Sian wasn't sure about that, but it sounded plausible. She sat down, began to run through exercises designed to enable automatic speech, but Jess would not pay attention, kept following the birds. The berries were all gone by the end of the session.

Finches were nothing if not efficient.

Today Jess's attention is not on the outdoors. She's staring across the ward. The other three patients sit together, chatting, not consciously excluding Jess, but not including her.

'Hi Jess!'

Sian waves. Jess, does not turn, does not respond. Sian knows there is no problem with her hearing.

'Hello, Jess!' Louder. 'Hello, Jess!' Louder still.

This time Jess turns, but not with recognition, more in non-specific response to noise, any noise. Sian smiles, waves again. Jess looks. Does not wave. Are the corners of her lips dancing slightly? Sian wonders if they are. Broadens her own smile. Perhaps this is, after all, a beginning.

'Excuse me.'

'Sorry.'

Sian steps back to let the female ambulance driver pass. Ah. This must be the girl who visits Jess. What's her name? Janet? She's heard about Janet, hasn't had the luck to catch her yet. The most regular visitor, according to the nurses, and the one Jess seems happiest to see. Sian has wanted to meet her. Now, she stands at the door, watching unobtrusively.

'Hi there, Jess.' The green-clad girl smiles, perching on the bed. 'And how are things?'

'No,' says Jess.

'That good?'

'No.'

'Hmm. My day's been a bit like that.' Janet reaches into her breast pocket. 'Brought us a Caramel Log. Fancy one?'

'No.'

'Good. Here you go.' She tosses the brightly wrapped biscuit to Jess, begins unwrapping her own. 'I don't like sweet things usually,' she says. 'But I really go for these. Don't you?'

Jess is having trouble with the wrapping. The skin on the fingers of her right hand is still raw. The damage was extensive, and has been slow to heal, infection after infection in the grafted areas. Janet sits waiting, patient, does not offer help. Jess gets there slowly, holding the biscuit in her right hand, painstakingly and clumsily peeling with her left. Janet does not begin her own biscuit till Jess's is unwrapped.

'Guess what, Jess?'

Jess raises her head smartly.

'Want to hear the latest?'

'No.'

Sian is struck by the conversational tone, by the natural body language Jess is using.

'Kev and me. It's all on.'

'No.'

'Yes. We went Salsa dancing last night.'

'No.'

'It's not so much dancing as sex with clothes on.'

Janet bites into her Caramel Log. Jess looks at her. Sian is watching very carefully. Jess looks at Janet. Jess looks at Janet, almost smiles. Takes the initiative.

'No?' Her voice is bright with mischief, keen with question.

Janet grins. 'None of your business!'

The afternoon light has veered from autumn to winter, sun slanting low across a changeable city sky. That would never be a summer blue, thinks Sian, calling her thoughts to order, bringing her attention to bear on the room, on the patient. She is trying to encourage Jess to vocalise, trying to persuade her to make any sound but No. She's having little success. Perhaps it's simply too late in the day. Jess will not co-operate, keeps allowing her attention to wander, her gaze to drift. Sian tries a new tack.

'Ella was telling me you had two visitors this afternoon, even though Dan's away. Ken and Janet.'

'No.'

'Did they come together?'

'No.'

Sian knows they didn't.

'And how was Janet? Was she f i n e?' Sian stretches the word out, repeating the question.

'How was Janet? F.. i ..?'

'No,' says Jess.

There's much less variation in the quality of communication in that single syllable than Sian heard in the earlier conversation with Janet.

Sian tries again.

'Nice to have a friend to visit. How was Janet? F.. i ..?'

'No,' says Jess.

'And Ken?' Sian moves on, shaking her head. 'Is Ken fine too?'

Jess's face, till now lacking in any expression but the startled openness of Barbie dolls or beauty contestants, suddenly looks sad. Almost definitely sad. Almost definitely frustrated.

And she laughed at Janet too, Sian remembers.

Interested, Sian pushes Jess, just a little; keeps talking about Ken. She's come to like him. Knows the gossip, of course. The recent divorce. Much of the hospital sympathy (for what that's worth) has run with him.

'What are you trying to tell me, Jess? Something about Ken?'

'No.'

'We can do it in simple words. One word if you like. You can tell a one word story. We've talked about that, haven't we? What's Ken's story? Happy?'

'No.' Jess sighs.

'Sad?'

'No.'

'Chocolate biscuits?' Sian offers a distraction here, suggesting Janet's visit.

'No.'

'Dancing?'

Jess nods. 'No. No.'

'You are fond of Ken, aren't you? Y.. e.. S?'

Jess says nothing. Sian is still trying.

'And Janet, you're fond of her. Aren't you? Y.. Y..'

'Eh.' The sound is so small Sian can hardly hear it.

'Good, Jess. That's really good. That's another word! That's magic, Jess. *Another word*. That's so great! Well done! Try it again? Yy..'

'Eh..'

Sian feels like hugging her. Fights to control her obvious emotion, keep her own voice steady. 'That's so great, Jess.'

She is greatly moved, unable to say anything more for several seconds. She smiles. Jess smiles too, blushes, fiddles with the paper on her trolley. Silence stretches between them, stretches till a young auxiliary nurse darts into the ward, her broad smile trained on Jess.

'Jess! A postcard for you. See? It's only just come in the internal mail – went to another ward this morning. And it's been round the whole of Scotland, look at it – redirected *four* times! It's a wonder it ever got here!'

All three bend their heads over the scrap of card, an image against blue sky of an ancient standing stone carved with intricately woven birds, wings and beaks enmeshed.

'Wow,' says Sian, finding her voice at last. 'Let me read it for you, Jess. Would you like that? Yy..'

'Eh.'

Sian turns the card over, squinting at the postmark. The place of posting is illegible, the date a little clearer. It has somehow taken weeks to reach the ward.

'*Good to meet you. Keep in touch. Michael.*' She hands it back. 'That's all. Who's Michael?'

'No.'

Jess stares at the picture, lost in the interwoven intricacies of the design. The Michael who sent it gets short shrift, little attention. The picture, though, that moves her.

She seems, Sian sighs, to have frozen out so much of her life, set it in amber. The memory loss preferentially disrupting interest in people, in relationships. Ward staff have found it difficult explaining that to friends and colleagues, all so sure *they*'d be remembered, all so hurt, offended, when they were not.

'You look tired,' she says. 'I'll come back later. Bye for now. Bb..'

'No,' says Jess.

'I know.' Sian smiles. 'You're tired.' She stands up, patting Jess's shoulder. 'I'm proud of you. That's a big, big step you've taken today.'

Dan

THE SUN HAD SWEPT so low, street level was in deep shade. Dan found it difficult to choose the right key for the door as he swept down with bags and boxes of food to the hired car. Living on the fourth floor had had its effect. He was fitter. Lighter. He was glad to finish here though, glad to be leaving. Glad he had his licence back.

He smiled a little as he humped the very last suitcase down the last flight of stairs. He'd been up and down these steps a dozen times and met no-one. This did not surprise him. He'd been in this building months and never met anyone on the stairs, not once. Other folk did live here at night you could hear their radios, their television sets. They seemed to be invisible.

A flat near the Tron had sounded a good idea; central, certainly. But traffic noise roared late into the night, invasive without double-glazing. Triple-glazing might, he thought, actually be necessary. Even that might not keep out the yells and shrieks that shattered the night's peace, the indecipherable shouts of joy or panic, drunkenness, fighting; all the irregular clamour of a city centre. It had never been possible to get a full night's sleep, even in the first weeks, even in that binge. Now he'd taken a new flat in a genteel terrace in Merchiston. It should be a great deal quieter. He'd like to let the house in White Street go.. once he was able to discuss it with Jess.. once he could be sure she understood what he was saying.

These had been the loneliest weeks of his whole life. Drifting every day from the cold and noisy flat to the hospital where Jess no longer screamed, but would not notice him. He knew she could communicate, after a fashion, with the nurses. He'd seen her nodding at the staff, shaking her head. He'd even heard the odd automatic word. No. She never spoke to him. Would not respond to him. When he came near, she assumed.. no, be more precise.. her face assumed.. a fixed expression, closed. It was as if she could not bear to see him, did not want him near. As if she thought he might be going to hurt her.

'It's a post-traumatic thing,' Sian, the young speech therapist assured him. 'Not something she's able to control. Not something we can really help her with until her language and other communication skills improve.'

'That's not a comfort.'

'No.'

Sian didn't lie. He liked that.

On this occasion she turned to him and said, 'You'll have to dig deep, rely on all that strength I know is in you, Mr McKie. Jess is going to need support. An infinity of it. You're all she has.'

Dan almost broke down then, almost confessed to Sian how imperfect the relationship had been.

'I expect,' she went on, 'you're thinking that you're only human, that life wasn't perfect anyway before the accident. Or maybe you were different. Maybe you and Jess had that unusual thing, a good relationship.'

'Not exactly,' said Dan, thinking how distancing that *Mr McKie* was. She was always formal with him. She called Jess *Jess*.

'We all have our cross to bear.'

Not you, thought Dan. Your life must be so clear. Uncomplicated.

Sian was still speaking.

'Life's rarely straightforward. What is simple and obvious is that Jess is going to need months, perhaps years, of selfless support. Are you up to that?'

'I think,' said Dan slowly, 'I'd need support myself.'

'That's what we're here for,' Sian nodded. 'That's exactly what we're here for. Counselling would help too, help you through all the frustration.'

He hadn't been sleeping well. The street noise didn't help, but it had surprised him how often he found himself thinking about Sian. Her measuring stare seemed challenging, addictive. It reminded him of someone. She was, perhaps, a little like his sister Grace? And not unlike Jess.

Well, that was the flat clear. He pushed the keys, as directed, in the caretaker's letter box. He'd never once seen the caretaker. Presumably one did exist. This was a surreal world, this empty city tenement, rented out to visitors. It must be visitors. No-one else would find it easy to survive here. What you could put up with for a week is one thing, what you needed for daily life another.

He took himself for one last stroll down the High Street. It had been his habit to walk from the flat to Holyrood and back each night. There was always something happening. There was always the chance of meeting Sian.

He knew her flat. He'd known that since the first evening; which close she lived up, which square. He'd seen her at her window. It did no-one any harm, walking these quiet streets at night. Exercise was beneficial. Got him away from the whisky, from the silent phone. From the TV.

That *Mr McKie* was very distancing.

It was what she called him even when they met outside the hospital.

Even when, like tonight, he was strolling down the street lost in thought and didn't recognise her till she was almost past. Why would he? It was Hallowe'en. Scurries of tiny witches and warlocks clogging the pavements. Death-heads, Munch-white *Scream*-heads wavering in and through the shadows, laden with plastic carriers, these bulging white supermarket bags at odds with the funereal costumes. Hallowe'en had changed. It used to be enough to wear your sister's coat, your mother's headscarf. A football strip. He's seen himself do that.

Avoiding two miniature Harry Potters, he stumbled into two girls, arm-in-arm, swinging out of a close.

'Sorry.'

He would have walked right on, but one of them stopped, reaching towards him.

'Mr McKie,' she said. 'Hello. I thought you were moving.'

'I am,' agreed Dan. 'I'm just getting a bit of air before I go.' His gaze switched from Sian to her taller friend.

'Let me introduce my twin, Jamie. Jamie, this is Dan McKie.'

Jamie stretched out a hand. 'Hi there.'

She was taller than Sian, taller than Dan. Red hair hung to her shoulders, dancing over them. She looked to have a great deal of humour, but she was not at all like Sian. Not like a sister, never mind a twin.

'Good to meet you,' Jamie grinned.

She knows, thought Dan. *She knows*.

'Hope the move goes well,' Sian smiled. 'We'll be thinking of you.'

'Och, it'll be fine. The new place will be quieter. I'll get more sleep. Well,' he hovered awkwardly, 'I ought to be off.'

'See you next week.'

'Aye.'

He sauntered on. Did not look back until he was a good three, four blocks down. They'd crossed the road, still arm-in-arm. Women, thought Dan. That touch, that warmth. By the time he was making his way back up the hill, they were no longer in sight. He walked, head slightly bowed, into the drizzling dark.

Jess

'HERE'S YOUR CHOCOLATE, Jess,' the young nurse slaps the mug down on the bedside table, spilling brown sweet liquid everywhere. It floods the melamine top, lapping the postcard Jess has been staring at.

'No!' There's real distress in Jess's voice. 'No!'

'What is it, Jess?'

Jess holds up the card. 'No.'

'I'm sorry. Look, give me your towel. Give me your towel, Jess,' the nurse asks, 'Hurry, before the stuff sinks in.'

Jess reacts quickly. Stretches across the bed and throws the nurse her face cloth.

'That'll do. There you are.. well done! You'd hardly know now, would you.. it's the quality of paper they use nowadays. Jess!' the girl stops, amazed. 'You gave me the right thing. Nearly the right thing. Look, Jess.. your towel.. *look*. L. L..'

'–ook,' Jess finishes the word.

'Jess! That's another word! Another w.. W..'

'.. orr,' finishes Jess, staring at the postcard, tracing the birds' interlocking beaks, following the intricacy of their ornate wings.

The girl, who's been watching Sian at work, races off to the nurse in charge. Jess goes on caressing the birds.

'Look,' she says. 'Look.'

When the staff nurse comes Jess waves the postcard at her.

'Look.'

'Very good,' the staff nurse says. 'Very good. But don't forget your chocolate. Don't want you losing sleep, do we?'

She looks carefully at the card. 'The words are still there. Look, it says *keep in touch*, see? And who's Michael? Is he nice?'

'No,' shrugs Jess, slipping the postcard into her drawer and picking up the dripping mug. She wipes the bottom of it on her face-cloth before she drinks.

'No.'

Dan

THE MERCHISTON FLAT was certainly much quieter, more settled-feeling than the open-plan, not-quite whiteness of the Tron. This new flat, in fact, was almost too quiet. Three bedrooms, kitchen, lounge; with its comfortable furniture it felt house-like, home-like. It had been painted jewel colours, from the kitchen's dark-oak green to the hall's deep river-blue; the lounge, with its perfect proportions and generous bay, was a cheerful yellow Dan could not quite name. Sunny? A cliché. Daffodil? This was gentler, warmer. He'd sometimes seen this particular shade in a rosebud, but not in any other flower; the hint of sand that was in it. This art of naming colour, choosing words to signify exact shade, was not straightforward, not easy, a philosophical exercise if ever there was one.

He was conscious that he lived by words but never thought about them beyond a cynical belief in his own prowess. It hadn't been that necessary to consider niceties of colour, of shade, when reporting football. Total football – speed, motion, elation, disappointment – he'd spent years of his life describing those; and the odd thing, really, the oddest thing of all, was that it had always been himself, his own dreams, his own feelings about the world, about the game of chance that was life, that he'd been trying to get down on paper.

He spread an Edinburgh map across the kitchen table, sipped the first cup of coffee he'd enjoyed in weeks. It was not that far from Merchiston to the Royal Mile, though his evening walks would look rather odder now. He would miss them.

At the Central they kept telling him Jess was improving. He was not stupid. He could see she was stronger physically. He still could not bring himself to look at her scarred shoulders. Nor her fingers. Her hands were not the hands they used to be. Her face was not so different, not the features, no, but the expression.. gone. This might be Jess, but not Jess as he'd known her. The world, the new world blaring from worrying headlines on every newspaper, every news report, was rougher, harsher. Odd, how much more he noticed these now that he was not competing in the journalistic fray – affray? And Jess left innocent, unable to comprehend the world, its anger, its bitterness.

Jack had told him, urged him, not to judge her. Dan kept trying not to. Trying. In White Street, surrounded by the pictures and furniture amassed over the years, he had found it impossible to feel anything beyond unreasoning anger. It drove him, rode him. How could she bring herself to do it? Over and over he imagined Jess sharing her white soft body with a shadowy other. Had she enjoyed it? Orgasmed? Faked it? There were times, with him, he had known she was.

Like after the clinic, when he had to tell her, persuade her, to go for that check-up.

Odd how these things stayed with you.

He remembered that perfume she was wearing.

Flowery. Light.

'You're early,' Jess looks up from the salad she's preparing, the table strewn with vegetables and cut flowers. Not good hygiene.

'That's a problem?'

'Dinner won't be ready for another hour.'

He hovers, not knowing quite how to begin. Temporises.

'I'll read the paper then.'

'Good idea. Put your feet up. Coffee? Tea?' She laughs at his expression.

'Okay. Beer? Wine?'

'A glass of wine would hit the spot nicely. I'm up to here with it,' Dan sighs. 'What about the Merlot we opened the other night?'

'You finished it. And the second bottle. There's only white wine left. Would you cope with Chardonnay?'

'What's for dinner?'

'Now that would be telling.'

'And what would be the problem in that?'

'Well,' Jess smiles, 'as Isabella says.. a little mystery is no bad thing.'

'And what has Isabella got to do with it?' Dan's voice grates with displeasure. 'What's going on, Jess? Why were you discussing me with Isabella?'

Jess has stopped working. The hand holding the knife hovers above the tomato she's been struggling to carve into an unnecessary rose.

'Why were you talking to her?'

'Pardon?' Confusion shivers in her face, her tone.

He is furious, his stomach still churning at the memory of the phone call that sent him rushing from the office, striding the Glasgow pavements trying to walk off guilt and anger. At the other end of the line, Isabella's voice advising him flatly, matter-of-factly, to go for a check-up. *You didn't use a barrier, Dan. And even if you had, chlamydia can linger. You'll need to get Jess to see a doctor too; Jess and all your other partners.* What was she on about – other partners? Dan had believed himself in love. Dan had been faithful to Jess till Isabella's Italian darkness came his way. She dismissed him. *Speak to you later, Dan. I've calls to make. I suggest you make a list and do the same.*

Her voice still burning in his ear harsh as an internet link.

He glowers at Jess.

'Have you been pestering Isabella?'

'Dan, what is this about? You're tired. You've been working too hard for weeks now, you know you have. All those late nights. Look, sit down. I'll open the wine.'

'Christ!' he shouts. 'What exactly are you trying not to say?'

Jess's face is now as white as the wall behind her.

'Very good,' he shouts. 'A good act, Jess. A good angle. I'd almost.. almost.. believe you didn't know!' Her misery drives him on. 'I suppose you thought I'd never find out? These things go back years,' he turns away, 'these *intimate* infections.'

Jess flinches.

Dan carries on, shouting. 'Women act as carriers. You didn't have to tell me. There's always the.. odour. Why do you think I've been avoiding sex? Working late? Working all the hours God gave?'

'Dan? I don't understand..'

This shifting of perspective, presenting itself as he goes on, seems clever, appropriate; timely too. Righteous indignation, always a winner. Dan sounds so convincing he almost believes himself.

Jess says nothing. Leaves the room.

The front door opens, closes, quietly. She does not come back that night.

Where she goes, what she does, Dan will never know.

She won't tell him and it will prove impossible to ask.

'How's Jess?' Jack looked around the new sitting room, nodding approval. 'How's she coming on?'

'She's not.'

'No?'

'I don't know, Jack,' Dan sighed. 'I can't tell where this is going.'

'What do they say at the hospital?'

'They think she's getting stronger.'

'That's encouraging.'

'They're wanting to discharge her.'

'Good. Don't you think so?' Jack stared at Dan. Dan blushed. 'What's your problem? Don't you want her home?'

Dan whistled through his teeth.

'You're scared. It's that simple, isn't it?'

'Fuck off.'

Jack shrugged. He'd been afraid of this.

He and Margot talked about it, had seen it coming from the start, from the moment Dan told them he'd insisted Jess be kept in Edinburgh. Jack had tried to persuade himself that it was a good thing when Dan took the Tron flat. Wasn't he nearer Jess, at least? But that flat was a disaster, and as far as he could make out, Dan spent his days avoiding the hospital. The sabbatical had not been such a good idea.

Jack opened his mouth, made as if to speak, then changed his mind, sat back in the sunny yellow armchair, trying to decide the best approach. At least the new flat was good. A big improvement. Almost as comfortable as the White Street flat Jess spent so many years fixing up. Dan obviously couldn't face it. Yet.

'I was up in Sutherland last night,' Jack said slowly.

'Oh? And?'

He ignored the peevish note.

'God's own country, but you know that. Outside my grandfather's house, and all along the road up to it there are trees, Dan, silver birch, rowan.. and the rowans bent double this year, like young cherry trees overburdened with fruit.'

Dan drained his beer glass.

'Yeah. Right.'

'No, you should see them, Dan. Vibrant! The red fairly leaps out at you.'

'Get to the point.'

'No point. Just.. it's the heaviest crop of rowans I've seen this decade or more.'

'Are you waxing lyrical for practice? Or maybe for the benefit of educating lesser mortals?'

Jack sighed. 'The point is this, Dan. It will be a heavy winter.'

Dan stared, confused.

'Sorry. I don't get it.'

'It's the old saying; the heavier the rowan, the harder the winter. Just like the one you're facing with Jess. Margot and I.. we can't bear all your burden, but we'll help, you know. If you'll allow us.'

'What are you getting at?'

Jack looked at his friend for a long, serious, moment. Dan found it hard to bear the scrutiny, looked away.

'You'll need support, Dan, to get through this. And friends. It's bad, but it could be worse. At least you still have the chance..'

'What chance?'

'To make a go of things.'

'Fucking fat chance!' Dan groaned. 'I'm tied, Jack, tied to a brain-damaged freak.'

Jack frowned. 'Has anyone told you Jess has permanent brain-damage?'

'Not as such.'

'Then why are you saying it?'

'She can't fucking talk!'

'You told me yourself the understanding was coming back. You told me yourself she's stronger, communicating more with the nurses.'

'Jack,' said Dan. 'She won't even look me in the eye.'

'Have you asked yourself why? Do you ever, Dan McKie, think of anyone but yourself?'

Dan jumped to his feet, walked to the window, stared down on the street. No rowans here. He turned back to his friend.

'Is that fair, Jack?'

'Yes, I think it is,' Jack paused, sipped his drink. His voice dropped almost to a whisper. 'She's your partner, Dan.'

'I'm not sure of that.'

'What are you saying?'

'Just.. this isn't Jess. Not the Jess I knew.'

'It is.'

'I can't see that.'

'You must. You do.' Jack drank the last of his beer. 'Fuck it, Dan, who else is she? Who else has she got? You'll cope. You love her. Look at all the years you've been together. You're strong.'

'Sometimes,' Dan glared down at the empty street, 'sometimes I wonder.'

'Wonder a bit more,' said Jack. 'Wonder a bit more about how you're going to cope when it's time for her to leave the hospital. You'll have to get your head in better order.'

'What I really wonder,' Dan shrugged, 'what I really wonder is why she felt she had to run for that fucking bus.'

Not the most successful or sympathetic conversation he'd had since Jess's accident. It stayed with him. He couldn't dismiss Jack's words. Even in this comfortable flat in Merchiston. The thought of being tied to a partner who could not or would not communicate with him was something he'd rather not consider.

Why? Why that bus?

What if Jack was right? What was it he'd said?

What's sauce for the goose..

Why can't he get his head around it?

Why couldn't he be satisfied with Jess? Why couldn't she be satisfied with him? *What's sauce..* Shut up, Jack!

What was sure, certain, was that his needs in this new and harsher world were simpler, less intense. And in the ward today they'd had a kind of breakthrough. Jess was looking at a card, a postcard, nothing special, just a postcard of a carved stone. Pictish carving. She'd really taken to it, the complex intertwinings of the pattern. He'd seen stones like that in the Chambers Street Museum. He was sure he had. He could find her more of the same. Perhaps a book? It was not much. It was a start.

Ken

KEN WAS SPENDING more and more time with Jess. Ella made a mental note to speak to him about it, but it proved difficult finding the right moment, the ward always so busy, so many people flitting in and out of the duty room. When finally she broached the subject, she was all too aware of both her own embarrassment and the possibility of interruption. She made coffee for them both and pushed the duty room door firmly shut, as if a ward meeting were in progress.

Ken looked up, nodded at the door.

'Everything okay, Ella?'

'Just a word, Ken. I've been wanting to speak to you in private.'

'About Liz?'

'No.' Her voice had an edge to it she'd rather had not been there. 'Not Liz. Jess. All the time you're spending with her.'

'Ella!'

She sat down. 'Ken. You know the hospital. You know the grapevine. There will be rumours. Are. They say.. you know exactly what they say. They link you with Jess.. and Janet. And Sian.'

'Hospital gossip,' Ken laughed.

'Don't you mind?'

'No. There's not a shred of truth in any of it. Come on, Ella, words, just words. Hot air. Sticks and stones. None of it will hurt me. Or Jess. Or Janet. Or Sian. Talk about something more sensible.'

She shook her head.

'Don't say I didn't warn you.'

'If they're talking about me, they'll leave someone else alone.'

'That's never how it works.'

'Ella,' he turned, exasperated. 'What would you have me do? Who else visits Jess? She needs as much visiting, as much stimulation, as possible. You know that as well as I do. You've been with her since the first day.'

'I know,' Ella sighed. Her promotion had coincided with Jess's move out of High Dependency. 'That Dan McKie,' she said, 'is a waste of space.'

'He'll come round. Wait and see.'

She frowned. 'You're blinkered by optimism, Ken. He's hard-bitten as they come.'

'I don't think so. I don't mind Dan so much these days. Have a drink with him now and then.'

'Rather you than me.'

Ella turned away, cradling her coffee mug. You could take a horse to water. You could try, but when the horse was mule-like, stubborn, there was nothing you could do.

'Ella..' he said tentatively. 'I.. I was going to ask..'

'What?'

'I know you sometimes see Liz.'

Her eyes narrowed. Ken blushed, looked down. His voice seemed steady enough.

'Is.. is she okay? Only someone told me..'

Ella finished the sentence for him. 'That Ruaraidh's leaving? He is. Off to London. I haven't seen Liz to talk about it. I did hear,' she added, relenting, 'he'd be travelling alone.'

Ken seemed to have developed a sudden and overwhelming interest in the off-duty chart. Ella let the silence grow. Ken had to toughen up, she thought. Move on. He didn't show much sign of it. He still looked shaken, thin, though it had been a full year since the marriage folded.

'Are you memorising that chart? Anyone in particular whose off-duty you're querying?'

Ken shrugged.

'I don't know what to do,' he said at last. 'Do you think I should go and see her? Would it do any good? She must be needing a listening ear.'

Ella shook her head. 'I wouldn't advise it.'

'You're right. You're right.' He stood up, straightening his shoulders.

'Not the advice you wanted?'

'I want to rush right over. See her. Tell her..'

'Would she listen? Feeling as she must be feeling?'

Ella sighed. Ken looked away.

'You're right.' He bowed his head, straightening the pile of notes on the desk, shifting and rearranging them. 'If you see her, Ella..'

'I don't often see her.'

He knew that was not strictly true. Not true at all.

'Ah well. I'll go find Jess. Thanks, Ella. Thanks for the coffee.'

He turned to leave, just as the lunch trolley bumped past, its grey-painted mass blocking the duty room door. It was followed by Janet, with Kev in tow.

'Fit like, loon?'

Ken's answer, his unforced smile, baffled Ella who always found Kev too cocky by half.

'Chavin awa. Fit like yersel?'

'Chavin.. most definitely. Ella, quine, can we nae pop in an visit Jess a minutey?'

She hated being called quine. 'Don't put her off her lunch.'

'As if we'd dae that!'

Ella's eyebrows stayed firmly knit. 'She won't look at cold food. And she needs every calorie that's going.'

Ken frowned. 'She's still losing weight?'

'Won't look at the supplements. You should hear her!'

'My, that's grand,' said Kev. 'We've been practisin expletives. I wisna sure she'd remember.'

'Expletives, eh? That's a long word, Kev,' said Ella. 'Explain it to me.'

'I fear,' laughed Kev, 'Ye're ower young.'

'Out! Out of here!' Ella's patience evaporated. 'Off with you. Five minutes. Five minutes max. Not a second longer.'

'Keep yer hair on!'

'Come on, Kev. Lunch break will be over by the time you two have finished arguing.'

Ken pushed the still-protesting Kev out into the corridor.

'Five minutes, Ella,' he promised. 'You have my word.'

Jess

JESS IS SITTING by her bed, a tray of food in front of her. Soup, salad, fruit. She's made no effort to start eating. The plaster might be off her leg but her hands remain a problem, skin grafts struggling. Her speech is slow. Her memory has not returned.

So many weeks on, she still seems fragile, lost. And this is not a good hair day. Sometimes they manage to dress her hair so that it seems less patchy. Not today. All the gaps show, exaggerated by new early growth sticking out at odd angles.

Ken finds her curiously unmarked, for all that. Knows her for the Jess he met on his first day away from home, in the slowly winding queue for hall-of-residence dinner, only her eyes betraying bewilderment, then and now. Then and now she turns toward him, smiling.

It must, he finds himself suddenly thinking, be very hard for Dan, with whom she refuses to communicate; whom, he'd almost say, she resolutely refuses to recognise. That's how it seems. She cuts him off, ignores him.

This is unlike the old Jess. Out of character. Jess was never cruel. This seems, if not irrational, non-rational. Ken nods. That's it. Her reasons for cutting Dan out of her life seem tied to her still mute response to life. Until the words came back, who could understand any of it? Who could tell the story?

Though things are improving, he reflects, as he follows Janet and Kev along the ward, returning their banter without listening to any of it. Yes, things are improving. Jess can respond, as he is now, automatically. She will, sometimes, communicate directly too. Her vocabulary is growing day by day, as if a flood of dammed-up words have been released, although she still has difficulty, her speech slow and halting, the wrong word slipping out more often than the right.

She has recently been moved to the eight-bedded ward furthest away from nursing station. Her corner bed, next to the window, overlooks the rain-soaked Meadows. She spends hours staring through the window, ignoring the ward, ignoring the other patients; focused on the view, on the quivering, dancing trees. She's pale and thin. Too pale.

'Hi Jess,' Janet calls out gaily.

'Fit like?' Kev sweeps across the room, hugs her. 'Chavin awa, eh?'

Ken waits at the foot of the bed. Jess smiles, confused. She is, you can see, wondering what to say. She shakes her head, nods at them. Sometimes she spends minutes searching for the phrase that will not come.

'Fuck!'

'See?' says Kev. 'Expletives. Fit did I tell ye? You and Janet, Jess.. fit a pair of roustabouts!'

'Reprobates, I think you mean!' Janet interrupts. 'Only a loon from oil-rich Aberdeen would make that mistake.'

'Roustabouts is fit I said, and roustabouts is fit I meant! I dinna ken, Jess, far this quine gets her manners fae. Nae fae you, that's certain.'

'No,' Jess blushes, reverting to the monosyllable that serves so well.

Words still elude her. Profanities come easily. Unasked.

Perhaps because of this, she will not play the language game with strangers. With other patients in her ward she is as mute, as unresponsive as she's ever been. These women, coming and going every few days, never think to challenge her lack of communication. They fail to notice, or are embarrassed by her. With them, Jess might as well wear a cloak of invisibility.

Ken bends down. 'Jess? I only came to say hello. I've a meeting this afternoon. I'll come back later. I'll leave you with these tearaways. I'll be quite late, after tea, probably. Take care now.'

'And quine,' says Kev. 'If ye dinna tak yer dinner that reid-headed charge-nurse will be on oor backs. Get suppin!'

'Shall I peel your orange? Or do you want to try yourself? It looks like one of those mineolas. Not difficult.'

'No.'

'Okay, I'll leave it for you.'

'No!'

Janet laughs, starts peeling.

Sian

KEN SWUNG ALONG the corridor, wondering what had made him leave the ward so precipitately. He wasn't angry with Ella. How could you be angry at straightforward honesty? You could, he found; you could. It was easy. But that wasn't the problem, wasn't what made him turn tail and leave – it was seeing Janet's eyes on Kev, the shared good humour. He and Liz had been like that. They could have been walking down a corridor like this, a busy cluttered corridor, and seen and heard no-one but each other. That couldn't all just disappear, couldn't be lost forever.

'Ken! We need to talk.'

He looked up. 'Sian?' The crowd parted, flowed round them. Ken took her arm, moved her to one side, his face relaxing.

'Have you had lunch?'

'Yes.. no. No,' he said, remembering. 'No, actually I haven't.'

'Good,' she smiled. 'I wanted to talk to you. About Jess.. can we do lunch? Pick up a sandwich? Have you time?'

He checked his watch. 'Not sure.'

'Won't take long,' she shifted a heavy pile of case-notes from one arm to the other.

'You shouldn't carry notes around like that,' he said. 'You should take a trolley.'

Sian ignored him. 'Look, you run and buy a couple of sandwiches. I'll boil the kettle. Tuna for me, please. See you at my office.'

'Sian, wait!'

'What now?' she turned back. 'What?' Ken didn't, she thought, seem quite himself.

'What is it?'

'Any special sort of bread? Brown? White? Ciabatta? Sun-dried tomato?'

'Any kind at all. You'll probably find there's not much left.'

'Right.'

'Oh, and Ken..'

'Yes?'

'If there's no tuna, just take anything. Anything at all. I'm starving. I could eat a horse!'

'Horse,' he repeated. 'Right. I'll ask. They don't always do horse.'

'And hurry up!'

Half an hour later, settled in the office, he seemed in no great haste to leave. With the sandwiches (prawn) he had bought Danish pastries, napkins and fruit, which he'd spread across the desk and lingered over, lounging in the one comfortable chair beside the window.

'Well,' said Sian. 'I never eat this much for lunch.'

'That,' he said, 'is obviously why you never grew.'

'There had to be a reason?'

'Nurses,' he nodded slowly, 'who as you know, rule the world, will tell you there's a reason for everything.'

'Right.'

'Never cross a nurse,' he warned. 'Ward philosophy is powerful stuff. Especially in calligraphy, framed. So what about you, Sian?'

'What about me?'

'What do you think about life.. life, the universe, the reason for everything?'

'Forty-two.'

He smiled. His eyes lit up.

Sian had never noticed quite how kind they were. Almost green. How could she have missed them? Her eyes locked on to his. Uncomfortably. It felt like focusing on breath, remembering to breathe. With an effort, she dragged her gaze away, and standing up, refilled the kettle.

'I don't,' she stared past him, into the greying afternoon, 'have a theory of life. Not a general theory.' She should have stopped there. 'But what we tell ourselves, that's the thing.' What was she doing, burbling on? Sentence after sentence. 'What we tell ourselves about *ourselves*, the stories we choose, affect not only personality – who we *are* – but what we *do* – how we respond to what life throws at us. The good, the bad, the ugly. We don't,' she looked directly at him now, braving those – yes, green – eyes, 'have to take it all on – life, the universe, everything. We just have to find a form of words that gets us through, balances the possible, holds all our narratives in equilibrium.'

'So you'd have no moral values? No genetic personality traits? No good and evil?'

'That's not what I'm saying. These all exist! And love! Without love,' her voice grew hoarse, 'the world would fail. Civilisations would fall. Love – and the word – get us through it.'

Ken found himself breathing hard. Said nothing

'You're allowed,' she blushed, 'to disagree. It's one of my obsessions. Hobby horse. Don't get me started!'

He looked down, away. The table before them was piled with the detritus of their lunch; sandwich wrappers, paper plates, screwed-up napkins. He wanted to look up, look beyond all that, but if he looked at Sian now, who knows what might happen? There were moments in life when the threads of fate swung before you, visible, tempting; when it seemed you could actively bend life to your will. Choose the future. Sometimes, as now, you chose by not responding.

Sian's cheeks burned. Why, oh why had she not kept to her prepared script? What on earth had prompted her to give so much away? Ken, it was obvious, was embarrassed. Why had she mentioned love? Why had she used that word? Wasn't it clear she'd not meant *that* – not anything personal – no?

Silence stretched. The kettle saved them, rattling to the boil.

'More coffee?'

'Please.' He made an effort to appear, sound, normal. 'What was it, Sian, you wanted?'

She looked startled.

'You said,' he prompted, 'when we met. Something about Jess.'

'Oh,' she rinsed and refilled their mugs with coffee, gathering her thoughts. 'Jess..'

He reached for an apple, closed his fingers round it. Brown on red. Sian found herself distracted. Hands told you so much. How they held things, how they played around an object, formed it.

'And about Jess. I've a question.' He bit the apple, set it down. 'Why do you think she suddenly improved?'

Sian shook her head. 'Who can say?'

Ken leaned forward. 'Do you think the aphasia.. You'd almost call it *mutism*.. was mainly psychological?'

'No.' Easier, this. Professional questions, professional words. 'No, there was definite anatomical disruption. You know that. You've seen it. You must have noticed how often she uses the wrong word.. has problems selecting, doesn't she?'

Much easier. Sian felt competent. In control. 'They're rarely completely wrong, the words; more often they're related, a part of whatever she's trying to say.. but the memory thing is more than that. Global, not just language. She's left with so little of her past. It's very hard. And limiting. I think it's why so few of her friends came back.'

'If she'd been in Glasgow..'

'It wouldn't have made any difference. It's.. it seems to me.. as if none of her relationships was strong enough; as if she had no really close friends. The partner didn't seem to know anyone we could call on.'

'Doesn't fit with the Jess I knew. But from what I can gather they've been living fairly separate lives.'

'City life needn't have much glue to it.'

'Well,' Ken sighed, 'where do we go from here? Where do you take it? She's too young to give up on. Too intelligent.'

'What do you think?'

He sighed again. 'I think.. don't laugh.. I think Jess has forgotten who she is. She's like a princess in a tower. Rapunzel without the hair. How can you ever get beyond that?'

'Well, input from Neuropsychology will help – she's been assessed – but, for my part, what I'd like to do,' said Sian, 'is make a book. I mean, get Jess to do it.'

'A book?'

She set her cup down. 'A portfolio.' She frowned a little, stretched up to pull a folder from the shelf above Ken's head. 'Here's one I made earlier. It's a standard thing, rather personal of course, but I don't mind showing you. A portfolio like this can help rebuild the stories that make us. Help us share them, tell them. Even in a small way.. even without words. We're nothing without our stories. And Jess.. Jess is doubly unfortunate. Normally the subject has a stronger sense of who they are, of their background.'

Ken took the leather-covered album, 'Tell me about it, then. Tell me how you set about this.'

'It's better in a group,' Sian shifted in her chair, sat forward, her eyes growing bright. 'See, Ken, you get the client and their main carer along with a small group of folk with roughly similar problems. You explain that you want each of them to fashion a book about *themselves*, that they'll have to gather all the bits and pieces for it.. oh, like photographs of people who are or were important to them.. maybe bits of writing or drawing.. postcards of special places they've been to.. menus from the café down the road where they go every day. Stuff like that.. all the small important stories that make them what they are. They bring it all in, then decide as a group what would be best included.

'I know, I know, you'll say it's a small thing, a daft activity for a group, but honestly, it works. It does! Having the portfolio really does build a new sense of identity, helps to. Each person can see and re-experience the things they love. They're no longer scattered, lost in silent pockets of life. They can be relived, looked at, shown to anybody, any time. And of course, they've already had the affirmation, the benefit of sharing with the group. They feel much less alone.'

'Can't see Dan going for this.'

Sian shook her head.

'No. Not that I've a group on at the moment. I thought,' she continued, quieter, more diffident now, '*you* might perhaps consider working on a portfolio with Jess? Ella says you knew her really well when you were young. That's why I'm showing you mine. I wondered if the two of you might work in parallel.'

Ken opened the folder, flicking through it. 'Don't suppose it would do any harm.'

'You might,' warned Sian, 'be surprised what it releases. You'll learn a lot about yourself in the process. A kind of personal archaeology.'

'Appropriate enough,' Ken laughed, 'when I come from Orkney. Come on, let's see what you've uncovered here.'

He glanced from Sian to the pages before him. Pictures of Sian and her sister from babyhood, of the couple who must be their parents. Student pictures too, and views of the Central. Theatre programmes, recipes, film and book reviews. Wedding invitations. Odd gaps, where photographs had obviously been removed.

Ken didn't stop to think.

'What was here?' he asked. He could almost read the name half-rubbed out below the gap. *Matt*? Did that say Matt?

Sian shrugged, shook her head.

'Life changes. The process,' she nodded, 'can be painful. You have to realise that.'

'Ah,' Ken snapped the book shut. 'I'll borrow this. May I?'

Dan

DAN WAS MUCH less keen. Sian found him at Jess's bedside later that afternoon. He had perched himself, as always, on the bed and Jess, overcome by his proximity, shrank back against the pillows, as far away from him as the mattress would allow.

'Mr McKie,' she smiled. 'What have you got there?'

Dan looked up, grateful. He has nice eyes, Sian thought, smallish, but rather a pleasant blue. He shrugged.

'I brought this book. Daft really. It's like that postcard, the one with the birds. I thought, maybe..'

Jess wore the blank, defeated look she seemed to save for Dan. At no other time did she seem quite so lacking in warmth, in physical expression. She looked half her normal size.

'May I see?' Sian asked.

Dan handed her the book, a shiny hardback.

'Ah,' she nodded, turning it over. 'Michael Hurt.. Yes. *The Riddle of the Picts.*

I've seen this.' She turned the book over, stared at the author photo inside the back page. Dark curly hair. Blue eyes. 'Good-looking.'

Dan glanced over her shoulder. 'You think so?'

She ignored this, racing through the pages, skimming.

'Complex text,' she said, 'but there are lots of pictures too. Why don't you leave it with me, Mr McKie, and Jess and I will work through it?'

Dan grew unenthusiastic.

'Fine,' he said at last. 'Probably better. It's not really my scene.'

'Is it yours, Jess?'

Sian realised she had been drawn, as always with Dan, into treating Jess as if she wasn't there, as if she could not communicate for herself.

'Do you like the look of this?'

Jess stared grimly ahead.

'Here,' said Sian. 'Why don't you take a look at it, see what you think? I want to speak to Dan. Give him some homework to do. We'll use my office and come back later. Okay?'

Jess accepted the book but did not open it.

'Right,' Dan stood up, stretching for the coat he'd slung across the chair. 'After you.'

'Leave your coat. Won't you be coming back?'

'Oh, I think she's had enough,' he said, 'for one day.'

Sian raised her eyebrows.

'Okay Jess, see you shortly.'

Dan made no move to touch Jess; did not say goodbye. This was his usual way. And though Sian felt it masked the depths of his defeat, the nurses were appalled at his lack of caring.

'So this is where you hang out.' Dan felt stifled in Sian's office, a narrow space cluttered with books and shelves and filing cabinets.

'Have a seat. Coffee?' The kettle was still warm. She switched it on.

'Thanks.'

'Milk? Sugar?'

'Black.'

'Drat. I'm out of coffee. Need to borrow some. Make yourself at home.'

Dan nodded. He sat down, folded his arms. The noticeboard above the desk was littered with notices, photographs. The desk was just as bad, piled high with sandwich wrappers, scraps of paper, pads. Even two unwashed cups. This room surprised him. He would have predicted that Sian, with her reasoned approach to language, would prefer a structured environment. He did not himself, these days, keep a tidy desk. Nothing tidy in his life. Nothing. The phone on the window-sill rang out six, seven times, switched to voicemail. Sian's voice.

Hello. This is Sian. You've reached my office, but I'm not here. Just leave your name and number and I'll try to get back to you as soon as I can.

The caller cut off. No message. Dan hated that.

Rachel phoned last night.

How she got the number she didn't say. He didn't ask. Her voice still held that clear London edge. Why wouldn't it? What would have changed? Dan shrugged. The kettle stuttered to the boil. Sian's phone rang again.

Again the soft tones:

This is Sian. You've reached my office, but I'm not here. Just leave your name and number and I'll try to get back to you..

'Ring me on the mobile, will you?'

No name, number. A Scottish voice. Female. Probably the sister. That girl with all the hair. Dan shrugged. She must have had her knife and fork into him the minute they passed. She'd seen. She knew.

Rachel phoned him twice last night.

He sighed. Sian was taking a long time to get the coffee, longer than he'd expected. The phone rang again, cut off this time after three rings, just as Sian herself backed into the room bearing a coffee jar and a plate of biscuits. She was out of breath. She had to clear a space for them on her desk.

'My secretary was out, sorry. I'd to run to Outpatients. Got caught on the phone.'

'The phone here's been going too. Someone wants you to ring them. Sounded like a friend.'

'You took a message?'

'Voicemail.'

'Ah. I'll catch that later. Biscuit?'

Dan looked at the plate. Jammy dodgers. Gypsy creams. Shook his head. Sian stirred the coffee, handed him a mug.

'Thanks. What was it you wanted exactly?'

'Sorry?'

'What did you want to talk about?'

Sian put her cup down, looked directly at him. It unsettled Dan, how much she looked like Jess, a younger Jess, that hairstyle, the brown eyes.

She hesitated. He leaned slightly forward, ashamed of himself; eager too.

'Well, Mr McKie,' she said at last, 'I wanted to ask how you thought things were going, generally,' she waited, picking her coffee cup up again.

'You mean with Jess?' he slumped back in his chair.

'That too. But more than that.. what's happened affects you both. Now that she's getting stronger, nearer discharge, we have to decide what plans to make, which support systems should be brought into play. And with you moving back to Glasgow it'll be that little bit more complicated. I'd normally,' she apologised, 'have talked to you about this before, but Jess began to make such huge strides that it has been difficult to decide. It's still,' she added, 'such a fluid situation. She comes on so much every day.'

This brought no answering spark.

'I don't,' he said at last, 'recognise that. I haven't seen any progress beyond her gradual return to strength.'

Sian sighed. 'No,' she agreed. She cast around for an open way to ask the next question. 'We.. we talked once,' she said, 'about counselling.'

'You talked about it. I don't think it would help.'

His tone left no room for negotiation. Sian stared out of her window. Not half an hour ago, it had been Ken who sat in that chair before her; Ken, whose abstracted smile wrung her heart. Ken who had known Jess for years; even before Dan. Had they been a couple? Had they lived together?

'How do you see yourself managing with Jess at home?'

She hadn't meant to put it quite so baldly.

Dan held on to his coffee cup, stared into it, watching the dark fluid scald the shaking brim, forming concentric interfering circles. This was dreadful coffee. How could anyone drink such stuff? His hands were shaking.

Rachel phoned him twice last night.

He'd lain in bed, the curved brass bed in his sky-blue bedroom, thinking about Rachel, the long sweep of her loin. He didn't know whether he wanted Rachel back, but he knew for a certainty he could not cope with Jess, not as things stood.

Sian waited. Dan said nothing.

'Well, we can think about these things,' she offered, at length. 'Don't have to make decisions now, today. But there is another matter.'

'Oh?'

The tone was so offhand it verged on insolent. Dan cringed as he heard himself, conscious that he sounded like a thwarted teenager.

Sian seemed unperturbed.

'Mr McKie,' she said slowly, evenly. 'I'm trying to help.'

He lifted his cup slowly to his lips, drank the now lukewarm coffee, bitter as it was. Drinking, he didn't have to look at her, didn't have to measure the expression in her eyes. Not that it mattered what she thought. Why should it? She was nothing to do with him.

And Jess felt equally unrelated. The mute woman in the ward was not the Jess he'd loved, not the Jess he'd lived with, nor even the Jess he'd lost. He was not at all sure who this new Jess might prove to be; he was, he realised, afraid to find out.

Sian had a great deal of patience. She could see Dan wasn't in the most helpful mood, but she persevered.

'In fact,' she smiled, 'this is such a little thing. It will be no trouble to you, I'm sure and it could help Jess enormously.'

'What do you want?' He stared out of the window, watched students swarming across the paths below. He'd been like them once, free, untroubled. 'What?'

'It's an exercise I do with certain patients. More a project, really.'

'Yes?'

'I work with them on building what we call a personal portfolio,' Sian looked directly at Dan now, smiled. 'You can look on it as an attempt to do very much the same thing as you were attempting with the Pictish text. Just a little more direct.'

'Portfolio?'

'Yes. An affirmation. A regrouping of aspects of identity in the face of lost or diminished language.'

'Don't give me the psychobabble! What is it you want? Where do I come into this?'

Sian came close to losing her temper here but controlled the irritation. If she snapped now, Dan would have won.

'We need photographs, personal things for Jess to work with.'

'Photographs? What photographs?'

'All sorts of photographs. Folk who were important in her past, folk who are important now. And other things,' Sian added, 'Postcards, programmes, books, writing, drawings. Evidence of the person she was and is.'

'No use,' Dan turned away again. 'I've none of that stuff here in Edinburgh.'

'I imagine,' Sian pointed out, 'there will be plenty in Glasgow.'

Dan was silent.

'Mr McKie?' Sian prompted at last.

'I'm not prepared to touch any of that,' he said. 'I've shut up the flat. I'm going to clear it, sell it. All that's over and done with.'

'It can't be,' Sian was calm but firm. 'It isn't and it can't be. You cannot just get rid of Jess's things like that. It's her past. Her one chance to reconstruct her life. '

'It's not as if she wants the stuff; not even as if she knows it's there.' Dan had come to a decision. He realised he'd been working towards this for weeks. Rachel getting back in touch had been the catalyst, not the cause, of what he was about to say. 'I'm going to do a bit of travelling. Sell the flat. Put Jess's stuff in store. If she ever needs it, it can be retrieved.'

'You'd leave her, just like that?' Sian allowed her dismay to show clearly in her tone. 'When she's so vulnerable?'

'Look,' said Dan, 'let me put it squarely to you. We haven't been a couple for years. I wouldn't be good for her. I'd be the opposite of good. It would be dangerous for her to be alone with me.

She wouldn't want it anyway. Look how she hates having me around. You've seen how she turns away from me.'

'She's been through so much.'

'Sorry. Can't help,' Dan turned, balancing his cup on a pile of books on Sian's desk. 'Can't go there. Was that everything?'

She sighed. 'You brought the book,' she pointed out.

'Much good that did,' he shook his head, looked firmly at the floor.

Sian recognised a lost cause. Or a temporarily lost one.

'Maybe,' she said, 'if you're not prepared or are unable to help, you might know someone who would be?'

Dan shifted in his chair, uneasy.

'Not off-hand. But I'll think about it. She has no relatives to speak of. Not that we were ever in touch with.'

'Did you want to be?' Sian asked.

'That's not the kind of fucking man I am.'

Sian bristled. Afterwards she would regret what she said next, think it unprofessional. It just slipped out.

'Oh you're a fucking man, are you?'

Dan blanched. Opened his mouth as if to make an angry retort, but seemed to think better of it, shrugged, picked up his coat and left. He shut the door so quietly Sian thought he'd left it open.

night and day

Dan

THAT GREEN SNAKING plant had always been dangerous. There was a hunger in the way its paired leaves lunged at you; the energy and intent of movement almost dragging the plant from its lacquered pot, almost overturning the scratched and narrow table the pot rested on. It was a pot Dan had always liked, dark blue, shiny, with shimmering oranges and apples red as blood, so red that if you stretched out your finger to touch them, as he did now, the blood dripped, curdling offered skin. An odd thing that.

Odd, too, how stiff his finger was becoming, how stiff and blue his arm felt, looked. How cold it had grown. How, suddenly, he could not breathe; how, suddenly, he found himself stretched thinly round the stale, stiff compost binding the ball of tradescantia roots. He'd never realised how hard roots pushed against a pot, with what determination they attempted to invade; or how, unsuccessful, they adopted different strategies, swarming now across, then up and over, inner paler surfaces; winding themselves with sullen and unpleasant speed round and round the narrow neck of the confining pot.

'I'll check,' he heard the usual midwife say, 'the cord isn't around the neck.' Fingers tugging at the roots strained to relieve the choking pain. 'Scalpel! Forceps!'

Dan was choking. Could not breathe. Paired green leaves, succulent green stems, and whiter, fibrous roots snaked about his neck, all as tight and high as if he'd been the original Giraffe-necked woman. 'I can't.. can't release the cord,' the midwife's voice again, panicking. There was no breath left in him.

He sat up, choking.

The landing dream again, the midwife dream.

He hated it.

At least it hadn't progressed to the stage when the plant, tugging itself off the high scratched table, flew downstairs, crashing on the lowest step, freeing its roots, leaving the pot bleeding, aching. When the dream went that far it left him in pain for days and days; difficult to force the smell of blood and compost out of his nose. Difficult. And sometimes (he shivered as he thought of this) the plant threw itself through the window. That wasn't so clever; the window stood twelve feet above ground level, twelve feet or more.. and the window glass (once broken) was razor sharp. Neither plant nor pot survived that version.

He'd never been able to work out what the dream might mean. Why should you worry about a plant as peaceable, as meek, as Wandering Sailor? And the landing. Why should he always imagine himself hanging about the landing, staring at the flats, the electric flats, where people had no fireplace, no stairs (not in the house)? He had never, to his knowledge, spent much time on that landing. It was not as if he sat there hour after hour setting the world to rights, thinking, worrying. He didn't remember spending much time in the house. He was always over the field playing football with the boys who didn't go to the Catholic school. Oh, his sisters stayed at home, banned from the field after someone grabbed a wee girl near the canal; his sisters helped around the house, watered the plants, polished the furniture. Maybe they hid on the landing, reading. Maybe they stared from the window, jealous of freedoms he took for granted, but Dan had never noticed the landing, never thought about it; not till the dreams began.

When had he last been touch with his sisters? He thought about it; could not remember.

Somewhere below him in the building a door banged. Dan lay down, pulled the quilt round his shoulders. He was shivering. He had torn himself panicking, sweating, from the landing dream and now the cold night air attacked on every side. He hated sleeping alone. He missed, he thought, the kindness of human breath playing beside you, and that kindest, most reassuring thing of all – the tender press of warm flesh against your back. He almost wept when he thought about it.

There were footsteps on the stairs now, footsteps retreating.

The outer door creaked open, banged shut. More footsteps on the pavement, and the high-pitched electronic bleep of car doors being unlocked. The quiet click of a door opening was followed by the soft metallic clump of closure. An engine revved, purred, faded. Dan could not, somehow, settle in the silence that folded round the room, the flat, the street.

He hated sleeping alone. Hated spending his days alone. He found himself eating out more and more often just to invite the possibility of conversation. He went shopping frequently, bought things in smaller and smaller amounts, for the same reason. They knew him well in the corner shop along the road, and in the off-licence too. When he went in they had his papers ready, or reached for the bottle of Syrah. The banter was building up nicely in both shops. Often this was the only human contact he had throughout the day so that by evening he found himself marooned in silence.

Visits to the hospital were always bad. Jess flinched, said nothing. Nurses glowered, didn't trust him. Only Sian Kinnon spoke to him with any attempt at civility. What were they to think – with Jess behaving as if he'd been responsible for all her pain? He'd have read things the same way himself if he'd been the onlooker. Stands to reason. Nobody behaves like that for nothing.

He shivered again. How long was it since he'd been in touch with his sisters?

Dan lay on his back, eyes open. Two am. The footsteps long gone. Who had been creeping down the stairs and out into the night? He'd done his share of that.

Rachel phoned last night.

It could have been him slipping into the December darkness. Midnight assignations. He used to rather like those early drives; the city streets surprisingly quiet, sometimes frosty. Stars penetrating the inky sky. It could have been him. He could be there again, if..

Why was he so fickle?

How long had it been since either of his sisters phoned? Did he even have their numbers? Jess would have them somewhere. They'd be in the flat in Glasgow. He had no idea where to start looking.

He turned on to his right side, staring in the dark towards the heavy folds of the creamy curtains screening the window. Where would she have put those numbers? They could be anywhere.

He rolled onto his back. They'd be in the study. No. They might be in the bureau in the hall. The kitchen drawer. Maybe. Oddly restless, he turned over on to his left side.

Maybe he should take himself through to Glasgow, look for those addresses, those phone numbers? Perhaps, the thought came unbidden, perhaps he should take Sian with him.. she could go through the flat, look for whatever she needed for that project she'd mentioned. Yes. That's what he should do. He shouldn't have been so rude. Unforgivable. He yawned. He'd phone the hospital tomorrow. Apologise. No. He'd do it now.

Sian

NINE O'CLOCK FOUND torrents of hail, street-vicious, stunning the New Town and the Old, biting the cheeks and eyes of any passers-by, stabbing, startling. They might have been drifts of cherry blossom, for all Sian noticed, as she drifted along narrow streets. Glowing.

Yesterday had started slowly enough; busy clinic, then that pleasant lunch with Ken, who'd agreed to help with Jess's portfolio. Hadn't she spent days deciding whether or not to approach him?

Dan McKie was not so helpful. Though she'd expected that, she had not expected him to storm out of her office; and for her to have lost her temper quite so badly, let it show.. she shook her head. Let him complain if he wanted. She'd done nothing wrong. She had nothing to be anxious about. It wasn't Dan McKie she'd lost time and sleep over.

Though she had been sufficiently shaken to tell Jamie about it.

'You said what?' Her sister's tone, thinned to querulous by telephone wire, gave her pause. 'You said what?'

'Jamie,' she pleaded, 'don't.. don't tease. If he complains I'll have to apologise, that's all.'

Jamie laughed. 'Don't worry. He'll probably be the one to do the apologising.'

'Don't think so. No. I don't think that man's ever apologised in his life. I don't think he's about to start.'

'But you quite like him, obviously.'

'I feel sorry for him.'

'Sorry?'

'Don't know why. He's like a terrier. Bites first, wags the tail as he sinks the teeth in. But yes, I do like him.'

'Tell me more,' asked Jamie, 'more about this other guy, this Ken.'

Sian stared at the television where the news still flickered, sound turned off.

Afghanistan.

'No. You tell me more about this conference in Kraków.'

She found herself unwilling or uneasy to talk much about Ken.

'It's arranged? You're definitely going?'

'Easter, at the end of the holiday. I'll have to get my paper together.'

'Tell me the title again.'

'Don't change the subject, Sian.'

The bell rang. Sian laughed.

'Not to change the subject, but that's my door. I'll ring you back.'

'Make it tomorrow. I'm off to visit Cass.'

'Give her my love.'

'I'll do that. Ring tomorrow.. after ten.'

'Okay. Have to run.'

The bell rang out again as Sian replaced the receiver. She glanced at her watch. Nine fifteen. And the weather blustery and fierce, even in the relative shelter of the court. Not a night for being out and about. Rain clattered the kitchen window and the door, spattering Sian as she opened it, astonished.

'Ken? What are you doing here? You're soaked! Are you wise, walking in this weather?'

'I brought your portfolio back,' his voice oddly gruff. 'Thought you might need it.'

'Tomorrow would have done. Come in.' She focused on the practical. 'Come away in. Give me your jacket. It's drookit! Isn't that the word? I'll hang it in the bathroom.'

Coming back with a towel, she found him perched on a stool in the kitchen, dripping, hair moulded to his skull, shirt and trousers as wet as the jacket she'd carefully hung over the bath. He looked younger, oddly shy.

'This isn't going to be much use.' She handed him the towel. 'Ken, take yourself through to the bathroom, and get out of those wet things. You can borrow my bathrobe.'

'*Your* bathrobe? I know I'm not tall, but..'

She laughed. 'It's unisex. One size fits all. All but drowns me. It should just about fit you. I'll put the kettle on. You must be chilled to the bone. Are you hungry? Have you had anything to eat?'

'I haven't stopped since lunch.'

'Ken! You of all people ought to know better.'

She was rattling round the kitchen, scrambling egg, juggling toast, when the phone rang again. It was difficult to stir the egg (now at a critical state) and talk.

'Hello? Hi Jamie.. what? You forgot what? What am I doing? Making supper. No, I know it's not like me. It's not for me. Ken Groundwater's just come in, looking like a drowned rat. Hold on a minute, Jamie..' she swung round, smiling at Ken who came back in, wrapped in her bathrobe.

'Sorry, Jamie? No. Don't think so.. not sure of that one either.' she hesitated. Ken looked so *relaxed*. At home. 'Look, we'll talk tomorrow. Bye.' She put the phone down, shrugged. 'My sister. Trying out titles for this paper she has to give at Easter. In Kraków.'

'You've a sister in Kraków?'

'No. Jamie – my twin – you'll have seen her picture – is going to a conference there.' She set two glasses on the table. 'Hope you're hungry.'

'Sian, you shouldn't have.'

'I'm hungry myself. Cutlery's in that drawer just behind you. Could you? Great. So.. glass of wine? And what did you do with your clothes?'

'Left them in the bathroom.'

'Did I switch the radiator on?'

'Think so.'

'I'll check. Help yourself to bread and salad. Maybe,' she ran on, far too quickly, 'maybe you could make yourself useful. Open the wine? Corkscrew's in the drawer with the cutlery.'

She slid from the room. Escaped.

The bathroom was not that warm, but the radiator was on. Rehanging Ken's clothes, Sian wondered what she was doing, why she was behaving like this. Daft! Every bit as bad as she had been this afternoon. What was going on? What had got into her? What?

The feet, she thought. The problem was those bare, perfect feet. Most men would have kept their socks on.

She bent, straightened his shoes. Ken's shoes. Leather. Tan.

Her heart lurched, wild.

No.

She clung to caution, fought for breath. In – out. In and out. Yes. Better now. Nearly. *Nearly..*

'Sian? Are you okay? What are you doing through here? Anything the matter?'

A knock on the door. Ken pushed it open.

'Sian?' he said again. 'What's wrong?'

Sian made her next mistake. Looked up.

Jess

'MORNING, JESS.'

Early morning. This is Ella's favourite time, favourite time of year too; next week she'll be on annual leave. A good time of year for leave. She always takes time off now, gets all the Christmas stuff out of the way, or most of it. She didn't do quite as well as usual last year; couldn't find the computer game Matthew wanted, and had to order Gavin's pogo stick. Who would have thought there'd be a run on pogo sticks?

'How are you, Jess?' she smiles, sitting herself down on the edge of the bed. 'You're looking nice and rosy. Not long awake?'

Years of training kick in. Every time she sits by a patient, even relatively fit patients, Ella finds her fingers straying to their wrist, her eyes drifting to her watch. She even does it with her children.

'How are things?' she says again, her fingers seeking, measuring.

'Are you okay? Jess.. Jess, are you okay?'

Ella frowns, looks more closely. Jess's pulse is weak, thready. Difficult to feel.

'What is it, Jess? Are you in pain? Where is it sore, Jess?'

Jess is flushed, sweaty too. Breathing fast.

'What's wrong? What is it? Can you tell me?'

Jess shakes her head, seems to have trouble responding. Ella can see she's struggling to breathe.

'Where is it bad, Jess? No. Don't try to answer. I'll get the young doctor in.'

She rushes back to the duty room.

'Jess, Jess,' she sighs. 'You certainly didn't need this..'

The resident takes several minutes to answer the pager. Ella paces round the duty room.

'Come on.. come on!'

The phone rings at last. She pounces on it. 'Ruth? Hi, Ella

here.. yes. Could you come up to the ward right now? It's Jess. Jess Kavanagh. I'm worried. Think she's going off.. maybe an embolism.. yes, yes I know it's late for that, but she's very breathless, pulse difficult to find. Calves? Well, they seem okay. Good. Thanks, Ruth. I know you've had a busy night.'

She moves swiftly back to Jess's bedside, rattles the curtains round the bed.

'Okay, Jess. Young Ruth is on her way. You'll be fine. Just fine. Try and relax. We'll maybe have to do more tests. I think you might be doing with a little of this in the meantime.'

Ella eases an oxygen mask over Jess's head.

'If you want to speak, just pull it down, eh, Jess? Okay.. ah.'

Ella smiles, relieved, as the resident pops her head through the screens.

'Here's Ruth, Jess. She must have run all the way! And hardly out of breath at all.'

Ruth smiles, blonde hair slightly dishevelled, straying from the clasp attempting to confine it at the nape of her neck.

'I was through next door. Now, what have we here?'

Ella watches anxiously as the young doctor examines Jess, listening to her heart, her chest. It seems to her that Jess's breath is growing fainter all the time, faint and ineffectual as sleet streaking the window, silvering the grimy pane.

Dan

DAN HAD SLEPT later than his usual six thirty, having tossed and turned all night. This, in itself, was not like him. All his life he had woken without the aid of an alarm, unable and unwilling to sleep longer than six thirty. He'd turn the radio up, increasing the intensity of the morning's sports reportage.

That morning however, he woke to silence. The radio alarm had run its course and stuttered into blankness. When the phone rang, he stretched blearily towards it, assuming it was still the middle of the night.

'Hello? Dan McKie.'

'Mr McKie, it's the hospital. You'll have to come in straight away. Your wife is less well.'

'She's not my wife,' the reflex answer. 'Jess is my partner, not my wife.'

'Ms Kavanagh very unwell this morning,' said the nurse. 'We're sending her back into High Dependency. Try and get here as soon as possible.'

The tone, the message, hit hard. Dan pulled his clothes on and raced along the stormy streets, slipping, sliding his way to the taxi rank on the main road. No taxis waiting. None in view. Hail scything his cheeks, his face, stinging as he made his uncertain way through the Meadows, towards the hospital.

By the time he reached the main gate his trousers were soaked from the ankle to the knee, his shoes wet through, his jacket thick with hail. He couldn't bring himself to go in. He hovered on the pavement, shivering.

It was not until he saw, in the distance, Sian's grey-clad figure that he saw a way forward, a way out of this dilemma. He didn't even wait till he was sure she'd had time to reach her office before he started ringing. At first, he reached the answerphone. Doubt struck him. Why should she come with him? After yesterday, why should she help? He had rung in the night, left a message about that portfolio thing, but even so. He tried again. And again and again till Sian's voice answered.

Sian

SIAN PULLED HER coat off the minute she got into the office. As she'd walked, hail gathered on her shoulders, clinging, melting. Her boots were soaked. She took them off, thrusting her feet into the open sandals kept at work for just such occasions.

Outside the world dissolved in grey confusion. It was cold, cold and damp. Why was her radiator set so low? She turned it up, started leafing through the pile of new referrals on her desk. Clinic today. With any luck she might be free till then. She shook the kettle. Half-full. Switched it on.

She ran through the mail again, checked the answerphone.

Too early for messages from Ken.

She didn't know, couldn't bring herself to dwell on what might be happening between them.

Nothing simple. Nothing straightforward.

Or perhaps all too simple. Sleet rattled the window. Perhaps, she thought, last night was simply comfort in a storm.

She gazed across the room.

'Ms Kinnon,' a voice startled her. She'd forgotten the answerphone. 'Dan McKie here. I.. wanted to apologise. I was out of line. You were only trying to help. I thought.. maybe we could look at Jess's things together. You would have a better idea of the type of thing.. We'll speak soon. Well. That's all I really wanted to say.'

No message from Ken. He had not rung.

Sian wished he had.

Wished he would.

Wished so hard for the phone to ring that when it did she stood bemused, staring at its sharp insistence. The voice at the other end was not Ken, was Irish, troubled, hard to place, as if the call were being made from a mobile on a train. She found it almost impossible to decipher the words.

'Mr McKie?' There was no answer. Sian tried again. 'Dan? What is it? Dan?

'I.. I..'

'What is it? What's the matter?'

'It's Jess,' he said. 'I'm sorry. I shouldn't trouble you. There's no-one else. They've just phoned about Jess.. going back to High Dependency.'

'Sorry?' Sian was utterly confused. 'What did you say? What's happening?'

'I don't know,' Dan whispered. 'I can't make it out. Can't understand. They said I ought to come in. I wondered.. wondered if you might come up with me.'

'I've a clinic later. Are you coming in right now?'

'I'm here already. At the front door,' he confessed. 'But it's just.. it's like a nightmare. I can't face that ward alone.'

'Don't move, Dan. Well, I mean, come in out of the weather. I'll be right down.'

Sian raced out of the room. As she reached the stairs, her phone rang again. The voicemail soothed.

This is Sian. You've reached my office, but I'm not here. Just leave your name and number and I'll try to get back to you.

Dan

ELEVEN AM. DAN sat slumped in the darkest corner of the hospital café, oblivious to the sticky table, the sagging chair. The smell of soup was harder to ignore. The cafe thrummed with noise, every table full. They had been lucky to find a seat at all. Arms folded against his chest, he stared into the distance, not seeing anyone, anything.

He should have been expecting this, should have known. The landing dream had always been an ill omen. Always. He'd talked to Jess about it; remembered sitting in the Café Gandolfi, telling her. Why? Wasn't she working on an article on dreams? Yes. A commission from one of the bigger magazines, well-paid. And in those days he insisted on taking her out for dinner every time he came back from a longish trip, though, now he thought about it, silence had been settling on them even then.

They had become like strangers, offering anecdote, opinion on only the safest subjects.

But that night Jess asked Dan what he thought about dreams.

He shifted uneasily in the high-backed chair, wishing they'd been shown to a table with less flamboyant seating.

'What do you mean?' he asked, his tone distinctly cagey.

'Just what do you think about dreams?' she repeated mildly.

'In what way?' Dan squirmed. 'Do you mean do I think dreams predictive?'

'If you like.'

Jess nodded, lifting her fork, spearing the olives from her *salade niçoise*.

Dan looked away. It was still early, the café half-empty. no-one famous lounging in wooden style.

'Are you asking if I think they're a psychological safety-valve?'

'If you like.'

His steak tartare melted in the mouth.

'Be more specific, Jess.'

'It's a non-specific question,' she waved an olive.

'Are you trying to ask if I get recurring dreams?'

'Do you?'

She looked directly at him.

'Yes, actually.'

Dan could not meet her gaze, looked down, away.

'Then have you thought about *them*?'

'Okay, Dan?'

'Sorry?'

'Are you okay? It's been a long morning, worrying too. Look here's your coffee. Not great. Hot and wet. That's about it, I'm afraid. I brought you a croissant. Thought you maybe didn't have time for breakfast.'

'Thanks. Thanks, Sian.' Dan brought himself back with difficulty to the plain surfaces of the hospital café, the plastic trays, polystyrene cups.

'I know,' said Sian. 'Tacky. We should have gone across the road. I told you.'

'It's fine,' Dan nodded. 'Fine.'

'No, it's not. But every hospital is the same, all those that I've ever known. And it's still a white-out out there. Talk about fierce.'

'Odd to have weather like this so early.'

'Don't think I've ever seen it.'

He sipped his coffee, frowned.

'Do you take sugar?' she asked. 'Sorry.'

'Not as a rule,' he said. 'Don't think it would help much.'

'No.'

'Sian..' he was almost frightened to ask this, 'Sian.. when do you think they'll know?'

'As soon as they've done the scan.'

'What do you think?'

'I hope,' she said, 'it's only an infection. But either way she's had a bad knock. This will hold her back.'

She kept her eyes focused on her cup.

'You're really fond of her.'

'Yes.'

'I..'

'What?' Sian looked up now, saw, Dan's face working with pity and perhaps with grief. 'What?'

'I don't understand,' he said. 'Can't quite work it out. You never knew her, not before. You didn't know Jess, yet you seem to treat her like.. like family. How can you do that, Sian? Without words?'

She took time to frame her answer. Sipped her coffee. Sighed. She put her cup down, shrugged. 'It's easy for me, Dan. I like my patients, but there's a safe distance, always.. professional. It's harder for families, I think.'

You are, thought Dan, less distant than you've ever been. Why? Why now?

Sian smiled, went on, 'And you know, Dan, speech isn't all of communication. Yes, and there are ideas, stories, things we can't easily share without words, and the pictures they paint. But liking, loving.. *they* don't depend on words, do they?

When you're watching films, so much of the action is just that.. *action*.. There are lots of ways that stories are told without spoken words. If you watch and listen for them. Sorry,' she blushed, 'long speech. Boring.'

'No,' Dan shook his head. 'Not boring. No.' He sipped his coffee, slowly. Sian too picked up her cup. They did not speak again till it was time to go back to the ward.

'Ready?'

'Okay.'

'I'll slip back after the clinic. Soon as I can. And Janet will be there too.'

He nodded. 'Fine.'

'Have you,' she hesitated, 'have you phoned Ken?'

Sian

SIAN'S CLINIC OVER-RAN. It was nearer five than four by the time she finished. There had been no word from Ken.

Don't think about him, she told herself. Don't think about him. Focus on the here, the now. Get through the day.

Jess had pneumonia. It would take its toll – and time – would slow up an already slow recovery. But Jess would pull through; that was the important thing. First thing this morning, it had all seemed touch and go.

Touch and go. Sian stopped, listening. Touch and go. Odd words. A narrative, an image. Touch and go.

Her head was aching.

Why hadn't he called?
This felt like migraine. She hadn't had migraine for a while.
Why hadn't he called?
'Mairi.. Mairi? I'm popping out for five seconds, need some paracetamol. I'll be back.'
Don't think about Ken. Don't think about him.
Five o'clock. The day gone. Outside these busy corridors, beyond the closed hospital world, rain spattered, lanced the thickening dark.
Serious rain. Spectacular rain.
Glasgow rain.
Edinburgh normally couldn't hold a candle to it.
But I'm nearly there, thought Sian. Nearly finished. Just check the office, ward visits.
Coffee first.
Don't think about Ken.
'Right,' she turned the corner. 'Right. Where was I?'

Forty minutes later, she tiptoed in to Jess who lay, apparently asleep against a mountain of pillows. She no longer wore the mask, but nasal cannulae; still on oxygen, then, though the drip was down. Her hair was plastered against her skull as if she'd just stepped out of the shower or swimming pool. The sleeveless nightdress clung damply, revealing shoulders barely healed, shoulders intricately scarred. She looked painfully young, oddly worn, half-starved.

Was she eating enough? Sian had never thought of her as thin. Was it the infection that rendered her ethereal, almost intangible? Life, thought Sian, was such a risk. What was it that had kept Jess going through it all, the accident, the pain? Most would have succumbed, turned their face to the wall. Sian had seen that happen.

But for all the trauma, lost as Jess had been – isolated as she was by the aftermath, the pain, not to mention the loss of language, of memory – giving up, defeat, had never for an instant seemed a likely outcome. She was thin, though. Tired. The months had taken their toll.

Dan sat by the bed, seemed older, sadder.
'Dan.'
He looked up, nodded. He was, she saw, holding Jess's hand,

caressing, stroking it. She had never seen him do that. Janet was there too, dozing, her head against the chair-back, eyes closed. Her mouth hung open, in that vulnerable way it does when someone sleeps upright in a chair. She'd have a stiff neck if she didn't wake up soon.

Sian brought a chair over, settled it silently at the foot of the bed. She smiled at Dan. She'd wait for a few minutes.

Jess might waken. Just to see her, just to smile, would be enough. The girl was ill, as the charts at the bed-foot testified, the mountainous temperature, erratic pulse. Really, it was better not to look at them. But she didn't appear nearly as frail as she had that morning, and Sian knew the ward staff were pleased enough with her condition. Fighting the infection would take time. It was a setback, certainly; it could have been much worse.

Her gaze fell again on Dan, on that restless hand, moving back and fore, back and fore. She blushed as he glanced up, reading her eyes. He seemed to feel the change in her, seemed almost to know; he smiled, shrugged, went on stroking. They both looked down, away.

The man, she thought, was not as black as he was painted.

Complex, yes. Selfish, probably. This morning when he thought he might be losing Jess, he'd been at his wit's end, beside himself. All the way upstairs, all the way along the endless, busy corridors, he clasped her arm, clinging tightly to her, as if she were solid, secure, the one thing he could trust in an uncertain world.

Ken had done the same last night but, then – last night – today was tomorrow, and tomorrow another day.

And tomorrow Dan, like Ken, would disappear, revert to type. *Don't think about Ken. Don't think about him.*

Last night Ken had needed her. Needed her. Sian shook her head. Last night spoke of comfort, not love.

She closed her eyes, heard the ward door open, shut. Heard it swing closed, banging softly. And footsteps, brisk at first, then slow, footsteps of a given weight. She had not known she knew them. She had not known how completely you could deduce living flesh from the simplest sound.

She ought to turn her head, look up; be brave enough to smile

– as to a friend – she ought to show him it didn't, wouldn't, make a difference, hadn't mattered.

But it had. It had.

She found she had no words, none helpful; none at all.

PART TWO

FLEDGES MERCHISTON with cherry blossom, stippling clotted earth with crocus, and window-sills with hyacinth that strain and groan towards the light. Tulip and daffodil (dwarf varieties; this is Merchiston after all) spike window boxes; pansies smile; primulae splash bright and sharp, shocking muted borders. Sitting at her desk in the small front bedroom, Jess can feel the grass change, minute by minute, can see over the sandstone walls across the road, watch winter grey warming to tousled green. And the birds! All of a sudden so noisy, so early. She writes it all down, savouring each syllable, conscious of the possibility, the probability, that any word, every word, may be clumsy, inept. Still she writes, records it all, everything. How the sun fondling her skin feels gentle, warm. How her fingers work better in temperate heat. She remembers words like *temperate* now, words like *remember*. She sighs, leans back, closing her eyes, letting the golden-pink warmth take over. Yes. That's good. Good. She cannot remember having felt like this before. She feels good now. Now. In the last six months there have been few moments as golden and safe as this, few moments when nothing actually hurt. *Nothing actually hurts.* Jess takes this in. Checks herself all over. Nothing hurts; her body, her mind dissolve in equilibrium, in equal, balanced freedom. She writes that down, goes on ordering words, sentences, paragraphs in her beautiful notebook with its soft suede cover – a convincing duck-egg blue – blue-green, perhaps, like the sky in deepest winter on one of those short cloud-free days when endless frosted dawn devolves into freezing dusk. The colour of those skies, always the farthest lowest corners, floods her mind's eye now; her fingers, her nose, her toes, twitch, freezing. She can see her breath frosting a cold car window as the phrase floats back into her mind. Duck-egg blue. Why duck-egg? She can't dredge up that image, but the notebook's paper, thick and rich, feels good against her fingers; and though her handwriting is almost illegible, unconstrained by lines, Jess takes pleasure, endless pleasure, in covering these soft sheets, page after page. Not a journal, not a diary, not even (as she will keep writing, never seeing the mistake) a *dairy*; simply a record of how she feels, a record for no-one but herself. No-one else ever sees it. Not Janet, not Sian. Not Dan. Certainly not Dan. She shivers, sighs. Has the sun dimmed a little? She lays her pen down, closing the notebook, picking it up, winding the blue leather bootlace tie over and over, tucking the ends carefully about and round the pages, in a pattern too intricate to be copied. No-one could open this without her knowing. 'Why the secrecy?' asked Janet, once. Jess had no answer for her.

Dan gave her the notebook. It lay waiting for her on the desk in this small quiet room, with a stack of new pens, each one seeming to Jess to hold endless promise, endless possibility. A pen, any pen, felt right in her hand, despite the pain too many hours of writing could induce; each time she laid a pen down, life became less full, less familiar, strange as the room, the flat, seemed strange, were strange. She had never to her knowledge been in Merchiston before. There'd been talk about moving back to White Street, but White Street and Glasgow are now as shadowy as a partially forgotten dream. To be leaving the Central, moving in with Dan was logical enough, though her past life with Dan is far from clear in her memory. It's hard to cast her mind back before the accident; hard for her to remember long episodes of her hospital experience.

Michael

IT WAS HARD FOR Michael, coming back to Scotland. The fact that he was flying made the journey a little easier. And to Glasgow, not Edinburgh, no direct memories of Jess, though he expected, every moment, to see her; found himself signing books in the palatial bookshop in the city centre, to a huge turnout. Who'd have thought so many Glaswegians would be into Pictish Stones?

He kept thinking she'd come, kept waiting for her right up till the last customer had gone, till the publicity girl smiled, 'Come on then, Mick. We'll go catch a bite to eat.'

He hated being called Mick. Of all the variations on Michael that was the one he liked least.

'Tired, Mick?'

'Yes,' he said, 'I am, a little. And, actually, the name is Michael.'

'Ah, well.. Michael,' her tone grew a shade cooler. She didn't even blush. 'Right. Michael. Where will we go to eat? What kind of food do you like best?'

'Well,' he glanced at his watch, 'actually, I thought I might look up an old friend. Don't worry. I can see myself back to the airport.'

'Are you sure?'

She was wondering, he could see, whether she had seriously offended him; or if he was sleeping with someone he shouldn't be; or last (least interesting) about to look up an old friend.

'If you're sure?'

He nodded.

'Okay. Thanks so much. That was a cool reading, Mick.. *Michael*. We'll meet again.'

He shook her hand. Escaped. How, he wondered, best to make for White Street? The tube, yes. Buchanan Street Station was mobbed. He scoured the crowd, sifting faces, moving quickly on. Plenty of smallish dark-haired women, plenty of sharply dressed women. The publicity girl had been beautiful, he had to admit, but she was not Jess. No, not Jess. And there was no Jess on the trundling orange train.

Stepping out into the relatively fresh air of Byres Road he felt as if in the few stops he'd changed cities, continents. Byres Road always did feel that bit different. Little Italy. *Délices de France*. New York? That thing they do with tenements in Glasgow, the corner feature.

As a student here Michael coveted a corner flat on Byres Road. White Street was, he remembered, towards the far end. He walked down the street taking in all the new restaurants, the changes in shops and cafés since he last paraded these pavements. It didn't look so different, though traffic was heavier than he remembered; crossing the road away from the lights seemed to take hours. Was that different? Was it?

The Peckham's at the bottom of the road enticed, windows rich with paté, biscuits, pyramids of wine. What should he take Jess? Wine? Cake? He bought a bunch of flowers, almost immediately regretting it. Roses seemed so obvious. Perhaps he should have bought wine after all? But no, they were pink: pink roses spoke friendship. Not love. Not.

He trailed the length of White Street twice, spying out the door, before building up courage to approach it, knock, ring the bell. And after all that, no answer.

A sash window slammed upwards in the flat above.

'Hey you!'

Michael looked up, amused. It might have been Kerry leaning out and over the sill, blonde hair swinging. Kerry with a Glasgow tinge.

'They're away but. Been gone ages.'

'Oh,' he said. 'Thanks. Sorry to disturb you.' He hesitated. 'Could you use these?' he waved the roses, tiny triple closed buds nodding, nodding.

'You're no wantin them yersel?'

'I'm not staying,' Michael shrugged. 'Passing through. Tell you what – I'll prop them on the doorstep here. You give them a home if you like. Bye!'

'Must have been my hairspray but!' she shouted down the street, after his retreating back. He laughed, shook his head.

'What are you on about?'

Her flatmate was immersed in a re-run of *Friends* on satellite TV, Jennifer Aniston smiling from the ad, assuring the world that she was worth it.

'It's jist like the hairspray advert.'

'Naw it isnae. She says it's science, an she's *worth it.*'

'*No this advert, dummy. The one that goes When a man you don't know buys you flowers..*'

'In Glasgow?' the flatmate snorted. 'Tell you this. If you don't get a move on, they'll be history. How long do you think a bunch of flowers will lie there on the doorstep?'

Jess

THE DAY SHE came to Merchiston was raw and damp. Jess remembers her panic as she walked up the stone stairs to the flat that first time, weak, legs wobbling, overwhelmed by unremitting sensory richness. After the confusion of the rush hour traffic, the calm, white-painted door; the treads scuffed, sculpted by feet running up and down, happy, sad, year upon year; the bannister polished to warm honey by stray fingers; the chipped cream of the thick-glossed walls. So many textures to relearn. So much..

The cleaner at the convalescent home hugged her, waved goodbye, wiped a tear from her eye. 'It's lovely, you getting home at last. That man of yours must be right glad.' She stuffed a scruffed-up pink tissue in the pocket of her orange-yellow tunic, her thin face softening.

Jess shook her head. Since the pneumonia, when Dan spent every waking minute with her, she has grown less unsure in his presence. What he means to her, what he has been, she doesn't know. In her current invalid state, she is dependent on him – for everything, food, the roof over her head. That's hard to understand; she'll have to get her head around it at some stage, when she's no longer weak, no longer an invalid. When she's finally, once and for all, *valid*.

She sighs. It's easier to focus on the moment, on day-to-day existence. Easier to mark new growth, the ever-changing cityscape, spring's pleasure in the city's confined opportunity.

A dandelion clump in a rone four storeys above ground can distract and entertain; the changing, rising light straining further, deeper, into the city gardens, gilding the recesses, forcing new life, new direction, even as it sweeps narrow city rooms, unmasking winter's lack of heart. Thoughts like these fill pages. Yes. It's easy to find words for the positive, the new.

Harder to know what lies seeded, germinating.

Dan

DAN WALKED DOWN town, crossing Princes Street a little defiant. He'd left early, far too early, had to linger over coffee in Waterstone's before making his way to Charlotte Square and beyond to the private address Sian had written on a piece of scrap paper.

'You'll be fine.'

She knew it was big deal, difficult. She raised her eyebrows at him.

'Don't expect instant results. It doesn't work like that.'

'Fine,' he snapped.

What was he expecting?

Not the neat Edinburgh street. Not the door onto the street, perhaps the finest door he'd ever seen, huge, squarish, with a central handle. It looked as if his counsellor owned the whole block. There was money in counselling, then. And what did a counsellor look like? Maria, opening the door to him, was a tiny sparrow of a woman with brown hair scrunched half-up, half-down.

'Dan. You must be Dan. Maria. Follow me.'

She led him through a dusty hall and up a flight of stairs steeper than any he'd encountered (even in Amsterdam) to a sitting-room of perfect proportions, with varnished wooden floors and working shutters. Dan glanced around, assessing the original artwork; not entirely to his taste, but there was a sense of *rightness* in it. A huge cheeseplant blocked the light from one window, wavering leaves unhealthy, browning at the edges. That's cheeseplants for you, thought Dan. They never last. Date you precisely.

'So,' Maria spread her hands, open, on her lap. 'It's never easy to begin. Tell me what's in your mind?'

'At this precise moment?'

'If you like.'

'That there's money in counselling.'

He hadn't meant to let that slip out. Maria took it well, burst out laughing. In some ways this felt worse than if she'd been offended. That she was surprised was evident.

'We don't actually own the whole building,' she giggled. 'Just the first two floors. The door is rather special, though. Makes most folk think we must be millionaires. Right,' she said, 'now we've got the real estate out of the way, tell me what you think I can do for you.'

Dan sighed. 'I have no idea.'

But in the next hour he found himself revealing more about himself than he had ever shared; more than he offered Jess even in the early days; more, even, than he would own to Jack. Maria let him talk without interruption. When at last he ran out of words, she sighed a little.

'So,' she said, 'your problem is?'

'I've just told you all the problems.'

Maria shook her head.

'You've told me something of your story. What do you see as the problem or problems?'

Dan was mystified. What more could she want?

'You're the counsellor.'

'Yes, counsellor, not judge. What I see as a problem may not bother you at all. Between now and the next visit, I want you to think about what you've told me. Think about it deeply, Dan. See if you can work out what you want to change or understand.

'That may take a little time, or no time at all. Do you want to come back next week? Or do you want to leave it, go away, think about things? Obviously, everything you've said will remain confidential, won't go beyond these walls.'

'Obviously,' he nodded, nettled.

'So, next week? Same day? Same time?'

'Fine.'

He left the house as quickly as he could; desperate to find a way to put the morning's rigours behind him. It was not perhaps the wisest decision to go up to the Central to look for Sian.

Jess

JESS LAYS THE notebook aside. She should be working, as she'd promised Sian, on her portfolio. That's much harder. Another book, larger. The sort of book you might stick cameras in; not, not. Not cameras. What you do with cameras. Frames. No. Not. Not frames. Not printers. People. Faces. Face-frames. That is not the word. Not glasses. What you do with cameras. Leave it. Leave it. The words for plants and gardens come so easily, but other things are more difficult. She sighs. It's like one of those river-things in the Highlands, one of those river-pillows. Sheets. *Beds*. One of those dry beds where the river does not sleep or lie, its swirling path written in water-rounded pebbles, wide, tumbling tracts of stones, the only water flowing a tiny, weakish stream. That's how her words are now; except when she has her notebook, and her newest pen. New pens release more words, Jess does not know why. If someone else has touched a pen she won't use it again. Throws it away. Take a new pen, on its first day, and the words for the notebook force their way, a stream in spate. (She holds a new pen between her fingers now, and the word *spate* flashes through her mind, through her mouth; her cheeks, her tongue form the sharp edgy single syllable. *Spate.*) New pens make the word business much simpler. Maybe, Jess thinks, maybe what she needs to do is use other pens for the portfolio. A good word *portfolio*, hard to say. It rolls around the mouth like thunder in the city. *Portfolio.* Yes, different pens might help. Old pens, perhaps? Pens from the old flat? She must talk to Janet about pens this afternoon. They should look in the other room, in the boxes. She and Janet look in the boxes every day, though they are never sure what they are looking for.

The portfolio has a bright blue cover. Plastic. Hard. It hurts the skin. When Sian first showed it to her, handed it to her, Jess recoiled from its alien surface.

'What's wrong?'

'It's cold,' Jess lied. 'Cold.'

The folder had the wrong feel, thin and sore, too shiny. She smiled uncertainly at Sian.

'It's blue.'

Sian nodded. 'Blue. Do you like blue?'

'Don't remember.'

'You don't remember how you used to feel about it. How does it strike you now?'

Jess put the album down on the bed, trying to focus on the colour.

'Glad. Glad I know.. for.. the word.'

'But do you like it?'

'Mmm.'

'You wouldn't prefer red?'

Jess shook her head.

'Okay,' said Sian, 'we'll run with blue. The blue team. Tell me, what does blue mean to you? Can you think of any words blue goes with?'

'Blue sky?'

'Yes.'

'Blue-collar?'

'What does that mean?'

'Don't remember.'

'Keep going.'

'Blue.. bell?'

'What's that?'

'A blue bell? No. Flower.'

'Any more?'

'Blue.. heaven?'

'Nice,' Sian smiled. 'And?'

'Blue.. stone? No. No.. Blue moon? Right?'

'Yes. And lucky too,' Sian smiled again. 'We can call this your Blue Moon book. It's going to make your dreams come true.'

Jess shivered.

'What's wrong?'

'I had the falling dream again.'

Sian shook her head.

Dan

DAN STRODE JAUNTILY enough back along Princes Street. Counsellors? Who needed them?

It was, after all, a lovely day, late spring, shops bulging with summer clothes; Princes Street Gardens busy too, teeming with daffodils, primulas, and couples (off their heads – it was still too damp, too cold) lounging on the grass, lost in conversation, in each other's eyes. He smiled as he ploughed through the midday city, footsteps muffled in the crowd. Sian would be busy; he was prepared for that. To find that she was not at work surprised him.

Her secretary offered a cup of instant disappointment. No-one in the building drank anything else. Dan accepted. By now he'd become inured to the coffee, could knock it back with a smile, to the bitter dregs.

'Phoned in with flu. Says she'll be back tomorrow.'

He stayed on for a good half hour.

Mairi was something of an ally; Mairi knew about football. She had known who Dan was from the very start.

'Well, better make tracks,' he stood up, stretching, as the phone interrupted for the twentieth time. 'You'll tell Sian I called?'

Mairi waved, dismissing him.

'These women,' he reflected all the way along the corridor, 'work so hard, and for what? Not money. The pay could be doubled easily; should be. No. Self-respect. Love. They work out of love. As I do. Did..'

A flower-stand, partially blocking his way, distracted him. Odd that he'd never noticed it before, never consciously noted the thickly-packed plastic buckets. Now he was stopped in his tracks by the bright incongruity of petals glazing varnished brick. On impulse he chose the biggest, brightest bouquet, then felt conspicuous walking Edinburgh's dusty streets with such a colourful burden. But Sian had been such a help, such a support, he reminded himself. He and Jess owed her a great deal. Everything.

He had wondered at one time, whether she and Ken.. but he might have picked that up wrong. The girl worked too hard. It was little wonder she'd contracted flu. She needed a bit of fun, a bit of spoiling.

He could do with a bit of fun himself.

These last few months had proved both lonely and disconcerting. Jess's accident was shocking enough; the aftermath worse, blow after blow. The slow pace and sheer grind of recovery amazed and depressed him; Jess had become a burden, her loss of memory perhaps the hardest thing, even worse than her inability to talk about it.

She did not at first show any emotion towards him other than fear, though she seemed to have got beyond that now, living for the moment in careful detachment. What could that mean? Was it a strategy? What did she think about?

Dan stopped walking. What, he wondered, *does* she think about? Who does she think he is? Who does she think *she* is?

Who is she? Who are they to each other?

He felt trapped, imprisoned. Since Jess's discharge, his days had been taken up with hospitals, with getting Jess to them for therapy sessions; getting her home again. Officially he was writing the definitive book on football reviewing, a critical text for which he had received a handsome advance, an advance he was currently doing little to justify. What he was now was housekeeper to Jess, housekeeper and nursemaid. Cook. He worried as much about her as if she were a young child. Worse than that. Less capable.

He couldn't go on this way.

Couldn't.

Not that he didn't try to help her. Fostering independence and judgement was the hardest thing. He made her go out every day alone, sending her to the shop, worrying that she wouldn't make it, worrying she'd get lost, that something untoward might happen on the way.

On the few occasions it had, he shouted at her, made her go straight back out again; much the same treatment that had been meted out to him whenever some difficulty in childhood had sent him asking help from either parent. That's the crux of it, he thought, the rub. He was now in *loco parentis* to Jess. Not a role he'd ever have expected. He was a time-served hack, a wordsmith, for Christ's sake! Not a nurse! Every day, a dozen times, a hundred times, he caught himself wishing he'd held to his decision to sell up, go abroad. That he hadn't was a mystery to himself as much as anyone.

The morning he'd been called back into the hospital, the morning Jess developed the pneumonia, that's what had set him on this path of defeating self-denial. He wondered now what made him so desperate, so suddenly sure he could handle a future with her. He'd found himself praying. Not that that had lasted. Things would have been easier if it had.

Maybe. Maybe not. That morning, it had felt like love.

He had never, quite, given up the habit of praying in tight corners. Never, he corrected himself, taken it up either. Lourdes put the last nail in that coffin. Dragged there, at nineteen, his mother insisting he accompany her on what she called pilgrimage, Dan had almost died of embarrassment. A package holiday. Pay and pray.

He told no-one he was going. Lourdes did not sound cool.

'Any plans for the summer?'

'I'm off,' he bent the truth, 'to the Pyrenees.'

At first he hated Lourdes; hated the plastic Madonnas, the constant call to prayer. But what he found he did like was standing on the hill in the early evening above the vast Domaine, watching real pilgrims walk in procession, each bearing a glittering candle. They sang while they walked; a swelling river of gold, sighing, shimmering. He'd never, to this day, seen anything more beautiful. It explained, perhaps, his passion for women in gold lamé. They always made him think of Lourdes, of gold gentle movement over sinuous hills though, in truth, few women could look subtle in cloth-of-gold as Lourdes, blowsy in daylight, did by night.

He made his last confession there.

'Bless me Father for I have sinned. It is three years since my last confession. I have harboured impure thoughts, Father. And masturbated. And enjoyed it. And Father, I have known the flesh of women. I have slept with each one of my three girlfriends. Also..'

He knelt in an open cubicle gouged out of rock. The priest, on the other side of the grille, could not be seen, and the rough wooden prayer stool was acutely uncomfortable. Dan wanted to get this over as quickly as possible; seduced by the nightly beauty of the candle-lit crowd he had decided to give the faith another chance. He'd get everything, sex and all, off his chest at once.

'Also..'

'You haven't been to church for three years?'

The question, offered in a stab of Gallic anger, startled Dan. He was quick to correct factual error.

'I've been to church, Father. In the holidays. I have to go to church when I'm at home. My mother makes me.'

'And the Blessed Sacrament? You have partaken of that?'

'As I said, when I'm at home..'

'When were you last at Mass?'

'This morning, Father.'

'You accepted the Blessed Sacrament?'

'Yes, Father.'

'When you haven't been to confession for *three whole years*?'

'No, Father.'

Dan was now more than a little bemused. Far from demanding the gory details of Dan's sexual exploits, the priest made him examine in exact and precise detail the number of times he'd gone to Mass and taken Communion without the umbrella of the Sacrament of Penance. He berated the boy at length and in a Pyrenean accent imposed the penance of twenty-three decades of the rosary, one decade for each time the host had passed unshriven lips.

Dan didn't say the penance. After the holiday, when his mother insisted he go with the family to Mass, he declined the opportunity; explaining he dare not add to the weight of his already considerable burden. His mother, a woman of principle, did not give up easily, but Dan now had the ultimate authority to back his natural inclination.

'He didn't even ask,' he told his sister, 'if I took precautions!'

'I suppose,' Mary replied, 'that might have caused another argument.'

As mixed a blessing as Lourdes had been, the enduring love of candlelight and movement still occasionally coloured his dreams. And good days always followed, so that now, loping towards the Royal Mile, he wondered uneasily, superstitiously, whether he should not revert to prayer if there were a chance it might help him, help Jess? Hadn't he seen an article about that in a Sunday magazine? A reference to the *British Medical Journal*?

No. He shook his head. Lourdes and sex had become integrally fused in memories of adolescence. What was wrong with him was simple enough. Sex. Lack of it. He'd not had to satisfy the urge by masturbating, not in years. And with Jess in the flat, so childlike, even that small comfort seemed out of bounds. As he'd confessed to Jack, he had seriously considered other options.

'Massage parlours?'

'No,' Dan was horrified, 'cold showers. Squash.'

Jess

JESS FLICKS THROUGH the first few pages. There she is; that's her on the front page, in a photograph.. yes, that's the word *photograph*, taken while she was still in hospital.

'You'll maybe want to change this, given time,' suggested Sian.

Jess shrugged. She looks tired in the picture, certainly, and strained, but she does look like that. It's definitely her. Not like the next one, a picture of herself with her parents. A young, rounded girl smiles from that page, unmarked by life. A stranger. Oh, the parents are real. She remembers them, remembers actual incidents, strong images; like her mother outlining pale lips with bright red lipstick, all the thinning hair on her head teased over rollers and held in place by elastic ties. And her father's sleeve, the wrinkled sleeve of the old sports jacket he used to wear to work. Somehow she remembers that, can still see that sleeve moving against a background of leather-covered steering-wheel and the shining wood-finish interior of his car, the dashboard.. is that the right word? Why would anyone call that bit at the front of the car the dashboard? Would you be dashed against it, crushed, in any accident? How would you know? How could you find out things like that? It has become very important to know why a word means one thing here, another there. The history of words, of letters.

Jess turns the page.

Dan in White Street. She doesn't like this photograph, normally skips over it. Today she stops, wondering why. On the surface it looks fine. Dan's sitting at the window, glass in hand, looking up, alert, but with an odd expression. Not anger, not sadness. Not happiness either. Not just wariness. Jess cannot find the right word for it. This picture was included because it is the one Dan chose. She shakes her head, passes on quickly.

On the next page, Janet. Then Ken, but not Ken now; Ken in Aberdeen, Ken in Johnston Hall, lounging in her room. It's as different from the photograph of Dan as it could possibly be. Ken is stretched out on the floor, back to the wall. He's laughing, shouting, wriggling, trying to escape the cushion flying through the air towards him.

For all she finds it difficult to remember what has happened in the last few months, Jess remembers quite a lot about her student days, and the image that comes to mind most often is not of Johnston, but some other hall – she can't bring the name to mind.

It must perhaps have been the end of term; yes, they were up at university in the holidays, and had moved for a few days, perhaps a week, into a different hall, into its annexe, a large converted house in a street of ancient buildings.

Ken's window overlooked the next door garden where the lecturer (it was, they thought, a lecturer's house) must have had children.

'Look, Ken!'

Jess is fully dressed. Ken is shaving, the razor grazing his cheeks, his chin, dredging foam. He's staring in the mirror, concentrating.

'Ken!'

'What?'

'Come and see the rabbits.'

Two large rabbits, flop-eared, with soft grey fur, rule this garden.

'Look! They're in the cabbages again!'

'I never saw rabbits move so slowly.'

'No?'

The towel round his neck is sweeping her shoulder now, offering that fresh, oddly sweet, part-toothpaste early morning smell. His chin, still wet, rests on her head.

'They're never in the hutch.'

'That's why the herbaceous border looks so thin.'

'You'd think a cat would get them.'

'What? Hulking brutes like that? They can defend themselves. I bet they've got some kick!'

'You think so?' Jess sighs. 'I like their ears. Lop ears. Long and strong. It must feel good to stroke them.' She twists round to face Ken. 'Don't you think?'

He dries his chin.

'Better ask the rabbit. Jess, if we don't get along the road for breakfast we'll miss it altogether. And it's so good. Look. I'll open the window. You can smell the bacon.. go on, smell it.'

He stretches in front of her. The skin on his shoulders is smooth and firm, rich.

'You never,' she says, 'see the children in that garden. There must be children, surely?'

Ken isn't listening. 'We might still make breakfast. What d'you think? Shall we run for it?'

A hundred-yard dash follows, along the cobbled road to the nearby hall of residence where breakfast lies in wait, a much-upgraded breakfast, designed for the conference currently filling the Easter-empty hall. Students from the annexe are offered the same luxury bacon, and Jess still remembers how delicious it was; though nowhere near as good as the enticing smell dragging them, leading them hungry in the soft spring air.

The granite street, the rabbits, Ken's face, even the itch from the fleas that attacked as they lounged in the hall's upholstered chairs, swim in her memory whenever she smells bacon frying.

Similarly, granite buildings, Ken's face, or a bad itch always leave her hungry.

Come to think of it, wandering that street with Ken – pelting towards the breakfast they knew was waiting for them, chasing alternating sun and shade – that had been good, better than good, just about perfect.

Michael

KRAKÓW IN APRIL. Rynek Główny spreading in polite sunlight beneath the high blue sky, unfurling mediæval vastness, the largest market square of its era in Poland, in Europe. It was beautiful (reminded Michael of Venice without sea) but cold, unseasonably so. And like Piazza San Marco, this space, when first defined, must have seemed overwhelming. The tyranny of space. He'd never thought about that. Buildings, yes – buildings sang with power, breathed it – space, he realised, whispered. With more effect.

He shivered, wishing he'd brought his leather jacket. It should not have been like this. He'd checked the five-day forecast before coming; to be more accurate, Lesley checked it for him, printing it out. The BBC weather page had promised weather at least five degrees warmer. Still, standing in the centre of the square, somehow deriving little or no shelter from the generous enough lee of the Cloth Hall, he was glad he'd decided, after all, to come, to give his paper. His room in the university residence on Garbarska was simple, comfortable. Spotlessly clean. It had obviously been recently refurbished but the building retained a monastic air, the hidden square offering a spark of the surreal.

Michael's window looked out over a large walled orchard where the base of every tree had been painted white, lending it the oddest appearance, as if all the leafless trees were swathed in metre-high bandages. He asked the domestic bursar why this should be so. She did not understand the question and Michael was forced to repeat it, slowly.

'The trees in the orchard. On the other side of the wall. I can see them from my room.'

'Yes,' she nodded. Of course he could see them. That was a problem?

'Why are they painted white?'

The woman shook her head again.

'I do not understand. I will ask. Come with me, please.'

Michael was forced to repeat his question to everybody in the residence office. None of them understood any better than the bursar; they did not understand, he thought, the *question* any more than the language. Surely everyone, they seemed to nod, must know why trees were painted thus? Wasn't it obvious?

He retreated, none the wiser, conscious of heads shaking, of amusement at foreigners. Wished he'd brought a camera to record this sight, this high-walled hospital of trees.

He backed along the corridor, escaping into ul Garbarska. He was only five minutes from the centre of the old town and yesterday he'd discovered a pastry shop in the centre where they made real Italian coffee.

They seemed to be digging up the paving all round Rynek Główny. Even Michael tall as he was, found sand and dust whipped by the biting north-east wind into his eyes. He spent a full half hour examining the postcard stands round the Cloth Hall choosing, eventually, winter views of the square – night views, the sky navy, brilliant with stars, Renaissance buildings and churches bathed in softening lamplight. There were no police vans in the pictures, though last night there were always two or three, prowling. Not that there was any sign, any hint of trouble. The square had been busy with tourists, with young Krakóvians taking the night air.

Michael straightened up, aware that the stall-keeper was watching him with some suspicion. He handed her half a dozen cards.

'English?' she balanced her cigarette carefully on the edge of the counter.

'Scottish.'

'You like stamps?'

'Please. For Britain.'

'Of course.'

She seemed insulted, grey curls tightening.

'Thank you very much.'

She relaxed a little, handing over cards and change.

'Your first visit to Kraków?'

'First to Poland,' Michael smiled.

She nodded. 'You have chosen our finest city.'

He smiled again, turned to leave. Dazzled by the sun's harsh brightness, his eyes watering in wind and dust, he blundered right into a tall girl waiting behind him, crushing her toes.

'Sorry,' he said. 'Przepraszam.'

She frowned. Was that the right word? He'd probably pronounced it wrong.

'That's alright. Don't worry. I'm fine.'

'You're Scottish?'

She was tall, not quite six feet, reddish hair sweeping her shoulders.

'You're sure you're okay?'

'Fine, absolutely fine.'

'But your feet?' he insisted.

'Fine.' She was laughing at him.

'I should buy you coffee, apologise properly.'

'Not necessary, I assure you. I'm meeting friends.'

'Well, if you're sure?'

'Really, I'm fine.'

Dismissed, Michael hovered for a moment longer.

'Stamps?'

The shopkeeper interrogated her new customer.

'Please. For Britain.'

'But of course,' grey curls rustling. 'But certainly. Where else?'

Jess

A HARSH BUZZING in the hall makes Jess jump. There it goes again. She lays the folder aside, stands up stiffly, hobbles to the front door.

'Yes?'

Her voice sounds strange, unused. The intercom crackles.

'Only me, Jess. I forgot my key. Can you get the door?'

'You're early.'

'I'm late,' Janet laughs. 'We'll not get much done this afternoon.'

She sprints up the stone uneven stairs to the open door on the first floor. The hall is empty, as are bedroom and lounge.

'Jess? Where are you?'

'In here, Janet. Tea?'

It staggers Janet, always, to see Jess moving round this colourful flat, to see her in the routine dailiness of home-life, making tea, rinsing cups; to see her face crinkle into a smile. Her conversation gets better every day, the words freer, more fluent. Her reading, it seemed, had been little impaired and her written work, if illegible sometimes even to Jess herself, has brought definite sparkle and depth. She obviously needs to write. Janet herself could live without the written word, as long as she had cinema.

Now that's something they ought to do, thinks Janet, slinging her jacket over on one of the high hooks at the side of the hall. They ought to take in a film. She'll check what's on.

'What time are you expecting Dan?'

In the green, mirrored kitchen, Jess concentrates on pouring freshly-boiled water in the brown ceramic pot.

'No.'

'Just wondered when Dan would be back.'

'Don't know,' says Jess. 'I slept late this morning.'

'Did he not leave you a note?'

Since Jess came back from hospital, Dan has taken great care to leave clear information of where he might be found whenever Jess is left alone. At such times, the flat is littered with notes.

'No.'

Jess had searched the kitchen three times. And the hall.

'When did he go? What time?'

Janet pours milk into the cups, not looking at Jess. If she had been looking, she would have seen Jess's hands shake a little.

'No.'

Janet looks up. Jess's face has resumed its old wooden look.

'Something wrong?'

'No.'

'No you won't tell me? Or no there's nothing wrong?'

'No,' says Jess again.

Janet does not push it, sits down, pours the tea. 'This is really grand, Jess. Thank you. Just what I need. The rush I had to get here even this late.'

Dan

DAN LOOKED UP at the upper storeys of the buildings crowding over him. He was well down the Royal Mile; past the tavern, past the church. He'd have to take it carefully or he'd miss Sian's turning. It had been months, months, since he walked this way.

Where was the courtyard?

Ah, he'd missed it, gone too far.

Slowly, he retraced his steps and there it was: the close narrow at first, opening to a broader arch, the courtyard beyond drenched in light, in cherry blossom, the ground below the central group of ornamental trees thick with dropped petals, even the pavement below his feet carpeted. A good sign, cherry blossom, a fortunate omen. Dan picked up handfuls of the pink floss, smiled. Let it fall slowly, drifting through his fingers like confetti.

Now, where was Sian's window? He turned, squinting up at the third floor of the building. He liked the clear, uncluttered lines.

Yes.. *that* was her door; so her window must be..

No.

Dan shivered, stared. He shrank against the wall. There must be some mistake! His chest grew heavy. Tight. It was Sian's window, yes. She was standing at it. Not alone. A taller, broader figure was silhouetted on the glass beside her, a male figure, close. Too close. Her head sank on his shoulder. Dan turned away. Moved back into the shade of the sheltering arch.

She was not ill, then.

No. Not ill.

People often did this kind of thing, took sick leave as informal holiday. Not Sian. He had expected more of her.

When he looked up again, the window was empty. The glass refracted white ceiling, pine cabinets, green walls. Dan stood a full five minutes in the close, then turning, propped his flowers against the wall.

Jess

JANET RAISES HER cup, takes a first sip. 'Some folk,' she offers, 'can't make tea. Ella, for instance. She drinks coffee and what she'd offer you for tea is either so weak and watery it's never seen a tea-bag, or lukewarm and so stewed my mother would have called it tinkers' brew.'

Jess doesn't answer. Janet, watching her skulk behind her raised cup reflects how little we are able to hide.

'Jess,' she says, 'did you buy a paper?'

'Yes,' Jess nods.

This is something she does every day. The short trip to the newsagents' was terrifying the first few times she made it, but now it's a regular journey down the street and along the two intersecting avenues to the corner shop. They know her so well at the shop she hardly has to speak, for which she is grateful even now. Speech tends to drift away, disintegrate, when she is nervous. The least thing can shake her.

Like the day a toddler fell off his tricycle in front of her, bumping his knee on the pavement. It bled. He yelled. Jess went home that morning without the paper, had to make another, later trip. Dan insisted.

Or the time there was a drunk in the queue in front of her, or rather, someone who behaved as if they might be drunk. The next day the newsagent explained the customer was ill, diabetic.

'Sometimes,' he said, 'when he goes like that, I give him sugar and send him home. Sometimes I have to phone his wife.'

There had been no problems today. She made her way to and from the shop, returning with rolls, newspaper, milk. Dan was still out when she got back. She'd not expected that. It was somehow disappointing to find the flat still empty.

'Here, look,' she crosses the room to the sideboard, lifts the paper, tosses it to Janet.

'What do you want it for?'

'I fancy a film. What about you?'

Janet takes Jess's lack of negative response as an affirmative.

'Something light and warm, eh? Let's see what's on offer.'

She flicks through the pages.

'*ET*? No. *Monsoon Wedding*? Jess, that's supposed to be really great. Look, the next screening starts in half an hour. If we hurry, we can make it. Go and get your coat. I'll call a taxi. The Lugano isn't that far, but we'd have to run to get there.'

Jess isn't even given time to put the cups away. In less than twenty minutes they're lounging in the cinema's cocooning dark. Janet is lounging. Jess sits upright, tense.

She isn't sure how she feels about this, isn't sure she can go the distance. She still has difficulty tuning into different voices, never mind different languages, different ways of living. It's hard enough watching television; she tends to slip out of the room whenever Dan turns the set on. And the sheer size of the cinema screen is daunting, all those acres of eyes, lips, nostrils, hair.

Michael

THE PASTRY SHOP was full, every single table taken. Michael turned, wandered back along St Anne's Street – ul Św Anny – where there was, he'd been told, a café in the cellars, very reasonable, famous for its żurek and pierogi. He found it easily enough, the entrance marked by the strangest wooden statue, half-tree, half-human; as like a tree in agony as anything he'd ever seen. He might, it struck him, be missing a connection here. Or perhaps it was to do with the name, Salad Bar Chimera?

He bent his head, descending, blinking in diminished light. A series of vaulted cellars unfolded before him, crowded with tables, walls busy with murals, chairs variously and ingeniously constructed from bed-ends or church pews. Recycling with style. This café was huge. And nearly full.

Michael squinted at the menu, following the queue, relieved to find the girls behind the counter all spoke English. By the time he had moved along to the cash register, his tray was heavy with salad, soup, bread and Żwiec, the local beer. He managed to find a small table vacant in a corner of the second cellar. Here, he could watch and eat, enjoy the music, Cat Stevens and Leonard Cohen, so far. He could play spot the foreigner, the non-Pole. Not that it was easy. There was no great difference in hair styles, in clothes.

Everyone he saw wore designer jeans, matching tee-shirts.

After the first few minutes, he came to the conclusion that what marked out the visitor, as in Britain, as anywhere, was a slight air of hesitance. Like the tall girl from the card shop who wandered through the room, a little lost. So much for her tale of meeting friends.

Michael considered offering her the other seat at his table. Too late. She swept by, pale green scarf trailing, brushing against him. Not till she was well past, in the next room, did he notice the scarf shining at his feet.

He bent down, picked it up. Hesitant.

If he stood up, followed her, would they clear his tray? Would he lose his place? The Chimera waiters, he could see, were nothing if not efficient, clearly bent on maximising throughput at the busiest time of day. Torn between gallantry and hunger, he compromised, slinging the scarf across the back of the chair opposite, where he would not forget it, where she would be bound to see it if she came back through.

He'd put this in the next postcard to Lesley. It would make her smile.

He never, he complimented himself, thought about Jess these days. Hardly ever. Some day it would be as if they had never met. As if nothing had happened. It had been a good decision, coming here. In Kraków he did not expect to meet her, did not look for her.

His drifting thoughts settled on the music now. Leonard Cohen was growling, *Suzanne* giving way to *Bird on a Wire*. Next thing, any moment now, *No Way to Say Goodbye*. Michael stood up, draining the last of his beer, finding it good. On a whim, he took the green scarf with him. He'd look for the tall girl, return it. Anything to help a fellow Scot.

Ken

KEN HOVERED UNEASILY beside Sian's kitchen window, thinking he should not have come; wondering why it had seemed such a good idea.

She'd changed things round. He did not remember the table in the corner. Nor did he remember the kitchen being green. (He remembered blue.) Best not, perhaps, to dwell too much on what he could or could not remember. His smile was rueful. He shrugged, raising his eyebrows, his embarrassment almost tangible.

'You do look awful.'

'Thank you.'

'You know what I mean. You should get to bed.'

Sian looked almost as green as her walls. Felt it too, her bones aching, her throat on fire. Talking was like stumbling through forests of broken glass.

'I was in bed, Ken before.. you came.'

She stuttered to a halt. Ken, for his part, blushed, looked away. She pulled her shawl tighter round her shoulders, sniffing, blowing her nose defiantly.

'So what is it you want? Why are you here?'

'I only came to say..' he broke off. 'I can see you're not well enough.'

'Not well enough for what?'

He seemed uncomfortable, jolted.

'Look, I'm sorry. This is a bad idea. I'll come back tomorrow.'

'Tomorrow I'll be back at work.'

'I don't think so,' he sighed. 'Not by the look of you. Is there anything you need? Anything I can do?'

She shook her head.

He hadn't even taken his jacket off.

It was like the fable of the wind and the sun, she thought miserably, the wind and the sun and the man with the jacket.

Ken tried again.

'Is there nothing you need? Shopping? Anything I can get you while I'm here? A drink, perhaps? Coffee? Tea?'

'Couldn't face it.' Sian stood up with an effort, tried to take a step, but the room had lost its shape, its solidity. Table, chairs, walls began to float, swim about her. She swayed a little, staggering. Ken moved quickly across the room. Just in time he caught and steadied her.

'Sian,' he whispered. 'Don't be silly. Let me help you.'

She slumped back into the curved wooden chair, her hands covering her face.

'Go home, Ken. Just go home.'

Her skull was exploding, imploding. What she needed, wanted

most, she could not have.

'Thing is,' he said, 'that's what I came to tell you. Why I'm here. I am going home. Back to Orkney.'

'What? What do you mean? When?'

Why should he feel the need to tell her this?

'Next month.'

'Next month?' she repeated dully.

'Yes.'

'Sorry, Ken,' she shook her head. 'The brain's not working. This flu,' she approximated a smile. 'So, a holiday?'

'No. I'm leaving, Sian.'

'Leaving?'

'Leaving the city, the Central. Got a job in Kirkwall. I had to give the usual notice, of course, but I've built up a backlog of annual leave one way and another.. anyway.. that's the long and the short of it. I've been meaning to tell you for weeks. Haven't seen you.'

Sian blew her nose again. She'd been working hard at avoiding him. Her eyes betrayed her, filled with tears, streaming.

'And Liz? How does she feel about this?'

She had to strain to catch his reply.

'Liz? Liz won't come.'

Anger flooded; infinite.

'And you come running here for sympathy!'

'No, Sian,' Ken looked and sounded wounded. 'It isn't like that..'

'Then tell me what it *is* like!' she flared. 'Paint the picture for me. You asked her? Of course you did.' The tone was scathing. 'You asked her, didn't you?'

'Of course I asked her.'

'Then what,' she asked weakly, 'what on earth are you doing here?'

He stared at her, bewildered.

'I don't understand. Don't know what you're getting at.'

'Then that makes two of us,' she groaned. 'I don't understand either. Not a thing. Obviously I never did.'

She pulled herself together with an effort. Her limbs hung dull and distant, as if they belonged to someone else, as if they'd drifted a long way off. Her head grew light, unfocused. 'Go home. Go home, Ken,' she whispered weakly. 'Sort out your life. I,' she shrugged, limp now, exhausted, 'I really do need to get back to bed.'

She pulled herself up, and shuffled weakly across the room, turning at the door. 'See and lock the door on your way out. Thanks.'

Ken stood frozen, staring at the spot where she had been. Safe behind the bedroom door, Sian lay in bed, lay rigid, holding her breath, willing herself not to cry, not to cry. Her head grew sorer by the minute. Her throat, her heart, her skin, her bones. Everything hurt. Everything.

Jess

AT FIRST THE pace and sheer vibrant colour of *Monsoon Wedding* threaten to overwhelm, but Janet's obvious pleasure means Jess cannot give up on the film, slip out, dragging her friend behind her. As the minutes pass, she realises she's enjoying the story. To catch all the spoken words she'd have to come back two, three times more. But words don't appear to be all that necessary. She loses herself in the visual, the emotion.

'Wasn't that absolutely fucking great?'

In the pub afterwards, Janet bubbles with enthusiasm, though the pizza they've ordered is almost inedible, the wine lukewarm.

'Sorry, Jess. Shouldn't swear. Kevin's always telling me to stop. But wasn't it the most fantastic bloody film? Couldn't you almost smell India?'

Jess shakes her head. She's tired now. Coming out of the cinema she felt strong, happy. That's fading.

'I don't know. Don't think I've ever been there.'

'Neither have I,' Janet sighs. 'But Jess, you're too literal. You mustn't always take words at face value. I only mean it felt so rich you could almost touch it, smell it. Didn't it make you feel like that?'

Jess nods slowly. 'Yes. Yes. It.. did. It did.'

It made her feel other things too, other things she hasn't thought about for months, many months, things she can barely recognise. The monsoon of the wedding, the rain drenching each and every one of the characters, soaked her just as thoroughly.

Janet burbles on. 'Almost makes you feel like investing in a sari. And that eyeliner stuff. What do they call it?'

Jess shakes her head. 'Not coal? No.'

'Actually,' says Janet, 'it is kohl, yes. Not coal but kohl. Well done, Jess. Good grief, that's never the time?'

Jess follows Janet's eyes to the clock on the wall. A heavy pendulum clock, at odds with the otherwise modern style of the bar.

'Seven forty-five. Where did the afternoon go?' Janet sighs. 'I'm going to have to rush. I'm meeting Sian at seven.'

'Seven?'

'She'll not mind. I'll ask the barman to phone a taxi for you.'

'No,' says Jess, quite firmly. 'No.'

'Jess..'

'Janet.' They're at the door of the pub now. Jess hesitates. 'Words are my problem, not.. not the map. No, not that. Not. And not the way out,' she sighs. 'No, not. That's not. You know. I'm tired. But I know how, why, to go.'

Janet gives her a quick hug.

'Of course you do. I'll see you tomorrow. Okay?'

Independence is, Janet reminds herself, a valuable and necessary thing.

'Take care now, Jess. Straight home.'

Jess sighs. 'As if.'

Janet races away, is soon lost in the evening crowds. Jess turns, begins the short walk back to Merchiston.

Walking city streets is easy enough if you know your way. Treading pavements is not that hard, even if you don't. You can go a fair distance in a short time, if you're fit and able. Jess isn't, not quite.

At first she feels confident, enjoys the cooling breeze that plays round her face, ruffling her hair. Then, a little too cold, she stops to fasten her jacket. She still finds buttons difficult. The finger tips on her right hand have not regained full sensation, and her left hand is clumsy too. This jacket has far too many buttons. All too small. Finnicky. Janet says they should go shopping, buy an easier one. Jess has resisted this suggestion. Shops are confusing. So is the profusion of these streets she's wandering through.

She's cold, and she doesn't recognise any of them, doesn't realise she's drifting further and further off her path. Each street looks so similar to the next; three, four-storied buildings with shops and cafés at ground level, flats above. Often, where the shops have gone out of business, the doors are boarded, the windows stiff with Windolene, or something like Windolene. That is the name for that white stuff, isn't it? It used to be the fashion for folk moving house; Jess remembers windows rendered opaque, swirls of clouded white denying those outside the merest glimpse of what went on within. Once everything was safe and set in order, just before white net was draped across the glass, the windows were wiped clean, shining. For a brief few minutes there was no *apparent* barrier; nothing but clarity between the household and the world, each visible to the other, transparent. Net curtains always went up, baffling.

And net is still in fashion. Nearly every flat Jess passes hosts this form of urban camouflage. She studies the windows, beginning to wonder if she might have lost her way. These are not the stylish nets of Merchiston. These are more gaping, meanly stretched. The net is different too. Merchiston net is denser, richer; sometimes it's muslin, pulled to one side, draped over a retaining thing like a huge fancy door-knob. There is a word for that, but Jess cannot get excited about the word, just as she cannot ever muster any hint of enthusiasm for the thing itself.

Ken

CELLAR BARS WERE the same throughout the world, dark and dingy, places to creep into and hide, oddly good for meeting where bright light might prove too intense, put too much emphasis on an evolving friendship; sanctuaries where couples might disguise or polish the patina of love, work consistently to harvest pleasure or pain; where men could none the less meet noisily, play darts, debate the latest results, football, rugby, boxing. Ken drained his pint, signalled to the barmaid who began to pull another brimming glass. She brought this over to him on a tray.

'Thanks.'

'No problem. I was glad to leave the bar. That Irish guy is getting me down.'

'Irish guy?'

Ken hadn't noticed anyone else in this part of the snug. Tucked in the corner, in the ingleneuk, he was hidden from three quarters of the room which, conversely, offered him a much diminished view.

'The red-haired fellow. I only took him on because he sounded so much like someone from home. Och, fair play to him, I suppose. He's not a problem, really, just maudlin. A long story, sick girlfriend, invalid wife. I think. May have got that a bit mixed up.' Her own accent was Irish. Belfast.

'Is he coming on to you?'

The barmaid was small, so slight she looked like she'd blow over in a gentle breeze; chicken-boned. Her hair, though, was more peacock than farmyard, a true and rather shocking blue; the cut asymmetric, winging from ear to jaw. She had to be an art student. Singer, maybe. Ken could imagine her strutting her stuff on stage. She'd look good. He'd go and see her any time.

'Not so's you'd notice. But if things get out of hand, all I have to do is call for Jake. You get tired,' she shrugged, 'listening. Sometimes.. you know?'

Ken nodded. 'I do.'

'There he goes again.' The girl turned. 'Banging the counter. I'll bring your change.'

'Keep it.'

'Thanks.'

When she was once more established behind the bar, Ken slid along the bench, glanced furtively at the cause of all the trouble. He was not somehow surprised to recognise Dan McKie.

'Dan,' he called. 'Come over here and join me.'

Why was he saying this? Not just to help the barmaid. Ken supposed Dan to be in difficulties. He'd seen him in the distance at the hospital these last few weeks, a change in him, a cloud around the man, almost furtive, making for Speech and Language Therapy. Sian. Ken had not talked to him, not in weeks.

He found it easier, simpler, to distance himself from all of them, Sian, Dan, even Jess. There was no way he could work on the portfolio.. not after that November night in Sian's warm kitchen.. no way he could go back to a simpler world where nothing complex had happened, where vulnerabilities remained unexplored, unexposed. And, conveniently, the pneumonia left Jess ill and weak for so long he was able to let the commitment die quietly, convince himself he wasn't needed. Perhaps that's what – no. He knew

ANNE MACLEOD

perfectly well what Sian had not been saying this morning.

He stared at his glass, at the rim of froth clinging where beer no longer assuaged the emptiness. He had not contacted Sian, not rung.

He lifted the glass, raised it to his lips. This was good beer. Good. Beer with body, heart. Not that it helped. He set the glass back down, watched the creamy bubbles sliding, settling.

Seeing Sian in High Dependency the day Jess became ill again more than proved the point. Though he'd sat beside her calmly enough, though she'd followed his lead, acting cool, acting, if anything, colder than she'd ever been, he could recognise, feel her need. For wasn't he the same with Liz?

And, whatever had got into him the night before, he was not going to compound it, make everything worse, hurting someone who ought to remain a dear friend, nothing less, nothing more.

Except, as his truthful conscience kept pointing out, he already had.

'What are you doing here, Dan?'

'Drinking. Logical enough. More to the point, what are you, life-guard Ken, doing drinking yourself to perdition this early in the day? It can't be much after five.'

'I think,' breathed Ken, 'I'm looking for logic. Like yourself.'

Dan laughed at that. 'A man after my heart. I'll join you.' He picked up the two shot glasses before him. 'A like mind. A soul-friend.'

'Don't know about the soul-friend bit.'

'No? And you been my soul-friend since Johnston days.. how long ago is that?'

The barmaid raised her eyebrows, heaved her shoulders heavenwards. Thanks and sorry, she nodded.

'Two coffees, please,' Ken pushed the table out a little to make more room.

'Irish,' Dan insisted.

'Black,' Ken shook his head, asked again, 'What are you doing here?' as Dan collapsed unsteadily on the bench beside him, bumping the table.

'Sorry,' he raised his glass. 'Clumsy of me. Slàinte.'

Michael

'EXCUSE ME. I think this may be yours.'

Jamie looked up. The guy from the Cloth Hall again. She frowned.

'Sorry?'

'I think you may have dropped this.'

Michael let the scarf drift gently to the table beside her. Painted silk, it floated from his hand like gossamer, gliding, shimmering – a banner, a pennant. He knew someone (well, he once met the son of someone) who'd spent years studying how best to make cloth quiver in the slightest breeze. They cost a fortune, those banners, these silk scarves. And though this pale yellowish green was not his favourite colour, he had to admit it suited this girl, this woman. She must be twenty-four, twenty-five perhaps? *Not* pleased at his interruption. Her pointed chin rising, combative; green eyes narrowing. It amused Michael that she should be suspicious of him.

'Good design. Energetic,' he nodded. 'I've always liked triskels.'

He moved away, but not before noticing the address on the postcard on the table before her. Edinburgh, Scotland. Not Canada, not USA, not Australia, but Edinburgh, heart of Midlothian. And for Midlothian, read universe. Read love.

Jamie followed his retreating figure. Shrugged. It was indeed her scarf, the one Sian gave her at Christmas. She was glad to have it back, hadn't even noticed its loss. She'd have been hunting all over the old town for it, might never have found it. She ought to have thanked Cloth Hall Man, but the guy gave her no chance to retreat, apologise. Oh well. They were unlikely to meet again. She turned back to her postcard, describing the scene, the lost scarf, the tall and brooding stranger, teasing the narrative into a detective style, Chandleresque. It might cheer Sian up. Something had to.

She'd spent the morning combing the Cloth Hall for gifts, admiring the amber, the folk art, the lace, the chess sets. She hadn't been able to decide what to buy her twin. Vodka, maybe? Żubrówka, flavoured with bison grass from the Białowieża forest? Sian might like that, might even share it.

Time to go. Jamie rose to her feet, her scarf now safely looped round her neck, postcards tidied away in her shoulder bag. The conference was due to start tomorrow. She'd done her homework, checked out the university building, and the Collegium Medicum where she was due to meet, in less than five minutes, the conference tour to Oświęcim. There would be a small party of them, five in all. Jamie was glad of that, glad there would be company.

Jess

JESS SIGHS. SHE should have been off this road by now. She takes the next turning, finds the shops thinning out, though the flats, the tenements, go on and on. Keeps walking. Twenty minutes, thirty.

She knows she is hopelessly lost. It's getting dark. Each new street looks exactly like the last. She has not seen a taxi. Parked cars line both side of every street (some triple-parked). She has not brought her phone, has not noticed a phone box.

Her leg has started aching. Her shoulders and neck are sore, chafed by the strap of the handbag she is no longer accustomed to carrying.

She tries not to panic. She ought to find a shop or pub, needs to find a phone, the number for a taxi. As she's thinking this, a taxi runs slowly by. Jess lifts her arm, waves, waves frantically, but the driver does not see her. Perhaps he has another fare already booked, or maybe he doesn't like the look of this slightly desperate woman, staggering through the thickening dusk. He does not stop, and Jess stumbles on.

She can't have far to go, surely?

Michael

'MICHAEL! WHAT ARE you doing this afternoon?'

Ul Św Anny no longer bathed in sunlight, shivered in freshening wind.

'Jan, hello. What are you doing here?'

'We're going to Oświęcim – Auschwitz. I know you didn't actually book the trip, but there is space in the taxi. You could come.'

Michael shook his head.

'I've still a little polishing to do on the paper.'

The small group standing round Jan added their remonstrations. *No. Come.. Come!*

They huddled on the college steps, all shivering; occasional students, pushing past them, swept into the college. Michael stood on the road till a passing car forced him back on to the pavement, into the group.

He marvelled at the generosity, the hospitality of his Polish hosts. Take Jan. Jan was one of the local academics who met them at the airport, himself and Marek and Joe. They'd all been on the same flight from Gatwick, a little disconcerted to find soldiers guarding the bus that swept them across the tarmac from plane to terminal building, no more than twenty metres, if indeed that far.

'Yes, come with us,' Joe added his entreaty.

'I'm not sure.'

Michael meant to visit Auschwitz alone, was not sure how he'd cope in even such a small number. But he found himself wavering.

'Make up your mind quickly!' Jan consulted his watch. 'We're waiting for just one more. Does anyone know a Jamie Kinnon? No? Any idea what he looks like?'

He peered along ul Św Anny. 'Anybody met him?'

Now Michael found his attention drifting. The red-haired girl from the Cloth Hall was striding along the street, silk scarf flung around her neck, fluttering. Butterflying. He wondered what she could be doing in Kraków, what she would be doing this afternoon.

She looked hesitantly at him, at the assembled company.

'This is the tour for Oświęcim?'

Jan nodded.

'And you are?'

'Jamie. Jamie Kinnon. From Cambridge.'

'Ah,' he smiled a little, raising his eyebrows, ticking Jamie's name off his list. He left the group, running a little way along the road to the waiting taxi, a people-carrier, new and rather shiny.

'So are you coming, Michael?' he called after discussion with the driver.

Michael still demurred. It had begun to snow, thin white flakes that at first seemed like fine ash, wood ash. He turned his collar up.

'Of course he is,' shouted Joe.

All eyes focused on Michael. He blushed.

'Yes, well.. okay, Jan. Yes.'

'Come on,' Jan called. 'All of you. Into the taxi. We're short of time. It's a sixty kilometre drive and the museum will close at four thirty.'

The snow seemed to be falling from a clear blue sky. Michael looked up, shivering.

'Snow,' says Joe. 'Don't you get snow in Scotland?'

'Mostly on the mountains, Josef.'

Joe laughed. Michael sighed. He'd never seen snow falling so thin, and from such a high sky. It was not blue now, white cloud thickening. Why, he wondered, did the sky here seem so high? Was it because they were so far from sea? Scottish skies never looked like this, were always low, straining to soothe, caress the earth.

'Mostly on the mountains,' he murmured again.

And Jamie, strapping herself into the seat in front of him found herself humming a tune from long ago, a skipping rhyme she had not sung – or even thought about – since primary school. Odd to have remembered it here and now, to be hearing it in Sian's voice. She hummed the words, soft and low.

On the mountain stands a lady.. who she is I do not know..

The taxi purred through narrow streets, carving its way through the old city into thicker traffic defiant with snow, into the suburbs, and beyond them into the country, less green now, more white, tarred roads thickening, disappearing. The sky dipped towards the land. Not a sign of blue. Jamie did not realise that she was singing openly, audibly.

On the mountain stands a lady..

Jess

JESS IS STANDING forlorn at the gates of a brewery when the police car pulls up.

'Are you alright, madam?'

She is shaking. This is a busy enough street, but dark, industrial; two cars have already stopped.

The first had followed her.

'Are you alright?'

Jess shook her head. 'Not. Not.'

The young policewoman on the passenger side gets out of the car. 'Are you ill?'

Jess cannot answer her. She's cold and frightened, confused.

'Can we help you? Are you feeling okay?'

They ease her into the back seat of the car. Jess looks round her wildly. Doesn't seem to understand what's happening.

'There, lass, you sit in the back,' the policeman soothes. 'We'll give you a lift. Where do you need to go?'

Jess remains mute.

'Tell you what, we'll take you to the Station for a cup of tea, and maybe you can phone someone? Okay? Will that be okay?'

Jess says nothing, and the car swings round, purrs away.

'What's your name?'

Jess cannot tell them.

'She's shivering,' the policewoman says. 'I think she may be ill, Jake. Her pupils are okay. Don't think it's drugs. We should take her to Casualty at the Central. Maybe we can contact relatives from there.'

Ken

THE CLOCK IN the cellar bar struck nine. Ken, listing across the sticky bar, listened to Beata, to whose mother, half-Polish, she owed her saintly name.

'Beata *Blessed*?'

'Can you imagine living with a name like that?'

He laughed. 'At least she didn't call you *Bea*.'

'They did at school. Can't you just hear it? All that *blessed Bea*, year after year. I suppose if she'd been Spanish it might have been worse.. imagine what they'd have done with Pia! Coming, Jake!' she answered a call from the other bar. 'Ken, I have to go. Tell you what, though, your man Dan.. when he comes back through you'll have to get him home. Jake's up to here with it.'

'I'll see what I can do. And if I don't see you, Beata, good luck with that degree show.'

'I'll make sure you get an invite, right? God, here he comes. Would you look at him.. Dan the man!'

'What did you call me?'

'Oh, I think you heard.. well enough. It's time you were on your way.'

'Come on,' Ken stood up, 'I'll walk with you. It's a grand evening for a walk.'

'How do you know? How can you tell? Have you got the sight, perhaps?'

'Well, it isn't raining any more.'

Dan swung round, arms akimbo.

'How can you know that? No windows in here. Unless..' he held on to the bar, steadying himself, 'they're invisible?'

Ken laughed. 'No paranormal in it, Dan, just logic. None of the folk coming in now are wet. Are they?'

'Ah.'

'Come on. Let's get you home to Jess. She'll be worrying.'

'Don't think so.'

Dan made as if to sit down.

'No, come on.. come on, now.'

'I've not finished my drink.'

'Yes you have..'

Ken pushed Dan firmly toward the stairs, nodding over his shoulder to Beata and Jake.

'Goodnight, guys. Thank you.'

Dan slowed down, fighting the inexorable pressure between his shoulder blades.

'I'm hungry.'

'Tell you what,' soothed Ken. 'We might buy chips on the way.'

Dan seemed to like the sound of that.

'Okay. 'Night, Beata, Jake. See you again!'

'Not,' hissed Jake, 'if we see you first.'

Dan, luckily, did not hear. Ken kept him walking. Fresh air seemed to help. He steered him through the Meadows, on past two or three chip shops. Greasy, heavy food would not be all that great an idea, not with Dan this well on.

'Do you need me to come up?' he turned the key in the lock of the outside door and handed it back to Dan. 'Will you be okay?'

'Fine,' Dan dismissed him. 'Don't want to fluster Jess. You come and see her another time.'

'I'll do that,' Ken promised. 'Tell her I'll see her soon.'

'G'night.'

Dan paid him no more attention, rolled into the house, slamming the door.

A thin rain had begun to fall.

Back at the cellar bar, Beata was cleaning tables.

Nice fellow, that Ken. Not bad-looking. Almost dishy for his age. She shrugged, dismissing him, thinking of the orange net tutu she'd made for the next gig. The guys didn't know yet. She couldn't wait to see their faces. Perhaps they'd win the Battle of the Bands. Maybe there would be an agent in the building. Maybe they'd be spotted and offered a recording contract and her degree show would have to be put off. She sighed. It might be put off anyway. She was behind with the sewing. As usual.

Jess

THE YOUNG PC and WPC, after some discussion, take Jess into Accident and Emergency. She's shaking so much she can hardly walk, goes on shaking quietly, even after a second cup of tea. Called through by the nurse, she remains silent, unable to speak her name, seemingly unable to comprehend the questions she's been asked. The nurse stares with suspicion at the scars on her hands, her neck.

'May I take your blood pressure, dear? Do you mind? We'll need to have your jacket off for that. Just the one arm would do.'

Jess makes no move to help. As the nurse leans forward she flinches.

'Don't worry, lass,' the nurse says, 'We won't do anything you don't like. Stay there. I'll be right back.'

She doesn't pull the screens quite together as she leaves. She slips into reception.

'Jean.. have we been notified of any missing persons? Anyone gone missing from a ward?'

'No, says Jean. 'I checked.'

Helen sighs. 'I'll give it another go. Thanks anyway.'

As she walks the length of the ward, she can see Jess through the splaying curtains. And Jess looks different now, less worried. She's nodding, as if there's someone else in cubicle beside her. There is.

'Dinna fash yersel,' a disembodied voice advises. 'I'm awa hame in aboot half an ooer. I'll tak ye hame, Jess.'

'Kev! What are you doing in here?'

Kevin stands up, glowering at Helen. 'Did ye nae ken Jess, then? Efter a that work ye did on her? This is Jess.. remember Jess.. Jess Kavanagh, Janet's pal. Is she nae lookin fine? I dinna ken fit's happened, fit she's daein here, but the quine could dae wi a lift hame.'

Helen shakes her head, has the grace to look embarrassed.

'Jess, I do apologise. It's been how long.. six, seven months? I'll check on the computer.' She turns to Kev. 'We'll need to look her over. For the record.'

It's after eleven when Jess lets herself back into the flat.

'What the fuck d'you think you're playing at?' Dan strides into the hall, rounds on her, his voice grating with anxiety, anger. 'Jess, where the hell have you been? I've been worried sick.'

He stops there. Kevin has followed Jess into the pool of light, Kevin and Janet too.

'Dan,' says Janet. 'She needs to get to bed. She's all in.'

'What's going on? What the fuck is going on?'

Dan fails to rein his anger in, includes them in it.

'Where have you been, more to the point? We would have phoned,' shouts Janet, 'if you'd left a number!'

He blushes. Janet motors on.

'You've been away all day. Don't bother making excuses. We don't want to know what you were doing that was so important, so secret.'

'Where has she been?' he asks again.

'Lost,' Jess shouts. 'Lost!'

'What?' Dan swings back to her. 'What did you say?'

'Lost,' she says again. 'Not. Not, anything. Not talking. Lost. Get lost.' The venom in her voice surprises them all. 'Dan. Lost.' She swings on her heel, turns towards her room, stops suddenly. 'Tomorrow, Janet?'

'Yeah,' Janet's smile is sheepish. 'I'm sorry, Jess. I should have come back with you.'

'You should have *what*?' says Dan.

'Not!' Jess insists. 'Not a baby! Not!' She does not turn to face them all, but her shoulders, stiff and rigid, speak volumes. 'No. Not words. Not.' She sweeps into her room, slams the door behind her.

They stand a long time in the hall staring at Jess's door; Janet, Kevin, Dan, saying nothing. The air vibrates with unasked questions.

'We'll be awa then.'

'Where did you find her?' Dan's voice breaks.

'The bobbies found the quine,' says Kevin. 'an took her to A&E. She'd been wanderin aa nicht. Couldna speak. Couldna get a word oot. Nae even her name. It wis just lucky I wis on the nicht and kent her.'

Dan blushes even deeper, sighs. This does not mollify Janet, not in the least.

'Dan McKie you are the biggest fucking idiot..'

'You might be right at that.'

'We've aa had a fright,' says Kev, 'we'll nae forget in a hurry.'

Janet turns on her heel, reaches for the door. Dan follows her as if to continue the argument.

'Guys,' says Kev. 'Dinna forget the quine's okay. She's safe. She's hame. Nae real harm done.' But long after the footsteps have echoed and died, long after the stiff outer door has banged shut, and Kev's noisy Renault roared and drifted away, Dan stands in the hall gazing at Jess's door.

Beyond the stripped and sanded pine, Jess lies sleepless, curled up on her bed, the quilt pulled round her shoulders, only her face visible, all her clothes still on. She can't get warm. Trailing endlessly round the unreadable streets had been all too familiar, too much like losing her way again, losing her mind. The words had disappeared so quickly, so completely. That was what had scared her most.

The streets grew darker, less hospitable, greasy with the light spring rain. She was soaked, rain dripping from her hair down her face, her back. She was cold, uneasy. She could not decide what to do, how to ask for help, ask her way. All the words had left her. Abandoned her. Gone.

She was panicking before the first car stopped.

She ignored it, kept walking, but the car followed, stopped again, and again, pinning her closer to the high black wall.

A middle-aged and wrinkled driver leered across the car, opening the door, suggesting something Jess could not decipher. She did not like his expression.

She screamed, backing away, trying to get back the way she'd come, back into darkness. The car was so close to the wall she scraped her legs on jutting brick. She screamed and screamed again. That can't have been why the second car pulled up, but as it did the first shrivelled off into the night and the second driver drove on too.

Jess pressed herself against the wall, into the shadow.

She could not think.

She could not breathe.

She could not move.

Before, she'd been uncertain. Now she was consumed by fear, a fear that flickers around her yet, though she's safely back in her bed.

She can't get warm.

She can't get warm at all. She shivers again as if the house were cold. It isn't cold. She knows it isn't cold. She's cold. She can't get warm.

What if the words were to desert her again? In the police car she couldn't understand what the girl was saying. Nothing made sense. Hospital was just the same. Nothing but noise and mounting fear till Kev came. Kev had come charging across A&E towards her.

'Hi Jess! Fit like?'

And she understood. She understood. It all came back.

'Chavin,' she said, as you did in the Doric, 'chaving awa, Kev. Fit like yersel?'

Till that moment she'd been teetering on the edge, clawing desperately. Then for Dan to shout like that at her friends, her friends who saved her, brought her home; Dan who hadn't been there. Not. Not here. Not. Never. Not. She's struggling now to stave off tears. Why not. Why not here? When? Not when. Not if. As if. Not warm. Not warm. She hears a knock at her door. Dan.

'Not,' says Jess.

The knock comes again.

'Fucking not!' she shouts.

'Jess. I want to give you a little whisky. It'll help.'

She burrows deeper in the quilt.

'Can you hear me, Jess? I know you're not fond of whisky, but there isn't any brandy, nothing else that will help. I'm coming in now, Jess. Okay?'

'Fucking not!'

The door swings open slowly. All Dan can see is the heaped quilt, shaking. He sets two glasses of whisky on the desk and comes over and sits beside the bed.

'I'm sorry. Sorry, Jess. I really didn't expect to be so late.'

She pays no attention to him, goes on lying still as a stone, under the navy quilt.

'I want you to drink the whisky, Jess. Just a small one. It'll make you better. Drink it and I'll go away. I'm sorry. I don't mean to intrude. This is your space. I'm sorry for shouting at you. You're right. You're not a child.'

He waits a few moments longer.

'Look, you ought to drink it. Please, Jess. I don't want you getting ill again. Drink it and I'll leave you in peace. Jess. Please. Did you ever,' he sighs, 'hear me say please so often?'

'Not.'

The quilt moves a little. Dan stretches out his hand, slowly, slowly, and lifts it off her face. It frightens him, how thin she has become, how fragile. He feels in his pocket, takes out his handkerchief and wipes the tears away from her hot cheeks.

'Come on, sit up, Jess. Here, I'll fix your pillow.'

He stretches behind her and eases the large square pillow into an upright position.

'Okay? Right, you sit up, that's right, gently does it. Yeah. Good. Don't move. I'll get your glass.'

He hands the shot-glass to her.

'Sip slowly. That's right. You'll soon feel warm. You'll sleep better for this.'

Jess sips, says nothing. Her head feels ragged, wet. Dull. There are no words, just the jumbled images of a monsoon wedding on cold Edinburgh streets. She sips again. Dan is speaking, muttering away, waiting for an answer.

'I'm sorry Jess. I should have left you a number. Taken a mobile phone. I didn't think.'

'No, Dan. Not,' Jess sighs. 'Not. Not. '

He swings round, shocked at the reproach in her voice. She sighs again, tries to make things clear.

'Bodies,' she shrugs, 'Not words. Not.'

Her expression, the shrug, the few words, make her meaning clear. She knows he is lying, knows it. Dan flushes. His eyes narrow to slits as he stares at the wall ahead. He drains his glass slowly, gets up without another word, leaves the room.

Michael

THE WORST THING about Auschwitz is not the cynical *Arbeit Macht Frei* above the gate, though that makes them shudder, all of them, as they follow their guide through the thin snow, shivering.

The worst thing about Auschwitz is not the remaining blocks, two-storey, substantial, huddled together, too close.

Michael trails a little behind the group, passes the wooden camp kitchen, where every day the orchestra played the lines of prisoners in and out of the gates, marching in step which, as their guide explained, made it easier to count them, check the numbers.

The worst thing is not the film, and not the wall of death where prisoners could be shot after summary trial, facing the bullet naked, barefoot, so the wooden camp clogs and rough grey clothes could be re-used.

Nor is it the gallows.

Nor the tons of shaved-off hair bleached white or yellow with dust and years.

Nor the suitcases clearly marked with their last owner's name, the mountains of worn-out shoes, toothbrushes, kitchen utensils.

These things are all impossible, unimaginable, but neither they nor even the undemolished gas chamber (swept clean, still dank, surprisingly small) affect Michael as deeply as the photographs hung along the corridor of the last building they visit – monochrome epitaphs to men, women, children, full-face, profile and three-quarter views – helpless human beings facing death in prison gear, hair hacked off, eyes betraying fear or blank defiance.

Nowhere do you see the reflex smile for the camera that sometimes hovers inappropriately in official photographs they've

THE BLUE MOON BOOK

seen earlier of prisoners on the move, prisoners waiting at the railhead, or walking slowly, herded on their last short journey. In those, the young, the old, the less perceptive, are occasionally fooled by the pointed lens, confused into a smile.

All such have been weeded out. Those who reached this far into the camp, beyond the railhead gas chamber, all these knew the score. Michael finds himself checking dates of entry, dates of death inscribed on each set. The braver, more defiant, lasted a shorter time.

'But why the three views?'

'Ah,' their guide shakes her head, 'They changed so quickly. Lost weight. Became unrecognisable.'

The worst thing about Auschwitz, Michael thinks, is it that it ever was. It blighted life, changed all, by its very existence.

And did this place merely reflect, perhaps enhance, inherent human darkness, forcing disguised aggression to the surface?

Was humanity, despite postmodern denial, engaged in a timeless duel between good and evil – an endlessly insoluble equation; respect, generosity pitching against cruelty, and greed? Were kindness – *good* – philosophical impossibilities? Disinterested good acts non-existent? Apparent benificence no more than a tool in some ancient power struggle? As for love? Did that exist?

Or like some modern notions of evil, sin, was love dependent on its loss? *No sin without remorse* (who said that? Michael cannot agree, not that sin is what he'd call a bad or wrongful act. Acts, ideas, could be and were wrong; as Auschwitz plainly proved.)

But could love exist, or happiness, without loss and sorrow? Could love – the possibility of love – endure?

It had to. Love did exist, in all degrees and definitions; love shared, fulfilled – love without hope or possibility of its return. Love that is, that was, that would be. Michael shakes his head. Is he not living proof?

He sighs. He had not meant to come here, not today. But Auschwitz in its offered memory of darkness, of cruelty, of evil that words fail to define, explain, has somehow brought him back to this.

To love.

He needs to believe in love. He does believe in love. How

else, he thinks, can we survive?

He'll write to Jess again. But not from here, not from here. From the city, from Kraków; a postcard from the square. That their love should ever have existed seems to him, somehow, a consolation. Even here. Even now.

Their little group scattered, silent. Walking back to the entrance building, they were lost in thought, disparate. In nearby Birkenau, they stared at the gas chambers, railhead and gate house. Said not a word. Most of the huts had been demolished; chimneys stood, bare concrete trees, weeping. No-one talked till they had left Oświęcim's bleak streets well behind; sweeping through the countryside they kept their voices low. Not till they were back in Kraków did the sombre silence lift.

'A drink?' This was Jan's suggestion. All agreed, almost too readily.

The flurry of late snow was gone. They found themselves cheered, glad to slip into the bar above the Chimera, a warm room, rather formal, walls heavy with the heraldic pride of Kraków's traditional guilds. The waitress brought them bread and beer.

Slowly, slowly, the ice in their bones began to melt.

Michael found himself sitting between Marek and Jamie. Pale faces round the table were gradually regaining colour, warming once more to life. Michael wondered what had been in all their minds, who they had been thinking of, remembering. Impossible to spend an afternoon as they have spent it without yearning for those you loved, aching to protect them. Impossible to hear Jamie's song – how did it go again?

On the mountain
stands a lady
who she is I do not know

Now he could see her. Jess. Jess Kavanagh. Sometimes he lost her face, her voice. Her laugh. She was back now, bright, bird-like. He raised his glass, saluting Jess, saluting all around the table. 'Na zdrowie!'

'Very good,' nodded Jan. 'How would that go in Pictish?'

'Slàinte?' guessed Michael. 'Slàinte mhòr!'

'Jacobite Picts?' Jamie raised an eyebrow. 'Na zdrowie!'

'Na zdrowie!'

'Na zdrowie!' The toast passed from one to another. 'Na zdrowie!'

Jan set his glass down, banged the table with a spoon.

'I think I've mentioned this to one of two of you already.. but we're meeting tonight at Cherubino, a Tuscan restaurant. We'll be there at eight, myself, Marek, and others from the conference. You are *all* most welcome. Cherubino is not difficult to find.. it's on ul Św Tomasza. Well. I have to leave you now, I'm sorry. Departmental business. If I don't see you tonight, tomorrow at the conference. And so..'

He stood up, straightening his chair precisely, shaking hands with them all.

'Well,' said Marek, 'what are you two doing now?'

'Going back to Garbarska,' Michael pushed his chair back. 'I really do want to get a little work done.'

'But we'll see you tonight?'

'Very probably. Yes.'

'And you?' Marek turned to Jamie. 'What about you?'

'Not tonight,' she smiled. 'I'm meeting friends.'

Michael caught her eye.

'No, I really am!'

He laughed out loud.

'But I'll come with you, Michael, back to Garbarska.'

'You're staying at Garbarska?'

'Quite a few of us are.'

Jamie pulled on her coat.

'Watch out! You'll lose that scarf again!'

Green silk wafted to the floor behind the chair. Jamie shook her head.

'I seem determined to do that.'

'Such a lovely thing. It would be a shame.'

'My sister would never forgive me.' She wound the scarf twice around her neck, thrusting the ends through a button-hole.

Marek lent forward, kissing Jamie on the cheek. Three times, Polish fashion.

She smiled. 'So. Till tomorrow, Marek.'

'But I'll see you tonight,' Michael shook his hand, 'at Cherubino.'

'Shall I come to Garbarska for you?'

'That's out of your way.'

'There may be other new arrivals. I promised Jan I'd check. Let's meet at seven thirty, in the hall. Okay?'

'Look forward to it. Seven thirty.'

Michael held the restaurant door open for Jamie. They flinched in the sharp evening air.

'Well,' she turned, 'I don't know about you, but I'm going to invest in some Polish vodka. There's an off-licence on our way. Beyond the traffic lights. Don't think I'd sleep without it. I'll have to get some wine too, for the friends I'm visiting. They're *real*.' she insisted. 'Live in Nowa Huta.'

'I believe you,' Michael buttoned his jacket and pulled the collar up, wishing again that he'd brought a warmer coat. 'Thousands wouldn't. So, Jamie of Nowa Huta, you have a sister?'

'In Edinburgh. A twin.'

'You'll be close, then?'

'Close enough.'

They came quickly upon the set of traffic lights. Michael shoved his hands deep in his pockets.

'Don't you find these confusing?'

'Only,' said Jamie, 'because I keep watching the adverts on the wall over there.'

Across the road, on the corner of ul Karmelicka and ul Krupnicza, a huge electronic billboard flickered, offering, as far as they could tell, films, plays, hairsprays, cigarettes.

'Distracting,' observed Michael, 'perhaps even more so when we don't understand the subtitles – no words at our disposal. No language.'

'My sister,' Jamie nodded, 'would have a view on that. The words.'

'She's a writer?'

'A therapist. Speech and language. Specialises in aphasia.'

'Aphasia?'

'Loss of language. Here we go,' She pulled his arm, dragging him across the road. 'Sorry. If you wait too long, you're left behind. Those trams are lethal.'

Michael laughed. 'You don't hang around.'

'Sian's more patient than me. Older.'

'I thought you said she was your twin?'

'She is. Five minutes older.'

'Therefore more patient.'

'Right. I'm younger, more impetuous. But taller, much taller.'

'Ah.'

'And this,' said Jamie stopping suddenly outside a narrow shop front, 'is the off-licence. Coming in ?'

Jess

JESS SIPS THE whisky slowly, laying the empty glass on the dark pine cabinet beside her narrow bed. Warm at last, she dozes off, is still dozing when Dan storms back in, belligerent, flinging the door wide, so that it bangs against the bedside cabinet. She wakes with a start.

'What gives you the fucking right,' he shouts, 'to judge? How come you're so perfect? Do you think I don't know what you can't fucking remember? Or do you remember, Jess? Talk about my body telling the truth.. is your body lying when your mouth no longer can?' He flinches as she shrivels back against the pillows. 'That's right. Go on! Make out I'm the monster! I'm not a fucking monster!'

He bends over her, still shouting, and Jess covers her face with shaking hands. He flinches again, cannot bear the sight of those scarred fingers. Jess's hands had been beautiful, shapely.

'Why can't you leave me alone?' he cries. 'Why can't you fucking leave me fucking alone!'

She turns to the wall, cowers away from him. This enrages Dan still further.

'I said fucking leave me alone! Christ! Why am I bothering?'

He stamps out of the room. The door bangs shut behind him.

Jess tunnels deeper in the quilt, moaning, whimpering. Gradually, gradually, the shaking stops.

Much later, she gets up, slips off her clothes, and pulls on pyjamas and dressing gown, wrapping the belt twice around her waist, tying it tightly, safely. Then she folds all her clothes neatly on the bentwood chair, taking great care, as if that will help, as if folding the clothes were important, as if she might be going somewhere, packing for a long, difficult journey; then she stands by the mirror, brushing her hair. Slowly. It's come on, her hair, looks better than it did; no longer so thin, not so patchy. The doctors keep warning her not to expect miracles. Jess doesn't. For long enough she could not remember what a miracle was.

Dan's right. They can't go on this way.

She feels calmer, now, more balanced, back to what passes for normal. But this can't be normal. Can't be. Surely normal is better than this? It has to be.

This is me now, she thinks, *and now is not normal. Was not.*

She stares at the face in the mirror, the bones of it, dark shadows haloing the eyes, hollowing cheeks. She marks each contour, each scar, leans closer, stretching her finger towards the cold, unfeeling glass.

Coming round, after.. after what she now calls *that day*.. left without words, left without anyone who could explain who she was, what had happened, why she found herself in such pain, lost, Jess had begun with mirrors. She recognised, somehow, the bruised, scarred features the mirror, any mirror, offered.

No words necessary. What she saw was what she was, separate from the pain, from ward machinery. What she saw was, in the early days, all she had to hold on to.

Sometimes it still feels like that.

Oh, she has endured the months since *that day*, and yes, she has regained, patchily, her childhood, the years before. Nothing has come back of the years with Dan; nothing, though the photographs, photos from the White Street flat, are ample evidence of time spent with him.

She does not know why she is here, why she was ever here, the mirror faithfully, wordlessly, reflecting her confusion. She stares long and deep into its proffered truth, tracing the remnants of tear-tracks; her cheeks are dry now, tight, her nose no longer puffy. After a long moment, she sighs, turns away.

She finds him in the kitchen, slumped in a chair, clutching his empty glass, snoring a little. She sets her own glass down, not that quietly. He does not stir, does not move.

'Dan.'

She stretches a hand towards his thinning hair, hesitates,

changing her mind; she bends towards him.

'Dan?'

Sits at the table, opposite him.

'Dan.' Louder.

His eyes open slowly.

'Dan,' Jess says again, firmly. 'Not again. Not. Not.'

Dan is not awake. Far from sober.

'Jess, I'm sorry, sorry. I didn't mean to shout like that. It's not as if.. And we've both had a rough night, rough – and you're so tired, there's no way I can follow what you're trying to say.'

'Fucking not!'

He sighs.

'I hate it when you swear. You never used to swear. Where are you going? Jess!'

She sweeps from the room, comes back with a pen. A new pen, and paper.

Dan, she writes, angrily, *can't go like this*.

'I can't read your writing, Jess. You know that fine.'

He is lying, playing for time. What is coming now? He holds himself aloof, trying to appear unworried, calm. Jess covers the paper, her words sprawling across the unlined white.

Dan, bodies speak. Tell more truth. Don't be angry. Don't lie.

He reads this, says nothing.

Today. Missed. You. Don't like alone.

He tries to look into her eyes, but she is concentrating hard, still writing; he can't guess what she feels. He stares at the emerging words which are unusually clear, unusually distinct.

Maybe – you – need away. I think I remember – you – away. Learn. To be. Myself. Better apart. Talk. Tomorrow. Tired.

She stands up, leaving him the paper. As she brushes past, he catches her wrist, strokes it.

'Jess. I've said I'm sorry. I am. Truly sorry. I don't know what came over me. This has not been not easy. God alone knows it's not easy for you either.'

She shakes her head, and Dan stands up.

'Goodnight, Jess.'

He lets go her hand, aims for a lighter tone. 'Off to bed with you.' He lifts the glass. 'Another dram? No? See you in the morning, then.'

Jess closes the door with what seems to Dan exaggerated care. He sighs. Where can they go from here? For him to have made the scene he did.. for her to have written what she has written. He sits long into the night staring at Jess's words, reading and re-reading them.

Dan

AT SIX O'CLOCK the radio lurched into spitting life. The news was bad. Bombs. Riots. A car crash. A Dutch politician shot. Dan took it all in, a litany of woe predicating the coming day. The presenters bounced it out, too happy, too cheerful, their tone in no way suited to raking the morning's entrails.

Why did he listen to this effluent day after day? You would think, he shivered, turning over in the bed, too hot, too cold, muscles aching, bed squeaking, head a little sore, you'd almost think (and it's odd he's never noticed this before) they were selling something. *Ice cream. Irn-Bru. MacDonald's Happy Meals.*

It was not appropriate. Any one of these incidents spelled out months, years of misery for faceless human beings, unnamed heroes and antiheroes. So much loss, so much pain, so much critical readjustment, hopeless recovery – couldn't he tell them?

But these guys – these guys seemed just delighted with it.

He clicked the radio off, turned away from the window, away from the light sneaking round the heavy curtain. He didn't normally pull the curtains shut, not since the early days with Jess. But he had shut them last night, blanking out the world. Hadn't slept a wink, couldn't, with their faces floating insistently before him. Sian, Jess. Jess, Sian.

And now, oddly, he could hear Jess stirring too, moving in the next room.

This was not usual. Jess never woke before eight or nine. Even before the accident, she'd not been an early riser, never bright in the mornings, quite the opposite. She tended to work long into the night. But that was definitely her, up and moving.

A dragging sound made Dan raise his head from the pillow. He sat up, listening hard. There it was again. And again. He stretched for his dressing gown. Since Jess left hospital he'd felt uncomfortable raking round the flat undressed. Come to think of it, before the months in hospital he hadn't seen her without a dressing gown, not in years.

The scraping noise continued, intensifying, punctuated by silence, the odd thump too. Dan stood in the hall outside Jess's door, considering whether or not to knock. A loud crash, the waterfall echoing of broken glass, persuaded him.

'Jess?' he banged on the door. 'Jess?'

He did not wait for an answer, pushed the door, alarmed to find it would hardly move. He yelled through the crack.

'Jess? Are you okay? What the hell is going on in here?'

No answer.

Anxiety mounting, Dan put his shoulder to the door, shoved hard. The resistance remained, but the door gave way a little. The resulting gap proved wide enough for him to slip his head round, peer into the room.

Michael

BREAKFAST IN THE Dom Professorski on ul Garabarska was a sociable affair; much of this due to the affable decor, a cross between traditional family dining room and Spanish restaurant. A cold continental breakfast had been laid out on the high counter tucked behind the door. Guests served themselves to as much cold meat, cheese, pickle, bread, as they could eat. The coffee pot was refilled by a silent woman hovering in the kitchen; and bread, rolls and butter were plentiful and good. Michael rolled into the dining room, setting his key on the largest table.

'Good morning, Jamie. How are you?'

'Just fine,' she nodded. 'Yourself?'

'Well, thank you. I'll be straight back. More coffee?'

'No thanks. '

Joe slid slowly into the room.

'And how did the rest of your evening go?'

'Not too loud, please,' Joe shook his head. 'I'm.. a little.. under the weather.'

'Would you like some coffee? Black? A roll, maybe? I'll bring it for you. I'm sitting over there, by Jamie.'

'That's kind.' Joe's movements were slow, exaggeratedly careful.

Institutional breakfasts, Michael thought, were never any different. Took some getting used to. He rediscovered that every time, every conference. He filled his own plate, piling rolls and butter on another.

'Here you are. Now, coffee. Jamie, you're sure you don't need a refill?'

'Actually,' she changed her mind, 'That would be kind.. but can you carry three cups?'

'Watch and learn!'

He carefully balanced two saucers in his left hand before picking up the last in his right.

'You've done that before!'

'Natural talent,' he sat down. 'Got me where I am today.'

'Which is?' Joe's head might be sore, but his sense of the ridiculous persisted.

'Garbarska, obviously, though,' Michael shrugged, 'I have to say I got in by the skin of my teeth last night.'

'What happened?' Jamie sipped her coffee. 'May I?' She picked a tiny Danish pastry from the heaped plate in the centre of the table.

'Of course. That's why I brought them. Help yourself. What time did you get in yourself?'

'Not late. Ten.. ten thirty. Why?'

'And was the gate open?'

She nodded. 'Why?'

'Well, when I rolled back from Cherubino, midnight, maybe, it was firmly shut. And you know the button Marek showed us to press, the one on the post that's all lit up?'

'Yes.'

'It didn't work.'

'So what did you do?'

'Kept pressing.'

'And?'

'It still didn't work. And it was very cold.' He shivered at the memory. 'I didn't fancy loping over the wall.. all that razor glass.. and that gate is well designed. Hard to climb.'

'Problem.'

'Yeah.'

'So? What happened next?'

'Well,' Michael spread butter on a roll, 'I thought about it. Tried the button again. No response. I walked out in to the street, through the tunnel, to find a signal for my mobile. Rang the hotel.'

'Should have thought of that.'

'No answer.'

'Ah.'

'So, I went back to the button. Still no luck.'

'You must have been freezing. It was cold enough at ten. This is unusual weather, you know. It's normally quite warm by now.'

'It was cold,' Michael owned. 'I was shaking with cold. Went out to the street again, tried to think.'

'And?'

'Couldn't come up with anything. Except the wall. So I came back.'

'Through that dark tunnel. I don't much like it even in daylight,' frowned Jamie. 'And so you climbed over?'

'No. On my way back in I noticed a fence post without a fence, on the left, half-way between the tunnel and the gate. It had a lit-up button too. I pushed that.'

'And?'

'The gate slid open. Thank the lord.'

'Fuck,' said Joe. 'I climbed the flipping thing.'

'How on earth did you manage that?'

'I found a wheelie bin,' he said. 'Stood on it, scrambled over. But look at the state of my hands this morning.' He held them out. Two fingers, three, were covered in plaster. 'Tonight,' he said, 'I'm coming home with you.'

'Or,' Michael laughed, 'For a small fee I could show you the button.'

Dan

DAN PRESSED HIS shoulder to the door, pushed hard. The resistance remained, but the door gave way a little. The resulting gap was wide enough for him to slip his head round, peer into the room.

Jess was in the far corner, bending over, charily lifting, piece by piece, fragments of broken mirror, the mirror that had hung above the fireplace. He could see at once why it had fallen. She had moved all the furniture; the single, heavy wardrobe, overbalancing, had slumped against the wall, and the fashionable clumpy sleigh bed was blocking the door.

'Don't touch that with your bare hands! You'll cut yourself to ribbons!'

She ignored him, went on retrieving splinters, shards, dropping them, one by one, into the waste-paper basket. Dan shoved the door again, gained another inch, enough leeway to wriggle through the gap, stumble over the awkward, springy bed.

'Jess! *Please* don't do that. I'll get the brush and dustpan.'

She looked up. 'An accident.'

'I can see that. Don't touch that glass. Jess..'

'It isn't ours.'

'Don't worry about the mirror. Or the wardrobe. Or the wall,' Dan noted the splintered wardrobe, dented plaster, shrugged. 'Don't worry. These things can all be replaced, fixed.'

Jess still looked despondent.

'For any's sake stop! Stop now! Come away from there, come on. Come and sit down.'

'Can't leave it.'

'Sit down, Jess. I'll get the brush.'

Dan scrambled back over the bed, squeezing his bulk through the door, conscious that he needed to lose weight again. He'd lost a fair bit in the Tron flat, but it had been harder here especially since Jess came out. Cooking for two made you eat more; and he had found it difficult building enough exercise into their uneasy routine.

'Sit down! Wait!'

The dustpan and brush were nowhere to be found.

'Jess!' he yelled from the kitchen, 'Where have you put them?'

'What?'

'The dustpan? The brush?'

'What?'

He poked his head around the door again. She was holding the dustpan.

'Jess? Jess! Why didn't you say you had them here all the time? Why weren't you using them in the first place? Honestly..' He wriggled back through the gap. 'What were you doing anyway? Demolishing the room? It's not that bad. No, don't go under there!

It doesn't look safe. Let me shift that wardrobe first.'

He raised the wardrobe slowly. It was awkward. Top heavy.

'No wonder it fell. You should have come for me.'

He pushed it slowly, slowly, flat against the wall. It still lurked, leaning forward.

'Pass me a book, Jess. Now!'

The first thing that came to hand was her portfolio.

'Not thick enough,' he slid the blue plastic folder under the wardrobe, tilting it back. 'I'll need that other book as well.'

Jess looked round. *The Riddle of the Picts* lay on her bedside table.

'No,' she shook her head. 'No.' Offered him a couple of magazines.

'The book would be better.'

'No.'

Dan sighed. 'These will just about do it, for now. What? There's blood all over this. Jess? Look, you're bleeding. I told you you would cut yourself. Let me see!'

He stood up, took her hand. 'Look.'

The palm of her left hand was scored, oozing blood from thumb to little finger.

'Och,' Dan pulled a handkerchief from his pocket and wrapped it round the injury. 'Hold that tight. Still, it doesn't look too deep. Don't think I need to take you back to Casualty.' He stood, holding her hand in both of his. 'Sit down. Sit you down, Jess. You're a white as a sheet.'

She did not argue. Dan crouched by the bed, beside her, holding her hand, wondering why he suddenly had such a strong feeling of déja vu. It was not the room, no, nor the broken glass, nor the gilded mirror frame abandoned in the corner; it was something to do with the blood seeping through his handkerchief. He folded the edges round and over the oozing.

'Press that harder.'

Why did it feel so much as if he'd been here before? Scarred fingers, the handkerchief, the blood. He could not remember, could not articulate. Blood always made him queasy; he was queasy now. He had to let go her hand, sit back against the edge of the bed, his breathing fast and shallow.

'Dan?'

He made no answer.

'Dan? What is it? Dan?'

She laid her uninjured hand on his shoulder.

'Nothing.'

He struggled to control his voice, sound calm.

'Feel a little dizzy, that's all. I should lie down for a while. Better go through.'

But when he tried to stand, the room rose round him, spinning. He sat down promptly, this time on the bed. 'Sorry,' he said, faintly. 'I'll.. I'll go in a minute.'

'No,' Jess prevented him from rising, pushed his head back against the pillow, lifting his legs up on to the bed. 'There.'

He felt better lying flat. From time to time she checked his pulse. Dan, for his part, noted his panic settling. Jess stayed beside him, silent, occasionally patting his shoulder. It seemed so odd to be lying in this deconstructed room, lying helpless. Dan was struck by the absurdity, the reversal of their roles. His inability to help himself. Whenever he raised his head, the room swung violently about him. He gave up, lay quiet.

Five minutes passed, maybe ten. He closed his eyes, drifted.

Michael

JAMIE AND MICHAEL lingered so long over breakfast that the woman in the kitchen went off, leaving them to it.

'More coffee?'

'Don't think I could.'

'Your sister. You were saying?'

Jamie played with her cup, set it down on the table.

'Sian,' she said, 'works far too hard. There's always some big case or other she gets too close to. Not in a bad way for the patient.. I don't mean that.. but she takes her work home with her, worries at it. All the time. I worry about her, but if I tell her that she only shakes her head, and says I don't understand. Maybe I don't. Just now, for example, it's this woman, a journalist. A really bad head injury. She had this freak accident, last year, during the Festival. Fell off a bus in Princes Street.'

'In *Edinburgh*? Last year?'

'You know about this?' Jamie looked up at Michael, frowning.

'I know about an accident much like that. Only, in this case, the woman died. But it happened in Edinburgh. There can't have been two incidents like that. Too much of a coincidence.'

'Certainly sounds odd.'

'You're sure this happened at Festival time?'

'Think so. Yes.'

'A journalist? A tour bus?'

'It must be the same one.' Michael had turned so pale that Jamie reached across, took his hand, squeezed it gently. 'But the woman wasn't killed,' she insisted. 'She was very badly injured. Lost her memory. Her speech.'

'God.'

'But they're coming back. Slowly. Or the speech is, anyway. Michael,' her voice dropped to a whisper, 'you must never tell anyone I mentioned this. Sian shouldn't talk about her patients, shouldn't tell me. She has no-one else.'

He cleared his throat. His voice stayed hoarse. 'I was on that bus. Someone told me.. I'm sure they did.. the woman died.'

'She nearly did. She's not had an easy time. Appalling, actually.'

'God,' he said again. 'No speech. How would you cope?'

'It's always different,' Jamie shook her head. 'I've never heard two stories the same.'

'Yesterday,' Michael raised his cup, stared into it, 'at Birkenau, when they talked about the hut that was the camp school.. where the prisoners were forced to learn commands in German,' he looked up now, and Jamie saw tears filling his eyes, 'that shook me, really shook me? You know? As if those poor women were being stripped of language as easily as they'd been shorn of clothes, of hair. Of names. What was left? What could they rely on?'

'But this is different, surely? This woman's family and friends, those who love her, must be grateful just to have her alive. Even without memory, without speech.'

'It's harder than you'd think. The consequences..'

Michael stared up at the high window above them, the grille suddenly drenched in blinding sunlight.

'I know what you're saying, and not saying, but Jamie, she's alive! There's hope. I never met your sister's patient, but our paths crossed at what was for me a critical time – don't ask any more than that – and that she didn't die seems a promise. A gift. It's like.. oh, like.. like *anything* could happen. Anything, Jamie. Everything good. It's wonderful that you should be able tell me this. You have no idea how I've grieved about it.'

'Without knowing her?'

'I was on the bus. Heard the screaming.'

'Awful.'

'Much worse for her.'

Jamie hesitated. 'You know, if you were in Edinburgh..'

'Sorry? What?'

'If you're going to be in Edinburgh I think Sian would like to see you. Perhaps you could get together.'

'Me and your sister?'

'No. Well, yes. Sian and..' Jamie broke off. She must never use a patient's name. Sian had impressed that on her, often and often. 'You and Sian and her patient, I mean. If she agreed. If you wanted.'

'It's wonderful to know she's alive,' he said again.

'Michael! Jamie!' Joe hissed from the doorway. 'Are you coming to this conference or not? Have you come all the way to Kraków for breakfast?'

Jess

'BETTER?'

Dan finds a cool wet cloth against his forehead. Even with his eyes open wide, the room has, thankfully, stopped spinning.

'Yeah, much better.'

Jess is kneeling beside him. 'Jess, don't stay there. There'll be splinters on the floor. Bound to be. You'll cut yourself again. I'll move over, look.' He slides across the bed leaving room for her to perch on the edge. 'You've got slippers on, at least?'

She laughs, sliding her bare feet on to the bed.

'Jess,' says Dan. 'Jess.'

She leans against the bedhead, folds her hands on her lap.

Dan stares at her. He can't read her expression.

'What are you thinking, Jess? What are you thinking about?'

She shakes her head. He pulls himself up on one elbow, watching;

watching Jess sitting, lying beside him.

It's been so long.

She's so near, so close. It's like the old days. Their first time. Her hair as dark, as unkempt, and her skin – he leans across, kisses her forehead lightly.

Jess lies still, says nothing.

Encouraged, Dan brushes his lips against her cheeks, her chin, her ears.

'You like that, Jess? You like that? Yes?'

He kisses her lips, and she lets him kiss her, does not kiss him back, makes no move, no response. It's as if she'd never known his lips before, or any others; as if she's observing, wondering at the whole thing. Still, she lets him hold her, lets him ease the soft silk of her dressing gown down and off her too-thin shoulders. Her thinness, the scars, don't repel him now. Dan kisses them, sighs.

'You like this, Jess? Jess?'

It's not till he opens his own dressing gown, not till the reddish hair on his chest curls against her breast, that she stiffens, drawing back.

He covers himself, reaches for her.

'It's okay Jess, okay. No, don't worry. Come back here. My fault. Too early, too early. Come back, come back, baby. Come back.' He draws her back into his arms, folds her head gently against his chest. 'Shhh. It'll be okay. It'll be okay, pet, you'll see. It'll be okay. All better. Don't cry.'

But Jess sobs as if her heart is breaking, sobs while Dan cradles her, kisses her hair.

'Shh,' he croons over and over again. 'It'll be okay. It'll be okay. Shh, Jess. Too much too soon. But it'll be okay. Shh.'

Dan

WHEN DAN WOKE, Jess was gone. The room remained chaotic. He found himself spreadeagled across her bed, coughing a little. Sunlight strafed his face, the scattered pillows, dust hanging in the air, sharp with the dissent of withered daffodil and fresh, strong coffee. He pulled himself up to sitting, uneasy.

Checked his watch. Eleven fifteen. Eleven fifteen? And Jack

coming at ten.

'Fuck!' he jumped out of bed before remembering the mirrored splinters broadcast on stained wood. He cast around frantically for his sandals, stretched for them before standing up to lift the heavy wooden bed gently into the centre of the room. As he set it down, fragments of glass grated, rasped beneath it.

'Jess?' he called out. 'Jess?'

'Awake at last? I don't know, McKie,' Jack lounged against the kitchen door, shaking his head. 'Must be getting soft. No golf today. You know what they're like in St Andrews. We've missed our slot.'

'Christ, Jack!'

'It's okay. I phoned them. Charged it to you.'

Dan laughed. 'Let me just jump in the shower.'

'No hurry. Jess and I are going out. Take your time.'

'Out?'

'We were leaving you a message. We'll be an hour, maybe two.'

'Where are you going?' Dan made no effort to mask his surprise.

'The National Museum. To see the Pictish stones. Some of them are in her book. Tell you what, why don't you meet us there? For lunch.'

'At the museum?'

'Yes. I think so. The museum.'

'Okay.'

Hovering behind Jack, Jess already wore her denim jacket. She glanced up at Dan, half-anxious. He nodded. Smiled.

She smiled back, then looked away too quickly. Dan thought about the morning. Those lips, those cheeks. The gently curving breasts; how soft, how much like silk her skin still felt.

'Let's firm up this arrangement. I know you Jack. And you, Jess. I've spent weeks of my life, no, years, trailing after both of you. One o'clock at the tower door of the museum. That's when we'll meet, and where. Just inside if it's raining, just outside if it's not.'

Jack laughed. Jess grinned.

'Got that? Both of you?'

If I didn't know Dan, thought Jack, if I didn't know Dan as I do, I'd almost think he was flirting with Jess.

'Oh, and Dan,' he called over his shoulder from the door, 'if Margot calls, tell her to meet us too.'

'Is she in Edinburgh today?'

'There's a good chance she may be.'

Jess hung back a little. 'Dan,' she whispered urgently.

His heart was in his mouth. What could she want to say?

'Janet isn't in. She was coming this afternoon.'

He hid his disappointment. 'Did you leave a message on her mobile?'

'Yes. But..'

'Leave it to me. I'll talk to her.'

Jess smiled. 'Soon.'

'You're a nag,' he raised his eyebrows. 'Nothing but a nag.'

'Jess!' Jack called from the stair-foot. 'Taxi's here.'

Dan shrugged. 'Better hurry. See you later.'

Jess nodded, still anxious.

'And I'll phone Janet. Don't worry. Run along. Jack is every bit as impatient as me!'

The flat had only the one bathroom. Since Jess moved in, Dan had found this more than a little inconvenient. It did, however, come with a statue of Aphrodite perched between bath and sink. Now, as he stepped into the white enamel bath and eased the shower on, Dan examined Aphrodite, the rounded naked breasts, hair drawn sedately back, smooth unblemished arms. A woman of plaster, unscarred. Even the bathroom's steam left this woman, this seeming goddess, impregnable, untouched. And did Greek goddesses not, he struggled to dredge up what lingered of a classical education, did Greek goddesses (sundry) not renew their virginity by regularly bathing in the sea? Perhaps shower-steam worked the same?

Perhaps if he got to the museum early, he could catch up with them, show Jess round himself? No, he changed his mind. No. Let Jack do it. Leave Jess her space. The more she had to talk, the more practice she had in communication, the better.

He washed his hair, shaved, found himself applying his most expensive aftershave. Why? And why was he pulling on one of his favourite shirts, his newest, best-cut trousers? (It got to the stage when you couldn't wear stone-washed jeans any more; it just snuck up on you. Jeans looked ridiculous. These linen trousers, on the other hand, looked the part. Just as well when you considered what you'd paid for them.)

He had locked and left the flat before he remembered Janet,
had to let himself back in to find her number. The home number
rang and rang till the message service clicked in.

'Janet? Jess and I are out for lunch today, with Jack. You know.
My editor. Jess tried to ring before. We'll speak tonight.'

He left a similar message on her switched-off mobile, before,
on a sudden whim, phoning Sian at the Central.

'She's still sick,' Mairi told him. 'Can I leave a message?'

'I was looking for Janet,' Dan frowned. 'You wouldn't have
seen her?'

'No. Why don't you try Sian?'

'Don't have her number.'

Mairi reeled it off.

'I hope,' warned Dan, 'you don't hand out that number to every
Tom, Dick and Harry.'

'Dan McKie,' said Mairi, sounding cross. 'Do you think I'm
that daft?'

'You just gave it to me.'

'Well, you're not Tom, Dick or Harry!'

'No, but..'

'Don't be silly, then.'

Sian's phone rang so long Dan was almost reconciled to the
answering machine. Sian must be out.

'Hello?'

'Janet,' Dan sounded almost pleased. 'Good. It's you I'm really
looking for. Jess was trying to ring you. We're out for lunch this
afternoon. She'll get in touch tonight.'

'What's wrong? Is she alright?'

Janet's sharpness irked.

'Of course she is.'

'Then I'd like to speak to her, if that's okay.'

'It would be okay,' Dan almost hissed, 'if she were here.'

'Where is she?'

'Janet,' he said quietly, 'what the fuck are you inferring?'

'I imply. You infer. I want to speak to Jess. Now.'

Dan hung up. Slammed out of the flat.

As he clicked downstairs he heard the phone ring out. And out. And out.

Janet

'WHAT WAS THAT about?'

Janet slammed the phone down, punched out the Merchiston number. No answer. She dialled again.

Sian tried again too. 'What's going on? Who are you trying to ring? Who were you being so abrupt to?'

'Fuck!' Janet flung over her shoulder. 'I'll have to go round there. He's not fit to be looking after her, Sian. I've told you before!'

'What are you on about? '

Sian was flushed. She still had a temperature, felt weak and shivery.

'Dan won't let me speak to Jess. Virtually forbade me to come round this afternoon.'

'Janet, that doesn't sound like Dan.'

'You didn't see him last night. That man is a bully.'

'I'm sure he can be.. firm. But I don't think he'd bully Jess.'

'No?'

'What exactly did he say? Word for word?'

Janet cast her mind back. Struggled to remember. 'Said they were going out. Said she'd been trying to get me, which she hasn't. You know that. We've been here all morning. '

'She wouldn't know you were here. Doesn't have my number. She's a patient.'

'Dan obviously has your number. Where did he get it?'

Sian shook her head, weary.

'He said they were going out for lunch.'

'Then they're going out for lunch. Why doubt it?'

'If that was the case,' Janet sealed the case against Dan, triumphant, 'why couldn't I speak to her?'

Sian's head was swimming. 'Janet, I don't know. Maybe she wasn't there. Maybe she'd gone on ahead.'

'Not Jess. Remember what happened last night.'

'She may have gone on with someone else.'

'If she was going out for lunch she'd have told me.'

ANNE MACLEOD

'Maybe it was a spur of the moment thing.'
'Too many maybes,' Janet frowned. 'I'm going round.'
'They won't be there, Janet. They're out for lunch.'
'I don't believe that. His story's just a front.'
'Janet,' Sian sighed. 'Janet, shut up. Shut the fuck up!'
'That's what he said.'
'I'm not surprised. Janet, you haven't even checked your mobile.'
Janet looked surprised. 'No.'
'Have you got it with you?'
'Yes.'
'Check it then.' Sian waited as Janet fished her mobile out of her coat. 'Switched off?' Janet looked sheepish, nodded, checking the voicemail. 'And?'
'She's going out for lunch.'
'See?'
'With someone called Jack.'
'Dan's editor.'
'That's what he said.'
Sian sighed. 'Janet, I think you owe Dan an apology. And I think,' says Sian, 'you're more than a bit over-stressed. What's eating you today? Something between you and Kev?'
'Don't want to talk about it.' Janet shrugged. 'Did you know I'm off on holiday next week?'
'Yes,' Sian moved across the kitchen and switched on the kettle. 'Yes, I was remembering.'

Jess

JESS THINKS SHE does remember the museum. It's familiar in the slightly hazy way scenes from early childhood can be, and as oddly strange. The space and whiteness of the upper hall confuse. She's glad when Jack shepherds her down to the lower chambers, to the less insistent light of the Early Living exhibition, to the Pictish Stones.
She recognises them from the illustrations in her book. Jack loves them, seems to know a lot about them. She follows slowly, trailing in his wake. He's a big man, energetic. She must have worked with him for years, must have known him well, though none of that has surfaced. Jack is a friendly face, a friend of Dan's

218

who visits, whose bright smile she instinctively trusts. A good face; Jack is one of those men who manage to look at the same time strong and baby-faced, having lost their hair.

She never thought of that before. Not that she can remember. There are still huge gaps, blanks she trips across, falls into.

Sometimes she tries to force it, fishing for her past, baiting the line with photographs, perfumes, garments. Clothes are the least successful. Since the accident she's lost weight. Nothing feels familiar; trousers, skirts slide off her, and blouses hang like smocks.

Smell is more evocative, not always in a helpful way. Dan's aftershave, for instance, leaves her uneasy. Her teeth clamp themselves together, the muscles in her shoulders knotting tightly. Her head feels taut and sore. Waking up with him this morning, though, she hesitates, was not like that. Not at all. This morning felt familiar, right. Which was daft. The bed was too small, far too small.

'Jess?'

She starts.

'See?' Jack's voice rings with pride. 'This is the stone in your book. Hilton of Cadboll. Amazing, eh? Just look at that carving. Did I ever tell you,' his tone alters, becoming confidential, ruminative, 'I grew up in the Highlands? My father was right into this kind of thing, stone circles, standing stones, decades before they were the fashion.

'We didn't understand, but he was that determined. Trailed us all.. the whole reluctant family.. round the countryside to see them. Nigg and Shandwick. Sueno's Stone in Forres. Strathpeffer.. the Eagle Stone. I thought,' he says, 'that one was something to do with the comic. Remember the *Eagle*?'

She shakes her head.

'Too young? No brothers? The *Eagle* was the hot boys' comic back in the Fifties, early Sixties. No relation to the stone. None. I don't need to tell you, I was one disappointed boy by the time we found it somewhere in a wee back lane behind Strathpeffer, fine carving though it is, impressively ancient though it is. See, I'd been expecting Dan Dare.. you've heard of *him*, no?

'Well, anyway, I like the Eagle Stone now. You would too, Jess. You ought to go and see all these stones while Dan's off, while you're still recuperating. Not,' he muses, 'that you can always get close to them these days, not like you could. But this stone, the Hilton of Cadboll; this stone here,' he nods again, 'this stone is arguably the finest of all. Look, Jess, look at the detail on it!'

There's something about the stone that makes Jess think of blue. What's the connection? she wonders. Why blue?

Jack goes on muttering, 'See the woman in the centre, riding side-saddle? She's important. Unusual. Women are hardly ever represented on these stones and she's plumb in the centre. The one with power. Some say she's the Virgin Mary, that's why she's riding side-saddle. In the middle of a hunt? I don't think so.'

He swings back round, facing Jess, smile darkening. 'It shouldn't be here should it? This place.. it's great.. don't get me wrong; I like it, really do. Beautiful as museums go. But what are museums for? The stones, stones like this, should be in their own surroundings, left in the place they were set up in, even if they have to be protected from the weather.' He hesitates, marshalling his thoughts, wondering why he is telling her all this. 'After all, whatever their purpose, and for all that we've lost the Pictish language, these stones spoke to the land they stood on. They can't do that here. This guy too..' He points back to the Viking grave reconstructed on the floor of the museum. 'Do you think that's where he wanted to finish up? Don't you think he objects? Am I talking through my hat?'

Jack has never talked so much before, not that Jess remembers. She smiles, shakes her head.

'No. Not.'

He sighs. 'I am. I'm talking too much. You look very tired. Coffee? Shall we find the café? Dan won't be here for ages yet. Or shall we take a look at the museum shop?'

'Sure.' This a new word. Jess finds it useful. 'Sure.' People seem to like it.

She nods, though she is indeed feeling very tired. The carving, the stones, even the room, have had an unsettling effect on her. There's something important, something integral missing, something.. blue? Something so basic to her understanding of the stones, of the room, that its absence renders the space void.

'Oh dear,' Jack sighs. 'I've bored you solid. Margot would kill me if she knew. Wait till I tell her. She may join us, you know. I told Dan to tell her where we were if she got through in time. Come on.

Shop first, then coffee.'

'I'm not good in shops.'

Jack nods. 'You need more practice, Jess, that's all. This'll be easy. A dawdle. Help me choose a present for Margot. It's nearly her birthday. I'm struggling. It gets difficult finding something right, something different. You'll be a great help. You up for that?'

Jess nods, smiles.

'Sure.'

The shop is busy and bewildering. It's noisy, for one thing, a space partitioned off from the old museum hall, catching the ricocheting rise and fall of voices; it's bewilderingly full of books and mugs and posters.

'Look,' Jack catches her arm, points to the A-board by the door. 'Look.. there's your man!'

Jess is confused. She can't see any man.

'The poster, see? Michael Hurt. The Michael Hurt who wrote your *Riddle of the Picts*. Heading up a conference. You ought to go.'

'Yes,' says Jess, not attending.

'Not often,' says Jack, 'that they'll use a picture of a man like that for advertising.'

'No.'

Jess doesn't see the picture. She's in a panic now.

This happens in crowds. Her heart thumps. Her breathing goes wrong, somehow; she can't get enough air in. Feels that everyone is scrutinising, judging her. They're not, of course. Why should they be? She's talked this through with Janet and Sian.

'Then why,' said Jess, 'do I feel like this?'

'Any, every, invalid does,' offered Sian. 'You're out of the way of mixing. You don't *look* odd, Jess.'

'Just a little startled at times,' volunteered Janet.

'Startled?'

'Like you do now!'

'Leave her alone, Janet. Jess, don't worry. Think of it this way. What's happened to you is a little bit like Rip Van Winkle.'

Jess had no idea what she meant.

'See, you've woken to a world you know but don't know, a world you don't have information for. It'll come back, given time.

Won't always be confusing. Aren't things getting easier?'

'The worst,' Jess frowned, 'is when people say they know me and I don't remember them. They get so hurt. Annoyed.'

'Tell them the truth.'

'How can I?'

'You must,' said Janet. 'It's the only thing you can do.'

'What if,' Jess's eyes were glinting now, full of mischief, 'they say I owe them money?'

'Blackmail?'

'Pardon?'

'We may laugh,' said Sian, 'but it's not that daft a question. There are all types of debts, things we owe. Friendship not the least of them. I suggest, Jess, that you say that since the accident you're finding it difficult to recognise folk. If they ask for money, refer them to Dan. Or me.'

'Or me,' Janet insisted firmly.

'Remember,' said Sian, 'you're a good judge of character, Jess. You don't need to worry too much about this.'

'No.'

'And you don't look odd. Not at all. You look very pretty.'

'Quite normal,' Janet added.

Sian laughed. 'I think that's what we in the trade would call a back-handed compliment! Talk about damning with faint praise.'

But Jess was pleased enough with normal. Standing as she now is in the museum shop she feels far from normal, far from health, feels every eye in the place must be on her; that the women standing together in the corner near the A-boards, for example, are talking about her, pointing at her, wondering.

No. That cannot be true. None of her scars show in this jacket, other than her hands, and those women are too far away to see them clearly. She's misinterpreting, over-reacting.

'What do you think of this? Would Margot like it?'

Jack demands her attention. Jess turns away, dismissing the women by the door. He is standing by a tall case displaying jewellery; silver and gold brooches, ear-rings, cuff-links, spinning slowly.

'Yes?'

'This one, see?' He indicates a silver brooch on a shelf a little high for Jess to inspect easily. She stands on tiptoe, stretching, to follow the two herons, intricately carved, endlessly entwining.

'Beautiful,' she breathes. 'You know, I have a postcard just like that.'

The herons glide round and round again. Their beaks meet, tip to tip; finely feathered wings cross, chastening the centre, while elongated bodies complete the circle, tangling. More Celtic than Pictish, still beautiful.

'Look,' she says. 'Look, Jack. You can even see the eyes. Real birds. Real feathers.'

'We'll go for that one, then.'

He looks over to the counter, raises an eyebrow. The assistant comes running. Jess smiles. Is it the height? The eyes? The way Jack assumes service, natural authority? It never works like that for her. While the brooch is being wrapped, she scans the bookstand by the counter and a small, rather pretty book catches her eye, a book of Celtic verse.

'Any good?'

'Yes. Lovely.'

Jack turns to the assistant. 'We'll take this too.'

'Jack! No..'

'Don't be silly, Jess. It's just a small thing. I come from a large family, love giving presents. And after all you had to stand and listen to me all morning, me on my favourite hobby-horse.'

'Jack, you're being silly.'

'No. Come on. Let's get that coffee. Tell you what though. I think we should go out of the museum and sit in the café-bar across the road where we can keep a look-out for Margot and Dan. We've taken rather longer in here than I planned. Sound okay?'

'Sounds fine.'

As they're leaving the shop, Jess feels a tap on her shoulder.

'Jess? It is Jess, is it? I wasn't sure. Jess Kavanagh?'

The woman confronting her is tall and grey-haired. Over sixty, Jess guesses. She cannot place her, cannot for the life her remember ever having seen this person. She blushes, smiles shyly.

'Yes. Jess Kavanagh, but..'

'I thought it must be you. How are you, my dear? Good to see you out and about again. Have you come through from Glasgow for the day?'

'No. No.. I..' Jess blushes.

The woman waits.

Jess, stuttering, miserably goes on, 'I.. since the.. the.. accident, the memory is.. poor. Patchy. Let me introduce Jack. Jack Patience.'

'Jack Patience of the *Standard*?'

'Yes,' Jess and Jack reply together.

'And you,' says Jack, 'would be?'

The woman holds her hand out to Jack, shakes his firmly.

'Goggins. Doctor Julia Goggins.'

'Ah,' smiles Jack. 'Good to meet you. I know your work, naturally. I've been introducing Jess to the Cadboll Stone.'

Julia's expression shifts, a subtle inflection, which Jack translates correctly.

'I should say re-introducing. And she has the book, of course.'

He nods at the posters Julia's carrying.

'*The Riddle of the Picts* played a part her recovery. Dan stumbled on that book with its wonderful illustrations.'

'It is rather wonderful isn't it? But then Michael is lovely man. Scottish, though he's currently in Oxford.' Julia watches Jess carefully. Not a flicker of recognition. 'And how are you, my dear?'

'Well,' says Jess. 'the memory is not so good. Yet. Gets better. So I'm sorry, if..'

'No, why should you apologise? It's not your fault.' Julia shakes her head, 'Goodness, if I could only forget half the folk I know, what a blessing that would be!' She stops, as if suddenly conscious of the enormity of what she's said. 'God. There I go again. Please forgive me, Jess. If you remembered me, you'd know I'm the most supremely tactless hag that's ever graced the world. At least, so Kerry says. Though *graced* is not precisely how she'd put it.'

'Kerry?'

'My niece? No. No.. I don't think you met. Just ignore an old idiot. That's the best thing. Jess?'

Jess has dissolved in giggles. Julia and Jack can only look on.

'Julia,' Jess gurgles, between fits of laughter, 'I wish I remembered you. Can't think I'd forget you again.'

Julia smiles, her narrow features softened, eyes a little misty.

'No. You never were afraid of me. I never fooled you for a

moment. You know, that's quite like Kerry, whom you haven't met, but when she comes back over we'll arrange it. Yes. Yes. Where are you staying now?'

Jess has at last stopped laughing. Her ribs are sore.

'Dan has a card,' she sighs. 'I should carry some.'

'I have one here.' Jack fishes in his wallet.

'Merchiston Crescent? Very nice,' Julia nods. 'We're in the New Town. Look. I'll phone. Can't promise not to blether. It's my way. Kerry says I'm bossy, speak too loud, but then that's habit. My husband's deaf, you see.'

Jess wipes her eyes. 'Do please phone, Julia. I'd like that.'

'Bless you, my dear.'

Julia surprises herself by leaning forward and hugging Jess, kissing her cheek. This is not Scottish, not an Edinburgh thing to do; and Jess feels slight, insubstantial in her arms, like a female barn owl someone once let her hold, its feathers striking, delicate in their tracery, gold and fawn filigree. That bird looked substantial enough, but its woven feathers hid a frame not much bigger than a wren.

No, that was an exaggeration. Still.

'Bless you,' says Julia again. 'I'll be in touch. Soon.'

'She will, too.'

They watch Julia race off through the museum.

'You might live to regret this day, Jess.'

'I don't think so.'

'We've still time for coffee,' observes Jack. 'But only if we don't meet another Julia. Jess, if anyone else talks to you, ignore them. Pretend you didn't hear.'

Jack

AS MARGOT EASED off the motorway towards Milngavie, Jack closed his eyes.

'Tired?'

'No.' His eyes sprang open, meeting hers in the mirror. 'Thinking, that's all. What an odd lunch. Odd day. Weird.'

'I know what you mean,' Margot slid into the right-hand lane. 'Dan retains the ability to surprise. I'd never have believed it if I hadn't seen it for myself. Will it last?'

'You know him as well as I do.'

'No,' she shook her head. 'Don't think I do. None of us knows Dan as well you.'

Jack sighed. 'I'm fond of him. We go back a long way. And he's a good writer, Meg.'

'Yes.'

'But I've never seen him like this. This is new. Interesting.'

'Ancient Chinese curse?'

'That,' said Jack, 'is what I'm a little afraid of. Jess too.'

'Interesting,' Margot nodded, said no more.

Dan

DAN SWITCHED ON the enormous yellow lamp. Warm light flooded the corner, rendering the room comfortable, relaxing. He'd always sneered at limpid descriptions of rooms furnished with armfuls of cut flowers, pools of light – purple (no, yellow) prose – where did you read such stuff? But this lamp worked, he had to admit that. This flat was good to come home to.

'Tired?'

'Mmm.'

Jess flopped into the nearest yellow armchair; eyes closing the instant her head hit the cushion. He would have liked to sit beside her, doze, lay his head on her shoulder, but that might have worried her. After the morning.

And there was her room to fix.

He slid through, shaking his head. He couldn't, he mustn't, push the furniture back. This was, fuck it, a bid for independence. At last. But he could at least make sure the room was safe, free of glass. He pulled the vacuum cleaner out, and all the dusters. Half an hour later there wasn't a single splinter left, not one; every corner, every gap in the floorboards was clear. Jess had slept through all the noise.

She would need a mirror, though. He wandered through the flat, assessing possibilities. The small one in the bathroom was fixed, screwed to the wall. The only mirror in his room, the master bedroom, was firmly attached to the antique dressing table. Might there be one in the boxroom, stacked among the pictures and books and broken chairs?

Odd that the owners of the flat should choose to leave so much stuff stored up here when renting it out. And such different taste, as if it belonged to a former life, former partner. That was it, he grinned, former wife. Former lover. Going through the pile felt very much like eavesdropping on a private conversation.

The paintings, all original, varied in form and medium. Water-colour landscapes, still-life in heavy oils, well-enough executed, but not to his taste, just as the vibrant abstracts currently quickening the walls were not, either, what he would have chosen. No mirror, not among the pictures. There was, however, yet another neat stack of frames on the highest shelf. He ought to look up there. He set up the folding steps, climbed to the top, and was just about to start exploring this new area, when the doorbell buzzed. He sighed, climbed down.

'Hello?' He wasn't expecting visitors. Sometimes kids rang the bell and ran away. 'Hello?'

'Why aren't you answering the phone?' a woman's voice blared, belligerent.

'Janet. How nice. Hello.'

'Why aren't you answering?'

'I am. I'm speaking to you now.'

'I rang a dozen times.'

'I didn't hear.'

'I'm telling you I did!' the intercom rasped with impatience.

'I don't think,' teased Dan, 'This is the best way to have this conversation. Are you coming up or not?'

'Not,' said Janet, 'till you open the door.'

He left the flat door open, retreating to the boxroom, where he climbed the steps again. Janet saw herself in.

'What the fuck are you doing?'

'Moderate language, Janet,' Dan sighed, 'unusually moderate. What does it look like?'

'Would I ask if I knew?'

'Here,' he said, 'make yourself useful. Hold this.'

He handed down the smaller pictures, one by one. They were better, more interesting, than the larger ones.

'Shame they didn't leave these up.'

'Dan,' Janet tried again, 'what is this about? What are you doing?'

'Jess had a small accident today.'

'I knew it!' Her arms full of dusty pictures, Janet dared not move, could not drop them, had nowhere to lay them down. 'I knew there was something up!'

He ignored this. 'Drat,' he sighed. 'No mirror.'

'What are you on about? Where's Jess?'

'Thanks.'

He started taking the pictures back, one by one, restacking them. 'Where is she?'

'Who?'

'Jess.'

He took his time. 'Got to make sure these are stacked safely. Don't want any more glass flying about this house.'

'Where's Jess? What happened?'

'I'll show you, in a minute. Thanks, Janet. That was a big help.' He climbed down, folded up the steps. 'We'll just have to buy a new one.'

'Dan, you're not making any sense. Where's Jess? What accident? What happened?'

'Let me show you.' He picked his way across the hall. 'Come on, come and see.'

Janet followed him, suspicious. 'What's this all about?'

He threw open the door to Jess's room.

'I *think*,' he said, 'it's a good sign, actually; her trying to do all this on her own.'

Janet was unprepared for the chaos that met her eyes, furniture half-moved, out of kilter, the bed, unmade, slanting across the room, the heavy wardrobe partly blocking the window. The gash above the fireplace was an incomplete story; Dan had removed the splintered mirror-frame.

'Where is she?'

'In the living-room, asleep. Do you fancy a cup of tea? Or would you,' Dan smiled sweetly, 'like to check the floor for splinters? I think I've got them all, but glass gets everywhere and I don't want her cutting herself again. It's good you've come, Janet. Handy. Maybe when she wakes up she can decide where to put all this. Better with two of us to do the moving, don't you think? She'll just have to use my mirror overnight. We'll get another tomorrow. Cup of tea? Glass of wine?'

He glanced into the living room. Jess was still fast asleep.

'Let's not wake her,' he said. 'She was up at the crack of dawn, then all round the museum with Jack; kept bumping into folk she couldn't remember. By the time I came for lunch she was exhausted, but we had to stay and eat. Then Jack's wife Margot turned up. Big, big day. So much happening. After last night too.'

'About last night..'

Dan blushed.

'I'm sorry I shouted at you.'

'No,' said Janet. 'I owe you an apology. It was all my fault. It was me left her after all. I'm sorry, Dan.'

'I think,' he looked away, uncomfortable, 'I was more at fault than you.'

'That's not what Kev said.'

'Ah well,' Dan grinned. 'Kev's a sensible man, except..'

'Except?'

'Except nothing. Wine it is, then? Come on through. We'll sit in the kitchen, give Jess a little peace. I'll make a start on tea. You'll stay to eat?'

'Be honest now.. can you cook?'

'Can I cook? You've known me all these months, and you ask can I cook? Is the sky blue?'

'Not often in Scotland.'

'Wrong. The sky is always blue. Just the clouds hide it sometimes. Like life. The blue is there, Janet, whether you can see it or not,' Dan shivered, suddenly. His mother would have said *someone stepping on my grave*. He didn't hold with such nonsense. He smiled. 'Let's get that wine. Couldn't you do be doing with it? I certainly could.'

Janet

The blue is there whether you can see it or not.

Janet shook her head. Was Dan an optimist then? She didn't herself, feel quite so rosy. How could she? It had been a rough twenty-four hours. Starting with Kev, starting with that phonecall.

'Janet, quine. Jess is back in A&E!'

But these things were straightforward enough, weren't they?

You loved someone or you didn't. They made your veins sing or they didn't. If one person did it for you, no-one else had a chance. And, Janet sighed, when one person really did it for you, and you couldn't have them, when they let you down, then you had to salvage pride, show it didn't matter. It was all quite simple.

Things hadn't felt so simple in A&E.

Kev was on with Lynne MacMath.

'Jess!' Janet rushed to hug her. 'Are you okay?'

Jess burst into tears.

'What happened, Jess? Can you tell me? Are you too tired?'

'Tired,' said Jess. 'Want to go home.'

'They're waiting for the medical registrar to come and check you over. They want to be sure the loss of speech was only panic.'

Jess nodded. 'Panic. I need to go home.'

'It won't be long now. I'll stay, Jess, don't worry. Helen didn't recognise you, you know. But then she hasn't seen you since the day you had the accident. It's not surprising. '

'No.'

'Shouldn't be much longer.'

'No.'

'You know,' Janet suggested, 'you could lie on that trolley, close your eyes.'

'No.' Jess shook her head. 'No.'

'Sure?'

'Sure.'

'Have they phoned Dan?'

'I told them. No.'

'Jess, they should have phoned him.'

'I'm going home.'

'Jess.'

'Home. Now.'

'I'll check how much longer we're likely to be.'

Leaving the cubicle she'd walked into the young medical registrar, who rushed in, glanced perfunctorily at the history, checked Jess's eyes, tested reflexes. Five minutes, it took.

'Helen,' complained Janet, 'we've been waiting an hour for that?

I know, I know. Thank you for looking after her. Where's Kev?'

Kev was sitting with Lynne MacMath in a secluded corner, drinking coffee, smiling, chatting ten to the dozen. That girl, thought Janet, had make-up inches deep. Fluttered her eyelashes all the time as if she were the female lead in some Hollywood teenage soap. Like she'd be kick-boxing next! And all to impress some poor deluded male.

What really bothered Janet was that they had officially been off-duty for twenty minutes. Half an hour. Lynne should have been long gone, not lingering, making eyes. Janet smiled at Jess, glowered across the room, hunched her shoulders.

'Let's get this flipping show on the road!'

The argument with Dan had been inevitable. Outside the flat, furious, she turned on Kev.

'What were you bloody thinking of?'

'Fit?'

'I said, what were you thinking of? Taking his side against me?'

She couldn't see his face.

'Janet, quine.'

'Don't quine me! Go and quine that fucking Lynne! As if you weren't already so far in your boots are hanging out!'

'I dinna follow.'

'No! Of course you don't. You spend the whole evening eyeing up the talent, fine. That's up to you. You side with a drunken sot against me when you know.. *know*.. exactly what he's like. That's up to you. And now you *dinna quite* follow my line. Fine. Dinna fuckin follow it!'

She'd turned on her heel, sprinting down the crescent. Kev's car, tightly wedged, faced the other way. Five minutes later, racing along Bruntsfield Road, running so fast she felt almost sick, she saw him pull in to the kerb before her.

'Janet!' he climbed out of the car, shouting again, 'Janet!'

She pretended not to hear, darted blindly across the road, so that a car cruising up the hill had to swerve to miss her. Kev stood staring. In the end, he jumped into his car, slammed the door, revving the engine so hard she could hear it half-way across the Meadows.

Dan

DAN ENJOYED WORKING in the green Merchiston kitchen, candlelight reflecting in the mirror-tiles behind the hob and work-surface. Glasses sparkled, shone.

'Do you like your new room, Jess?'

He wiped the sink clean, tossing the tea-towel to dry on the pulley in the scullery.

'Are you pleased with it?' he asked again.

'It used to be too dark.'

'It is the smaller room. Do you want to swop? We could.'

'No. I like the bed. It's comfortable.'

'So's mine. But maybe,' Dan said slowly, 'you should give it a try. We could swop over for a night or two. See what you think. The mattresses are pretty much the same. You might like the light better in that bigger room. I'll go and change the sheets.'

'You changed them the other day.'

'It wouldn't take long.'

Jess sipped her tea. Hot.

'You don't need to change the sheets. You're clean.'

Dan blushed.

'We could give it a try,' she continued, 'if you like.'

'I suggested it, didn't I?' He changed the subject. 'We'll miss Janet, next week. You'll really miss her. I hadn't realised quite how often she was coming round.'

'She needs the holiday.' Jess frowned. 'She isn't quite.. quite.. you know. Tonight.. what do I mean? Not quite.. I'm tired. Hard to find.'

'Tell me about it. Listen, Jess. I hired a video this morning from the shop. Someone,' he glowered, ' had to go or we'd have had no milk!'

'Video?'

'Steve Martin. Quite an old one. *Roxanne*. Remember that? You used to like Steve Martin.'

'Don't know.'

He shook his head.

'Wish I could show you the cover. If they'd only leave rental videos in the original box, so you could read the blurb. This isn't much help.' He waved the clear plastic box. 'I think it was made – ooh – ten, twelve years ago, something like that. It's good fun. Fancy it?'

'Sure.' Jess nodded. 'Why not?'

'You haven't said that before.'

'What?'

'Why not?'

'I said what, not why.'

'No, you said, "Why not?"'

'Did I?'

'Jess, shut up. Go through. I'll make another pot of tea. Go on. Off you go. I know you're tired, but you slept so long this afternoon you won't sleep if you turn in early. Not first night in a different bed.'

Jess slipped into the living-room, glad she could give up the struggle to make more conversation. Words were impossible. The video seemed a good idea. She settled herself on the yellow sofa.

'Good,' said Dan. 'We'll fast-forward the adverts, eh?'

'Can't we see what's in them?'

'Jess. That's what you always say!'

'Do I?'

He raised his eyebrows in mock despair.

'Always. Okay. Okay. We'll let them run.'

He leaned against the mantelpiece, ostensibly fiddling with the video controls. He'd have liked to stretch out next to her. 'Look,' he said, 'if I push the coffee table closer.. like so.. and put a cushion on it.. there.. hey presto! You can sit with your feet up. And so can I!'

He flopped down on the other end.

'Dan,' warned Jess. 'Take your shoes off!'

'That's what you always say.'

'Sorry to be boring!'

Dan could hardly speak. He stretched across the yellow sward between them, reaching for her. *Give her enough space*, he reminded himself. Warned himself. *Don't rush. Don't rush anything.* 'Jess,' he took her hand, squeezed it. 'You're never boring. Never. You're lovely. Now, the film. Here we go.'

He turned back to the set, folding his arms, pretending not to see the delicate flush rising on her neck.

Jess

NEITHER JESS NOR Dan sleeps well. Towards the dawn Jess dozes, cuddling a pillow, half-burying her face in it, so that when she wakes, the cotton creases have transferred themselves to her skin. She's wakened by the radio. Dan, in the other room, hears it too; creeps through to switch it off. Seeing her awake, he hovers in the doorway, hesitant.

'Sorry. I should have thought.'

He looks as tired as Jess feels. Crumpled, sleepless.

'Did you have good night?' She can see he didn't. The bags under his eyes.

He shrugs, 'First night in a new bed.. you know. How about you?'

'Not.'

'We'll get on better tonight.'

'Tonight?'

'Did you want to swop back?'

'We should. Go back. This bed is too big for just me.'

'King-size. I like that.'

'It's cold,' says Jess. 'I'm not a king.'

'You always say that.'

'I don't.'

'Yes you do..'

'No, *you* always say that.' She frowns.

'Say what?'

'You always say *You always say that* like.. like I'm doing it all wrong.'

'Jess,' says Dan, 'you're not doing anything wrong. I don't mean that. That's not what I'm saying at all. It's just..' he breaks off.

'What?' she sits straight up now, fierce. 'Just what, Dan? It's just what?'

Dan sighs. He wants to hug her, comfort her, smooth the hair back from her face. He can't. She's exhausted, angry. The time just isn't right. Maybe – he can't escape the thought – maybe it never will be.

'It's.. good.. to see you coming back,' he offers, simply. He crouches at the foot of the bed. 'Couldn't sleep last night. I've been doing a lot of thinking. The stuff you wrote the other night. Do you remember, Jess?'

THE BLUE MOON BOOK

She looks away.

He sighs. 'I don't want that. Don't. Don't want, or need, to be away. But we're in this weird position..' he goes on slowly, feeling his way. He hasn't worked this through, though for much of the night, for weeks now, it's been fevering his brain. 'See, you don't know who I am, Jess, don't remember the years we spent together. And maybe, Jess, maybe there's a reason for that. We weren't so good, not at the end, but we weren't so bad either that you should have been frightened of me.

'I don't understand any of that. I may have.. *did*.. cause you to be unhappy, lonely. But I never ever hurt you. Not physically. Not once. You have to believe that.

'I can't get my head round the way you were in hospital. Other things too.. no, don't say anything, not yet. Please. Let me finish.'

He looks directly at her, straight into her eyes. *You're a good judge of character*, Jess. Sian said that to her once. This man beside her is telling the truth. She can see that, feel it. Whoever he was, is, he's hurting.

'Jess, I'm asking you to give it time. It won't be easy. I'm not an easy man. But you've nowhere else to go. So.. this is what I want to say.. I think you should stay with me till you're properly well, Jess, till.. till you're able to decide who you are, what you want. Who you want to be with. Where you want to go. Then do exactly as you please. There'll be no pressure. Think about it, Jess.'

She nods.

He runs on quickly. 'And I ought to say. Should have told you the other day, when I was out, what I was doing. I went to see.. to see.. a.. counsellor. Found it difficult. Drank too much afterwards. Again. But I'll stick with it.' He shook his head. 'When we began, years ago, that day in Johnston Hall.. I know you don't remember this, but then, even then, the day we met, I told a lie, said I was unattached. I wasn't. It won't be like that any more. No lies.' He takes a deep breath. 'If we end up together, it will be on an honest footing. No, don't say anything, Jess. Don't make up your mind. Take time. Now I'll go and put the kettle on. Tea?'

'Please,' Jess closes her eyes, leans back against the headboard.

Johnston. Johnston Hall, Ken lounging on the floor. Her friend..

Marta? Long black hair? Someone else too. A room full of people.
A knock sounding above the chatter. She's been hoping for this.
Waiting. She can see her hand stretching towards the door.
Should she open it?
She can hear it, hear the knock again, feel her excitement.
Could it be? Is it *Dan* she's waiting for?

summer

MOST MORNINGS, WHILE Morna walked the boys to their school bus, Janet pounded Portnahurach beach, the collies yapping at her heels. She'd run, tide permitting, all the way along the bay, past the Free Church, on past the caravan site, run till her breath would let her go no further. She'd stand gasping, staring north across the firth to the sweeping hills of Sutherland.

Spring had come later here, slower than in Edinburgh, as if the hills were slumbering, unwilling to wake, resisting summer's brief assurance. But the soil, hill or plain, could not argue with drenching light. Early dawn succeeded late dusk, rain or shine. Ploughed fields turned sudden green, distant hills less brown, the very dunes less grey, plush with maram.

Today, Janet did not catch her breath, run further. She sighed, turning back towards the village where hedges and gardens were stirring, elder, gean, blackthorn, white against the glowing gorse. The gorse was wonderful this year, after the week they'd had in April, that week of unexpected sun.

'Blackie! Coll!'

She reeled the dogs in, started back.

Jess

THE MIRROR IS a little high, not too difficult for fixing hair. But this is altogether different. Jess stands on tiptoe, wiping the wet glass clear of steam, folding the towel carefully, laying it in the sink. Her new make-up bag seems very red against the towel's dampened white.

What did the girl say? Jess lays out everything she needs. She spent ages unwrapping this stuff when she got it home, disentangling each pot or stick from the endless folded information sheets she'd tipped immediately in the bucket. She should, she supposed, have kept them, read them, but life is too short for such caution. She briskly discarded every box, every scrap of paper.

First, foundation.

The girl showed her how to sweep the sponge across her cheeks, covering her eyes, hiding the dark rings, flattening out her features. Jess isn't sure about this, even now. It doesn't, somehow, look like her. More like the features of an older, paler relative.

Now, bronzing. The powder brush restores a third dimension, sable fibres gentle on her skin like.. like something she can't remember, not quite.. and today, as yesterday, ripples of the past shimmer towards the present as her cheeks warm to the touch.

Eyes. She did not like what the beautician in the shopping centre did to her eyes. She came straight home and cleaned the make-up off, every last bit of it. Subtlety. Care. That's what it takes.

She flicks the powder shadow, looks more closely at the face reflected before her. Brown eyes. A swirl of blue. What is it about blue? Why does she always choose blue? From the corner of her mind Jess snatches the slightest suggestion of a memory – perhaps memory – blue sky, blue silk? She doesn't have a blue dress.

Eye pencil. Mascara.

'Jess! Hurry up!'

Lips now.

She ignores Dan's knocking, outlining them in brownish pencil as the girl had taught her. Lipstick next. Like the foundation, this feels strange. Not the eyes, though. She's done eyes before.

Jess blots her lips, studying the new reflection. Her, but not her. Not quite now, not quite then.

She shivers, packs everything away.

One last look.

Nearly convincing, yes. More natural. Much better than yesterday.

Dan

DAN WAS UP at five, packing. His taxi due at ten fifteen. He banged on the bathroom door.

'Hurry up! Jess! Get out your butt out of that shower! Breakfast's getting cold!'

'Coming!'

'You said that ten minutes ago!' His bags stood by the door. His jacket hung on the chair, passport and flight details stowed in an inner pocket. 'Jess!' He checked his watch. Eight forty-five. He had time, time to spare, and he wanted to spend some of it with Jess. 'Jess!' he yelled again, breaking off as she slipped into the kitchen. 'There you are at last! What took you so long?'

'Nothing, Dan,' she sat down. 'Sorry.'

He glanced round, stared, stopped stirring the scrambled egg. 'Jess,' he accused, 'you've got make-up on!'

'And?'

'And you haven't worn make-up since.. since I don't know when.. I didn't know you had any.'

'Dan,' she blushed, 'it's a free world. I can wear make-up if I choose.'

'Yes, of course you can.'

He lifted the saucepan off the heat, adjusting the flame. She frowned.

'You don't think it looks stupid?'

He considered the effect for rather longer than she found comfortable.

'Good,' he said. 'Natural.'

'That's what I thought.'

He went on staring. She blushed, changed the subject.

'Are you sure you've got everything you need?'

'Jess. I've done a lot of travelling.'

'I know. But not for ages.'

He grinned, 'You don't forget.'

'I forget.'

'No you don't. You only don't remember. That's different. One day it'll all come back.'

'Do you think so, Dan? Do you really think so? I'm beginning to be afraid,' she sighed, 'a huge slice of my life may be gone for ever.'

'All the words came back.'

'Most. I still forget some of the more abstruse ones.'

Dan kept stirring the scrambled egg. It was just about ready, just about to thicken. It had that creamy texture. He switched the gas off.

'If you can remember abstruse you're not doing too badly in my book.'

'I'm not in your book,' she said.

Dan laughed. 'How do you know that? Tell me, how you do you know that? Have you been reading my private notes?'

'Don't be daft! I fail to see, that's all, how I could ever play a part in a book about football.'

'Wait and see.. wait and see,' he raised one eyebrow. 'You may get a surprise, that's all.'

'You're teasing.'

'Maybe. Maybe not. Sit down Jess.'

She toyed with her breakfast. Wasn't that hungry. It was good of him to make it, and it was delicious. And usually she loved the luxury of a cooked breakfast but today, somehow, she couldn't eat. Dan didn't seem that hungry either.

'Jess,' his tone changed, darkened.

'What? What is it?'

'What on earth have you done to your arm?'

Jess reddened. Her hand flew to the dressing on her left upper arm. 'Ah.'

'What's wrong?' he asked again. 'What happened?'

The flush grew deeper, spreading down her neck. Even as he worried, Dan wondered at the intricacy of that dappled spreading edge.

Jess tried to sound confident, unworried. 'Nothing.' She did not look up. 'Nothing important. This is really good, Dan.' She took a mouthful of scrambled egg, swallowed it. 'Wonderful.'

'Cold scrambled egg is never wonderful. Don't try to change the subject. What's wrong with your arm? Did you hurt yourself?'

'May I have some coffee?'

'Sure.'

His face had changed again.

There was that look on him Jess recognised these days, a look of carefully-assumed openness, determined lack of hurt. She came across it more and more, knew it for what it was. Dan offered her so much space she sometimes felt as if she were drowning in it, even while she battled to keep him at arm's length.

'All right, all right. I'll show you,' her expression less transparent, almost furtive. 'I wasn't going to mention this till you came back from Seoul.'

'Tell me in your own time.' He turned away, fiddling with the coffee pot. 'It's okay, Jess. Leave it. I'll make more coffee.'

'Dan! Don't sulk!'

'I'm not sulking. I'm making coffee! Okay? If you've hurt yourself again, had it seen to, treated, why should you tell me? No reason, I agree, no bloody reason at all. You're an adult. Independent.'

She stood up now, came round the table, stood beside him. She'd not been the only one putting on a face this morning. Dan, she saw, had gelled his hair. Cut himself shaving.

'Don't be like that, Dan. Don't be touchy. I didn't hurt myself. Not in the way you mean. And you'll think this daft, I know you will. I do myself.

'I'm not sure why I did it, but it's been in my mind for weeks and weeks. I thought it would be fully healed by the time you came home.'

'You're not making sense, Jess.' Dan filled the cafetière, settling the lid in place. He turned to face her. 'I don't understand.'

'Neither do I,' she said. 'Let me show you.'

She eased the edges of the white open-weave dressing off her skin, then slowly, slowly peeled the dressing back.

'Je-ess!'

'I knew you'd say that. It's not healed,' she pleaded. 'It'll look better by the time you're back. I think it turned out really well. I took the book with me and she copied it. The girl, I mean, the artist.'

Dan said nothing.

Jess grew pale.

'I thought you wouldn't like it.'

'No,' he said. 'it's okay. It's a little.. surprising.' He looked away. 'I'd never have expected you to want a tattoo – and not a *snake* – you were always so afraid of snakes.'

She shrugged, swallowed. 'It's Pictish. For rebirth. Sometimes it feels like that, Dan. Like I've been born again.'

'Mmm.'

He stared in disbelief and disapproval at the intricately curving image, at the spreading purple bruise.

'It means wisdom too. Healing. Fertility.'

'All that?'

'That's what the book says,' she tried to smile, looked anxious. 'With this on my arm I'll live for ever.'

'The book says that?'

'I made that up, that last bit.' She sighed, 'You don't like it.'

'Well, its very..' he stopped.

'Very what?'

His voice dropped. 'It's a bit – well – final,' he looked away, embarrassed. 'I've never liked tattoos. Never. But it's up you, of course. It'll probably be alright. You like it. That's the main thing. Does it hurt?'

'No.'

She turned away, stared out the window, stared across the yard at the copper beech fountaining the centre of the green; no leaves yet. Buds threatened, fat, tawny. She suppressed her tears.

'I like it. Really wanted to have it done. It feels.. right.'

'Good,' his tone was cool. 'These things are permanent. You can't do anything about it now. I think they can remove them by laser, but that would be expensive. Besides, it might be sore. Now, you don't want to go getting it infected, Jess. Go and put another dressing on. You have another?'

'Loads of them. They recommend vaseline too. For a day or two.'

'You'll need to keep it clean.'

He might, thought Jess, have been talking to a child.

'I know, Dan. I know. I'm not an idiot.'

He made as if to follow her into her room. She turned on him, angry.

'Dan. I'm going to change the dressing.'

'And?'

She faced him down. 'And this is my room. My space.'

'But my taxi will be here soon.'

'Then better make sure you've packed everything you need.'

Abashed, he turned at last, left the room slowly, unwillingly. Jess walked over, closing the door before she opened her box of dressings and with difficulty fixed a new one over the wound.

The taxi arrived five minutes early. Dan knocked on Jess's door.

'Jess. That's me. I'm off.'

She came to the door, opened it, her eyes a little red.

'Do try,' she said, aiming for lightness, 'not to say it's been a game of two halves.'

Dan sighed. 'Injury time, Jess?'

The last few months had not been easy.

He leaned forward, hesitating.

'Here's looking at you, kid.'

He reached out, touched her cheek.

Jess shut her eyes. Kept them shut. Heard his slow and heavy step on the dipping stone of tenement stair; heard the front door slam behind him; the taxi moving off, easing into the morning traffic.

Janet

THE KITCHEN WINDOW gazed north across the beach, the firth a silvered wash feathering the blue Sutherland hills. You could never, thought Janet, escape that light, never escape the sea. Nor could you, in Morna's house, expect a lingering breakfast. By the time she had finished her post-jogging shower, her older sister had swept the floor and cleared the table, which would, she knew from experience, still be a little sticky.

The post had already been delivered.

'How many today?'

Janet strolled into the kitchen, towelling her still-wet hair. It irritated her that none of the towels in this house matched. The one she held was lime green; Bart Simpson glaring from one corner, Homer from another. She threw the towel in the washing basket, sat down, poured herself a mug of coffee. As she raised it to her lips she realised the mug was chipped. She turned it round and round, seeking an intact area to drink from. There was no point in looking for another, unchipped one. Most of the mugs in this house were chipped. Morna didn't throw them out. She used them all the time; it was her style. Not one of the chairs round her scrubbed pine table had a matching partner; her plates were similarly mismatched. She and Morna could not, thought Janet, have come out of the same womb. Should not. Morna looked up from the pile of mail she was scanning.

'Twelve. We're building steadily. It's always like that. Quite promising, at this stage. There's still over a week. I'm going to do the final mailshot. Hoped you'd give a hand.'

'What do you want me to do?'

'Lick and stamp the envelopes.'

Janet frowned. 'Didn't you ask for self-adhesive envelopes? I told you, Morna. They're more hygienic.'

'Mairi didn't have any. There's a letter for you.' Morna nodded.

'Oh?' Janet feigned indifference, reached for it slowly.

'No, don't read it now! I need to get this stuff out on the first post!'

'You've missed it.'

'There's half an hour yet if I take round to the Post Office.'

Janet stuffed the letter in her pocket. It was from Sian, not Kev.

Kev had phoned only once; she found it difficult speaking to him. It was impossible talking on her sister's phone. He sounded stiff. Embarrassed. And Janet told him her mobile wouldn't work in the village, which was not true.

She thought about this as she stretched under the sink for the car-washing sponge (never used, as far as she could tell, for that purpose); she wet the sponge, set in a saucer by the growing pile of envelopes.

'Morna,' she said, 'do you think enough folk are coming?'

'Yes. Already there are more bookings than last year. The expenses are higher, though. Bringing Michael Hurt up, for one thing..'

'Is he expensive?' Janet stared at the brochure.

'Airfares. But his book's done really well. He's quite a draw.'

'Good,' said Janet, adding absently 'Jess has that book. She really liked it.'

'The girl who was in that awful accident?'

'Mmm,' nodded Janet, sipping her coffee. 'It was one of the first things she responded to.'

'Oh?'

Janet stretched across the table for more envelopes. 'I've been wondering if she mightn't like to come. Think I'll send her a brochure. Toss over an extra one.'

Morna paused now, thoughtful.

'That's quite a story. Human interest. Wouldn't it be good publicity? Couldn't you see the national newspapers running that?'

'No!' Janet was vehement. 'Don't be stupid. Jess is still recovering. Needs her privacy.'

'Just listen,' objected Morna, 'think about it. The Picts, overwhelmed, suffer centuries of silence – just like your pal, not that she's been ill for centuries, no – but their symbol stones survive, so powerful that even today they help her back to speech! A great story! I don't see that she'd mind! Why would she? You said she was she was a journalist!'

'She isn't a journalist now. She's struggling back to health. Morna, don't do this. Don't even think about it. I'm warning you seriously, if any of this, a whisper even, so much as reaches Mairi at the Post Office, I'll.. I'll..'

'You'll what?' Morna laughed. 'What, Janet? What will you do?'

Janet was reminded of so many childhood arguments. Morna taunting her. *Go on.. tell. I dare you.* This was more of the same. More difficult.

'For one thing, I'd never talk to you again.'

'Don't be silly, Janet. I didn't mean it.'

Janet looked at her sister drily.

'I know you. Believe me, I mean what I say. Anyway, it's not exactly a *scientific* story, is it? All a bit tabloid, eh? No-one, but no-one would take your conference seriously.'

Morna considered this. Could not resist teasing Janet, just a little longer.

'Any publicity is good publicity.'

Janet was probably right; it would draw the wrong sort of crowd. But it would draw a crowd, Morna was sure of that. She left it, for the moment. She might, she thought, run it by Michael in her next email. She finished stuffing envelopes, started busily tidying flyers away, neatly piling all the conference stationery in the basket she used as filing system.

Janet saw through her sister's apparent docility.

'And perhaps I should warn you that Jess's partner would definitely sue. Dan McKie would be a bad enemy.'

'Dan McKie? I know that name.'

'I should think you do. Dan McKie from the *Standard*.'

'The football writer?'

'Hard as nails. So if you want to keep the house, and not spent the next ten years subsidising Dan McKie's international lifestyle, you'll leave Jess out of your sound-bites, your photo-opportunities.'

'That's cheap, Janet.'

'Due warning. Now is that everything? Do you want these posted?'

'I'll run out with them right now. Want to talk to Mairi.'

'I'll get on with my letter then. Will you buy me a *Ross-shire Journal*, please?'

'Why?'

'Why do you think? For the Property section.'

Morna sighed, 'Janet. It's the wrong time of year. And you know we like having you. Okay, I'll get one.' She stopped at the door on her way out, looked back. 'You always were a rotten baby-sitter.'

'Yes,' smiled Janet. 'Pride myself on it.'

Janet ran up the narrow wooden stairs to the tiny guest room. She'd have to get her own place soon. She was used to silence, not the chaos of a family of three young sons. Charlie, working in Inverness, left each morning before eight, and was never home till nine at night. It would have made sense for them to move south, nearer.

'And lose all this?' said Morna, indicating the horizon, the clear white light, the village picturesque to a fault, curving round the sandy bay. Janet shook her head. It had to be said the house was rather special. On the outside.

Morna's bedlinen reflected her taste in mugs and chairs. It struck Janet suddenly that Morna would get on with Kev. She'd like his tartan plates. She might, God help her, like his brown dralon chairs. How could people live like this? The guest room was tidy because Janet had tidied it herself, stacking suitcases and books and sewing stuff in the side loft. Before, you could barely walk round the bed. She needed her own place, needed work, needed occupying.

Deciding to move north had felt like taking control, but giving up the flat, the job, had offered only temporary relief. She didn't miss the city. She didn't miss the flat, proud as she'd been of it, hard as she'd worked on it. She didn't, certainly, miss Kev. Who would waste time over a dork last seen cheek to cheek with Lynne MacMath? No. She needed occupation. Wanted something different. The Tarvat Dig might do for the summer, but it would not start up again till after the conference. Still, she meant to give it a try, looked forward to getting to grips with Pictish soil. Imagine, sweeping aeons of dust off hidden life, unveiling layers last exposed hundreds of years before.

She stretched out on the bed, looked at Sian's letter, Sian's large, excited writing, oddly difficult to read. Her letters were always thick with paper, scarce on words. This one looked even shorter than usual. Janet leaned towards the window, squinting at the deckled page.

Hi Janet,

How are you? How are things? I hope preparations for the conference are well in hand, that you're not quite as bored as you were last time we talked. I know you miss the city. Maybe, when you've had a good rest, after the summer, you might want to come back?

Ken Groundwater phoned last night from Orkney. He's loving it. Sounds happy. He asked about Morna's conference.. wants to come south for it.. suggested we could all meet up. I told him I couldn't make it. Shame. I would have liked to come. Couldn't, not with Ken there.

I'm off to Oxford this weekend. Haven't seen Jamie since she went to Kraków. She and Des are thinking about tying the knot.. Would you believe it? I'd have to be the bridesmaid. Imagine me in green.. I know she'll insist on green.

Oh, and Jess is fine. I expect she's been in touch herself. Dan's off to the World Cup but Julia Goggins will be keeping an eye on her. They really get on. Isn't it odd? I find Julia hugely daunting, but Jess just laughs at her. Maybe not so odd. She copes with you.. no, don't throw anything! Don't swear! It was a joke!

The Port, as you call it, sounds really beautiful. When you get your own place I'll come up and you can show me round Easter Ross. Better run, though, now.

Much love –

'Janet! Janet!' Morna yelled from the bottom of the stairs. 'Janet! Come down at once!'

'I'm getting dressed.'

'The kettle's on. And..'

'And what?'

'We have visitors.'

'Och, Morna, I've seen Mairi and Ailsa before. They won't mind if I take time to comb my hair.'

'Please yourself! We'll be in the kitchen.'

Janet sighed. Morna would never change. She looked at Sian's note again. She hadn't mentioned Kev. That made her feel.. made her feel..

She pulled the brush through her hair. The water here made such a difference. Her hair dried straighter, somehow; more natural. It had a bounce the city water never allowed it. And running, she thought, getting out on the beach every day had helped her skin She felt fitter, stronger. Maybe, as Sian said, after the summer, she might try the city again.

'Janet! Coffee's ready!'

'Coming!'

'You said that before.'

Janet had just pulled off her bathrobe and slipped into her jeans when the knock came on her door.

'Janet!'

'No.. don't come in! Christ, Sian, what are you doing here? You're supposed to be in England! You've just said so.. look!' She waved the letter in her friend's face. 'When did you write this?'

Sian smiled. 'I posted it yesterday. I must say I thought you'd be more pleased to see me.'

'Of course I'm pleased to see you. But you're not in the right place. And it's too early in the morning. What's going on? No, wait. Let me slip on my shirt.' Janet pulled it over her head, 'What's the problem? What?'

'What do you mean, what's going on?'

Janet buttoned the cuffs. 'Why are you here? Sit down. Tell me all about it.'

Sian shook her head. 'Settle! I came to visit you, that's all.' She blushed a little as she said this. 'You know I'm on holiday all week; not going south till Thursday. I thought I'd come and see the Port for myself. End of story.'

'Okay.' Janet could see she'd get no further, not at the moment. 'It's great to see you, Sian. Let's go down.. there'll be more space in the kitchen. And I expect Morna will have coffee on the go.'

Sian nodded. 'She didn't wait. Poured it already. Said we were lucky there were still some clean mugs. '

'We?' Janet turned, surprised. 'We?'

Sian started down the stairs. 'I got a lift. This is not the easiest place to reach on public transport.'

Janet clattered after her friend.

Maybe Sian was right. Maybe she should take herself back to the city. The village hadn't brought her peace, not the peace she'd hoped for. And she was, after all, more or less settled. Over Kev. *Well* over Kev. She'd find a different job. Buy a new flat. Start over.

'He was desperate to come,' Sian waited for Janet to join her at the foot of the stairs. 'I don't want you to get the wrong idea.'

'Who was? What idea?'

'Don't want you to think I'm here with Kev,' Sian whispered, nodding at the kitchen door. 'He came on his own account. I hitched a lift.'

'Kev?' Janet stopped short. '*Kev?*'

'I'm going to stay a day or two, find Bed and Breakfast.'

'Bed and Breakfast, nothing! You'll stay here. Sleep in my room. I'll move down to the couch.'

'Don't be silly, Janet.'

'Look, you're in the Highlands. We take hospitality rather seriously. We'd be highly offended if you went to Bed and Breakfast, no matter,' laughed Janet, 'that you might be more comfortable. Comfort doesn't come into it. Not an issue. Besides, you can help with Morna's endless mailshots.'

She was rambling, and she knew it. Kev. In Morna's kitchen. It didn't seem possible. Didn't seem probable. At least, she thought, the kitchen was clean. At least she'd combed her hair.

Julia

'FRIGGING HELL!' CRIED Kerry when Julia told her about the conference. 'Michael's going? And Jess? Haven't you told him? Haven't you told him about her accident?'

'Well, no.'

Julia rarely blushed. She was blushing now, perched on the edge of her green leather chesterfield, the one she and Dennis bought so many years ago that the springs had failed, causing it to sag in the middle.

'I couldn't tell him, Kerry. There wasn't an opportunity. I thought.. I wondered..'

'Go on.' Kerry knew what was coming, but gave her aunt no help.

Julia tried to sound soothing, natural; not that soothing was natural to her, nor how she felt. 'The two of you get on well. You and Michael. I thought.. maybe you could phone.. prepare him. He'd take it better from you.'

'You mean *you'd* take it bloody better if it came from me!'

'Don't be silly, Kerry. Even if you're right, and you are, there's no need to swear like a damned trooper.'

'Yes there bloody is!'

'Look, Kerry. I tried to tell him. You know. You know to your cost how direct I can be. In this case I.. I couldn't find the words.'

Kerry softened. 'Yeah.'

'You'll do it?'

'No. If you couldn't face up to it, how the hell can I?' Kerry realised her aunt was near to tears now; Julia, who never showed her feelings. 'Listen. When we get there, if there's a chance to do it gently – talk to Michael face to face – I'll do it then.'

'Kerry, you're a good girl,' Julia patted her arm. 'And you'll take to Jess, I know you will.'

Jess

JESS LAYS OUT all her clothes and shoes on Dan's bed, with her notebook, *The Riddle of the Picts*, her pens. Everything folded in tissue paper, neat and precise. Pens wrapped in polythene. A big thing, this travelling alone; and for the first time since the accident.

She catches sight of herself in the mirror on the dresser, pale and serious, bending over the bed. She stands up, stares. Who is she? Who exactly is the woman reflected in that mirror, Dan's mirror? What defines her? The make-up she's become so adept at using?

Or light? Life? Memories? How can she, Jess, retrieve the image, when she's shattered as the mirror she had broken? She slit her hand struggling to gather up the scattering glass; winnowed countless fractions of herself in the wistful, shining heart of every splinter. All of them caught her, every one.

This was her eye. Her chin.

Her lip.

The mirror, disintegrating, sieved a shredded face, offering nothing but the truth.

Like the young queen in the fairy-tale blindly guessing names, like the child whose warm heart froze when a sliver of ice embedded itself in his eye, she faced the near-impossible. Tethered to the present, lacking a coherent past, how could she hope to breathe again, complete? How can she trust the mirrored view, the single proof she'd held to through the silence?

It was Dan swept away the fragments, reorganised the room. Helped her find and carry home a new reflection.

Dan helped. Tried to let her choose; tried to be gentle, supportive, though returning memory showed him in different mode, so many moods. What had she been to him?

Who am I? Who were we?

The past is always relevant. Even without words, the body has its own ways of remembering. Not always happy. She and Dan both know.

Here's looking at you, kid.

A young Dan stretching across the white-clothed table of a dark and gilded Chinese restaurant – not stretching far, the table so narrow their knees meet, their feet would have been dancing slow avoidance had not their legs been intertwined. They haven't ordered yet. The menu lies on the table. Her hair is wet, dripping, plastered to her head. Dan looks at her in wonder, brushes her cheek.

Here's looking at you, kid.

An older Dan slamming down the phone, glancing warily, the White Street window bright behind him, unshuttered – unlike his face. He opens his mouth as if to talk, thinks better of it, looks away. And Jess sore, stiff, as if she's slept in a strange bed. Why is she so cold? Why is she so cold?

Here's looking at you, kid.

Words stopped her in the hall. Dan's voice. Dan's words. Who was he speaking to? Who? Jess says nothing; nothing. The silence has begun. Is beginning.

Dan looking at her, looking. Close, too close, on the huge yellow sofa, his body wrong. All wrong. Too short, too round. Her shoulders tightening, flinching. His shoulders sagging.

Here's looking at you, kid.

You couldn't lie, not easily, not with the body. Neither of them could. Neither she nor Dan. Which way, she thought, did time flow?

She is very careful next morning leaving the flat. Pulls out all the plugs, double locks the door. It feels as if she is setting out on an expedition. The taxi driver picks up her anxiety. 'Going abroad?'

'Just up north.'

It's a blue day, beautiful. Sailing across the city, Jess wonders at the world. So many people milling streets she should have known but cannot distinctly differentiate. So many people, all with purpose. They know where they're going. Seem to. And all so different, no two the same. Some exhibit briefcases, some sauntering with prams. Some armed with books, or bulging carrier bags. And the traffic.. cars and buses.. all so full. Most of all, the city's fleet of tour buses, garish, colourful, eye-catching.

'Lots of tourists, Miss,' the driver nods. 'Earlier this year. More folk holidaying at home.'

'I suppose.'

'We'll have a good season, mark my words. And we'll have a summer this year. Not like last one.'

Jess is intrigued. 'How can you tell?'

'My bunions,' the taxi driver laughs at her expression. 'No, seriously, Miss, my old neighbour always tells me. I don't know how she does it, but she gets the weather right. Every time.' The taxi's slowing down now, turning out of the traffic and down into the station. 'Here we are. You're in good time. Waverley Station.' He draws up at the taxi rank and jumps out, running round to take her luggage from the boot.

I must be looking old, thinks Jess. No-one ever used to do that.

'Hope you have a lovely time,' the driver says, and means it. There's a shine to this woman, though she seems so vulnerable. Like a snowdrop, he thinks, a primrose. That's it, yes. She reminds him of the early primroses that used to glimmer in the birchwood by his grandmother's house.

'Thank you. You've been so kind,' Jess smiles. 'I'll look forward to that summer.' She can already see Julia on the platform, outstaring the crowd; chivvying the tall blonde girl who stands beside her, laughing. *Tarvat*, thinks Jess. She takes a deep breath, turns to wave. The taxi is already gone.

Michael

'AND THIS IS your room. When is.. I mean..' Morna stuttered, 'we were expecting Lesley..'

He moved towards the window on the sea side of the room,

pulling back the curtains for a clearer view. You could breathe here, he thought, really breathe. He'd let Lesley deal with Morna. A mistake.

'So she's not coming?'

He turned. 'Nice room. Great view. Lovely to have two windows.'

Morna tried to keep her eyes away from the queen-sized bed, looming, white, before her. 'The food is really good. We wondered, though, whether you might want to eat with us tonight?'

'Best not, Morna. Things to do. But of course I'm looking forward to meeting your husband and the boys.'

'And my sister. Janet's on the conference team.'

'I didn't know you had a sister.'

'You used to read *The House at Pooh Corner* to her.'

'I did?'

'She's a lot younger. Well,' Morna turned. 'Better run. We're expecting Julia and her niece off the next train, with a friend of Janet's.'

'Kerry's coming? Julia's niece? Australian girl? '

'Don't know if she's Australian. Her name might have been Kerry. They're staying with Janet, not here. Janet's friend is the one I told you about, the one your book cured. She..'

Michael cut her short. 'Morna, I'm not comfortable with that. Not the sort of publicity I would have asked for. I wish you hadn't run that story.'

She looked past him, focused on the sea.

'I didn't, Michael. I don't know who spread it.'

'You copied that last email to the world and his wife.'

'Not knowingly! It was a glitch! My computer had that virus that was on the go. Kept doing those odd things.. our firewall didn't work.'

He shook his head. Changed the subject.

'What time did you say Kerry was arriving?'

'In about an hour. Janet's taking the Landrover down to the station to pick them up.'

'Good.' Michael turned away. 'Catch you later.'

He left her no alternative but retreat. Morna tried to smile, turned. The door swung closed. Her unwilling steps trickled along the corridor. After six or seven paces, she regained confidence, the briskness coming back into her stride, so that she fairly skipped down the stairs. No. Morna would never change.

Michael sighed. That stupid article. On the plane he'd decided to laugh it off, make a joke of it; but now the unnamed woman would be here at the conference. Morna had obviously engineered the whole thing. There'd be photographs, press. Well, he'd refuse to play along. He'd find a form of words to get them through it.

He unpacked, stowing his clothes in the old-fashioned wardrobe, arranging laptop and papers on the writing desk. She had left him a conference folder. No Kavanaghs. Why did he always look? After all this time?

A handful of papers tumbled from the back of the folder. Last-minute announcements. Last-minute delegates. He screwed the papers up unread, tossing them in the waste-paper basket.

Now. A walk. A walk on the beach.

He ran down the side stairs, and through the tartan-carpeted hall. No Morna. Good. The street was empty. From the doorway he could scan the gentle sweep of the bay. The tide was coming in. The sun was shining.

'Michael?'

He didn't recognise the dark-haired girl in jeans standing in the cottage garden to his right.

'It's Michael, isn't it?'

'I'm sorry. Have we met?' His tone was cautious.

'Janet. Janet Pringle.'

'Morna's sister?'

'I used to disturb your snogging sessions. But I was only thirteen, after all.'

Michael didn't remember. He frowned. 'Morna said I used to read you *Winnie the Pooh*. You were thirteen?'

'No, that was Martin Smith, her first boyfriend. I was little then. I don't know.. five or six?'

'Odd.'

'Sorry?' she hesitated. 'Odd?'

'You don't look a bit like her.'

'Thank goodness. Two Mornas? Who could cope with it?'

Michael sympathised with that point of view.

'Well.. I was going for a walk.'

'*À propos* of nothing..'

'Pardon?'

'I *remember* you being like that!'

'Being like what?'

'So confident. So sure that the world is – eagerly! – awaiting your intention. And only yours.'

He laughed out loud at that.

'More like Morna than I thought! You can go off people.'

Janet giggled.

'I really am off for that walk.'

'You wouldn't,' said Janet, 'prefer to come to Fearn, and help me entertain Julia?'

He was tempted, remembered just in time that Morna's miracle woman would be there.

'No! Tell Julia I was asking for her. Kerry too. Tell them to come and see me at the hotel.'

Janet turned away. 'Catch you later.'

Michael crossed the road, making his way through the empty car park towards the beach. The tarmac, gritty with sand, rasped against the leather soles of his conference shoes. He should have put on trainers, running gear. Should he go back and change? He stopped, looked around him. The sky had darkened, grown uncertain. It would rain, he thought, within the hour.

He felt more comfortable stepping out of the hotel in his track suit. First he ran along the road, the pastel string of houses, to the crow-stepped Christmas tree of a house at the far end of the village. *Harbour Haven*. A house with tiny windows, tiny doors, walls that must be four feet thick. You'd be safe in a house like that, he thought. Safe if Morna hadn't owned it.

The harbour wall ran out at right angles from the house, straight out in the firth, before it bent back, coiled with rope, stacked with creels. Fish boxes blocked the path, fishboxes stamped *Cetanea de Marisco*, and other, probably Spanish, words which he could not make out. At the end of the wall, beyond the only working boat, a small boy sat, legs dangling, plastic fishing rod extending above the few feet of water lapping below him. He paid no attention to Michael, squinted back at the village. Occasionally, he wound the line in, precariously attaching artificial bait to the small hook. Each time he threw the line out, the bait went flying.

'Are you managing?'

The boy shook his head.

'Nothing biting today. Mam says it's too bright, but it's going to rain.'

Michael nodded.

'And worms would be better, but she won't let me dig for them. Says the garden is covered in animals' *do*.'

'Animals..? I see,' Michael nodded again. 'When I was your age, I used to dig up lugworm. They were quite good.'

'That's what Dad said, but there aren't any worms in those sandy curly bits. I checked.'

'You have to dig below them. When the tide is out. Like now.'

'If I go home now she'll never let me out again. I should be at school.'

'Why aren't you?'

'I got sick in the bus.'

'Good enough.'

'She doesn't know I've come fishing. If I went back for the spade I'd be for it.' The boy's brown eyes grew large, his expression so serious that Michael could not smile.

'Well, see you later. Tight lines.'

'Wouldn't you think,' asked the boy, 'that a person of six is perfectly old enough to go fishing by himself at the harbour?'

Michael hedged his bets.

'I think that might depend on the person. And the parents. And probably also the weather.'

'That's what Dad says. Anyway,' he nodded. '*She's* too busy doing the conference to notice I'm not home.'

'I think,' said Michael, 'I know your mum. Morna Forrester.'

The boy shook his head solemnly. 'Everybody knows her.'

Michael pounded his way along the beach, the city counterpoint of traffic and tarmac blessedly absent. Here life was defined by the sough of waves, the slap of hard-packed sand, instigations of gulls, wailing, wheeling. A moody sun glittered sky and sea though the wind was rising, dark cloud thickening.

He closed his eyes, monitoring the body's movement, simple waves of energy, of being; the congruence of muscles contracting smoothly, arms swinging, legs flexing, extending. When he opened his eyes, sound and movement faltered. To hear, to really hear, he thought, you had to close your eyes, risk falling.

He must have run for fifteen minutes, twenty, before he felt the first drops spattering his face, his arms. He welcomed the coolness, the needling sharpness, but after a few minutes more turned back. He could barely make out the hills across the bay. The storm was sweeping south, strengthening.

As for Morna.. as for the woman in the case.. he'd simply ignore the whole thing, make sure they were never alone in the same place, never together.

Though.. it struck him suddenly.. she might feel quite as compromised by Morna's antics as he did himself. That she was travelling with Julia could only be a good sign. Michael brightened. He should have thought of that.

He is almost back at the village. The tide has swept in fast. He's been forced to run on higher, drier sand. It stings his legs. He gives up, breathless, striking a path across the dunes and through the caravan site beside the squat, grey church; a building still in use, unlike so many imposing piles across the county. Very obviously still in use. It must cramp the style of weekend caravanners. He stops to catch his breath, bends forward. As he straightens up, Morna's blue Landrover jolts past, and he registers Kerry's neat features, her blonde head. Kerry! He lopes after the vehicle, now rounding the corner into the sleepy village. The Landrover slows down, coming to a halt at the cottage next to the hotel. One by one the doors open.

Janet slides from the front, Julia from the back.

And yes.. there's Kerry hopping down from the near-side back door, all legs and elbows.

'Kerry!' he shouts. 'Kerry! Julia!'

Janet ignores him, goes on unloading cases, bags, from the back, stretching in for them, handing them to Kerry who, seeing Michael, drops the luggage she has picked up.

'Mikey! Wow!' she runs towards him. 'Mikey!'

He hasn't felt this happy in months.

Kerry.

He's hugging her, swinging her off her feet, when the Landrover's fourth passenger, descends a little awkwardly. Michael can only see her back, but there's something familiar about this person, smallish, dark. She straightens up, turns round, smiles at them, nods. Turns away.

'Where do you want these, Janet?'

Michael flinches, stiffens.

'Julia!' Janet shouts. 'Get the door?'

Julia swings round.

'It's not open.'

'That's what I'm asking you to do.'

Janet has two bags in each hand, one under each arm; doesn't understand Julia's confusion.

'Look! I'm full-handed!'

'Janet,' Julia offers faintly, looking from Jess to Michael, 'Janet, the door's still locked.'

'This is the Port. Everything's open! Michael, move!' Janet dismisses him, her patience running out. 'Come on, Julia!'

'I'll get it,' Jess sets down the cases she has picked up. 'There you go, Janet. There you are.'

'I'm glad that at least one of you is awake. Get the cases in! Out of the rain!'

The blue door slams. Julia groans.

Kerry is still in Michael's arms. He is sagging, head bowed, lost in her blonde hair. She is holding him up. Kerry stares at her aunt, helpless.

Julia shrugging, shakes her head, follows Jess and Janet into the cottage. The shower chooses this moment to intensify.

'Mikey,' Kerry whispers in his ear, 'It's okay. It's not how it seems, I promise.' She eases herself from his arms. 'Come on,' she soothes. 'Settle. If I wasn't wet before, I'm soaked through now. We need a drink. Where are you staying?'

He nods at the hotel.

'That close? Good.'

She lifts her bags, pushing them into the scrap of shelter offered by Janet's door.

'Why don't you run inside and jump into a bath. I'll change into some dry clothes, then come find you.'

Michael does not move.

Kerry looks at him again.

'Okay,' she says, slowly, stretching the word out. 'Will the bar in there be open?'

Michael doesn't answer.

'Come on,' she pushes him firmly towards the door. 'We'll ask.'

'Mikey..'

He's stretched out in the bath. Kerry, lounging on his broad white bed, has to raise her voice for him to hear, though the bathroom door is open and the quiet lapping sounds he makes as he moves reach her distinctly enough above the chuntering electric fan. She sips her glass of wine.

'I've never spent so much time drinking with a naked man.. one I'm not actually sleeping with.'

'Okay, I give up,' he ducks his head under the water, sitting up smartly, birthing a small tidal wave that swims noisily along the bath and over the edge. 'Sleep with me. Come on. Let's do it. Get it over.'

'Don't be silly. '

'Thanks, Kerry,' he lies back, smiling.

'It wasn't an invitation! I wish..'

'Sorry? Can't hear.'

She raises her voice again.

'I wish there'd been a way to tell you. I can't begin to imagine the year you've had. Both Julia and I felt sure you *must* know, must have heard what happened.'

'You should have phoned.'

'I did. You didn't answer. Julia tried too. We tried many times. How could we leave news like that as a message?'

'You could have asked me to phone back.'

'Mikey. The way you were when you left, the way I found you that morning at Maigret's, I didn't dare.'

He lies silent for several moments, weighing the truth of that, feeling the water's warmth gradually seeping into his bones, his skin. God. Even the slightest ripple, the slightest movement, is deafening.

He wishes he could disconnect that fan.

'She doesn't remember me at all? You're sure?'

'I don't think she remembers anything. She's lovely, Mikey. I can see why you.. I really like her. I don't suppose..'

He sits up again, sets bath water slapping back and fore across the bath, cascading over the side, splashing the already flooded floor.

'I didn't catch that, Kerry? What don't you suppose?'

Kerry sighs. She stretches out across the white bed, rumpling the sheets, her wet clothes moulding damp, small valleys in the cutwork of the bedspread. The imprint on her arms reminds her of Jess's scars.

'Oh, I don't know. What is it I'm trying to say?'

She rolls over, curling on her side, arms tightly folded.

'Mikey, I didn't know Jess before. I don't know if you'll know her now. It's my impression Jess doesn't know *herself*.

Mikey.. are you listening? Are you okay?'

He leans forward in the bath, staring straight ahead, counting the bland flowered tiles round the wall.

She loves him.

She loves him not.

Jess is alive.

Jess nearly died.

It wasn't that she didn't love him, wasn't that she'd *chosen* not to be in touch. She couldn't. She couldn't be in touch.

And there's a chance, a real and frightening chance, she never might. The worst thing, worst of all, is that she has no living memory of their days, their hours. No memory. No words.

'Christ.' He lies back, shuts his eyes as the water spills across his face, soothing, submerging. When he talked to Jamie, back in Kraków, when he blithely said that life was hope, he hadn't thought of this. He hadn't thought of this.

'Tell me again about the accident.'

'I don't know much about it. Except..'

'Except?'

'Julia said, right at the start, when we saw that newspaper report, that it must have been the bus you guys were on.'

'And Jess?'

'She doesn't know. Doesn't know why she was running for a tour bus. She can't understand it. No-one can. But I think..'

'What?'

'I think she saw you on it.'

Silence stretches between them. Michael's trying to reconstruct that afternoon, trying to feel what it was like being there, on that bus.

Yes. They are in the open air, right at the front, upstairs, laughing politely, sun on their faces, the slight breeze in their hair.

Yes. Julia is going on about.. about the dinner. Where they'll all sit at high table. How hard the committee worked to set the whole thing up.

He's trying to answer sensibly.

He can see nothing but Jess the night before, Jess that morning. He can think of nothing beyond her smoothness of her skin..

Kerry leans against the bathroom door.

'You'll be okay? You look a little less like death.'

She scrutinises his face, his chest, then looks quickly away. Too quickly.

He shrugs. 'I'm fine, Kerry. Got to catch my breath, that's all. Take it all in. I need time.'

She turns to go, stops.

'She's remarkable.'

'Julia?'

'No, Jess. Think of it.. she might have died. She fought her way back. All that surgery. The not being able to talk. The memory gone. And even her poor fingers.. but you'll see when you meet her. Tell her you've met, Mikey. She needs to know.'

'What makes you say that?'

Kerry shrugs.

'And the partner? This Dan?'

'That I don't know. Janet knows him best. See you at dinner?'

'You're eating here?'

'No. Morna's. Janet said you were invited.'

'I hadn't planned on going.'

'No? I am. Jess too. We'll maybe see you?'

He shivers. 'Don't know.'

Jess

JANET'S RENTED COTTAGE is a sparsely furnished space, white and bare.

'You couldn't have a better view.'

The firth, across the narrow road, swims angry, grey.

'Better still, no Morna! I've been here a whole week! I tell you, Jess, it's been bliss. I love my sister, but.. och. Julia!' Janet turns, calls through the door. 'Julia, how does Michael Hurt know Kerry?'

'From the conference last year,' Julia sails into the room. 'Jess met him too.'

'Someone else I don't remember.'

'He'd have looked different,' says Janet. 'Not wet. Not in a soaking tracksuit. Not red about the gills.'

'He was pale, not red,' Jess frowns. 'He seemed really upset with me. Do you think it was that article?'

'No,' Julia hastens to reassure her. 'Don't be silly. He can't be best pleased at the article; who would be? But no-one could be upset at you.'

'He was angry,' Jess insists. 'That's me unpacked.'

She turns back to the window.

His shock had been obvious. Michael Hurt had been plainly appalled to see her climb down from the Landrover. If it wasn't the article, it must be her, the way she is.

She makes people uncomfortable. What is it about her?

Not the scars. No. He couldn't have seen them.

She wishes, suddenly, that Dan was here. Dan stood between her and an alien world, knows her for what she is now. So, of course, does Janet. With Julia things are not quite so straightforward. As for new folk.. Jess rebels.

'Do we have to go out for dinner tonight? Don't think I could face it. I need a bit of peace.'

'Kerry and Janet and I have to go,' nods Julia. 'But if you want to pace yourself, Jess, why don't you take yourself to the hotel for a snack, then have an early night?'

'Good idea.'

'Do you want me to stay with you?'

'No, Janet. I've got a book. Several books, thanks to Julia! We almost missed the train building up my stock of books. And did

I open any? Not one! Don't worry. I'll be fine. Who's for coffee? Shall I make some?'

'You'll find it in the cupboard behind the kettle.'

'Kerry,' Jess smiles as Kerry pops her head around the door. 'I'm just about to make a cup of coffee. Want some?'

The kitchen is a small room at the back of the cottage. Like all the other rooms, it's painted white, the walls uneven, plastered; the window small, cut into the wall's full thickness. Mirrors flank the generous sill, gather restricted light, reflecting it further into the room. Jess stretches her right hand between the mirrors, waves it up and down. Scars on both sides stand out livid; back and front. Back and front.

In the bedroom. Kerry shivers.

'Janet, can I use the shower?'

'Any time. It's electric. Not bad. Gets quite warm. Reasonable power too. Look at you, girl! Covered in sand! Anyone would think it had been you running on the beach, not your boyfriend.'

'He's not my boyfriend.'

'No?'

'Sadly,' Kerry sighs, 'he's spoken for.'

'Doesn't wear a ring.'

'Is a ring necessary?'

'On a bike?'

Jess is suddenly behind Janet.

'No. That's not right, is it? Do I mean on a bell? No. I mean, on a bike, don't I? Isabel? Isabella? Necessary on a bike?'

'Jess. If you keep going round and round in circles like that, and with such crap jokes, I'll make you share with Kerry. Come on. We'll fix that coffee, let this girl get changed.'

Kerry slumps in the sagging leather armchair, glancing about the bedroom. Twin beds, light blue duvets. A single picture on the wall. A low-set window facing the tiny back garden and the neighbours' white-washed gable.

'This place isn't bad. If it wasn't a bit on the chilly side.'

'Get out of those wet clothes.' Julia doesn't look up, continues unpacking. 'Pop this on.' She throws a cotton bathrobe at her niece. 'You'll find it surprisingly warm.'

'And surprisingly smart!' Kerry holds it up. 'Who were you expecting to impress, Aunt Julia?'

'A difficult Australian. It's a present.'

'Julia! God.. can this be the first sign of Alzheimer's? Or guilty conscience?'

'If you don't be quiet, I'll take it back.' Julia drops her voice. 'How did he take it?'

'How do you think? We should have told him.'

Kerry stands up, begins to pull her wet clothes off. Julia remains, solemn, quiet.

'Of course,' the girl relents, 'he knows we were in a difficult position, had no firm information.'

'No.'

'But we should have got word to him somehow.'

'He said that?'

'No. I did.'

'You're right,' says Julia, nodding. 'Do you think he'll be okay?' She stops at the door. Her niece shrugs, doesn't answer. 'Christ! It's more than coffee I need! What I wouldn't give for good stiff dram!'

Julia doesn't mean to bang the door, but it resonates behind her.

Kerry shakes the folds from the bathrobe, slips it on. The fabric, slightly stiff, scours her naked skin. This will improve. Body heat and water will soften the waffled cotton, imprint her personality, her shape.

Even clothes have memory. Like old shoes. Clay.

Kerry knows about clay, how it holds the first shape moulded; how that native form will fountain in the kiln. No memory can be truly lost. Not lost. It can be not yet found. Yes, she thinks. That's more like it.

Michael

AFTER KERRY LEFT and he persuaded himself from the bath, Michael lingered at his desk, in theory, working. Above him and below, doors opened, slamming shut. Footsteps in the corridor ran to and from the stair, voices sang in the street outside, car doors clicked open – all of these interfering with his concentration – which was to admit he wasn't concentrating, couldn't.

For the last ten months, almost a full year, the seasons' turning, he had kept himself alive tendering the memory of finite, perfect love. It might have been love lost, but that had somehow rendered it more perfect, more complete. To find out that this memory was not a fact that could be shared, not even with the one he loved, was hard to bear.

Harder still to understand. And nothing he could do would alter the loss. Nothing.

Michael was bereft.

He stared beyond the screen towards the beach. The world went on. Waves danced, stubborn, clawing at the shore. Was the ebb-tide turning? He couldn't tell. Had it altered since his run? But the sea, he thought, never gives up, never languishes in grief. The sea works with the tide, works and waits.

Everything comes to him who waits. Everything comes. Everything. And life – wasn't life the same? His finger traced the pattern on the screen before him. Interwoven symbols. Pictish stone.

He and Jess had been bound to meet again. So many links, so many ways the strands of their lives turned and twisted.

He was in two minds, three, about dinner. He had, of course, turned Morna's invitation down. But Julia and Kerry would be there. And *Jess*. Perhaps he ought to go. Definitely he ought to go.

He dressed carefully, shaved, splashed on some aftershave, studying the modest, half-elliptical bottle. *Truth*. Odd name for scent. Citrus tones fading to flower and musk. Sherbet. Michael laughed. Everything, everything was sold by smell. Hadn't he found himself in the supermarket just last week reading coffee tins? A rare, luxuriant, fruity aroma, with overtones of – coffee. Even olive oil was sold, like wine, for its scent, its tang. Smell was important, smell was sexy, no doubt about that, and this one was, he thought, even cheerful. More than that. Happy.

Would he need a jacket? He studied the sky. Yes, though Morna's house was no more than a step along the street. He'd been soaked once already. Once was enough. Clutching his leather jacket, he went to find a drink.

The back stairs brought him to ground level next to Reception.

He had never in his life seen a hotel with such a hidden, difficult-to-find, reception area. It was a little disconcerting. Every time he'd passed it, there was someone standing there, pressing the bell, looking lost.

As there is now.

'Can I help?'

'You're not hotel staff.'

'No, but I'm staying here.'

'I know. You're Kerry's friend. I saw you,' she lifts her chin, 'when we arrived. I'm Jess. Jess Kavanagh.'

She holds out her hand.

Michael does not reply, does not take the offered hand. He's staring at her fingers. She blushes.

'God, I'm sorry. I didn't think. I never think. I shouldn't do this. Shouldn't.'

She lets the hand drop limply to her side, looks away.

Michael, appalled at his reaction, blushes redder than the carpet.

'Jess,' his voice is gruff, 'I didn't know.'

'It's not just you. Everyone..'

He reaches forward now, lifts her hand, cradling it in both of his. Says again, 'I didn't know.'

She's fighting back tears. 'I.. I ought perhaps to tell you, Michael.. isn't it?.. Michael?'

'Yes. I know you, Jess. We met last year.'

'Julia said. I have no recollection.. no memory of that conference. That was before..'

Again he nods.

Jess rushes on.

'And I have to tell you it was me they wrote about.. in that awful article. It was nothing to do with me. Or Julia. We don't know how it happened.'

'I think I do,' Michael frowns.

He's still holding her hand, will not let it go. Jess, he remembers, had such beautiful hands. That first day, that small hand on his arm..

These.. these are heart-breaking, the covering skin red and patched, lacking smoothness, shape.

'They're better than they were,' Jess offers, awkward. 'You've no idea.'

'No.' He turns the hand over and over, runs his fingers over wounds that for so long have failed to heal.

Jess isn't sure what to do. She cannot pull her hand away. Not easily. 'Are they sore?'

'No. Not any more. Not really.'

He lets her go, oddly reluctant. 'But,' he says, 'you're not staying here.'

'No.'

She's thin. Too thin. He hadn't noticed that this afternoon.

He looks at her, looks carefully. She doesn't remember. No. He can see.. he can't see.. in her eyes.

'So?' she says.

'So, what are you doing here?'

'Here?'

'At Reception?'

'At Reception? Oh.. I.. I wanted to ask if they had the internet. Need to borrow their machine.'

'Borrow mine,' he says. 'I've brought my laptop. Are you waiting for something important?'

'Not really, no. Email.'

'Come with me. Use mine. I insist. I'll set it up for you.'

'I couldn't.'

'Course you could. You don't remember, but we became friends, good friends. This way. Come on.'

Jess

JESS FINDS HERSELF trailing Michael up the tartan stairs and along the narrow, uneven corridor.

'Here you go. Sit down.' He pulls a chair out for her.

'Oh!'

A white room tinged with gold. Sun streams through cloud in the west; defining hills, shimmering above the mist. Clinging to the shout of land and sea.

'Yes, beautiful,' breathes Michael, stretching across her to attach the modem. He seems nervous. Why? 'I'm the lucky one, don't you think? Two windows? Will you manage now?'

She nods.

'I'll leave you to it, then. See you at Morna's.'

Jess shakes her head. 'I'm not going. Thought I'd have a quiet snack here.'

'Well,' says Michael, 'then maybe.. maybe I could join you? See, you switch this on like so.'

He stands up slowly, one hand on the back of the chair, grazing her shoulders. Close, so very close. He leans across, presses a button on the computer, a simple, quiet movement.

Jess stares at him, stares. This white and fragrant room has been teasing her, leading her somewhere, somewhere she hasn't been. Not in a long time. Where? What is it? What is she remembering?

Michael stands up.

'Let me check this last connection.'

He moves to her left side, as Jess, suddenly hot, too hot, unable to breathe, slips off her woollen jacket. She throws it on the bed, twists back to the computer. He freezes.

'What's this, Jess?'

'Sorry?'

'This?'

His fingers brush her arm.

The snake.

She shakes her head.

'Pictish.'

His eyes hold hers. Earnest.

'Rebirth, wisdom. Protection,' she shivers. 'See? I've read the book.'

He strokes the tattoo, barely touches it.

'Michael,' her voice has all but disappeared. 'I know you?'

'Yes.' He whispers. 'Yes, you do.'

Jess blushes. Taps the keyboard.

No email.

That's Dan.

Where will Dan be?

What will he be doing?

But Michael bends, drops a kiss on top of her head.

And suddenly it's there, the whole thing.

All of it.

beginning

The fourteenth of June dawns, like any other day that summer, tremulously bright. In Portnahurach, gulls wheel, lingering as inshore boats put out to sea. A sluggish stream of headlights begins to carve its way along the narrow road towards the A9; making for Inverness, Nigg, Invergordon. Farmers are already in the fields. Above Balintore, the Shandwick Stone still stands, beautiful, more permanent than oil rigs strung, Christmas-lit, across the Firth. Cats slink home for breakfast. Dogs howl to be let out.

Jess wakes briefly in the dawn, wondering what is different; hearing something, hearing syncopated rain amplified by vellux windows. It wakes her to the unfamiliar shadows of a Portnahurach room, its unclosed curtains; wakes her to this narrow bed, its crushed white cotton, and gentle, irregular, breathing. Across the room, curled up on the folding bed, Janet is moaning, dreaming.

Janet sees herself in the church at Portnahurach. She is kneeling in Old Tarvat Church, trowel in hand, scratching at the new-laid founds. Her fingers feel for words, slicing through the concrete, crumbling it like sand, brushing it away. Gradually, a shape is emerging from the rubble, a form she recognises, a breathing figure, rising. 'Kev!'

'Sorry. Did I wake you?'

'What?' Janet sits up, stares. 'Jess?'

'I didn't mean to wake you.'

Janet rubs her eyes.

'You didn't.' She yawns, 'Just the rain.'

In Japan, Dan McKie is dreaming too. Sees himself in Tokei-ji, the Divorce Temple; a sanctuary for wives for some eight hundred years, a Buddhist Temple set in plum trees, irises. Not yellow flags, not wild iris as they may be found on moorland in his native Ireland, but the full purple Japanese variety. Nightingales sing. In the distance, Jess floats in red kimono, eyes blacked, hands raw.

'Jess!' She doesn't seem to hear him. He raises his voice. 'Jess! Jess!'

'Dan, you're snoring. Turn over. Go back to sleep! You're off to Tsukjii early. Then the sentou, then Sapporo. Do you want some water?'

He wakes, stares blindly at his blonde companion. Her breasts are small, barely formed. She hands him a dripping glass.

'Thanks, Katya. Thanks.'

'Go to sleep.'

He sighs. Turns over. Not till they jumped into bed had he seen the snake writhing on the base of her spine. He recoiled, bitten.

Why did women do these things?

Jess, where are you? Jess..

Michael stalks the rising dawn; the beach disrupted by low-flying jets, six in quick succession. He walked here last night with Jess, sat with her on the pier, watching Kerry and Julia drift back from Morna's.

Midnight. Not completely dark. It would not get dark.

'I love you,' he said. 'Where do we go from here?'

Low tide washed the pier's foundations. Whispering.

'Michael,' she touched his arm, 'I don't know who I am.'

But she stared into the northern sky and leaned against him, leaned so close they might almost have been one; one word, one story.

What was it he'd thought yesterday? To feel, to really feel – you have to close your eyes, risk falling?

He shuts his eyes. Doesn't fall.

Some other books published by **Luath Press**

Driftnet
Lin Anderson
1 84282 034 6 PB £ 9.99

Introducing forensic scientist Dr Rhona MacLeod...

A teenager is found strangled and mutilated in a Glasgow flat.

Leaving her warm bed and lover in the middle of the night to take forensic samples from the body, Rhona MacLeod immediately pervceives a likeness between herself and the dead boy and is tortured by the thought that he might be the son she gave up for adoption seventeen years before.

Amidst the turmoil of her own love life and consumed by guilt from her past, Rhona sets out to find both the boy's killer and her own son. But the powerful men who use the Internet to trawl for vulnerable boys have nothing to lose and everything to gain by Rhona MacLeod's death.

A strong player on the crime novel scene, Lin Anderson skilfully interweaves themes of betrayal, violence and guilt. In forensic investigator Rhona MacLeod she has created a complex character who will have readers coming back for more.

Lin Anderson has a rare gift. She is one of the few able to convey urban and rural Scotland with equal truth... Compelling, vivid stuff. I couldn't put it put it down. ANNE MACLEOD, author of *The Dark Ship*

The Road Dance
John MacKay
1 84282 040 0 PB £6.99

Why would a young woman, dreaming of a new life in America, sacrifice all and commit an act so terrible that she severs all hope of happiness again?

Life in the Scottish Hebrides can be harsh – 'The Edge of the World' some call it. For the beautiful Kirsty MacLeod, the love of Murdo and their dream of America promise an escape from the scrape of the land, the repression of the church and the inevitability of the path their lives would take. But the Great War looms and Murdo is conscriptd. The village holds a grand Road Dance to send their young men off to battle.

As the dancers swirl and sup, the wheels of tragedy are set in motion.

[MacKay] has captured time, place and atmosphere superbly... a very good debut. MEG HENDERSON

Powerful, shocking, heartbreaking... DAILY MAIL

With a gripping plot that subtly twists and turns, vivid characterisation and a real sense of time and tradition, this is an absorbing, powerful first novel. The impression it made on me will remain for some time. THE SCOTS MAGAZINE

Milk Treading

Nick Smith

I 84282 037 0 PB £6.99

Life isn't easy for Julius Kyle, a jaded crime hack with the *Post*. When he wakes up on a sand barge with his head full of grit he knows things have to change. But how fast they'll change he doesn't guess until his best friend Mick jumps to his death off a fifty foot bridge outside the *Post*'s window. Worst of all, he's a cat. That means keeping himself scrupulously clean, defending his territory and battling an addiction to milk. He lives in Bast, a sprawling city of alleyways and claw-shaped towers... join Julius as he prowls deep into the crooked underworld of Bast, contending with political intrigue, territorial disputes and dog-burglars, murder, mystery and mayhem.

This is certainly the only cat-centred political thriller that I've read and it has a weird charm, not to mention considerable humour... AL KENNEDY

A trip into a surreal and richly-realized feline-canine world. ELLEN GALFORD

Milk Treading *is equal parts* Watership Down, Animal Farm *and* The Big Sleep. *A novel of class struggle, political intrigue and good old-fashioned murder and intrigue. And, oh yeah, all the characters are either cats, or dogs.* TOD GOLDBERG, LAS VEGAS MERCURY

Smith writes with wit and energy creating a memorable brood of characters... ALAN RADCLIFFE, THE LIST

Me and Ma Gal

Des Dillon

I 84282 054 0 PB £5.99

This sensitive story of boyhood friendship captures the essence of childhood. Dillon explores the themes of lost innocence, fear and death, writing with subtlety and empathy.

Me an Gal showed each other what to do all the time, we were good pals that way an all. We shared everthin. You'd think we would never be parted. If you never had to get married an that I really think that me an Gal'd be pals for ever. That's not to say that we never fought. Man we had some great fights so we did. The two of us could fight just about the same but I was a wee bit better than him on account of ma knowin how to kill people without a gun an all that stuff that I never showed him.

Quite simply spot on. BIG ISSUE IN SCOTLAND

Reminded me of Twain and Kerouac... a story told with wonderful verve, immediacy and warmth. EDWIN MORGAN

Ripe with humour and poignant vignettes of boyhood, this is an endearing and distinctive novel. SCOTLAND ON SUNDAY

Me and Ma Gal *was winner of the 2003 World Book Day* We Are What We Read *poll.*

Six Black Candles

Des Dillon

1 84282 053 2 PB £6.99

'Where's Stacie Gracie's head?' ... sharing space with the sweetcorn and two-for-one lemon meringue pies ... in the freezer.

Caroline's husband abandons her (bad move) for Stacie Gracie, his assistant at the meat counter, and incurs more wrath than he anticipated. Caroline, her five sisters, mother and granny, all with a penchant for witchery, invoke the lethal spell of the Six Black Candles. A natural reaction to the break up of a marriage?

The spell does kill. You only have to look at the evidence. Mess with these sisters, or Maw or Oul Mary, and they might do the Six Black Candles on you.

But will Caroline's home ever be at peace for long enough to do the spell and will Caroline really let them do it?

Set in present day Irish Catholic Coatbridge, *Six Black Candles* is bound together by the power of traditional storytelling and the strength of female familial relationships.

Bubbling under the cauldron of superstition, witchcraft and religion is the heat of revenge; and the love and venom of sisterhood.

Hilarious. THE MIRROR

An exciting, entertaining read... just buy it. THE BIG ISSUE

But n Ben A-Go-Go

Matthew Fitt

1 84282 014 1 PB £6.99

The year is 2090. Global flooding has left most of Scotland under water. The descendants of those who survived God's Flood live in a community of floating island parishes, known collectively as Port.

Port's citizens live in mortal fear of Senga, a supervirus whose victims are kept in a giant hospital warehouse in sealed capsules called Kists. Paolo Broon is a low-ranking cyberjanny. His life-partner, Nadia, lies forgotten and alone in Omega Kist 624 in the Rigo Imbeki Medical Center. When he receives an unexpected message from his radge criminal father to meet him at But n Ben A-Go-Go, Paolo's life is changed forever. Set in a distinctly unbonnie future-Scotland, the novel's dangerous atmosphere and psychologically-malkied characters weave a tale that both chills and intrigues. In *But n Ben A-Go-Go* Matthew Fitt takes the allegedly dead language of Scots and energises it with a narrative that crackles and fizzes with life.

I recommend an entertaining and ground-breaking book. EDWIN MORGAN

Be prepared to boldly go... ELLIE MCDONALD

Easier to read than Shakespeare, and twice the fun. DES DILLON

Bursting with sly humour, staggeringly imaginative, exploding with Uzi-blazing action. GREGOR STEELE, TIMES EDUCATIONAL SUPPLEMENT

FICTION

The Tar Factory
Alan Kelly
1 84282 050 8 PB £9.99

The Golden Menagerie
Allan Cameron
1 84282 057 5 PB £9.99

Outlandish Affairs: An Anthology of Amorous Encounters
Edited and introduced by Evan Rosenthal and Amanda Robinson
1 84282 055 9 PB £9.99

The Fundamentals of New Caledonia
David Nicol
0 946487 93 6 HB £16.99

The Strange Case of RL Stevenson
Richard Woodhead
0 946487 86 3 HB £16.99

POETRY

Tartan & Turban
Bashabi Fraser
1 84282 044 3 PB £8.99

Drink the Green Fairy
Brian Whittingham
1 84282 0451 PB £8.99

The Ruba'iyat of Omar Khayyam, in Scots
Rab Wilson
1 84282 046 x PB £8.99 (book)
1 84282 070 2 PB £9.99 (audio cd)

Picking Brambles and other poems
Des Dillon
1 84282 021 4 PB £6.99

Kate o Shanter's Tale and other poems
Matthew Fitt
1 84282 028 1 PB £6.99 (book)
1 84282 043 5 £9.99 (audio CD)

Talking with Tongues
Brian Finch
1 84282 006 0 PB £8.99

The Luath Burns Companion
John Cairney
1 84282 000 1 PB £10.00

Men and Beasts: Wild Men and Tame Animals
Valerie Gillies and Rebecca Marr
0 946487 928 PB £15.00

Madame Fi Fi's Farewell
Gerry Cambridge
1 84282 005 2 PB £8.99

Scots Poems to be Read Aloud
Introduced by Stuart McHardy
0 946487 81 2 PB £5.00

Poems to be Read Aloud
Introduced by Tom Atkinson
0 946487 006 PB £5.00

Bad Ass Raindrop
Kokumo Rocks
1 84292 018 4 PB £6.99

Sex, Death & Football
Alistair Findlay
1 84282 022 2 PB £6.99

The Whisky Muse: Scotch Whisky in Poem and Song
Introduced and compiled by Robin Laing
1 84282 041 9 PB £7.99

THE QUEST FOR

The Quest for Charles Rennie Mackintosh
John Cairney
1 84282 058 3 PB £16.99

The Quest for Robert Louis Stevenson
John Cairney
0 946487 87 1 HB £16.99

The Quest for the Nine Maidens
Stuart McHardy
0 946487 66 9 HB £16.99

The Quest for the Original Horse Whisperers
Russell Lyon
1 84282 020 6 HB £16.99

The Quest for the Celtic Key
Karen Ralls-MacLeod and Ian Robertson
1 84282 031 1 PB £8.99

The Quest for Arthur
Stuart McHardy
1 84282 012 5 HB £16.99

FOLKLORE

The Supernatural Highlands
Francis Thompson
0 946487 31 6 PB £8.99

Tall Tales from an Island
Peter Mcnab
0 946487 07 3 PB £8.99

Luath Storyteller: Highland Myths & Legends
George W MacPherson
1 84282 064 8 PB £5.00

Scotland: Myth, Legend & Folklore
Stuart McHardy
0 946487 69 3 PB £7.99

Tales from the North Coast
Alan Temperley
0 946487 18 9 PB £8.99

HISTORY

Scots in Canada
Jenni Calder
1 84282 038 9 PB £7.99

Plaids & Bandanas: Highland Drover to Wild West Cowboy
Rob Gibson
0 946487 88 X PB £7.99

A Passion for Scotland
David R Ross
1 84282 019 2 PB £5.99

Civil Warrior
Robin Bell
184282 013 3 HB £10.99

Reportage Scotland: History in the Making
Louise Yeoman
1 84282 051 6 PB £6.99

SOCIAL HISTORY

Crofting Years
Francis Thompson
0 946487 06 5 PB £6.95

Pumpherston: the story of a shale oil village
Sybil Cavanagh
1 84282 011 7 HB £17.99
1 84282 015 X PB £10.99

Shale Voices
Alistair Findlay
0 946487 78 2 HB £17.99
0 946487 63 4 PB £10.99

ON THE TRAIL OF

On the Trail of William Wallace
David R Ross
0 946487 47 2 PB £7.99

On the Trail of Bonnie Prince Charlie
David R Ross
0 946487 68 5 PB £7.99

On the Trail of Robert Burns
John Cairney
0 946487 51 0 PB £7.99

BIOGRAPHY

Tobermory Teuchter
Peter Macnab
0 946487 41 3 PB £7.99

Bare Feet and Tackety Boots
Archie Cameron
0 946487 17 0 PB £7.95

The Last Lighthouse
Sharma Krauskopf
0 946487 96 0 PB £7.99

Details of these and other Luath Press titles are to be found at www.luath.co.uk